I0587131

How Did
I Get
Here?

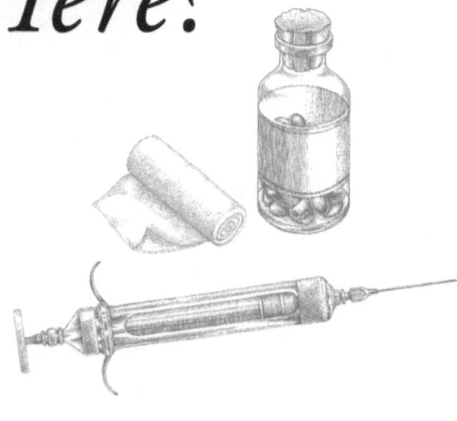

How Did I Get Here?

JANE MARLOW

RIVER GROVE
BOOKS

This book is a work of fiction. Names, characters, businesses, organizations, places, events, and incidents are either a product of the author's imagination or are used fictitiously. With the exception of well-known historical figures and events, any resemblance to actual persons, living or dead, events, or locales is entirely coincidental.

Published by River Grove Books
Austin, TX
www.rivergrovebooks.com

Copyright ©2018 Jane Mahlow

All rights reserved.

No part of this book may be reproduced, stored in a retrieval system, or transmitted by any means, electronic, mechanical, photocopying, recording, or otherwise, without written permission from the copyright holder.

Distributed by River Grove Books

Design and composition by Greenleaf Book Group
Cover design by Greenleaf Book Group
Cover image: ©iStockphoto.com/kvkirillov; chippix and Sathya Sudharsanan, 2018. Used under license from Shutterstock.com
Interior images: MATULEE and Channarong Pherngjanda, 2018. Used under license from Shutterstock.com

Cataloging-in-Publication data is available.

Print ISBN: 978-1-63299-164-5

eBook ISBN: 978-1-63299-165-2

First Edition

NOTE TO READER

This novel is dedicated to those who learn
from history's mistakes and triumphs.

The result of this expedition was one of the most
fruitless and lamentable that has ever occurred in
the history of warfare.

—William Howard Russell of *The London Times*

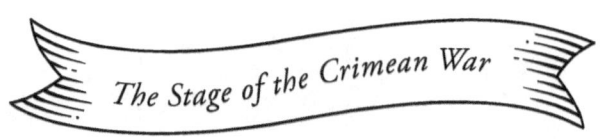

The Stage of the Crimean War

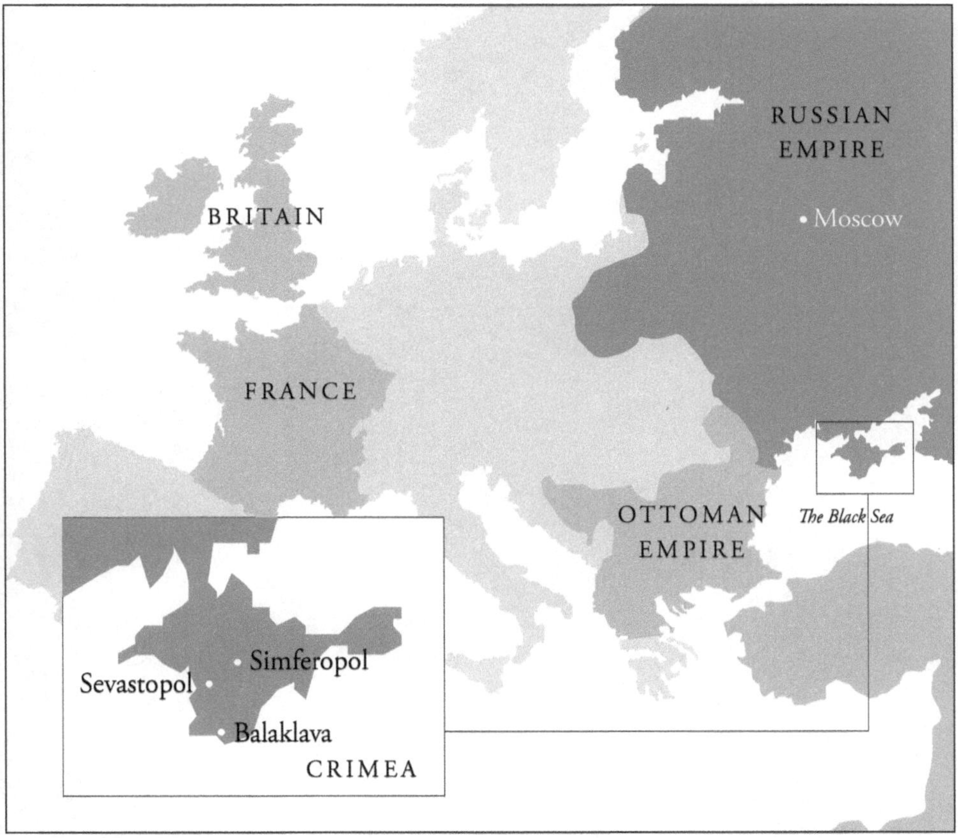

RUSSIAN
EMPIRE

BRITAIN

• Moscow

FRANCE

OTTOMAN
EMPIRE

The Black Sea

Simferopol

Sevastopol

Balaklava

CRIMEA

DATES

UNTIL 1918, RUSSIA followed the Julian (Old Style) calendar, which ran thirteen days behind the Gregorian (New Style) calendar that was, and continues to be, used in Europe and the Western world. Because this Russian story takes place in the 1800s, all dates herein reflect the Julian calendar.

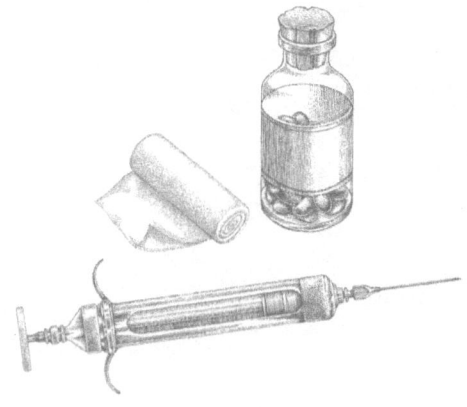

CHAPTER 1

November
1854

I NAB THE flea from my wrist, cleave the little scoundrel in half with my fingernail, then regret killing it so quickly. I should have tortured it.

But fair play is one of my exceedingly few strong suits, although God only knows how I came to possess such a virtue. To hold the flea accountable for my misery would be ethically wrong. The decision to place myself here—to travel, in my final year of medical school, to serve the Tsar's military at the Crimean front—had been mine and mine alone. And I say that with the fiercest regret.

"Idiot!" The word blows through my lips. The shaggy peasant driving the wagon swivels about, seeking the target of his lone passenger's vitriol. I ignore the shaggy peasant, consumed as I am with my internal flogging.

I never act impetuously. Never. Except that fateful moment two months and three days ago when my professor's proposition shone like a beam of hope. I faced a decisive juncture and dove in headfirst.

I'm now in the nightmarish upshot of that rash decision. Railways being non-existent south of Moscow, the army consigned a peasant with oxen and a wagon to haul me and a load of military supplies over the trampled earth that constitutes the roads to Sevastopol. I'm a mélange of blue and purple bruises from being tossed about in the bed of a springless wagon that reeks of its previous load of sour grain blended with pig feces. Every daylight hour, I sit jammed between packing cartons, my long legs folded like an accordion as we bump along kidney-bruising dirt roads that do their utmost to bounce my brain against the inside of my skull. Most of my time is spent in a stupor, numbed by vacant vistas broken only by sad little hamlets of no consequence.

The driver and I spend our nights in peasant barns, where I tussle with a smelly sheepskin blanket, its length only half that of my own, and share the dusty hay with droves of fleas. My fingernails are caked with blood from raking across fleabites. Meals are woefully inadequate, and I'm trying my darnedest to keep my galloping dysentery at bay. Hell, I signed up for this stint because I was half starved. Now I tie a rope about the waist of my trousers to keep them up.

THE FILTH-ENCRUSTED DRIVER and I have been together a little over a week when we arrive at the army encampment at Kursk, a provincial capital midway between Moscow and the Crimean Peninsula. With Russia beginning to pour its massive army into the Crimea, the formerly drowsy town has become overstuffed with regiments converging on the theater of war. Every donkey, mule, burro, camel, horse, ox, wagon, and bullock cart in the Empire seems to be traveling this road with us, all loaded to capacity in the Tsar's warmongering service.

Saliva froths in my mouth at the thought that the army mess hall might serve up a warm meal. Warm meal? Ha! Turns out to be a virtual banquet! Hearty soup so thick with cream, it could hold a spoon upright. Dumplings in sour cream. Thick-sliced bread. Pickled gherkins. Stewed pears. Then a second serving of each, a third helping of pears. The mountain of food will doubtlessly have a romping fun time with my already dysenteric bowels. But that's tomorrow's problem.

Daybreak arrives inordinately early. I'm climbing back into my wagon when a grizzled, bantam-sized fellow emerges from amid the endless rows of newly erected white tents.

"Zaitsev." He tosses his name up to me along with his canvas bag. Then he informs me that he is a physician and will be my traveling companion as far as the military post on the isthmus that connects the southern mainland of Russia to the Crimean province. After wedging himself among the stacked crates and chests, he gives me a once-over. "You ain't Pirogov, are you?"

"P-P-Pirogov?" The esteemed name leaves me, a mere medical student, mouth-gapingly dumbstruck. "You're referring to Nikolai Ivanovich Pirogov?"

"Could be the name. Supposed to be some grand and glorious physician. Rumored to be headed to the Crimea. All the army physicians—a bunch of bootlickers, every one of them—are tripping over themselves to meet him."

"Pirogov! One of the most respected physicians in all of Russia!" Receiving only a droopy-lidded gaze from Zaitsev, I proffer some details. "Author of *Pathological Anatomy of Asiatic Cholera*. And one of the first surgeons in Russia, if not *the* first, to use chloroform as an anesthetic."

Zaitsev heaves a *humph* and rolls a yellow-papered cigarette. "You're arriving at a good time. You missed the malaria season, and you're too early for typhus." He squints at me. "If you ain't Pirogov, who are you?"

"Rozhdestvensky," I reply. "Andrey Yevgrafovich Rozhdestvensky. Perhaps you could fill me in on what to expect when I reach Sevastopol? The kinds of wounds I'll be treating? The latest techniques in limb amputations?"

"Don't fret over the wounds, Rozhdestvensky. The minor ones heal themselves, unless they get maggots. Which, in the summer, they will. The fellows with bad wounds, they die. Simple as that. As for amputations . . ." Zaitsev strikes a match on the sole of his boot and fires up his cigarette. "For every ten I've done, nine gave up the ghost."

A ten percent survival rate? I take a deep swallow and redirect my questions. "Do you prefer chloroform or ether as an anesthetic?"

"Neither." Zaitsev blows smoke toward the sky. "The smart of the knife is a powerful stimulant. Helps keep the poor devils alive."

I'm at a loss as to how to respond.

"Disease and pestilence, those are the real scalawags," he continues. "Typhus in the winter. Asiatic cholera and putrid fever in the summer. I should know." He thumps his chest with his thumb, dumping ashes down the front of his greatcoat. "Saw my first deadly fever in the swamps of the Caucasus in 1828. Cholera in the Polish campaign of 1831. Same story in '49 when the Vomiting Death hit us in Hungary. Seen it all, scores of times."

His knobby forefinger motions me to lean closer. "I divulge this next piece of information in strict confidence." The old geezer roves his rheumy eyes about the wagon, presumably looking for eavesdroppers stowed away among the army's crates and bundles.

"I'm quiet as the grave."

"Those knuckleheads in St. Petersburg!" He spits his disdain over the side-boards of the wagon. "They're sending women here."

"Women at the front? You can't mean as soldiers!"

"Hell, no!" Zaitsev's confidential whisper detonates into a boom. "Supposedly as medical assistants. Imagine, women tending to sick men! I promise you this: for as long as you serve in the Tsar's army, you'll never see a single soldier with solid shit. Those women will take one look and, bah, they'll run all the way home, holding their skirts with one hand and their noses with the other."

"Your point is well taken."

Zaitsev sneers, flaunting his tobacco-stained teeth. "Consider this, also. Why would a handful of women want to be with twenty-five thousand men? Only one reason: loose morals. Just picture the legions of syphilitics we'll have to tend to once those jezebels spread their disease and pestilence."

"Perhaps it's just a false rumor?"

"I have my sources." The old physician nods with the wisdom of the ages. "And the army's making things worse with the food they're serving. Did you notice the beef in the soup last night? Remember from your dietetics class, fleshy foods lead directly to systematic excitation of lust? That beef will incite drunkenness and then, after the hussies arrive, out-of-control libidos."

"Sounds like a piece of medical wisdom you should share with the generals."

He brays like a donkey. "It's the generals who have the greatest carnal appetites. By the way"—his index finger rises to rest crosswise under his nose—"consider growing a mustache. It serves as a natural respirator, of obvious value in this malaria-cursed country."

THE FARTHER WE journey from Moscow, the more abysmal the roads become, slowing our travel to a nerve-wracking crawl. The irksome pontificator and I share meals of dried sausage, stale bread, salted cucumbers, and bitter green apples. At night, we continue to bed down in decrepit barns in nameless peasant villages, the ruthless ends of the hay turning my skin into a pincushion as Zaitsev snores with the vigor of a bull bellowing to a cow. At the rooster's first crow, we're once again bouncing along pot-holed roads, my stomach churning from the apples, and my head beginning its daily ache from the windbag's blather. Every moment of every day I'm tempted beyond measure to pitch the nonsensical old-timer over the rickety sideboards.

My blue-tipped fingers tucked into the warmth of my armpits, I once again hotly curse my impulsive choice. With an overabundance of time to kill, my demented mind traces back to that decision, the first and only moment in my insipid life when I felt hopeful. I should have known better. Disappointment has never been more than a stone's throw away.

CHAPTER 2

November

1854

MY CYNICISM ISN'T something I cultivated. Rather, it settled on me as a matter of course. Just as some families are notable for their stunning blue eyes, the Rozhdestvensky family is renowned for its grimness.

My parents had an unshakable conviction in Proverbs 13:24, "One who spares the rod hates his son, but one who loves him is careful to discipline him." All six of their children were strictly and severely raised to be amenable to the ways of the family, the Church, and the Holy Sovereign. I was the youngest, and my two twin brothers took their cue from my parents, showering me with innovative insults. I learned that yes, indeed, words do hurt. As do cuffs to the back of my head.

For a while, trepidation was my constant companion. But inevitably, I grew too large to hide under the bed. So I switched strategies and simply stopped talking. As a result, my fifth year of life was spent with the embarrassment of nonstop hiccups.

I reached, oh, maybe seven years of age when I began taking for granted people's false piety and ulterior motives. A shoulder shrug became my answer to almost everything.

During my early teens, my appearance also provided an easy target for mockery. To say I was of slender build was an understatement of epic proportions. My torso was as long and thin as an axe handle, with a chest so sunken, it gave the appearance of having been the target of a horse's hoof.

To make matters worse, I am the son of a priest. Rather than joining the rough-and-tumble world of the neighborhood boys, I suffered a childhood cloistered behind the impenetrable walls of the Church. My playmates consisted of my three older sisters, who were only slightly more charitable toward me than were the twins.

In no manner of speaking am I implying I was a prude. Quite to the contrary, I inherited my father's tendency to enjoy vodka to excess. And shortly after I sprouted pubic hair, I and the neighbor girl, Sonia Lepekhina, began spending countless hours in the church bell tower familiarizing ourselves with each other's bodies.

At no point in my childhood did I feel safe. My God-fearing, family-fearing upbringing is perhaps best summed up with an illustrative story.

One of the many ecclesiastical duties assigned to us three brothers was the cleaning and refilling of the incense burner. Once, on the Feast of the Intercession of the Holy Mother of God, the task was somehow neglected. During Vespers, Father swung the chain of the censer, and nothing happened. No celestial smoke. Not a hint of heavenly fragrance. My father's face reddened like a radish as he pumped more oomph into his swing.

The twins bolted to the sacristy, while I stood trembling. They located a tarnished, timeworn censer, added the charcoal, dumped in some incense, and meekly presented the dusty replacement to our humiliated father.

That evening, the twins, ever true to their pattern, conspired to pin the slipup on me. But Father didn't fall for their cover-up. He positioned the three of us shoulder to shoulder and spooned hot incense onto the back of each of our left hands.

"Never ever forget your obligations to God and to your parishioners!"

How could we? The scars would be our daily reminder. As would every nauseating sniff of incense.

Even more forlorn than our upbringing was our future. The three of us brothers were destined to join the family lineage of priests.

Priests are buttonholed into the Russian caste system, just like the nobility, merchants, peasants, and so on, all of whom regard themselves as superior to us "clerical dirt." The life of a cleric's son plays out in a predetermined manner. First, he attends a parochial school, followed by the Church district school, and finally the seminary. Shortly thereafter, he marries the daughter of a cleric. The loving couple then beget more of the same, each offspring obligated to follow the same bleak footsteps.

The ensuing oversupply of clerics is so excessive, priests have to vie for positions. Even those fortunate enough to secure an entry-level position at some tumbledown rural church reap wages too meager for the cleric to support his family. But here's the real rub: the priest's holy vows forbid him or his family to earn supplemental wages outside their virtuous vocation.

The end result? Priests, out of necessity, developed a fail-safe strategy to augment their income.

"Prayers for the sick?" An upward palm is thrust toward the parishioner. "A tin of tea."

"Wedding? Two rubles plus vodka. Don't have it? Then don't get married."

Rare is the young man who enters the priesthood because of a divine calling.

Nearly all join because they have no choice. I speak with the foremost authority when I say the outcome is an inert, moribund priesthood.

My three sisters were destined to fulfill their duty by marrying scantily paid priests. They craft their families' meals from their kitchen gardens and clothe their children by raising and spinning their own wool, bound to a life not a pittance better than that of their husbands' impoverished congregations.

The career path for us three boys was to attend a district boarding school for six years, then transfer to the seminary. As a youngster, I watched with mounting trepidation as the twins prepared to be thrust not only into an occupation contrary to their own preferences, but into a life devoid of respect, both from others and from themselves.

After my stint at boarding school, it was my turn to journey onward to the seminary. I packed my meager possessions and waved goodbye to my family, aware in my heart that I was permanently severing all ties with them. I walked out of our small town with shoulders pulled back in feigned confidence. But instead of heading to the seminary, I spent my few horded kopeks to secure passage to Moscow and its university.

Owing to a glut of priests and a paucity of physicians, sons of the clergy could legally pursue the medical profession, one of the very few options on an otherwise choiceless path. I managed to score decently in a couple of university classes and was admitted to the medical curriculum.

Having been sequestered from a normal childhood and adolescence, I was ill at ease with my classmates, and I shied away from their boisterous after-hours antics. I had grown into a gangly, loose-jointed fellow, the type of young man people customarily overlook. I did little except study, work, sleep, and eat, with damn few rubles available for the latter.

Then came that fateful September day in forensics class during my final year of medical studies, when I made an uncharacteristically abrupt decision.

AS I SLID into my seat that morning, I was so hungry I could have eaten a mule's ear. Tingly barbs stabbed my thawing toes. With Moscow's winter bearing down, I needed new soles for my only pair of boots, the uppers of which were a patchwork of repairs. And if I didn't replace my threadbare jacket with a stouter coat, I'd surely come down with yet another bout of bronchitis.

For too long, I had robbed Peter to pay Paul, and I found myself at wit's end. I was left with three choices. I could pay my share of the rent for the single-room dungeon I shared with four fellow students. Or I could clothe myself for the winter. Or I could eat.

"This morning's first announcement comes from your Tsar via his War Department." At the podium, a fleshy hand held the innocuous sheet of paper with lofty nonchalance. "Russia's escalating war on the Crimean Peninsula," the corpulent, gray-haired professor read, "has an urgent need for medical personnel to serve our military forces. You are hereby given the opportunity to voluntarily replace your final year of studies with practical experience."

As best I recall, at that moment my stomach cut loose with a lengthy clamor for food. I wrapped my belly with my crossed arms, as if they would conceal the grumbling from the ears of nearby classmates.

The professor cleared the morning hoarseness from his throat. "In exchange for serving our Motherland against the dissolute Turks and their co-conspirators, you would be provided with transportation to the front, plus food, shelter, and clothing." He adjusted the paper's distance from his spectacles. "Plus five rubles a month, and a full refund on your final year's tuition."

I held my breath while he pushed his spectacles higher up on the bridge of his nose. "In addition, you'll gain exposure to military medicine. And you'll benefit from the firsthand study of warm-weather diseases, such as malaria and the Crimean fevers."

The instructor lowered the paper and peered at his students. "At the end of which, you will be granted your medical degree."

Free tuition. Wholesome food. Warm clothes. A more agreeable winter a thousand miles south of frozen Moscow. This announcement was the answer to my prayers. Except I never pray.

But there was another consideration, one that was difficult to put a precise finger on but was nevertheless impossible to ignore. The Crimean conflict offered free passage out of my vapid life.

Ahead of me lay the mouthwatering promises of the Crimean War. The Russian soldier was renowned for his bravery and endurance. Surely those intrepid attributes would rub off on me, firming both body and character. The Crimea was my portal to a new identity.

A rare, buoyant confidence surged through my bones as I signed the indecipherable military paperwork.

Yes, Andrey—courtesy of my childhood reclusion, I've honed the skill of holding informative, usually admonishing conversations with myself—*you'll return to Moscow not as a submissive youth, but as a man of mettle, toughened by the exertions of war.*

Week after anxious week, I waited for the War Department in St. Petersburg to exchange paperwork with the university. Everyone knew the skirmish would last only a couple of months before the Russians (far and away Europe's largest military power) chased the English and the French permanently off its Crimean Peninsula and out of the Black Sea. Wouldn't it be just my luck if the whole fray ended before I ever stepped foot outside of Moscow?

To occupy my agitated mind, I scoured the maps at the university's library to learn more about what I'd gotten myself into, such as where, exactly, is the Crimea. The shape of the peninsula in the Black Sea reminded me of a splotch of bird droppings with jagged edges. If it weren't for the sliver of land that hitched it to the rest of the Empire, the land mass would be an island. Toward its south end lay the fabled naval base of Sevastopol, the site of the military action. The longer I perused the map, the deeper my brows knitted. Apart from Sevastopol, the province looked like ten thousand square miles of desolate hills sprinkled with a handful of insignificant villages.

After a month and a half, the university finally received the necessary military correspondence. I spread a moth-eaten blanket on my mattress, and in its center, I placed my few articles of clothing and a couple of handkerchiefs. Atop that, I set a comb, a razor, and a honing stone. My books were too heavy to carry. Better just to pawn them.

Last, I tossed in a deck of cards. Perhaps I'd meet someone who enjoyed the intellectually challenging game of skat.

After tying the blanket's corners in a knot, I theatrically flung the totality of my possessions over my shoulder. With a giddy sense of adventure, I indulged myself with ill-defined visions of Crimean hills, of dark-eyed women, of life-saving surgeries. *Andrey Yevgrafovich Rozhdestvensky, you stand at the threshold of a new life.*

How quickly fantasies can be replaced by reality.

I'm cold.
I'm sick.
I'm broke.
I'm lonely.
I'm regretful.

I'm scared.

I have no idea where I am.

And I'm ready to strangle Doctor Zaitsev.

Fortunately for my blathering companion's well-being, we finally reach his encampment, and I bid him adieu. My wagon is mercifully peaceful as it merges into the makeshift caravan of wagons and carts headed south across the isthmus and onto the Crimean Peninsula. I've been on the road just shy of three weeks, and a week's journey to Sevastopol remains, barring any unexpected delays.

But wouldn't you know, the weather turns downright mean, and bottomless mud slurries slow the convoy to a start-and-stop crawl. Even with a tarp draped over my head and shoulders, my thin jacket and tattered nankeen trousers are no match against battering wind and cold, bone-soaking rain.

During breaks in the rain, I join the driver on his wooden bench and watch the tails of the two oxen swish ceaselessly back and forth. I try to convince myself that things will look brighter in Sevastopol. However, the farther I venture onto the Crimean Peninsula, the deeper I sink in to an abyss of disbelief. Could the men, armament, and provisions of the world's largest army really be moving like a giant trail of ants along scars etched in to the earth by wheels and hooves? And is the transport actually being carried out by road-weary wagons, wobbly peasant carts, bony oxen, and shaggy little ponies?

On the right-hand side of the so-called road, a wooden direction post tilts forlornly with the prevailing winds, informing me that we're approaching the next unkempt Tatar village. Also alongside the road are a plethora of oxen carcasses in various stages of decay. To my left, a ragtag assortment of conveyances carries wounded soldiers north to the encampment on the isthmus, where they will be tended to by (Heaven help them) Doctor Zaitsev. Local people—lots of them, all with their animals and overflowing carts—are also headed north, away from Sevastopol. Are they fleeing? Fleeing from what?

Scattered amid the clogged mayhem in both directions are camels laden with produce that their dark-skinned, wild-looking owners will sell for eight to ten times the normal price. And whenever the rain lets up for even a few minutes, a squadron of angry green flies appears from nowhere.

Flea-bitten. Hungry. Filthy. Fighting dysentery. Deadened with cold and boredom. This isn't the life-altering adventure I had bargained for. Not at all.

Andrey, you incomparable imbecile, you don't belong here any more than a saddle belongs on a cow.

TWO DAYS SOUTH of the isthmus, as we creep toward the peninsula's center, the impromptu convoy comes to yet another standstill. My teeth clench as I and the neighboring drivers and travelers once again slog through the boot-sucking mire, preparing to push aside a hobbled wagon, another victim of the logs and rocks that give the road its local flavor. The road's edge had washed out, and courtesy of an oozy amalgamation of rain, mud, and animal excrement, the rear wheel slipped sideways into a small gully on the craggy hillside.

Crippled wagons along this road are as common as horse dung. What sets this one apart from the others is the half dozen women huddled beside it.

CHAPTER 3

November
1854

I APPROACH THE catawampus wagon, cold muck infiltrating my tattered boots and oozing between my toes. The women are clustered around a second conveyance, a two-wheeled peasant cart, inside of which lies another female. While the driver hurtles Greek curses at the mud-slick road, I and my fellow good Samaritans lighten the awry wagon of its load of suitcases, boxes, and barrels.

The women wring their hands as they console their injured companion. "How badly does it hurt?"

"Oh, you poor dear."

"We'll get you to a doctor straightaway."

Well, Andrey, I dialogue with myself, *didn't you come to the Crimea for the purpose of performing doctorly deeds?* As the men and oxen labor to replace the wagon in its rightful position in the road ruts, I summon the gumption to approach the women. "Are you in need of a physician?"

"Sister Ivanova is injured!"

"She's in pain!"

"She can't breathe!"

My eyes flick across the six faces. The women are in their late teens or early twenties, though age is difficult to judge, bundled as they are in cloaks, hats, and scarves. "I'm without medical supplies, but I'll do what I can."

"Oh, would you please?"

"That would be so kind of you."

"How fortunate you came along!"

My cold hands grow moist with sweat. I've never had sole responsibility for a patient. *Andrey, you impostor. Your aptitude falls far short of your bluster.*

Pushing aside these self-deprecations, I ask the prone woman where she hurts. Grimacing, she points a gloved finger at the left side of her rib cage.

"Would you mind opening your cloak so that I can examine you?"

Beneath her cape is a long, brown garment, as formless as drapery. A bulky gold cross hangs from a wide ribbon around her neck. Are these the "hussies" who caused Zaitsev such indigestion?

As my hands prod and the woman flinches, I tentatively diagnose a cracked rib. But what if her spleen is ruptured? Or her liver? Or perhaps her stomach is twisted? No. Her cheeks are rosy, and her lips, although pinched, are a healthy pink. Those ailments don't make sense, I reassure myself.

The covey of anxious women tightens like a corset around me, abetting my self-inflicted pressure to quickly reach a diagnosis. Eventually I almost fully convince myself that my original interpretation is correct.

I explain to the patient and the circle of ladies that simply remaining inactive for a couple of weeks will allow the rib to heal on its own. "If you take shallow breaths, it will hurt less. However, I fear traveling over this bumpy road will be painful. Where are you headed?"

"Simferopol," six female voices answer in perfect unison.

From the library's maps, I learned that Simferopol is the provincial capital, as well as the administrative headquarters of Russia's Crimean Army. The city lies in the center of the bird poop splotch, approximately fifty miles inland from the naval port of Sevastopol.

"Do you by chance have some bandage material?" I ask the shivering women. "If I wrap it snuggly about her ribs, her pain will ease somewhat."

The women bring forth a tattered blanket and tear off a long strip of wool.

I lower my eyes sheepishly. "I need to apply it directly to her skin."

They do an about-face, their backs to the cart, their shoulder-to-shoulder semicircle creating an impenetrable haven for Sister Ivanova. When my fingers, stiff with cold and inexperience, complete the task, the women heap unending gratitude upon me.

"Such a skilled physician!"

"A saint in disguise!"

"Bless you!"

"May we know your name?" This question comes from a large woman, twice the girth of the others.

"Andrey Yevgrafovich Rozhdestvensky."

In response, the women introduce themselves one by one. Their names go in one ear and out the other. Until I find myself peering into the bluest eyes imaginable.

"Sister Vasilisa Stepanova Abramova." She offers me a slight curtsy and a demure smile.

So ensnared am I by her dark-lashed eyes and melodic voice, I forget the final Sister is waiting to greet me.

"How grand that you came along at just the right moment."

I tear my gaze from the blue-eyed beauty to see the last Sister—the large one who had initiated this parley of name sharing—extending her hand boldly in the Western style.

"Sister Maria Ivanovna Kurbatova."

Her grasp is so strong, I grit my teeth to keep from flinching. Kurbatova is of medium height, oxen bones, and hefty flesh. Her pudgy, gloved fingers remind me of sausages with overstuffed casings.

"I'm pleased to make the acquaintance of each of you," I say, letting my attention drift back to the jeweled eyes. "May I ask . . . ? You call yourselves Sisters. Are you nuns?"

"No, we're Sisters of Mercy." The words pass between the impossibly full lips of Sister Vasilisa Stepanova Abramova. "We're on our way to be of assistance at the hospitals."

"Perhaps we shall see you there," says the large Sister. What was her name?

"I wish that were true. However, I'm stationed at Sevastopol."

The corners of the brawny woman's lips turn up whimsically, as if she has a secret she intends to keep to herself. "One never knows. Perhaps our paths will cross."

I bow to the group as a whole. "Let us be diligent in seeking out those paths."

As I walk away, expressions of gratitude trail after me. But these words of appreciation are smothered by my own ruminations about Vasilisa Stepanova Abramova.

CHAPTER 4

November

1854

OVER THE NEXT few days, while the weather fluctuates between damp-cold and wet-cold, my unchaste thoughts about Sister Abramova steadily heat up. The hint of mischievousness behind her sedate curtsy. The provocativeness of her beguiling eyes. The possibilities lurking beneath her dreary, shapeless habit.

Andrey, listen to me. You must, YOU MUST get reassigned from Sevastopol to Simferopol.

The clouds hang low like dirty fleece. Their chilly drizzle soothes my forehead, which throbs from the wagon's continuous pitching. As I sit on the bench beside the driver, my gaze mindlessly latches on to the repetitive to-and-fro of the rusty bucket that dangles beneath the military wagon ahead of us.

When the tedium becomes more than I can bear, I fold my arms across the top of my knees and drop my head onto them. Through momentary holes in the clouds, the sun warms the moist clothes clinging to my back.

With eyes closed and forehead bouncing off my forearms, I swear I discern every possible means of communication. The neighs of horses. Bellows of cows. Cries of camels. Bleats of sheep. Yells of the drivers in assorted Eastern and Western languages: Greek, German, Armenian, Polish, Bulgarian, Tatar, various Slavic regional accents. It's as if half of Russia and a good portion of Eastern Europe have converged on this pathetic trail.

The wagon tips into a steep decline, and I jolt upright. We're descending into the equivalent of a great amphitheater. Nestled in the wide basin is the celebrated city-fortress revered by every Russian.

"Sevastopol." The word whistles on my breath.

During the weeks when I impatiently drummed my fingers in the library, I'd learned that Catherine II's unstoppable ambition had forged the venerated fortress in the late 1700s. Besides being one of the Empire's most revered citadels, it is also a town of forty-five thousand inhabitants, the bulk of whom have ties to the military base.

Viewed from our hillside, the dazzling "Jewel of the Black Sea" lies on both sides of the soft blue waters of an elongated bay, which I hazard to guess is a half mile wide and ten times as long. Low afternoon sunbeams, sidestepping the dreary clouds, ricochet off blindingly white buildings. The City of Imperial Power could be mistaken for a seaside resort except for a few telltale signs, such as frigates at anchor in the long bay and mammoth piles of earth arranged in a fortifying ring along the southern edge of the town. Scores of skiffs and larger boats ply to and fro. The west end of the harbor opens into the sea, and farther west, at some indistinguishable place, the water meets the sky.

Oh, Andrey! Your whole life, mediocrity has clung to you like a gosling to its mother. But all that is about to change!

ONCE WE ARRIVE in town, the two oxen plod down wide, unpaved roads. The streets are laden with steamy mounds of oxen, horse, and camel dung, but simultaneously boast gracious private homes, stately public edifices, and dockyards unequaled anywhere in the world. Some of the multistory, neoclassical, stone buildings flaunt columns that would be regarded as colossal even by Moscow's standards.

As my wagon lumbers toward the city's center, the streets narrow and become clogged with gun carriages, piles of shot, and timber. Wooden carts with squeaky wheels are laden with bread and flour. Weathered brown men in multicolored garb sit cross-legged on little rugs, smoking long pipes. Pairs of Albanians in white kilts carry hulking bales of cotton suspended on poles between them. Greeks with red fez caps dicker over the price of hanging racks of raw lamb.

My mouth waters as we pass by wizened women hawking gingerbread and roasted pumpkin seeds. And I thirst after the younger Tatar women pulling their smocks high to step across puddles, exposing their bare legs.

After a month together, the driver and I part ways when he lets me off near the waterfront and instructs me to walk down to the bustling jetty and take a boat to the opposite side of the bay. There I'll find the hospital.

I board a ferry loaded with an assortment of soldiers and civilians alongside crates, barrels, baskets, and sacks of bulk merchandise. As we push off from shore, I look back at the evening glow of the sun radiating off crosses atop the steeples of Catholic churches, juxtaposed with the familiar round cupolas of Greek and Russian Orthodox churches. Our destination, by contrast, looks dismal and bare: a couple of large, low-slung stone buildings and some taller stone structures. Forts, perhaps?

As the sun begins to sink into the sea, I disembark on the idle quay of the north shore and venture up a hillside footpath. Leafless, scrubby brambles grab at my trousers until I reach what could loosely be termed a road. Lining the soggy wagon tracks, crisscrossed with gouges from rainwater runoff, are squat cottages of wood and rough stone.

Farther down the road is a spacious building. In front of it, to my monstrous relief, is a hospital sign. I step through the door, only to slam into a wall of stench.

Beds and cots crammed side to side and end to end.

Mattresses leaking pus and blood onto the wooden floor.

Men groaning, shrieking, and coughing in foul-smelling misery.

My nostrils clamp shut. My stomach contracts. My every hair springs into full-attention panic.

I'm about to back out the door, with the objective of running the whole way back to Moscow, when a man appears. Like me, he's tall and slender, though based on the crevices that radiate from his eyes and his thinning sandy hair, I'd peg him as between ten and fifteen years older.

He offers his hand. "Captain Daniil Filimonovich Berestnev, medical director of this hospital."

I identify myself, and he nods. "When I saw you freeze in the doorway, I thought you might be one of the students we've been expecting. Your eyes screamed fear, revulsion, and regret." Berestnev's grin is wide and easy.

"Is . . . is this . . . ?" I squeak and stammer like a schoolboy. "Is this the hospital?"

"Hate to be the bearer of bad news, Rozhdestvensky, but yes, it is. Shall I give you a quick orientation to the north side of the bay while I walk you to your sleeping quarters?" Berestnev's strides are long and fast like mine. "If it rains any more, we'll need paddles to get from building to building," he quips.

"My thoughts ran more along the lines of gills and fins."

He chuckles. "By the look of your boots, I can guess you haven't received your army issue yet."

My cheeks flood with embarrassment at the assorted patches. "I apologize for my shoddy appearance. These boots, poor as they are, are the only ones I have."

"You'll need good gear here. Crimean snow blows three months of the year. Crimean dust blows another three months. First thing tomorrow, go to the provisional office that services this side of the bay. Squatty, makeshift structure on your left." Berestnev's hand vaguely gestures down the lone road visible. "Buildings are few here on the north shore. A couple of forts protect the entrance to the harbor and ward off invaders sweeping in from the north. And there are some old biscuit factories that the army converted into hospitals, a slapdash response to the war."

Biscuit factories? A sterling beginning to your medical career, Andrey.

"Your home-away-from-home," Berestnev says as he opens an arm toward a square stone cottage.

Once we're inside, he explains, "It used to house the superintendent of one of the biscuit factories. It's enormous by Crimean standards." We amble through the kitchen, the dining room, the parlor, two bedrooms. "You'll share it with other medical personnel of various sorts. Find yourself an empty cot."

"Cozy," I murmur, winding through the congested maze of cots. I stow my small bundle beneath an unclaimed one in the former dining room. My despondency sinks to yet a grimmer level when I notice there's no pillow. A simple man with simple needs, I covet this sole luxury.

Back outside, we skirt the puddles as best we can in the inky night. At the officers' mess hall, the meal is noodles covered with a cream sauce swimming with mushrooms and chunks of meat, plus crayfish soup, pickled carrots, and wine. I lap it up like a starved dog.

Berestnev butters his hot roll. "What can I tell you about your duties?"

"I heard a rumor that Doctor Nikolai Ivanovich Pirogov will be working here."

"Is *already* working here. Our new consultant surgeon blew in like a cyclone about two weeks ago."

I lick the cream sauce off my lips. "There are also rumblings of volunteer women serving as medical assistants."

"Bad news travels fast, doesn't it." His chuckle is low and mirthless. "If they envision lending moral support to our patients, that's fine by me. If they want to hold the patients' hands, so be it. As long as I don't need to hold *their* hands. I have more than enough work to do without tending to fainting females."

"How did this idea come to be?"

"The most prevalent rumor is that Grand Duchess Elena Pavlovna created the Sisters of Mercy so women could help our wounded in the Crimea."

"And how would they do that?"

"Devil if I know. They're under Pirogov's supervision."

"Where will they be stationed?"

"Don't know that, either." He snickers and pats his mustache, which meets up with his cheek whiskers. "Best we move along to a more palatable topic. The primary hospital and first aid stations are in the main part of town, on the south side of the bay where you first arrived. The hospitals here on the north side are supposedly convalescent hospitals, but you'll see plenty of fresh wounds in all shapes and sizes. First thing you do is stop the hemorrhaging. Then you have two choices: bandage it or amputate it."

A burly man with coal-black hair and a lavish mustache sets his plate on the table next to Berestnev's. "Mind if I join you?"

Berestnev points his spoon toward the swarthy fellow, whose age I peg to be somewhere between mine and Berestnev's. "Andrey Yevgrafovich Rozhdestvensky, you'll want to treat this man with respect. This Tatar from Kazan is Ignaty Sadykov. He's our hospital purveyor. If you want lint, ipecac, or bedding for your patients, he can usually find it for you. Assuming, that is, there's any to be found. Give him whatever he desires, and he'll return the favor. Ignaty, this is one of the medical students we've been expecting."

I exchange nods with the densely muscled Tatar.

"Ignaty is honest to a kopek and a stickler for details," Berestnev elaborates. "If he orders twenty grains of morphine, that's exactly what he expects to receive, and not a tenth of a grain more or less. How his penchant for integrity has survived eight years of army life, I'll never know."

Sadykov smiles modestly, his head bobbing up and down, his white teeth glistening like pearls below his dark mustache. "Captain Berestnev has a penchant of his own: exaggeration. I'm merely a second lieutenant who tries to keep us from being robbed blind by the career officer above me and the noncommissioned officers below."

Berestnev's eyes roll. "Between graft and incompetence, our Tsar's army can be a complete circus. Just the other day, I tended to a soldier whose wounds from the Alma had yet to be treated. Removed enough maggots to fill a tin cup."

The double helping of dinner weighs heavily on my stomach.

"Are you familiar with the Alma?" Berestnev continues. "Our first battle. In September. About twenty miles north of here."

"Actually, I believe it's eighteen miles," Sadykov injects in an apologetic tone.

"Excuse me, eighteen miles," Berestnev corrects himself. He goes on to describe a clear and sunny day, and troops lined up in unyielding regimental columns with muskets shining and colors flying, itching for battle. "A glorious sight, by God! Except for the annihilation that followed. Over five thousand of our men, dead."

"The last count was 5,708." Indeed, Sadykov is a stickler for details.

"That's when we increased our medical capacity on the north side of the bay. Two battles have occurred since then. The road you traveled on, Rozhdestvensky, isn't far from the latest one, near the little village of Inkerman."

Sadykov bows his head and sways it dolefully. "That was a bad one. Ten thousand casualties."

I know nothing about war, but ten thousand seems like a hell of a lot.

"Not only do we have nowhere near the medical staff to handle that many casualties," Berestnev explains, "but there are only twelve *hundred* hospital beds in all of Sevastopol."

My mouth falls open. "But . . . but St. Petersburg predicts a speedy victory before winter sets in."

"Considering the strength of our opponents," Berestnev says, "St. Petersburg is making a wish and ignoring reality."

"And it's not at all clear we're going to win," Sadykov adds.

His words smack me so hard, my head jerks back.

Berestnev braces his palms on his knees to rise. "On that happy note, Ignaty, we'll bid you good night."

Berestnev and I leave the mess hall to find that a raw, damp wind has blown in from the Black Sea. As we retrace our earlier steps, his arm sweeps toward the pitch-dark oblivion of the bay.

"It's a superb choice for a naval station. A long, narrow bay, well protected by surrounding hills. Deep water, with a flat bottom. During the summer, the wind blows from the west during the day, then backs around at night from the east. Perfect for filling sails."

To me, it's cold and black and treacherous.

"Everything that's useful is on the south side of the bay," Berestnev continues. "The new admiralty buildings. Marine stores. Garrisons. Dry docks. Officers' library. Markets. Taverns. Entertainment. Most of the troops are camped on the outskirts of the city. Other than a few small houses, all we have here on the north side are hospitals and magazines that store gunpowder and grain."

"Where's the enemy, sir?"

"Look. I am your commander, your mentor, and your supporter. You and I will spend more time together than you'll ever hope to spend with your future wife. Let's dispense with the formalities. As long as we're not with patients, call me Daniil. Agreed?"

"Agreed."

"The enemy is about six miles south of here, on the far side of the plateau that surrounds Sevastopol. The British took over the tiny Greek fishing village of Balaklava, near the southern tip of the peninsula, and the French are headquartered a few miles up the coast from there. The truth is, every day the English, the French, and their Turk brethren dig their trenches closer so they can haul up more artillery to duel with ours."

"I thought the fortress at Sevastopol was impenetrable."

"Theoretically, it is. The maps show a trench system that connects an outer ring of eight earthwork bastions. Plus, there's the protection of a twelve-foot-high, six-foot-thick crenellated wall. Quite formidable on paper." Berestnev again pats his mustache, which seems to be a tic of his. "But in reality, these defense works are far from complete. The most important redoubts are isolated from each other. As a result, the existing fortifications are completely haphazard. The city is defenseless from the north and only slightly more secure from the south."

"That description differs vastly from the newspaper articles."

"I suspect so. I also suspect that the newspapers don't report this: If the allies ever cut the single supply road north to mainland Russia, we're finished."

The implication shudders through me. "All that keeps us alive is that one road I traveled on?"

He nods. "Basically, you and I and everyone in this city are under siege."

My throat tightens as I picture the noose the allied forces have placed around the naval base.

Daniil pauses in front of my cottage. "I'm not so old that I've forgotten those daunting first months out of medical school. I'll turn you loose in the hospital, but I'm always available if you need me. And I'll be watching over your shoulder these first few months, even though you might not be aware of it. When I see an interesting case, I'll call it to your attention. When I see you've made a mistake, I'll likewise call that to your attention. Fair arrangement?"

We shake hands, and as we part ways, an immense, throbbing loneliness settles atop my overstuffed stomach.

AN OIL LAMP sheds just enough light for me to find my cot. The cottage is quiet, if you don't count the card game at the kitchen table and the snoring from my dozen new housemates. I fold my Moscow blanket into a surrogate pillow and stare upward into the darkness, engulfed by bewildered thoughts and anguish.

That stinkpit of a hospital. How could any self-respecting physician work there? How will I force myself to enter that hellhole in the morning?

Can I simply renege on my agreement? Would the university allow me to resume my studies? Probably not. Besides, how would I pay for the journey back to Moscow? If only I had realized, that morning in forensics class, what an immeasurably foolish and completely irrevocable choice the Crimea was.

I'll be watching over your shoulder these first few months.

First few months! I had assumed I'd be back in Moscow by spring.

Basically, you and I and everyone in this city are under siege.

And it's not at all clear we're going to win.

My balled fist presses against my lips. The die has been cast. And it was my own doing.

CHAPTER 5

November

1854

THE NEXT MORNING, I wait for my army-issued supplies in a line that moves as slowly as my sleepless night. The counter at the provisions office is manned by a young, doltish guy with earlobes so pendulous, they almost rest on his shoulders.

A tin-plated wall clock ticks off fifteen minutes. Twenty minutes. Thirty. When I finally reach the counter, I state my need for clothing and basic supplies.

The clerk dips his pen in ink and poises it over a voluminous ledger. "You're in the infantry?"

"No."

"The artillery?"

I shake my head.

He shifts his weight from one foot to another. "The navy? Cavalry? Engineering? You're obviously not a Cossack."

His sneer sorely tempts me to shatter it with the heavy ledger. "I'm a medical student," I explain, "requested by the War Department to assist the physicians."

The clerk sets aside his pen. "If you're not in the military, I can't be expected to outfit you."

"You don't understand. At the university—"

The dolt's face darkens at the word.

"They told me that upon reaching the Crimea, I would be given the clothes and equipment I require."

His gypsy-black eyes narrow. "Do you have any paperwork to prove your story?"

My chest sinks as I feel every bit the fool the clerk assumes me to be. "The university has my paperwork."

"Then it's out of my hands." The knothead shrugs an apathetic shoulder that grazes the bottom of his prodigious earlobe. Then he looks around me to offer his assistance to someone who legitimately deserves his help.

I hold up my palm. "Listen, what is your name?"

"Corporal Kudin."

"Corporal Kudin, I fully understand that you cannot dispense supplies indiscriminately to anyone who walks in here. However, I am in Sevastopol in the service of the Tsar for the same purpose that you are—to win this war. Even though I am not officially in the army, navy, or any other branch of the military, I was assured I would receive the supplies I require to live and serve here."

Kudin, not about to be influenced by reason, raises a defiant eyebrow. "Without a regiment and a company number, I can't issue you a thing. Look here." He flips the ledger end-to-end to face me, then spins it back so promptly my eyes can't focus on a single word in the myriad columns. "Besides, I wouldn't know what color or style to issue if you're not in any battalion and you don't have a rank."

My thoughts pitch about frantically. I've never been skillful at persuasion or intimidation. I prefer that people treat each other with fairness, and I'm at a loss when that fails to happen.

"I'd like to speak to your commanding officer."

Kudin draws himself up stiffly. "He's busy. He doesn't have time for—"

"I'm certain . . ." I grope for an influential name to toss about. A major? A general? Coming up empty-handed, I seize the first name that comes to mind and fiddle slightly with the truth. "I'm certain Tsar Nicholas will be quite displeased that he personally selected top-level medical students and transported them to the Crimea, only to be told his army won't issue his recruits the most basic articles of outfit."

The little stooge snorts his disdain, then stomps to the back room and retrieves someone higher in the pecking order. The expanding line behind me abounds with heavy sighs and shuffling feet.

This new officer-asshole echoes Kudin's rejoinder. Eventually the conversation rounds a corner when, completely devoid of other options, I mention the name Captain Daniil Filimonovich Berestnev.

The officer-asshole mutters something to Kudin that sounds like, "Shit. Not him again."

Kudin retrieves a pile of clothes and shoves them across the counter. I'm informed that I'm obligated to pay for any lost or damaged articles.

"I don't suppose you have a pillow?" I ask, already certain of the answer.

"No!" He slaps some sheets of leather on top of the pile. "Take these to the regimental cobbler for your boots. There's enough leather for two pair."

Huh? "Why can't you just give me boots?"

"Because that's the way the army works. The cost of the cobbler will be deducted from your pay. Same with the barber."

I dig deeply, very deeply, to find a calm voice and words that Kudin can understand. "Here's my predicament. First: I'm not part of any regiment, so a regimental cobbler isn't an option. Second: I need boots *now*." I step around the counter to show him the left sole, barely connected to the upper, and my muddy sock. "The right foot is an exact match. Would you like to see it?"

In the line behind me, a voice growls, "Come on!"

Kudin blasts, "I don't have any damn boots! A cobbler is your only option!"

I clasp my hands in front of me to thwart my impassioned desire to yank his dangling earlobes clear off. "Here's my third point." I inhale to full capacity. "I have absolutely no rubles—none!—to pay for a cobbler. In exchange for my service in Sevastopol, I was promised a salary and tuition reimbursement. Is this office where I would receive those rubles?"

Corporal Kudin's eyes burn hot. "Headquarters in Simferopol."

Simferopol. Home of the dreamy-eyed Vasilisa, and now of my much-needed rubles! Everything of import is there!

WHEN I REACH the rancid, clamorous hospital, Daniil motions me toward a windowless supply room akin in size to a horse stall. It's infused with the pervasive aroma of camphor overlaid with the noxious effluvium of the main ward. At least the cubbyhole's stone walls dampen the moans and curses of the patients. A few wobbly stools, a tiny square table, and a cloud of steam from a gurgling samovar offer respite from the wet chill outside.

I begin to explain my boot predicament while Daniil fills two glasses with hot tea. Our conversation is cut short, however, when two other physicians wander in for tea and biscuits. The three doctors dive into an impromptu lecture for my benefit on the treatment of frostbite and hypothermia, both of which are certain to rear their heads soon. I suspect this storage room doubles as an unofficial meeting room as well as a sanctuary for the doctors.

All too soon, I step from the quiet of the supply room into the fetid chaos of the hospital ward. Orderlies, dressers, litter-bearers, attendants, and physicians hasten from patient to patient, carrying bandages, tea, vodka, fresh linen, surgical instruments, and stretchers. Sevastopol's yellowish mud is smeared in long trails from the main entrance into the cavernous wards. Bedpans, both full and empty, are strewn about. Soiled dressings clutter the stone floor. Knee-high heaps of trash occupy the corners.

My inexperienced hands rebandage several men, even though it's evident that death will soon take them. A shell has laid open a private's head, and his brain bulges through the hole. Another had his lower jaw shot off. Several men suffer with peritonitis secondary to abdominal wounds.

In addition to wounds, men are sickened by a variety of diseases, including erysipelas and catarrhal ophthalmia, which test my memory of textbook treatments. For almost all the patients, I find myself seeking advice from the experienced physicians. While I minister to the hollow-eyed, sunken-cheeked sufferers, I try unsuccessfully to block out the other agonies nearby. Some patients call for their mothers. Some curse. Some writhe. Some are stoic. Some beg to be shot.

Over the groans and coughs and sobs, I hear thunder. But when it continues for an hour, I realize I'm a dumbass.

It's a war, Andrey. Your "thunder" comes from cannons south of the city. Ours? Or the enemy's?

By midafternoon, my sinews are tied in knots from bending over beds and cots. I put my fists atop my kidneys and arch my back to stretch out the cricks.

"You're so tall," says a small voice nearby. "Would a stool help?"

Standing a few steps away is a freckled boy whose face has only a dusting of dandelion fluff. Probably age fifteen, tops. The youngster's boot nudges a low wooden stool toward me.

"You can carry it with you."

How is it that a baby-faced kid can get boots but a physician can't? "A splendid suggestion." I lower myself onto the seat, my knees threatening to scrape my chin. "Perfect height."

"You're new, aren't you?" He speaks with the callowness of a schoolboy, not a soldier. "I know everyone in this hospital."

"Arrived yesterday. I'm Doctor Rozhdestvensky." How strange the title feels on my tongue! "What is it you do in this hospital?"

The boy's eyebrows arch. "My duty lies with the laundry. I gather the dirty bandages and linens and haul them to the wash building. I get them as clean as I can with lye and cold water. Then I rinse them with boiling water, fold them, and stock them in the supply room." He holds up his left hand. "But then I got this."

A linen bandage encircles the flat of his hand, exposing his thumb and three fingers.

"There was a tiny cut on the first finger. It festered, and the whole finger swelled up and hurt and turned as black as a crow. So Doctor Berestnev cut it off. He's a swell doctor. Kept me asleep the whole time." The boy looks down at me over his upturned nose. "I asked Doctor Berestnev why my finger went rancid, but he didn't know. Do you?"

"No, I don't."

His shoulders shrug in acceptance of one of life's inexplicable phenomena.

Andrey, you need to get off this stool and move on to other patients.

But, I answer myself, *it's comforting to rest a moment and listen to the boy's cheery prattle.* "What's your name?"

"Colya."

"I may be new here, but I know this much, Colya. You're far safer in the laundry than you are on the battlefield."

I didn't know freckles could droop until Colya's did exactly that. "I'm not supposed to be in the laundry at all," he replied. "I was supposed to fight at the Alma. But I had a tapeworm."

"You couldn't fight because you had a tapeworm?"

"Yes, sir. They treated me with some liquid. I asked Doctor Berestnev if he was sure I was supposed to drink it and not put it, you know, where the worm was. But he said it was supposed to go in my mouth. I got the worst pains and almost pooped out my insides, and that's when the troops left for the Alma. By the time the battle was over, I felt better, and Doctor Berestnev got me this job in the laundry. It's not a hero's job, but I don't mind doing my part." Colya's cheeks swell with flushed enthusiasm.

"But wasn't the Alma a horrific battle?"

Colya straightens his spine, thrusting forward what little chest he possesses. "That's why I'm here. To fight for Holy Russia and our sacred Church, and for the persecuted Christians under Turk rule."

I cock my head at the incongruence of the boy's words and his fresh-faced look.

"Damn the bad luck," Colya concludes. "First, I missed the Alma because of a tapeworm. Then I missed Inkerman because of my finger. But I'll be in the final battle when we crush the allies. No doubt about that."

THE NEXT MORNING, chilly water again scoffs at my boots and shrivels my toes. My mood sours further with my first step into the rank hospital. The priest is gliding from bed to bed, sprinkling holy water on the bodies whose souls departed during the night. I know too much, lamentably, about the ignoble underbelly of the Church to tolerate its malignant men of piety. Complete avoidance of the black-robed bastards is my unflagging, lifelong objective.

I scurry to the storage room for the comfort of hot tea. Seated at the table are Daniil and five other physicians, all of them spellbound by a balding man with high cheekbones. The cocksure fellow, who looks to be in his mid-forties, is wagging his index finger in the air, saying, "Only a person who holds the welfare of suffering people above all other considerations has the right to call himself a true physician."

I intuit I'm in the presence of Russia's great physician, Nikolai Ivanovich Pirogov.

All the stools are taken, so I slouch against the wall, ankles crossed, my hands embracing a warm glass of tea.

"I estimate that on the combined north and south sides of the bay, there are four thousand sick and wounded," Pirogov expounds. "And their medical care is an abomination."

The physicians shift uneasily, and Pirogov is quick to amend his statement. "The fault lies not with you fellows. It's the system. Organized transport of the wounded is absent. So is basic warm clothing. Latrines are overflowing. Physicians are in atrociously short supply. In my estimation, there should be one physician for every one hundred seven men. Wars, like great epidemics, require a multitude of physicians. After all, war is merely an epidemic of trauma. Instead of the proper treatment, however, Sevastopol is engulfed in its own epidemic of mismanagement and graft."

The physicians' heads give a collective nod.

Pirogov continues to brandish a furious index finger. "Our soldiers are subject to maladministration of the grandest scale. They suffer a dearth of everything. Drugs, yes. But also lamps, lamp oil, candles. Even stools." He gestures toward me. "Look at that young man. He can't even sit down for want of a stool."

All heads swivel in my direction, shattering my assumption that I'm as inconspicuous as a fly on the wall. With Pirogov's blue eyes pinned on me, I uncross my legs and straighten my posture. I tend to lumber through life as quick-witted as a bear waking from its winter slumber, and today is no exception. My mind scrambles for an appropriate response, but my tongue goes numb.

Daniil rescues me. "Doctor Pirogov, this is one of our medical students from Moscow. May I present Andrey Yevgrafovich Rozhdestvensky."

"My honor to make your acquaintance, Doctor Pirogov." Perhaps not the most eloquent words, but at least they flowed out in sensible order and with a manful tenor.

Pirogov's eyebrows knit together. "Well, let's hope you learn something here besides ineptitude." He turns back to the others. "I have two priorities in the Crimea. First, curtail incompetence and slash corruption."

More head nodding around the table.

"Second, establish protocols for preventive medicine. It's a specialty too often overlooked and underappreciated, even though it's vital to any civilized society. How can we win a war without healthy men?"

With those words, he rises to his feet. It appears we are dismissed.

LATER THAT AFTERNOON, after treating a bomb victim's burns with oil and cotton, I rise from the bedside to see Pirogov blasting toward me at full force.

"Hello, young student! I'm spreading the word regarding my upcoming presentation, the first of a series of medical dissertations." Pirogov's eyes sparkle with enthusiasm. "My lecture will be Wednesday evening. Tell the others, will you?" Without waiting for a response, he breezes away, the bloodied tails of his white coat fluttering behind him.

I head toward my next patient.

"Young student! One other thing." Pirogov bounds back toward me. "I couldn't help but notice this morning—your feet sound like the bills of a pair of ducks, flapping up and down. When do you plan to see a cobbler about getting those boots repaired?"

"I apologize, sir, but I've yet to receive any pay. And I was promised reimbursement of my medical school tuition when I arrived in the Crimea. But the Sevastopol authorities told me I have to obtain the rubles in Simferopol."

"Considering the Byzantine code of regulations here, I believe that's undoubtedly true. Simferopol, you say?"

I can see ideas churning behind the broad expanse of his forehead.

"Your name again?"

"Andrey Yevgrafovich Rozhdestvensky."

"Here's what I propose, Rozhdestvensky. Tomorrow I'm traveling to Simferopol to make certain the Sisters of Mercy are settled at the army hospital there. Ride along with me. You can question the person in charge directly about your reimbursement. It's a lesson I learned long ago, to eliminate the middlemen if at all possible. They just muck things up."

I go bug-eyed. Simferopol and Vasilisa! "I'm very grateful, sir. Truly I am. I'll take you up on your offer. Thank you . . . thank you very much." *Stop stammering, Andrey.*

"Once I'm assured the Sisters are well housed and receiving courteous treatment, I'm headed to Bakhchisarai to inspect the facilities there. I'm certain you can find the means to return to Sevastopol on your own."

"But . . . but Doctor Pirogov, perhaps I misunderstood. If you're going to Simferopol tomorrow—Tuesday—and then onward after that, how is it possible for you to give a talk here in Sevastopol on Wednesday?"

Pirogov's brow drops until his eyes are in danger of being completely shrouded. "Hummm, yes. That's problematic, isn't it?" He hikes up his eyebrows, and his forehead crinkles cheerfully. "I'll have to reschedule the talk, won't I? See you in the morning, Rozhdestvensky. Seven bells prompt."

CHAPTER 6

November

1854

THE CHURCH BELLS peal seven times into the moist morning air. My driver sits hunched over his reins, snoring beneath a blanket. Standing alongside the supply wagon, I lean back against it with arms crossed, one foot folded behind me to rest on a wheel spoke. My head swings from side to side in dumbfounded astonishment.

In my life, good luck of any kind is a welcome stranger. Will fate remain in my favor until the rubles are clenched in my needy hand? Will good fortune linger long enough for me to woo Vasilisa off her feet and out of her stodgy brown habit?

"Down, boy," I quietly order. This time, I'm not talking to myself. Well, it's only somewhat to myself. My Little Soldier is part of me, but he also has a will of his own. I never know when he's going to snap to attention. And Vasilisa definitely garnered his attention.

Little Soldier's preoccupation with the image of Vasilisa's habit sliding to the floor is interrupted by Ignaty Sadykov passing by, his stalwart legs hurrying him to the start of his workday. Even though I've been in Sevastopol only a couple of days, eating with Ignaty and Daniil in the mess hall has settled into a habit, and their easy camaraderie helps allay my aloneness in this hellhole.

"Don't you dare return without my cigars!" Ignaty quips. In Sevastopol, cigars have become as rare as courteous corporals in the provisions office.

I grin. "They'll be in your hand next week!"

As Ignaty moves on, my smile plummets. *Come on, Pirogov! Don't fail me!* We have fifty miles to travel, and winter's daylight is short. My fist whacks the wagon's sideboard. The driver snorts and resettles himself.

At half past the hour, the great physician races toward me, arms bent at the elbows and propelling him forward like the coupling rods on a locomotive's wheels. He bounds onto the wagon's bench, scoots close to the driver, and motions me to squeeze onto the seat with them.

The driver shakes off his morning somnolence and slaps the reins.

"I just saw the most fascinating case," Pirogov exclaims.

At seven o'clock in the morning? "Oh?" I ask.

"A private was admitted to the hospital with complaints of aches in his limbs and joints. Plus, he feels weak. On physical examination, the only abnormalities I noted were his extreme thinness and sallow complexion. Have you a diagnosis?"

I try to arrange my face into a self-assured expression. "It sounds like rheumatism to me, sir."

"My diagnosis also. I told him he needed to stay in a warm bed for a few days and eat extra helpings of stew with plenty of meat and bread. That's when he told me that he could eat the bread, but his mouth hurt too much to chew the stringy meat. Guess what I found in his mouth." Pirogov's eyebrows arch. "Bleeding gums and loose teeth. Now what is your diagnosis, Andrey Yevgrafovich?" The physician closes one eye in a protracted wink. The other is agape with expectation.

I admit I don't know, thinking that if Pirogov keeps up this line of questioning, this will be a very long trip.

"I can't blame you for overlooking the answer. It's a condition not commonly seen in the cities." Pirogov leans into my shoulder and whispers, "Scurvy."

I pull back, as much in surprise as in an effort to put some distance between myself and the vociferous physician. "Scurvy? How can that be? We have sufficient food."

Pirogov sways to upright, shaking his head. "I fear those in the field do not, thanks to a few corrupt regimental officers who pocket the rubles intended to feed their men." The corners of his jaws clench and unclench. "It's a breakdown of the military system on the most massive scale. The right hand requisitions supplies, only to have the left hand steal them."

"Perhaps you can gain General Menshikov's ear on this matter," I suggest.

"Already tried. Heavens, how I've tried!" Pirogov peers at me and scratches his bushy sideburn, as if assessing whether a student can be trusted. "When I described to Prince Menshikov how miserably our men are suffering, do you know what he replied? He smiled and said, 'In the past, it was worse.' That was the sum of our leader's response. 'In the past, it was worse.'" He gives a dispirited shake of his head.

"So what is to be done to help our soldiers?"

Pirogov's answer comes slowly as he raises his gaze toward the Crimean hills. "I'm convinced the Sisters can help us."

"The Sisters?"

"I have faith that the Sisters will take matters into their own hands, as women are prone to do. I hold fast to the belief that we will enjoy cleaner, better supplied, more cheerful hospitals." He pauses to survey my baffled face. "Think about it. Women can't help but clean things up. It's part and parcel of their nature. Women, as a race of people, have been given admirable gifts that the Creator withheld from men. And these particular women volunteered for this mission out of feelings of altruism. Their own consciences compel them to be dutiful."

All right, Andrey, come up with a neutral response. "You hold high expectations for the Sisters."

"I do. And I hope your generation has enough sense to recognize the value of women." He bestows me with a weighty glance. "If a woman is raised and educated properly, she is just as capable as a man of adopting scientific, artistic, and social culture. And without relinquishing her womanhood."

A handful of the more radical students at the university are in favor of equality for women. They're a tiny minority, however, and are under constant scrutiny by the officials. Like the rest of Russia, I know the truth: women have distinct functions in life, including the time-honored, benevolent roles of motherhood and caregiving. They are best suited to their traditional position as housekeeper, food preparer, family tailor, and bed partner.

The sky is widening with light as Pirogov segues to a host of diverse medical topics, including his revised position on the proper handling of gunshot wounds, the need for expanded hygiene lectures in the medical curriculum, and his firm stance that alcoholism is both a disease and a social evil of enormous proportions. Eventually, even Pirogov grows weary of his own voice and lapses into blessed silence.

As the wagon pitches toward the center of the peninsula, I scowl at the countryside. The fog is receding from the bleak, unwelcoming hills and their deep, craggy ravines. Little scrub plants cling tenaciously to the stony slopes. Trails meander between thistles and boulders, traveled by both humans and small, skinny sheep.

Why would anyone fight over this godforsaken piece of land?

But I rescind my own question. The war isn't about land. The clash traces back to long-standing religious animosity and political resentment between Russia and the sovereign states of France, England, and Turkey.

For centuries, Russian rubles have maintained the Christian shrines located on the soil of Muslim Turkey. A couple of years ago, France persuaded the Turks to hand the keys of the main door of Bethlehem's Church of the Nativity to the Roman Catholic priests rather than to the Eastern Orthodox monks. To add insult to Russia's injury, Napoleon III, the self-proclaimed protector of Latin Christianity, placed a Catholic silver star, adorned with the arms of France, on the holy manger.

Orthodox monks tried to stop the symbolic gesture. The religious feud escalated into riots, and several monks were killed. Tsar Nicholas I, believing himself to be the guardian of Turkey's ten million Orthodox Christians, lashed out at the Turkish police for their failure to maintain order. He even hinted that the heathen Turks had contrived the "murders."

During the summer of 1853, bullying and name-calling eventually led to a few skirmishes along the Danube in the principalities of Moldavia and Wallachia, a buffer territory under the joint protection of Russia and Turkey. Following a series of negotiations and ultimatums, push came to shove, and in October, the Turks declared war on Russia.

In response, Nicholas mobilized his vast army, proclaiming, "Russia fights not for the things of this world, but for the Faith."

"A sham!" cried Russia's intelligentsia, convinced the religious war was merely a masquerade to conceal the Tsar's voracious appetite for more land. The weak Ottoman Empire was on the brink of collapse, and when the time came for Turkey to topple, Nicholas had every intention of being poised to pick up the choice pieces. Russia had long coveted a warm-water port, especially one that offered easy passageway to the Mediterranean and, in the opposite direction, access to the rich provinces in Eastern Europe and Western Asia.

And wouldn't it be delightful to turn the Black Sea into a Russian lake?

Nicholas's dream was Queen Victoria's nightmare. She predicted Russia would use its land acquisition as a springboard to expand into Central Asia and disrupt England's communications with India.

France, meanwhile, didn't want its power in the Mediterranean usurped by Russia, nor did it want the Tsar meddling with its North African empire. It did, however, want to reclaim its place of respect among European powers. Not to mention Napoleon III's hunger to fulfill his personal ambition: to achieve the glory and popular acclaim that his uncle Bonaparte had savored forty-five years earlier.

There was no love lost between England and France. Even so, in March 1854, under the guise of protecting the Turks, but with the ulterior aim of slashing Russia's size and power, the two military goliaths joined with feeble Turkey. Collectively, they were known as the allies.

Contemplating the whole mess, I chuckle aloud as the wagon rocks along the meager road. I always garner a perverse pleasure when the Church finds a useful purpose for itself, even if that purpose is to provide a pretext for a war that will claim the lives of its congregation.

ONCE WE REACH Simferopol, the world takes on a new flavor. The narrow, littered streets team with black-marketeers, booze sellers, and prostitutes. Packs of bony dogs dig through piles of garbage, and thick streams of mud and sewage flow along the streets toward the Salgir River.

Pirogov barrels into the hospital while I trail after him like a faithful dog. Straight off, the renowned surgeon locates the chief medical officer, Doctor Gavriil Gerasimovich Orshansky, and as expected, receives a deferential greeting. Pirogov's words are polite, but a sharpness cuts through his voice. The reason for his vexation is obvious. The hospital's conditions are beyond appalling.

Overrun with patients, Sevastopol hospitals transfer their excess to Simferopol. Once the provincial capital fills its existing beds, the remaining patients are scattered on straw on the floor. Rodents of all sizes scurry between the twisted bodies, which look out with pained eyes. Gaping wounds are left uncovered. Men lie in their own excrement. The noxious stink is so thick, it can almost be grasped.

Suddenly I understand why the Russian soldier prefers death on the field to sustaining a wound, however slight.

Tired lines fan down from the corners of Orshansky's eyes and lips. He tries to converse with Pirogov, but the words are drowned by the racket of coughing consumptives, clanging bedpans, and shouting hospital attendants. "Perhaps we should visit the overflow facility."

Overflow facility? I wonder if anyone else sees the sad irony that Sevastopol requires overflow accommodations in Simferopol, which in turn requires overflow provisions of its own.

The facility turns out to be converted horse stables that house well over a hundred ill and wounded men. Many lie without quilts or blankets of any kind, with only straw between them and the cold, earthen floor. The putrid straw is soaked with urine and pus. Any trace of equine aroma has long ago been overridden by the stench of rampant dysentery and rotting humans.

Orshansky bends Pirogov's ear about the hospitals' shoddy provisions, inadequate staffing, and endless delays in supply acquisition. He's of a mind to grouse on indefinitely about the fiendish circumstances that confront him, but Pirogov suggests that the dialogue be resumed over the evening meal.

Our host nervously turns up the ends of his moustache. "I was able to secure you a bed in one of the officers' quarters, but I thought you'd be traveling alone. I'm afraid I don't have any arrangements for your companion." His sunken eyes turn toward me, desperate, as if locating a bed might be the straw that ends up breaking his back. "I realize this is a shabby offer, but there's a loft up above. I can supply fresh straw and blankets." His eyes plead with me.

I consent to the meager arrangements. "I slept in all manner of barns on my way from Moscow and found them to be quite satisfactory. By any chance, do you have a pillow?"

"Pillow?" The word seems alien to Orshansky's vocabulary.

"I'll be fine without one."

Pirogov says, "Tomorrow, the young doctor has to tend to some personal errands, but after that, he'll have time to assist with the patients in this overflow facility."

I interpret the statement as a directive.

Orshansky offers dinner at his quarters, a cramped little bungalow he shares with other physicians. During the brief walk, I feel anger seethe from Pirogov's tense body. By the time we reach our destination, I'm prepared for a blowup. My expectations are met.

"That hospital is an unbelievable combination of Slav carelessness, Tatar filth, medical ignorance, chaos, and stink," Pirogov thunders once we're seated around the dining table.

"I agree with you, sir. It's an appalling state of affairs, to say the least." Orshansky's shoulders are bowed. His chest seems ready to cave completely against his spine. "The men lie in misery, but our hospitals are so short on supplies and space, we're like a cart with no wheels. I'm at a loss to know how to proceed. Twenty-five years in military medicine, and I've never been confronted with anything as overwhelming as this." His forehead drops into his palm.

"I expected conditions here to be better than at the front, not worse," Pirogov bellows.

Forehead still nested in his hand, Orshansky groans, "Sevastopol keeps sending more and more wounded. We're beyond our capacity to cope."

Pirogov's tone loses some of its sharp edge. "What is St. Petersburg doing to help you?"

Orshansky lifts his head. "What is St. Petersburg doing for me? Sending me goddamned women, that's what St. Petersburg is doing for me!"

The corners of Pirogov's taut mouth twitch. "As you know, I'm here to ensure the Sisters of Mercy are treated hospitably." His voice contains a thinly veiled warning. "What arrangements have you made for them?"

"I secured a decent house, which I acquired through the grace of sheer luck. The Sisters are crowded but relatively comfortable while they recuperate from their journey. But truthfully, Doctor Pirogov, I don't know how they'll survive in this nightmarish environment. I suspect they'll all succumb to typhus within the week."

"They'll have to survive as best they can. Just as the rest of us will."

"It's a living Hell, as you can see. What if they go into hysterics?"

Pirogov inhales deeply, calling forth some patience. "We'll give them a fair chance to show their worth. If they can't perform under pressure, home they go."

Stifled worries continue to erupt from Orshansky. "On one hand, the physicians don't want them here, and I fear they'll treat the women poorly. On the other hand, I don't need any romances between my doctors and those holy martyrs. The doctors barely have enough strength to get through the workday. I can't have them waste precious energy cavorting with women."

Pirogov's eyebrows form a severe line just above the pupils of his eyes. "Any untoward behavior on the part of the men will result in a reprimand. If not corrected, the offender will find himself digging trenches at Sevastopol."

I infer that the phrase *untoward behavior* exactly matches my intentions toward Sister Vasilisa.

Orshansky closes his eyes and sways his head. "No good can come of this," he says, nearly weeping.

The conversation is interrupted by servants setting out a meal of salted cod, deviled eggs, pickled cucumber, wheat bread, and strong Crimean wine. The food and drink mollify everyone's disposition, and at the close of the meal, Orshansky brings out a bottle.

"I tend to like a small nightcap before retiring." He pours the golden liquid into tumblers. "A little arrowroot in rum is a fine way to unwind."

I must agree. As the smooth concoction fills my belly with a warm glow, my eyelids grow heavy. When another physician enters the cottage and Pirogov immediately engulfs him in conversation, I reluctantly decide to return to the stench and moans of the stables.

As I climb the wooden boards that serve as a stationary ladder, I'm grateful nature ordained that heat rises. I settle into the surprisingly warm straw. A little rum with arrowroot is indeed a fine way to finish the day. As are dreamy musings about the pink swell of Vasilisa's lips and nipples.

THE NEXT MORNING, I follow Orshansky's directions to a white stone building. I'm greeted by a dull, thick sergeant whose terse demeanor makes Corporal

Kudin look like a bleeding heart. I produce the letter that Daniil graciously penned for me, verifying my status. The document holds little sway.

"Do you have your certificate?"

"Certificate?"

"Yes. Certificate."

"What certificate?"

"The certificate they gave you in Moscow substantiating your status and that you're entitled to reimbursement."

"They never gave me a certificate. They said you would give me the rubles when I reached Simferopol."

"Without a certificate, it's impossible, by all accounts."

"No one ever mentioned a certificate."

Round and round the conversation goes, until I'm told to return tomorrow. The sergeant requires time to discuss the preposterous situation with his superior.

Muscles taut with fury, I stride in the direction of the converted stables. Although it's only midmorning, street commerce is in full swing. Greeks peddle lemonade. Jewish moneychangers rattle coins in their leather purses. Tatars with turbans of lamb's wool barter with one another under bare-limbed acacia trees. Laughing, dark-haired boys offer to sell anything visitors want, including their sisters.

I occupy my afternoon working at the makeshift facility. During the evening meal, Pirogov announces that the Sisters of Mercy are settled in and ready to begin their hospital duties. "I'm calling on you, Andrey Yevgrafovich, to help orient the Sisters tomorrow."

Vasilisa! Tomorrow!

Tomorrow . . .

Damn it all! Tomorrow morning I must confront the sergeant about my tuition reimbursement. The discussion had better be short and with a suitable outcome.

Fuming, I run my fingers through my hair and eye the bottle of rum. Orshansky doesn't disappoint.

CHAPTER 7

December

1854

I'M FIRST IN line at the sergeant's desk, only to have my hopes trampled. Tucked behind stacks of precisely piled papers, the slow-witted ox snarls that my request has to be forwarded to St. Petersburg "to see if they can untangle this mess. Don't expect a response from the capital until after the first of the new year."

I argue that I've been promised the rubles and can't be expected to live without them. I toss Daniil's letter of support onto the green blotter, thump it with my index finger, and insist on speaking to the dumb ox's superior.

The ox ignores my demand and continues to seek refuge behind the security of regulations. He glares at me from beneath the rigid portrait of His Imperial Majesty Nicholas I, the same Tsar who beckoned me to the Crimea.

I erupt in a loud, abusive tirade at both the ox and the Tsar, stopping just short of sweeping my arm across the dullard's desk and shoving his fastidiously piled papers onto the floor.

He threatens to have me physically removed from the building.

What little lucidity I retain tells me to exit the building posthaste before I dig my own grave. Threading my way between the dung piles of various transport animals, I mutter every obscenity I know. Then, for emphasis, I link the vulgarities together in a string of profanities. A concatenation of foul expletives. A progressive hierarchy of vile curses. Despite my aptitude for cussing, my rage is still not fully vented by the time I reach the stable-turned-hospital.

I spend my morning consumed, first, with indignation at the sergeant and the army in general; second, in a cold sweat about my finances; and third, beside myself with anxiety about the Sisters' arrival. Fearful I might miss them, I obsessively traipse to and from the real hospital.

During my fourth visit, I spot Pirogov escorting a dozen females through the hospital wards. The women are prudishly attired in their identical brown habits, now with white aprons fastened about the waist. A white scarf, enormous as a frigate's sail, is secured under each chin with a prim knot, and a bulky gold cross hangs from every neck.

"Doctor Rozhdestvensky!" the great physician hails from the other end of the ward. "Greet some of our new arrivals."

I hasten toward them, my eyes scampering from face to face. The pent-up air in my chest vents in a sigh of relief as I spot the exquisite Vasilisa. The subtle swing of her skirt inspires my Little Soldier.

Pirogov is effervescent. "Sisters, may I introduce Andrey Yevgrafovich Rozhdestvensky. He is a medical student at the university in Moscow and is finishing his final year of studies with us. You see, in school, one learns the craft of medicine. In practice, one learns the art."

"Some of us already had the most wonderful pleasure of meeting Doctor Rozhdestvensky," responds one of the Sisters, whom I recognize from the overturned wagon.

I ask, "How is Sister Ivanova feeling?"

The heavyset woman is also among the group. "Still in some pain, but on the mend," she replies.

The corners of Vasilisa's mouth curve seductively upward as she explains to Pirogov, "When Sister Ivanova was injured, this kind man arrived at just the right moment and tended to our poor Sister." She turns in my direction and pours her gaze over me. I am altogether submerged in her full-bodied voice and the deep wells of her sapphire eyes.

The remaining nine Sisters introduce themselves to me. Despite their youth, most of them hold forth a matronly bearing. I note none of their names, focusing instead on the cinch of the white apron about Vasilisa's slender waist.

Pirogov interrupts my ripening fantasies. "I call on you, Doctor Rozhdestvensky, to escort these benevolent ladies on the final leg of their orientation—the auxiliary facility—while I tend to the remaining Sisters awaiting their tour." He gives the Sisters a cavalier bow of his head.

I crimson at Pirogov's aggrandizement. *Auxiliary facility.* Nothing more than a horse stable converted into a filthy piss hole.

"My pleasure." I smile at Vasilisa, whose moist lips return the gesture.

While the Sisters don their cloaks, I'm aware of the many eyes, both patients' and staff's, that sweep over our small assembly. On the way to the stables, Vasilisa falls into step next to me. I fix my sight straight ahead, trying to keep at bay the effect her closeness is having on Little Soldier. I've been celibate for quite awhile. Quite a long while.

The Sisters inundate me with tales of their ordeals en route to the Crimea. At times, eight or ten oxen were required to dislodge sunken wheels from mud holes

of the pockmarked roads. Never having had a dozen women chatter simultaneously at me, I'm at a complete loss. How can I possibly swing my head in so many
different directions, all while snaking between drunken soldiers, cursing camel
drivers, and heaps of filth?

Before we enter the auxiliary facility, I warn, "The conditions inside are far
from desirable. The staff are short-handed and do the best they can."

The big-boned woman asks, "When you doctored Sister Ivanova, didn't you
say you were stationed in Sevastopol?"

"You remember correctly. I'm headquartered at the front." The last words are
a pathetically boyish attempt to impress Vasilisa. "I'm temporarily in Simferopol
on an errand."

The square-jawed Sister continues her questions. "But while you're here in
Simferopol, you work in these overflow wards, correct?"

"Yes, I do. But please understand, it's not really a hospital. The army has made
use of all available buildings." I pray Vasilisa doesn't think I'm so low in the medical hierarchy that I'm assigned to a horse barn.

I keep the tour brief. Who in their right mind wants to look at a sea of miserable, rotting men surrounded by vermin and general debris? Yet the women
handle the conditions better than I expect. Several even pause to chat with some
of the men.

I'm reflecting on Vasilisa's high breasts when she turns her back toward me
and bends forward to speak with a bedridden patient. The brown fabric drapes
across her buttocks, and her hem glides above her high-topped shoes. Heat accumulates deep within me.

We move from the disarray of the hospital back to the pandemonium of
the street. Gentle gusts of wind whorl the blonde wisps that have spilled from
under Vasilisa's scarf. As the errant locks skim across her creamy cheek, I'm
sorely tempted to brush them aside and savor her softness against the back of
my hand. Then slide my fingers down the curve of her jaw. Untie the obstruct-
ing bow . . .

"I shall be assigned here," states the bulky woman.

"Pardon?"

"I'll request to work at the overflow wards."

"Of course, your assistance is needed everywhere, but why would you choose
to work here, in the worst of conditions?"

Her eyes, a placid green, focus on mine. "Something attracts me to this place. I
believe I can be of use here." The woman turns toward Vasilisa. "Sister Abramova,

will you be joining me in this overflow facility?" The woman isn't asking a question. She's issuing a challenge.

Vasilisa, who had been idly watching the bedlam of people and animals, swirls her head in surprise. "Why, no. I'll work in the main hospital, as planned."

The big-boned Sister's smile is smug.

"Well, I . . . I suppose I'll see you in the morning," I stammer, crestfallen that I won't be seeing the golden-haired beauty as well. "Good day, Sisters."

Vasilisa reaches her gloved hand toward me, and I lightly clasp the tips of her delicate fingers. Her gaze, rich with promise, holds mine before she sedately lowers her long lashes and bids me adieu. Am I mistaken, or did her fingers linger in my hand a tad longer than was necessary? Was there something suggestive in those hypnotic blue eyes, perhaps a promise that something special lies over the horizon?

The beefy woman thrusts her paw forward. "Good day, Doctor Rozhdestvensky."

Recalling the bullish strength of her grip during our first encounter, I brace myself and extend my hand.

The Sisters make their way through the lengthening shadows of evening until they disappear in the mass of humanity and animals and conveyances that clog Simferopol's streets.

That night, following dinner and rum with arrowroot, I lie on my straw, wishing I had a clean shirt to wear in the morning. I roll onto my side, Vasilisa's provocative voice pouring over me like warm caramel.

THE BIG WOMAN is already at work when I reach the stables. I use the term *work* loosely. She talks with patients, assists those who can't manage a spoon to eat their breakfast, and picks up littered bandages and linens as she moves through the ward. She gives me a cheery wave of her hand. I reciprocate and allow her to continue with what she perceives to be important tasks.

Later she strides up to me. "Good morning, Doctor Rozhdestvensky. I wasn't exactly sure what tasks I should be performing, and there appears to be so much that needs doing. So I merely started tidying up and helping the patients. Did you have something specific in mind for me?"

"Good morning . . . ?" I begin, unable to remember her name.

"Maria Ivanovna Kurbatova," she says pleasantly.

"Sister Kurbatova. Please continue as you have been. You seem to be helping the men a great deal."

With that, she continues to maneuver her unwieldy body through the tightly packed men, shoving soiled linens into a sack as she goes. She's built more like a barrel than a woman.

I spend the day on tenterhooks, contriving excuses to visit the main hospital and stumble upon Vasilisa. Each trip is nonproductive. Her desirability increases proportionately with her inaccessibility.

At sunset, I step from the stables into the frosty air, my listless spirits intent on a good meal and a nightcap at Orshansky's cottage. Kurbatova appears at my side.

"Excuse me, Doctor, but I wonder if I might impose upon you. I'm somewhat uneasy walking alone after dark and would be grateful for your company."

Considering her arms are the size of hams, I assume she could whip any man who dared to accost her. But I politely respond, "My pleasure."

"You mentioned you were in Simferopol on an errand." She matches her step to mine. "What sort of errand?"

I find the question intrusive to ask of a stranger, but I answer all the same. "The military owes me some rubles, and the authorities in Sevastopol said I needed to make my plea to headquarters here."

Her laugh is robust but feminine. "Nothing can run you around in more circles than the military. My father was in the army. Some of the things I saw! Pettiness on an epic scale. When are you returning to Sevastopol?"

"The day after tomorrow."

"So soon? How fortunate the Sisters arrived when we did and were able to express our gratitude again."

Kurbatova is obviously a nice person, leaving me with a sense of guilt for ignoring her all day. "Fortunate, indeed, that I was able to hitch a ride from Sevastopol with Doctor Pirogov, who came for the sole purpose of making certain the Sisters were well received."

She sighs. "Most of the physicians don't want us here. What about you, Doctor Rozhdestvensky? What do you think of us?"

I resist my reflex to respond, *Well, if you desire to act as chambermaids, that's your affair.* Instead, I set into motion my tried-and-true ploy of changing the subject. "There's no need to refer to me as a doctor. As Doctor Pirogov explained, I'm still a student."

"Yes, I remember. However, he addressed you as Doctor, so I thought you preferred the title."

"Only in front of patients. The truth is, I'm not at all used to being called Doctor."

"With time, I'm sure, it will feel natural."

"I'm curious. If you don't mind my asking, what medical training do you have?"

Again comes that pleasurable laugh, but I detect a hint of self-consciousness. "Not very much. I spent two weeks at a hospital, learning what I could."

"So you've seen wounds being dressed and surgeries being performed?"

"Yes, but scarcely a teacupful."

"And the other Sisters? What experience do they have?"

"About the same."

"Once your duties are finished in the Crimea, what will you do?"

"Probably return to Moscow, where I live with my sister, Vasilisa."

My heart thumps. "You don't mean Sister Vasilisa?"

She stops walking, so I follow suit. She bestows me with a long, oblique stare, the kind my sisters gave me when I exhausted their patience. "Sister Vasilisa is far too pretty to be a member of our family. All the way to Simferopol, she attracted admirers like flies. She knows exactly what those dreamy blue eyes can do to a man."

"Oh." I resume walking, but she remains still. I turn to look at her.

"This is our housing." She gestures toward the stone two-story structure.

"Oh," I say, trying to see through the windows. Is Vasilisa inside?

Kurbatova chews the inside of her lip. "Forgive me if I'm being forward, but were you able to obtain your rubles?"

I give a sad shake of my head.

"Please don't think me presumptuous, but it's possible I can help you."

I tilt my head as if intrigued, although internally I'm scoffing. What does she think she can do that I can't?

"I wouldn't at all mind accompanying you tomorrow to try again."

"Your offer is enormously generous, but I couldn't impose." I keep glancing toward the house. *Vasilisa, are you in there?*

"I didn't grow up a military daughter without learning a thing or two about how to grease a palm." She laughs yet again, a big, happy laugh that is somehow not overbearing. Looking at her full lips and broad smile, I decide she has at least one attractive attribute.

"I suppose we could go first thing in the morning," I concede. "It's worth a try. Meanwhile, I'm sure your evening meal is waiting for you."

As is my nightcap, I add silently.

CLUTCHING DANIIL'S LETTER, Kurbatova suggests I wait in the hallway while she deals with the sergeant. I sit on a straight-backed chair, offended that I've been excluded from the office. As the minutes pass, I work myself into a boiling fury and begin pacing the hallway. This is a waste of time. A far better use of my last morning in Simferopol would be scouting about the hospital for Vasilisa.

My pacing has about worn out what's left of my boots when Kurbatova pokes her head out the door. "You need to sign for your rubles."

As I enter the office, the obtuse sergeant fixes me with a nasty scowl. I return the greeting. After shoving the crumpled banknotes across the desk, he growls, "I assume you're returning immediately to Sevastopol to tend to our wounded."

I nod. "And I assume I'll be able to access my future pay in Sevastopol?"

If looks could kill, the sergeant would see to it I'd never get the opportunity to spend my rubles.

Before I leave the desk, I count each precious ruble. Two months' salary, plus fifty rubles for tuition. Having paid only the first half of one year's tuition, I'm entitled to only twenty-five rubles. The moral dilemma pauses briefly as it passes through my ethics censor, replaced with a mental note to purchase some rum and arrowroot before departing Simferopol.

As we leave the building, I ask Kurbatova, "However did you do it?"

"Everyone in the army has a commander, and every commander can be bribed. I demanded to speak to the captain, and I discovered he has a penchant for Turkish sherbet. Seems he can't find any here." On their way to Simferopol, she explains, the Sisters spent four days at the encampment on the isthmus, where she learned of a black market. "In my negotiations with the captain, I swore by all the saints that I'd have my contact send him some."

I hold forth a ruble. "Will this cover the sherbet?"

Kurbatova waves it away. "The fellow with the sherbet owes me money from a card game. Terrible card player."

Card game? I'm disinclined to inquire further. "My appreciation knows no limits. You've already lived up to your title of 'Sister of Mercy.'"

She smiles. "Matching wits with those rascals was rather fun."

"I hope your time in the Crimea holds many more amusements. Meanwhile, I'd best tend to some errands. I need to purchase some cigars and other items."

"I hope you don't smoke in the loft. If the hay starts on fire, the whole overflow ward will be in ashes." Her honest, unrestrained laughter bursts forth.

How does she know I'm sleeping in the loft?

"The cigars are for my friend in Sevastopol. Thanks to the siege, tobacco is as difficult to find as sherbet."

She responds with that inviting laugh of hers.

"You have my sincerest gratitude, Maria Kurbatova, for your assistance today. I wish you'd allow me to repay you in some way."

"I'll give it some thought." Then she paraphrases the words she used during our initial encounter. "I trust our paths will cross again."

CHAPTER 8

December
1854

ONCE BACK IN Sevastopol, I fall into the comfort of a routine. Unfortunately, that routine includes waking each morning to find I'm still in Sevastopol.

After bemoaning my lack of a pillow, I clasp my hands behind my head and conjure up captivating words to say to Vasilisa. In my fantasy she giggles, and dimples form at the corners of her mouth. I loosen the knot in her white scarf. Her blonde hair pours down her back and over her breasts. At long last, I unburden her of her puritanical attire . . .

My next twelve hours are spent in the wards, walking lines of beds, cots, and floor pallets occupied by men hacking up blood-tinged, yellow expectorate, or swaddled in sodden, redolent bandages where frostbite claimed toes or a nose. I usually share my evening meal with either Daniil or Ignaty. Then I retreat to my cot for the soothing comfort of rum with arrowroot and Vasilisa's suggestive eyes. Her caressing voice. Her tempting mouth. Her unveiled creamy skin. The taste of her many charms.

I realize I sound soft in the head, but Vasilisa's sensuality is tormenting me. Each night, Little Soldier wholeheartedly urges me to take my fantasies a step or two further.

IN MID-DECEMBER, YOUNG Colya begins to work with us at the hospital. Daniil could tolerate neither the thought of Colya living in a tent during the winter nor the possibility of what might befall the boy in battle. He was able to get Colya assigned as an orderly. "Just temporarily," Daniil told the youngster, "until that hole in your hand is fully healed."

Colya was as happy as a brass kopek. "I'll learn all sorts of medical things!"

I keep wondering why Daniil is so perplexingly fond of a boy who, within a year, will either be shipped home or end up in a shallow grave in the Crimea. How could anyone develop a deep attachment to someone merely passing through his life? Why bother?

One unseasonably mild morning at the tail end of the year, when ambling up to the hospital, I spot a horde of springless bullock carts that serve as ambulances. Moaning, blood-soaked men are being off-loaded. I race to grab one end of a stretcher.

"What happened?" I holler to the ambulance driver gripping the other end.

"An assault on one of our rifle pits," he shouts over the mayhem.

The wounded man's hand covers his blackened face. "Powder magazine blew up."

Inside the ward, cries for help ricochet off the stone walls. I speed from one ashen man to another, tying off hemorrhaging vessels with silk ligature. Shell fragments and splints can wait. As I wrap a tight compress around the bleeding stump of a sergeant-major's shin, the injured officer calls out in a clear, authoritative voice: "Hold on, brothers! We'll beat them down yet!"

At the next bed, the priest makes the sign of the cross over a legless body. "I give you up to God, Tsar, and Motherland."

Colya tugs at my sleeve. "Doctor Berestnev wants you in surgery."

This is my first time in the operating theater, and I'm of a notion that it more closely resembles an abattoir. The walls are spattered with blood. The corners are piled high with a welter of gore, which I soon recognize as disembodied arms and legs. The floor is both sticky and slick.

At each of the three tables stands a physician clad in an oil-cloth apron as bloody as a butcher's. A variety of surgical instruments lie on a side table—saws, knives, pliers, cleavers, probes, tourniquets, and forceps. Daniil, his hands rummaging around in a man's abdomen, glances my way. "Vetrov's been on duty since last evening. He needs rest. Take his place."

My eyes and mouth form three perfect circles of panic.

Daniil bolsters me with, "I'll be right next to you if you need anything."

Mimicking the other surgeons, I roll up my shirtsleeves to the elbows and don a surgical apron. I rinse my hands in a bowl of cold water while Doctor Vetrov sews up his patient as quickly as he'd button an overcoat.

After the patient is removed, an attendant uses a much-soiled towel to remove most of the blood from the tabletop. Two orderlies deliver the next patient. Doctor Vetrov administers chloroform and offers me words seasoned by experience. "An abdominal wound, eh? Good one to start with. You can hardly mess it up. Almost always fatal."

I give a satirical nod. "That's reassuring."

"When shot is lost in the cavity of the belly, you need not amuse yourself hunting for it," he continues. "Best to just administer opium via suppository to stop peristalsis, and give the patient absolute rest and no food. But sometimes it doesn't hurt to survey the damage. Cut him open and let's see what you've got."

My muscles are as tense as kite string on a windy day. I etch a white line on the skin with my scalpel. A second attempt scores a wee bit deeper.

Vetrov peers over his spectacles. "Apply pressure. *Slice* through the skin."

I do as instructed, petrified that my blade will cut too deep and nick an intestine. After what feels like decades, the abdominal cavity is laid open.

Vetrov's hand moves aside some intestines and clotted blood. "No good. You've got a liver wound and a torn bladder, each of them fatal in its own right. Sew him up so you can get on to the next one."

Aghast, I look at Daniil. He gives me a single, subtle nod.

Vetrov departs for a few hours of sleep. My hands, clumsy and slow, suture first the muscles, then the skin of this poor man who will be dead within a day. Nervous perspiration accumulates in my armpits and on the back of my neck.

My next patient has fat protruding from a lacerated abdomen. The soldier's eyes are wide with fear as the attendants transfer him from the stretcher onto the table.

"Relax, soldier. You won't feel a thing while we sew you up lickety-split." How can my voice be so steady while my insides quiver like plum pudding?

After the patient is anesthetized, Daniil asks, "Is it just omentum?"

My fingers explore the protruding material. "I believe so."

"Then stuff it back inside the abdomen and sew him shut. It gets a little trickier if intestines are poking out, in which case check them for punctures and sew up any holes. Peritonitis usually sets in within a day or two. Not one in a hundred will live, but at least you did all you could."

Next in line is a beetle-browed veteran of fifteen years. His foot dangles from his leg by a thread of tendon. "Lop it off fast, Doctor," he pleads. "I need to get back in the field."

Once the soldier is under the effects of the chloroform, Daniil explains, "It's not unusual that they're raring to go when they reach the hospital. And that has its advantages. High spirits on the day of battle help the soldier withstand the shock of surgery, which lessens mortality."

This theory doesn't hold true for my next patient, whose final breath flees as soon as the chloroform takes effect.

That's when I hiccup. And again. And yet again—whopping big ones that almost give me whiplash. The spasms play havoc with my unsteady, novice hands as they attempt to cleanly slice through skin or securely ligate hemorrhaging vessels. My cheeks heat with embarrassment.

Hiccup.

Hiccup.

"Someone must be thinking about you," Daniil says.

"Huh-cup?" I ask.

"Hiccups mean that someone is thinking about you. Usually that they miss you."

My hope is knee-jerk. *It must be Vasilisa.*

But of course, my hiccups aren't caused by Vasilisa or anyone else missing me. They're an emotional regression to the year I spent as an insecure, hiccupping five-year-old, a reemergence of my chronic fear of never being good enough.

I continue to fumble through the surgery, the hiccups settling at one *hic* per three breaths. Daniil advises me to inhale and hold until the hiccups stop. That exertion accomplishes nothing.

"Yawn really big," recommends a dresser. "Really, really big. Several times."

I comply, feeling not only foolish but also fearful. What if I give a frenzied burp, my hand lurches, and I slice through a major artery?

Halfway through my next surgery, Daniil finishes his foot amputation and comes to my table.

"I'll finish this," he offers. "Go stand against the wall and hold your arms out like a cross."

I comply, shrouded in embarrassment.

"Breathe in as deeply as you can," he directs. "Good. Now bring your hands together in front of you very, very slowly until they touch. And now breathe out as slowly and completely as possible."

Hiccup.

I repeat the whole humiliating maneuver.

Hiccup.

A litter-bearer advises me to plug my ears with my fingers, take a deep breath, and swallow five times straight without taking a breath between swallows.

Hiccup.

There's no end to the helpful guidance.

"Close your eyes and press on them while I hit you hard on your middle back."

"Pull on your ear while pinching your nose."

"Stand on your head." That suggestion is ignored.

Even one of the patients tosses in his two kopeks' worth as the orderlies are placing him on the table. "My grandfather told me if you think really hard about your next hiccup, it won't happen."

By now it's apparent my malady isn't going to politely retreat. Another physician arrives to take my place.

The tips keep coming, including one from the new physician. "Go to the mess hall. Ask for a spoonful of vinegar. Swallow it in one gulp."

"If that doesn't work, drink honey."

"Drink warm water."

"Drink warm water with honey in it."

"Plug your ears with cotton while you drink the honey water."

As I'm leaving the surgery room, Daniil calls, "If the mess hall treatment doesn't work, find a bed in the ward to rest on. And do everything we just told you to do, but do it lying down."

When nothing offers a reprieve, I manage to find an empty bed in the far corner of the ward and slide under the wool blanket. The flat, lumpy mattress is supposedly stuffed with straw, but it has the feel of crumbled pine cones. I start off on my back but quickly flip to my side. Then I roll to my other side. Again onto my back.

Gradually both my hiccups and my agitated mind begin to slow. I'm forced to accept that my disconcerting condition stemmed from anxiety. What a milksop.

"I have sinned most irredeemably."

I glance at the boy in the bed next to mine, a typhoid fever patient. A priest hovers over him. "Have faith in His mercy, son."

Have faith in His mercy. How many thousands of times had my father droned that phrase? My nostrils are singed by the resurrected aroma of candles, and my skin stings from the imagined sprinkle of holy water. I close my weary eyelids. There stands my father, demanding payment for saying last rites over me. His fingers are the upside-down claws of a raven. His hand demands rubles, more rubles. Over his shoulder peers the sorrowful gaze of the icon of Our Lady of Vladimir.

But the gaze doesn't belong to Our Lady of Vladimir. It belongs to Colya, his face framed by the fading sunlight.

"Doctor Rozhdestvensky? Why are you in bed? Are you sick?"

Only a dream, I reassure my galloping heart. *It was only another dream.*

I hadn't meant to fall asleep, but hooray, my hiccups have stopped!

"No," I tell Colya, "I'm not a bit sick. Merely resting for a moment." I don't know why I bent the truth. By tomorrow, the tale of the hiccupping medical student will have spread throughout the entire north shore.

I sit up and swing my legs over the edge of the bed. My back feels as though a fireplace poker has tunneled into it. How do those poor sick buggers lie day after day on these mattresses of torture?

"How's your new position as an orderly?" I ask Colya.

His blow-by-blow description of everything he's learned and done bubbles with more enthusiasm than I've ever felt about anything in my life.

Abruptly he shifts to a new topic. "Are you going to the award ceremony tomorrow night?"

"Award ceremony?"

"The Cross of Saint George will be given to the soldiers who stood their ground at the Alma and at Inkerman. I heard the Vladimir Regiment will receive it for their charge against the British Light Division. They're so brave; they maintained proper alignment the whole time."

"To be honest with you, I don't know what the Cross of Saint George is."

"You don't?" Colya's face squishes in disbelief, creating an entirely new pattern of cinnamon freckles. "It's a great honor. Sought after by sailors and soldiers alike."

"Is it the highest honor they can receive?" Not that I care about the answer. I have no patience for officers who pin so many trinkets to their chest that they tinkle like prisms in a chandelier.

"It's the sign of a true hero. That's my wish, to fight so bravely in battle that I'm made part of the Order of Saint George and become an officer." The adolescent voice fluctuates several octaves, his youthful zeal innocent of the battlefield's gore. "A lot of my buddies back in my village are chicken-hearted and did everything they could to avoid conscription. They put lye on their faces and their balls to make them have sores and swell up. My friend Akim, he made his gut come out his butt so he wouldn't get drafted."

"He made his large intestine prolapse?"

"I'm not sure about that. But I do know his insides came out his asshole."

I'm familiar with the use of lye as a means of avoiding conscription. But to cause one's own rectum to prolapse is a novel and extreme approach. How had the boy done it?

"Did he live?"

Colya shrugs an *I don't know*. "I was drafted. He wasn't."

"If you don't mind, Colya, let's move the conversation away from guts and assholes." I punch both fists into my lower back and arch my midsection. "These mattresses are atrocious—as flat as the Ukrainian steppes. You know your way around this place. How would I go about getting straw to stuff into them?"

Colya's expression tells me that he didn't grasp the analogy about the steppes. Nonetheless, he holds forth an answer. "I doubt you'll find any straw. The animals need it."

"Since when do animals get preferential treatment over humans?"

"The corrals are on the other side of the bay, along with the veterinary surgeons, the farriers, the butchers, all those animal people. But they're not going to give you any hay."

"I don't want hay, just straw."

"You can ask if you want." His lips slide skeptically to the left.

After the boy leaves, I put one hand on the top side of the mattress and one on the bottom side. I can trace my fingers through the smattering of filling. How do we expect men to heal atop such a travesty of a mattress?

I'm three steps from exiting the hospital when a voice from behind sends chills down my aching spine. "I'm so glad to finally meet you. I'm Father Matvei Grigorevich Arkhangelsky."

The odor of incense wafts off the priest's robes, storms my nostrils, and strangles my stomach. I'm trapped! I turn and force politeness between my lips. "I'm Andrey Yevgrafovich."

He nods. "One of the medical students. And your family name, Andrey Yevgrafovich?"

The question was inevitable. "Rozhdestvensky."

"Rozhdestvensky. A name that's quite common among the clergy." The holy man strokes his long beard. "Does your family belong to the clerical estate, by chance?"

"No, my family belongs to the petty merchant class." It is a flagrant untruth, but I don't care.

"Well, Andrey Yevgrafovich Rozhdestvensky, I don't believe I've seen you at our services. Father Popov or I say Mass every morning." Receiving no response, Arkhangelsky presses onward. "The government that we both honorably serve expects you to attend Mass twice a week. And go to confession and receive communion at least annually."

"That's been explained to me."

"You seem to be a bit wary of the Church."

Wary? The grossest of understatements. A more accurate description would be that hostility permeates my sinews and floods my veins.

Sensing my hesitation, Arkhangelsky grabs my shoulder. "Remember, a bad son of the Church cannot be a son of the Motherland."

I pivot and stomp from the building.

CHAPTER 9

January
1855

DANIIL SWINGS WIDE the door of his cottage. "Saints alive, it's cold out there." He rubs his hands together as Ignaty and I enter. "I heard the water is frozen at the pump."

Ignaty gives his characteristic up-and-down wag of his head. He cups his hand around the hoarfrost on his midnight black mustache and in a raucous whisper tells me, "This weather makes Daniil's job easier. When the wounded are brought in, their white breath gives him a clue whether they're alive or not."

It's the second day of the new year, and Daniil has invited Ignaty and me to his lodgings for an evening of sausage, cheap wine, and comradeship. Daniil shares a cramped, two-room bungalow with three other surgeons, none of whom are present tonight. At the small kitchen table, he pours wine from a clay jug into dwarf-size ceramic glasses, none of which match.

I lower myself onto a straight-backed wooden chair. Ignaty shrugs off his long greatcoat, allowing me to observe him at an upward angle. The bull-like man is a head shorter than me, but he outweighs me by at least twenty pounds. His sleeves seem twice the length of his arms, yet the shirt across his barrel chest appears to be in danger of bursting its seams. I have a feeling that despite his easy grin, Ignaty would be a plucky opponent for fisticuffs. Like a bantam cock in the barnyard, he evokes respect. Yet his incessant head bobbing causes him to come across as a rather queer fish.

Such an improbable friendship between these two! Fair-haired Daniil is well-spoken and highly educated, while dark, burly Ignaty doesn't seem to be the sharpest knife in the kitchen, as the saying goes. Here in the middle of absolute Hell, two people with nothing in common find camaraderie. I, on the other hand, found it impossible to make friends in Moscow, with its 350,000 people crowded shoulder to shoulder.

Sleet begins to tick at the window. From his pocket, Ignaty pulls out a knife and a block of wood about the same size as the wine glasses. Whenever his hands are empty, he inevitably takes to whittling. As he slices away at the wood, he asks me, "When you went to Simferopol with Pirogov, did he mention plaster of Paris?"

"Plaster of Paris? No. Why?"

"Yesterday he told me to begin stocking it." In response to two crinkled brows, Ignaty's head slams up and down with vigor. "On my word of honor, he wants a hundred cases of plaster of Paris delivered within a fortnight."

Daniil guffaws. "Within a fortnight? Is he cracked in the head? Nothing reaches Sevastopol within two weeks. A month, maybe. By spring, probably. But never a fortnight."

The back of Ignaty's hand rubs his chin's blue-black stubble. "He told me that the doctors unnecessarily reach for their saws to amputate broken legs and arms. He believes many of the fractures can be positioned back into place and then immobilized with plaster of Paris." More nodding. "The material is lightweight enough to allow the patient mobility while permitting the bones to heal."

Daniil entwines his hands behind his neck, his arms like wings beside his head. "I'm having a difficult time believing he said this to you."

"May lightning strike me on the spot if I'm making this up. And anyway, how would you know what anyone said yesterday?" The Tatar flashes his white teeth at me. "According to what I heard, our friend"—Ignaty aims a stout thumb in Daniil's direction—"having thoroughly enjoyed himself at the senior officers' New Year's party the previous night, spent all yesterday with his head in his hands while the champagne drained from his body."

Daniil tosses him an ugly look. "We celebrated the arrival of 1855 by drinking to the health of His Majesty. Can you fault us for that?"

"Oh, no. One cannot fault a toast to the Tsar. Followed by a toast to Mother Russia. Followed by toasts to every regiment stationed in the Crimea." Ignaty lowers his gaze to his whittling. "And what about the singing?"

"What do you find offensive about singing 'God Save the Tsar?'"

"Nothing." Ignaty continues to focus on his knife. "How many times did you sing it?"

"We weren't nearly as rowdy as the officers in the next tent."

"Whom you felt compelled to join."

"I'm sorry, I thought this was more my story than yours. Or do you prefer to tell it?"

Ignaty looks up from his block of wood. "Please, tell the story, especially the part about the rousing cancan you did with Major Korzinkin."

Daniil pats his mustache. "Who told you that?"

"The whole north side of the bay knows."

"Why don't you quiet your mouth and center your attention on that knife before you slice your finger off? The hospital doesn't have bandaging to spare on you."

Little buds of happiness burst open inside me. This tête-à-tête between the two friends makes me realize how profoundly I appreciate their companionship.

My eyes open wide. "Hey, hold on a moment. Did you say 'senior officers' party'?"

Ignaty stops whittling and looks up at me. "That's right. You are now looking at *Major* Berestnev."

I extend my heartfelt congratulations to my mentor. As Daniil pours another round of wine, I feel joy and gratitude that I now have two friends. Three, if you count Colya. Which is more than I've ever had in my life.

CHAPTER 10

January
1855

IN MID-JANUARY, I'M granted a half-day reprieve from the hospital, which I desperately need so I can visit the south side of the bay to replenish my rum and arrowroot.

Gone are the teeming crowds of carriages, wagons, horses, and vendors on the once-colorful Ekaterina Street. Instead, there are only soldiers and sailors, smoking cigarettes while shivering in their long greatcoats and earflap hats. Signs that once hung upright in front of shops and taverns now either dangle from a single chain in lopsided dejection or are completely absent. Many storefronts are boarded up. Even the Schneider Hotel and Restaurant, a favorite haunt of officers, is forlornly subdued.

I find a bottle shop that's still operational. The other customer in the shop is a gray-haired fellow who has just completed his purchase.

"I only had one bottle of rum," the proprietor informs me. "This man just purchased it."

"Sorry, pal," the gray-haired fellow remarks as he turns up the collar of his coat.

I shrug and try to make light of it. "I'm used to that sort of luck."

The proprietor interjects, "More rum may arrive today. But there's no guarantee."

Damn! "I'll spend some time in the officers' library and check back here in a couple of hours."

Stepping outside, the gray-headed guy says, "It's your day for bad luck, that's for sure. The library's damaged. Don't know if or when it might reopen. You stationed on the north side?" At my nod, he continues, "There's damn little else in town to amuse yourself with nowadays. But you're welcome to spend some time with me. At least it's warm in the barns." His grin exposes a quality specimen of a snaggletooth. "Alexei Alexeevich Puzanov, veterinary surgeon."

I reciprocate with my name and position and extend a hand to shake, Western-style. He clamps down on my bones as if cracking open a walnut. Recalling Colya's words that the "animal people" have the straw required to plump the hospital mattresses, I tell Puzanov that I'd be pleased to join him.

We head toward the southern outskirts of the city, where the sight of the damage inflicted by shot and shell sends a tremor across my shoulders. It's one thing to hear the pounding of the cannon from across the bay; it's quite another to see its ravages. Streets are littered with torn quilts, tree limbs, crumpled metal, and cannonballs. A heap of stones and clay marks the place where a building once stood. We sidestep the craters the shells have dug in the stony ground. From beneath the stubble, rats the size of tomcats glare at me.

South of the charred suburbs, hundreds of our soldiers are hand-building new batteries with walls of earth a dozen feet high and twice as thick. The riflemen's *pop, pop, pop* seems dangerously close, yet Puzanov maintains a steady chatter. At the edge of town, we come to a small, red-tinged stream that snakes its way toward the bay. As we trail the stream uphill, the air becomes saturated with a raw, acrid smell that contains hints of meat, urine, blood, offal, and animal feces.

At the stables, Puzanov removes his outer clothes and pulls on a lightweight jacket. He calls to his assistant, "Sasha, let's start with Lieutenant Shevchenko's mare. She's a gentle thing." He turns to me. "Anything you're curious about, don't hesitate to ask. Visitors are a rarity, so you're the highlight of our week."

Sasha returns with a chestnut mare, and Puzanov creeps his beefy, calloused hand down one of the horse's back legs. The mare swerves her rear end away and tries to bite the livestock doctor. *And this is a gentle thing?*

Several attempts later, Puzanov successfully lifts the horse's foot. With a hoof pick, he pries dirt from the sole. The procedure goes well enough until he gets a little deeper. In the blink of an eye, the mare reclaims possession of her limb and, in a show of force, stomps her foot.

I'm of a solid mind that choosing a career as a veterinary surgeon is indeed a reckless decision.

Puzanov repeats the process on the remaining three feet. When the pedicure is complete, Sasha leads the mare away. "What ails her?" I ask Puzanov.

"Another case of thrush. Given rest and treatment, she'll be fine. But she's temporarily out of service—something we can't afford right now."

"Because we're short of horses?"

"Oh, my soul, yes. We've had more than five thousand draft animals die over the past couple of months. And over half the remaining horses are unfit for service. Same with the oxen. This stony Crimean ground is rough on their feet." He sighs with deep vexation. "But the calamity is that most of it is just plain overwork. Wind puffs, ringbone, clap of the back sinews—they're all preventable with just a little common sense."

Puzanov spits on his dirty hands, rubs them together to loosen the grime, then wipes them on an empty sack of coarsely woven canvas. I decide this is one tough guy.

Glancing about at the stabled horses, I ask, "Where are the horses that were wounded in battle?"

"Son, those horses never make it to me. A bullet is the only kindness to a wounded horse in the field." He motions me to walk with him. "I need to check an officer's pride and joy. She's off her feed."

Puzanov and I meet up with Sasha, who's leading a dappled gray mare into a wooden stock. Puzanov strips off his jacket and shirt and yanks a rubber sleeve onto his right arm, securing it around his back with a strap. Although I guess the broad-shouldered man to be upward of fifty years, his physique is that of a fellow half that age.

Maintaining a healthy distance, I watch the veterinary surgeon move alongside the mare's rump, pat her croup, and lift her tail. The horse's back legs take to prancing. Despite Puzanov's soothing words, the mare persists in cavorting ill-temperedly. Sasha yanks repeatedly on her halter, but her attitude remains belligerent. One of her rear legs lashes out at the veterinary surgeon, but he's protected by the stock.

Puzanov informs the animal, "I don't like it when you don't listen to me."

He nods to Sasha, who picks up a wooden handle the size of a thigh bone. Attached to one end is a loop of small chain. The assistant grasps the horse's upper lip between his thumb and forefinger and slips the chain around it. I wince as he twists the wooden handle until the metal loop squeezes the lip like a wrung-out piece of laundry.

I wince again as Puzanov eases his greased glove into the mare's anus and evacuates feces. A considerable pile of steaming, dry excrement accumulates beside his boots. He fiddles around in the animal's rectum awhile, then announces, "Impacted." He withdraws his arm, and Sasha departs.

"None of the animals appear to be in particularly good flesh," I say.

Puzanov pulls off his rubber sleeve. "True enough. Haven't the slightest idea how we'll feed these animals the rest of the winter."

"Forage is scarce?"

"Scarce?" Puzanov's head jerks back, his snaggletooth protruding like a fierce dagger. "A deficient term if there ever was one! This peninsula produces little besides grapes, which means grain and forage must be hauled from the southern provinces. And that's if we can get it at all."

The assistant returns with a large bucket and rubber tubing as long as I am tall. Puzanov grabs the animal's nose with his left hand, and his right hand threads the tube up one of the nostrils. The horse remains astonishingly calm as over an arm's length of tube snakes its way to her stomach. I, on the other hand, feel the back of my throat fold over onto itself.

After sniffing the vapors coming from the tube, Puzanov raises its end to head height. The assistant attaches a funnel and slowly pours in a bucketful of clear, thick liquid.

I decide to use this lull in conversation to make my request. "I wonder if perhaps the barns might have some straw—not hay, mind you, just straw—that could stuff some tumbledown hospital mattresses. The mattresses are so grievous, our soldiers could use them to torture the enemy."

The veterinary surgeon swings his large and incredulous face toward me. "Mattresses? Impossible. Every fleck of forage, regardless of the quality, needs to go in these animals. Without them, there is no cavalry. And how do you suppose we haul supplies and ordnance, not to mention the food you eat? The saddle and transport horses will give us their all, if we merely feed and take reasonable care of them. The whole campaign depends on their lives." He shakes his head sadly.

My hangdog appearance and lowered voice bear witness to my shame. "Of course, you're correct. I didn't realize forage was in such short supply."

He continues to regard me as if I'm the most simple-minded creature in the Tsar's army. "Short supply? Dire straits is more like it. Do you realize how much feed an ox requires? Between lack of nourishment and the strenuous work over poor roads, they die faster than we can haul off the carcasses."

I maintain an apologetic tone. "Just thought I'd mention it. Obviously, the needs here are greater than the ones at the hospital."

Puzanov softens his demeanor. "I know you medical fellows face shortages, just as I do. A month or so ago, I begged the pharmacy for some bandage material for the horses' legs and was turned away. He said there was only a few days' supply in the whole city."

"We don't have enough of anything—morphine, blankets, laudanum," I say, seeking common ground.

By now, the contents of the bucket have disappeared into the horse. Puzanov slowly extracts the tube from her nostril. "Young man, we'll be lucky if a quarter of the draft animals make it through the winter. And I'm referring to both horses and oxen."

Bells peal in the frosty air, and I deferentially touch my hat. "I'd best be leaving. Dark will be setting in soon."

"Don't mean to sound gruff." Puzanov smiles to validate his statement. His snaggletooth is a beacon of amicability. "But these animals are our lifeline. More people should bear that in mind."

"I thank you for a most enlightening afternoon. I'd better check on the rum before someone else snatches it up." I nod my adieu. "I wish you the very best."

"As I do you."

Feeling like a scolded schoolboy, I retrace my steps to the bottle shop. The rum—hurrah!—has arrived.

As I carry my purchases down the embankment toward the jetty, I spot three women in huge white scarves boarding a ferry to the north shore.

Please, please, let Vasilisa be one of them!

CHAPTER 11

January
1855

I PUSH MY long legs to their limit in a sprint to the quay. The ferry is about to shove off when one of the three women spots me. "Wait! There's one more person." It's the Sister who obtained my rubles.

The ferryman obliges her, and I leap aboard. Panting, I scan the other two women's faces. A stab as sharp as a knife's plunges between my ribs. Neither is Vasilisa.

"Such good fortune to meet up with you!" exclaims the sexless slab of a woman. "Sisters, this is Andrey Yevgrafovich Rozhdestvensky. We met while he was temporarily stationed at the hospital in Simferopol."

The two women give me their names and explain that they're part of the newly arrived second group of Sisters. I mutter something I hope sounds welcoming.

"Several Sisters, including the three of us, have been assigned to Sevastopol," the big woman explains. "The north side. Is that where you likewise work?"

"Yes." I unsuccessfully grapple for her name. "How are the other Sisters? We've heard typhus is rampant in Simferopol."

"Unfortunately, that's true. Only twenty-two remain of our original twenty-eight."

I gasp. "Six deaths?"

"Five. One was sent home. Vasilisa took her flirting a step too far, and the head Sister sent her and her bags packing."

"Sent her home?"

The woman's eyes bore into mine. Her irises are the color of cold, gray gun metal. "You remember Vasilisa, don't you? The little tart?" Her words are drenched with sarcasm.

Rise to the occasion, Andrey. "Thank goodness you ladies stayed healthy. We have a good vantage point here. Perhaps you'll allow me to orient you to some of the landmarks."

The women are attentive listeners, but I hardly hear my own words. Vasilisa is gone. My daydreams lie shattered on the boat's bottom boards. I clutch my purchase to my chest, intending to put it to full use this evening.

Upon reaching the north shore, I help each of the Sisters off the ferry. The big woman smiles broadly. "I look forward to working with you, Doctor Rozhdestvensky."

"And I with you." I squint as I wonder if my eyes are deceiving me. Her eyes are currently the loveliest shade of jade green. They didn't actually change color, did they? Perhaps it's the reflection of the setting sun off the water.

THAT NIGHT, I knock back glasses of rum and arrowroot until I'm deep in my cups. Why couldn't I have been the one with whom Vasilisa took her flirting a little too far?

I and my headache are both in foul moods when we arrive at the hospital the next morning. Hospital gangrene broke out earlier in the week, so the entire facility reeks of rotted flesh and corrupted blood. The stink doesn't improve my disposition.

The big Sister, whose name still eludes me, is serving tea to the patients. She offers me a bright smile, but I veer around her. "I'll be back in a few moments to show you around." Fingertips pressed against my warm, aching forehead, I stomp to the supply room.

Hoping to settle my sour stomach, I slouch over the table with a glass of tea and a biscuit. An odious thought spears me as I look around the small room that serves as a peaceful respite from the patients. The women won't be allowed in here, will they? This will remain a men-only sanctuary, won't it? I snort. I wouldn't put it past that big Sister to elbow her way in here. And incidentally, why is she always showing up wherever I am?

I snap my fingers as her name comes to me. *Well, let's see what kind of mettle Sister Maria is made of.*

"First, we'll see a case of hospital gangrene," I inform her as I begin my duties. "It starts as a black spot the size of a thumbprint on a healing wound, and then it spreads rapidly until the whole leg or arm is rotten, evil-smelling, dead flesh."

I lead the Sister to the bedside of a private whose necrotic foot is threatening to slough off, and watch her carefully for signs of fainting.

"I saw cases of this in Simferopol," she says. "No one could tell me with any certainty what causes it. Some said it's spread by flies, but there aren't any flies this time of year. What do you believe brings it on?"

I'm slightly disconcerted that she's not the fainthearted lady in white gloves that I had supposed. "Yes, some believe it to be caused by flies. Others postulate that it's spread through touching, though obviously these patients do not touch one another."

"But what do *you* believe?" she repeated, as if my opinion mattered to her.

Being far more concerned with its accurate diagnosis and treatment, I've paid little attention to its cause. It doesn't sit right with me that she's more inquisitive than me on matters of my own trade.

"I haven't formed an opinion yet," I announce. "As you're familiar with the disease, perhaps you're also familiar with its treatment?"

"In Simferopol, we doused the sloughing stumps with aromatic spirits. Is that the correct treatment?"

"Yes, it is."

We move to the next bed. "This man has tetanus. Treatment involves dressing the inciting wound and administering large doses of laudanum or brandy to minimize the rigidity. If necessary to maintain nutrition, food is given through a tube that runs from the nose into the stomach. Have you ever seen a tube inserted through the nostrils?"

She hasn't, but she's willing to help me perform it. Although she requires instructions every step of the way on exactly what to hold and how to hold it, she's not nearly as put off by the procedure as I was by yesterday's mare.

The next patient's legs are dreadfully mangled. She asks the soldier, "How in the world did you manage to get so much blood on your head when you were hit in your legs? Your hair is so matted, you look as though you're wearing a helmet."

She receives nothing in response.

"He pretends to not understand a single word," I explain as I flush out the leg wounds. "He's French."

"French?"

"A spy. He was trampled by a runaway horse and wagon. Our hope is that after we patch him up, his greed and lack of patriotism will shine through and he'll agree to work for us as a double agent."

She bends low and utters something in French. The spy's rejoinder is brief. Her reply is long-winded, with many gesticulations toward his legs and hair. His response is slightly lengthier than his first. She retrieves a towel and a small basin of water and goes to work on his hair. They chat in French while she cleans off the blood and smooths out the mats.

"There. That certainly looks better," she says in Russian.

"It certainly feels better," he responds, also in Russian.

My gaze swings to the man's lips. For a week, the army interpreter has been trying to get the spy to open up. Yet within minutes of being with the Sister, he's jabbering in both French and Russian.

"You're quite fluent in French," I acknowledge as we move away from the bed.

"Foreign languages come easily to me. French. German. Even a smattering of English."

As we move from patient to patient, faces blossom into smiles in response to Sister Maria's questions or her tenderness when she adjusts their blankets. She promises several patients that she'll return later to write letters for them.

By now, my hangover is easing. I decide the Sister isn't a bad sort. She might actually be of some assistance. "You have the gift of sociability."

Her eyes, today a smoky green, settle on me. "One of the first things I learned in Simferopol was the value of asking soldiers how they were wounded. It comforts them to talk about it."

"The patients respond quite well to you."

"Why, thank you, Doctor Rozhdestvensky. Compliments are in short supply in the Crimea. In fact, if it weren't for Doctor Pirogov, the Sisters wouldn't receive any at all."

CHAPTER 12

January–February
1855

RUSSIA'S BEST GENERAL is winter. The well-known maxim was superbly evidenced by Napoleon's foiled plans in 1812. Even though Crimean winters are the mildest in all of Russia, biting temperatures remain a loyal ally of the Motherland as the French and British hole up in their respective camps.

During these raw, wet months, the campaign becomes a war of attrition as the two sides leer at one another, each wrestling with cold and disease. Although my surgical skills have progressed significantly, my days contain few mangled body parts. Instead, I minister to cases of frostbite and winter contagions such as typhus and pneumonia.

In early February, Daniil, Ignaty, and I again spend an evening together. Ignaty hoists his glass and bobs his head. "Here's to life!"

Daniil raises his glass in response. "To life. At all times uncertain, and even more so in times of war."

My glass clinks against theirs, and the sweet Crimean wine is consumed in a single tip of the hand.

"And here's to plaster of Paris!" Ignaty lifts his glass in honor of the swift arrival of Pirogov's casting material. The three mismatched glasses chime again.

While the gracious host pours another round, Ignaty pulls out a block of wood and begins to whittle.

"Not again!" Daniil chastises him, though little smile lines emerge at the corners of his eyes. "I'm tired of cleaning up your debris. You be sure, when you leave here tonight, you're not too drunk to take your droppings with you."

"I'll leave this place cleaner than I found it. You can bet your liver on that." Ignaty looks pointedly about the kitchen. "If cleanliness is next to godliness, I hate to even consider on which rung of Heaven's staircase you are."

I interrupt the mock squabble by asking Ignaty, "What are you making?"

"The Benign Savior. Colya requested it, to take into battle with him."

Daniil thrusts a candle into the neck of the empty wine jug and sets it in the middle of the table. "I wish I could find a medical excuse to permanently remove him from the fighting."

Ignaty nods with vigor. "It's a shame the boy is blind to the danger of battle. All he can see is its glory and high-minded principles." Then he tells me, "Daniil's son, had he lived, would be almost Colya's age."

Daniil pats his moustache. "Died at childbirth. Took his mother with him."

"Such a dreadful loss." I feel sincere sympathy for Daniil's misfortune. I truly do. But intimate conversations are the antithesis of my upbringing. I and my siblings were raised to be reserved in sentimentality. Wearing one's heart on one's sleeve was taboo, and we certainly didn't meddle in other people's emotions.

Daniil rises and gathers the rusty utensils and chipped plates for our meal.

Ignaty sets aside his knife and piece of wood, and with exaggerated actions orchestrated to attract Daniil's attention, he brushes his shavings into a small pile in one corner of the table. Then he painstakingly lowers his forefinger onto a wayward fleck of wood scarcely larger than a grain of sand. When it adheres to his skin, he shifts his hand to hover over the pile of shavings and flicks it off. Once the table is immaculate, the purveyor leans back in his chair and folds his arms across his broad chest. He smirks at Daniil, who is carrying food to the table. "Satisfied?"

Without so much as a glance toward Ignaty, Daniil deadpans, "There's debris on the floor."

Ignaty's swarthy face grows even darker. With a disgruntled *huff*, he plunges into the banquet of sausages and cottage cheese.

Following the meal, Ignaty slaps a deck of cards on the table. "Do you play, Andrey?"

"Not very much. Although I enjoy a good game of skat."

Neither man is familiar with the game.

"It's a German game. Three people play at a time, so we have the perfect number." I outline its complex rules.

"Thirty-two cards. Ace is high. Seven is low. The objective is twofold: First, the player's aim is to take no tricks. This is called 'nullo.' Second, he should win enough counting cards in tricks to make sixty-one."

The Tatar furrows his brow and scratches the black stubble on his square jaw.

Hopeless, I think. Nevertheless, I forge onward with my instructions.

"An ace is worth eleven points, and a ten is worth ten. A king, four. A queen, three. And a jack, two."

Ignaty, his cigar clenched between his teeth, says little. His short, thick fingers grip the cards, and his eyes narrow as he studies the hand he's been dealt.

As I predicted, Daniil is the quicker of the two to comprehend the game. But completely to my surprise, once Ignaty grasps the rules, he wins more hands than Daniil and I combined. The Tatar's success is a tribute to his keen attention to details and numbers.

When the cards are finally put to rest, we make plans for future evenings of sausage, wine, and skat. Ignaty offers a final toast. "To the Sisters of Mercy."

"Hear! Hear!" Daniil seconded. "My presuppositions have been entirely uprooted. The Sisters perform their work with zeal, punctuality, and compassion. And the patients respond to their attentions like a tonic."

"Plus, the walls got whitewashed," Ignaty says.

My head nods along with Ignaty's. "And the floors receive a regular scrubbing."

"Chamber pots are emptied," Daniil adds.

"And the doctors are more cheerful." His nose in his undersized glass, the Tatar gravitates his ebony eyes, slowly and purposefully, toward me.

"Pardon?"

"*Some* of the Sisters seem to have befriended *some* of the doctors."

"You're referring to . . . what?" I search Ignaty's face. Gaining no insight, I look to Daniil for answers. The major returns the gaze, a bemused half grin on his wine-wet lips. I sense my inebriated mind has missed some vital piece of the conversation. "Care to fill me in on the joke?"

"You and Sister Kurbatova seem to have become great chums." Ignaty's abundant set of pearly whites gleam at me.

"And . . . ?"

"Every time I see you, she's by your side, with a smile that seems permanently applied to her face with Pirogov's plaster of Paris."

Their implications suddenly make sense. My head rears back defensively. "You're joking, correct?"

Ignaty leans over the candle and lights his cigar with the flame. He blows a ring of blue smoke in my direction.

My face swivels toward Daniil, whose hands rest on the table, fingers interlaced, thumbs circling each other while he waits for my response.

Granted, it's true that over the past few weeks the Sister of Mercy and I have developed a comfortable repartee. But sweet Mother of God, surely people don't think I and beefy Kurbatova are having—I shudder at the thought—an *affaire d'amour!*

"What of it?" I demand. "She smiles all the time, regardless of whom she's with. Maria's quite gregarious. Plus—"

"Thank you for validating my point." Ignaty raises his glass in a salute to me. "How many of the other Sisters do you address by their first name?"

"Our duties require us to work side by side almost every day."

"And walk to the hospital together? And eat together?" Oddly enough, Ignaty's head isn't bobbing up and down. It's as steady as his gaze.

A flick of my raised hand dismisses the accusation. "This conversation is ludicrous."

The tip of Ignaty's forefinger slowly rasps the stubble of his beard. "So you wouldn't take offense if a virile, good-looking purveyor pays her a bit of attention?"

"Of course not."

"Good."

"BROOMS! WE MUST have brooms!" Maria's determination is unparalleled. Pirogov has just completed a demonstration of his new plaster of Paris contraptions, and the medical personnel are filing out of the mess hall. I had intended to do the same, but Maria lowered herself onto the stool next to mine, intent on having a lengthy chat about brooms.

"There's not a single broom to be had anywhere on the entire north shore." Her toe kicks a moldy biscuit from underneath the table. "Look at this place. Rotten food. Rat droppings."

For days, she has been on a quest for a broom. With the tenacity of a terrier, she scoured every nook and cranny of the hospital. There's a shortage of lint, soap, morphine, meat, spoons, scissors, basins, towels, bedding, beds . . . In other words, virtually everything. Even doctors. But it's the want of a broom that has set her off.

"What did the commissariat staff say?" I ask.

Her head drops back, and she stares at the rafters. "The same stale thing they always say. 'Brooms have been ordered and will arrive in due time.'" She heaves a sigh. "But the commissariat's office isn't the only one I'm mad at." She rights her head and turns toward me, her eyes tightened into accusing slits. "I'm also angry with you, Andrey Yevgrafovich."

Inwardly, I smile. She's so affable, it's impossible not to enjoy her company. Not that I'm in any way romantically drawn to her. Several weeks and many games of skat have passed since Ignaty made his accusation, and the topic, fortunately, hasn't resurfaced.

I fill my voice with exaggerated boredom. "What are you angry about this time?"

"You didn't notice my new hairstyle."

I study her long and hard. "How in the world am I supposed to notice a new hairstyle when you keep your head covered with that blanket all the time?" I give a playful tug on the corner of the white scarf that overlays half her back. "This behemoth could smother a banquet table."

"I don't wear it because I want to." She jabs at the knot under her chin. "But even with the scarf, you should be able to tell something is different."

I scoot my stool catty-corner so I have a straight-on view of her. Yes, there is something different. Short tufts of chestnut hair cover her upper forehead. "You have hair."

"I've always had hair."

"I mean, you have hair on your forehead."

She grabs a lock and holds it straight out from her head. "It's this short all over. Several of us did it. Whacked it all off."

"Why did you do that? Imbibed too much Crimean nectar one evening?"

"It helps keep out the lice."

"That's sensible. Who did the cutting?"

"I did. I'm a barber."

I scan the whimsical upturn of her lips. "Don't tease me. After a tiring day, I haven't the strength."

"I'm not teasing you. I was a barber in Moscow."

"There's no such thing as a woman barber."

"You're looking at one. My sister is one too."

"You just want me to believe your outlandish yarn so you can poke fun at me for being gullible."

"It's more common in France. A female barber is called a *coiffeuse*. It's time you acquire a little worldliness, Andrey."

I keep my expression skeptical as I try to recall how and when she transitioned from addressing me as "Doctor Rozhdestvensky" to calling me "Andrey."

"I swear to you by all that is holy, both I and my sister are barbers."

I lean an elbow on the table, rest my weary forehead in the hollow of my hand, and scrutinize her cropped bangs. "How did you and your sister come to be barbers?"

Maria explains that her father, a widower and a noncommissioned officer, put both girls in a school for military children, where Maria excelled in French and struggled with her other subjects.

"Military school?" I interrupt. "I didn't know there was a military school for girls."

"Only in St. Petersburg."

"What sort of classes do they teach?"

Maria's pudgy fingers playfully drum the table. "Which story do you want? The barber story or the school story? I can only tell one at a time."

She describes how she and her sister—named Vasilisa, as I now remember she has told me—always loved to tinker with various hairstyles. Quite fortuitously, the regimental barber took a liking to the sisters and taught them the tricks of the trade. The girls set up their own part-time business to bring in extra rubles for the family. Maria was fourteen when their father died of fever, and the sisters quit school to take up barbering full time.

"I think most of our customers simply felt sorry for two young girls on their own, eking out a living in such an unusual way."

"You have your own shop?"

She shook her head. "We carry our supplies to businesses where men don't have time to go to a barbershop. Banks, insurance companies, and the like. By the way, you could use a haircut. For you, my good friend Andrey Yevgrafovich, free of charge."

I lift my head from my palm and self-consciously smooth my hair. I suppose it is somewhat in disarray. Usually I run a comb through my hair in the mornings, glance in the mirror every couple of days when I shave, and forget about my appearance the rest of the time.

"I'll take you up on your generous offer. But only if you bring a broom to sweep up what you cut off."

Maria bursts forth with that happy laugh of hers. I contemplate her plush lips, broad mouth, and straight teeth. She has a magnificent smile. Too bad about the rest of her.

"If your business was flourishing in Moscow, what possessed you to join the war?"

Damn, Andrey, why did you ask that? She'll be long-winded for sure. I stretch out my long legs under the table and wait.

She places her elbows on the table, intertwines her fingers, and rests her chin on the back of her clasped hands. "Vasilisa became engaged, so I felt it would be best to move out of our small apartment to make room for her new husband. I couldn't afford to live by myself, and the Sisters of Mercy seemed like a good opportunity to start a fresh life. So here I am in the middle of a war, still cutting hair." She tugged on a lock of her bangs and smiled, but it wasn't the carefree smile that normally lit up her face.

"When the war is over, you'll barber again in Moscow?"

"Yes, I'll move back in with Vasilisa and rebuild my clientele."

"But I thought your sister got married."

"Two weeks before the wedding, he called it off. Vasilisa was crushed. When I left Moscow, she was still in a fit of depression."

"She'll find someone else. Someone better. More reliable." I'm button-busting proud that, for once, my perpetually dispirited thoughts have come up with an optimistic outlook.

Maria drops her hands to her lap, and her eyes flood with melancholy. "Vasilisa looks identical to me. Homely women like us are fortunate if we receive one marriage proposal. We never get second chances."

The self-satisfaction I felt for my well-intentioned comment melts away like hail in July. I know I should tell her that she's far from homely, but I doubt I could execute the fib in a believable fashion. Besides, she doesn't deserve to be told a lie.

She senses my discomfort. "Don't feel bad. I'm used to being unattractive. I was a fat, ugly duckling as a girl. I grew up to be a fat, ugly woman."

"But that's not true! Just a few minutes ago, I was thinking that you have one of the most beautiful smiles in all of Russia."

Her grin is pinched with skepticism. "When I was a child, I developed a devil-may-care personality to hide the pain when other children called Vasilisa and me 'fatties.' And through years of practice, I actually became the jovial, chatty persona I once hid behind."

I run my fingers through my hair, wishing I could either toss back some vodka or hightail it from the mess hall. There's no getting around the truth: her looks are as basic as bread.

"Maria," I begin, with no idea where my words are going. I lick my lips. "I meant it when I said you have a beautiful smile. And your capacity to put people at ease is unequaled. The doctors and the orderlies think the world of you. In fact, not long ago, someone asked me if you and I were romantically involved. He wanted to pursue you, but not if I had already beaten him to the prize."

She looks me in the eye. "And what did you tell him?"

Good job, Andrey, you've trapped yourself in a corner. "I told him that we are good friends and that your company is enormously pleasurable, but there are no romantic feelings between us."

She looks down at her folded hands and inhales, pulling her lips into her mouth until they disappear. She holds her breath. As she lets it out, she slowly raises her eyes. Moments ago, they were the color of malachite. Now they're leaden. But her smile is intact.

"That's a good response on your part," she says, her voice light. "Because I find *you*"—her index finger gives my upper arm a teasing stab—"only middling attractive at best."

CHAPTER 13

February
1855

THE ENEMY CONTINUES to hold the plateau south of Sevastopol, but they put forth only a token offense. "General February" has made mere survival our enemies' foremost concern.

On our side, bronchitis, scurvy, typhoid, typhus, dysentery, and frostbite chisel away at the troops. Wood is so scarce, burning it for heating is permitted solely in hospitals and public buildings. Daniil, Ignaty, and I take comfort in our weekly evening of skat.

In the middle of the month, the allies decide to probe the Chernaia River about three miles southeast of Sevastopol. Early reports assert that we put forth a "spirited defense," while the allies offered "stiff opposition." The physicians interpret this lingo to mean that an onslaught of wounded are headed our way.

Daniil seeks me out. "Listen to me closely, Andrey." He pats his moustache. "I'm assigning triage and first aid personnel to the site of the skirmish. You're one of them. Take one of the Sisters with you. Take Kurbatova. You two work well together."

Without a word, I nod my grim understanding and turn to walk away.

Daniil grabs my arm and swings me back around to meet his eyes. "You and Kurbatova be careful."

Maria and I squeeze next to the driver of a springless wagon, a twin of the one that brought me to Sevastopol. Beyond the outskirts of the city, as the wagon sways through countless dips in the stony road, I'm hounded by the somber look in Daniil's eyes. *You and Kurbatova be careful.* The back of my neck prickles, as if a legion of centipedes is crawling up it.

Without warning, a round shot escapes the colorless hills and howls past us. It knocks the forage cap off a soldier walking on the road ahead of us. The young man calmly picks up his dusty cap, slaps it against his pant leg, and places it with care back on his head.

I whistle. "That was a near miss."

Maria turns her mossy green eyes on me. "A miss is as good as a mile."

Such an exasperating understatement!

The wagon driver, a local contracting with the army, turns off the potholed road onto rutted tracks. In an instant, the wagon's bed tilts precariously to the right, and the cargo slides with it. A couple of tall crates topple over the side. The driver leaps off his bench and pummels the broken wheel with Greek curses. When his breath is spent, he removes his cap, scratches his head, and peers up and down the deserted tracks.

Maria suggests, "Let's walk, shall we?"

I cock my head at her. "Walk? Why should we walk? A wagon will come by sooner or later."

"Because it may be later rather than sooner. We've only a mile or so to go."

"Why would I walk when I can ride? Once we arrive, we'll be on our feet nonstop."

"Come along, Andrey. Or do you plan to sit there like a disgruntled mule?"

"Come along?" Sometimes I regret the easy familiarity our relationship has assumed. Try as I might, I can't remember how and when she glommed onto me.

Maria insists, "There's bound to be a whole caravan of wagons headed toward the wounded. One of them will pick us up along the way."

"Then why walk at all? Let's simply wait here."

"We'll be warmer if we walk." She descends from the bench and rummages through the disarray in the wagon's bed until she locates our two haversacks. Dark, threatening clouds obscure the weak winter sun, and I silently concede it might be better to walk than to wait here, exposed.

Making full use of his gloved hands, the driver pantomimes that a smaller dirt road branches off this one. That branch heads downhill to the site of the skirmish.

An eerie silence surrounds us as we walk. We pass a homestead, its house in charred ruins. At one point, rocks tumble down the hillside, and my heart freezes. I peruse the area but see nothing unusual. Sheer idiocy! Any snipers would have a heyday with us.

Maria stumbles over a large rock. If she sprains an ankle, I'll be damned if I'll carry her.

"We may as well make conversation." Her words are a frosty mist. "Time will go by faster."

Andrey, how did this woman wedge herself so firmly into your life?

"Very well," I begin. "I'm cold. I'm angry at the world in general. And I'm scared shitless. Is that sufficient conversation?"

Out of the corner of my eye, I see her lips purse. I hope the silence will last but know that's fanciful thinking on my part.

"I heard that you and Serpukhov clashed yesterday." She's referring to the captain who directs the preparation of the meals.

"It wasn't a clash, merely a difference of opinion."

"About what?"

The last thing I want to do during this unpleasant moment is discuss another unpleasant moment. "I don't agree with what he feeds the men."

"You think it's not adequately nutritious?"

"My exact words to the dietitian. Do you realize that because the Orthodox Church withholds meat and dairy products every Wednesday and every Friday—not to mention the fasts before Christmas and Easter, as well as the eves of all holy days—Russians don't receive proper nutrition half the year? That same nonsense is idiotically applied to those men whose bodies are trying to heal from wounds and illness, the very bodies that crave nourishment the most."

"I don't mean to pry . . ."

An obvious misstatement.

". . . but you seem to know quite a bit about ecclesiastical law. Yet you harbor such malice toward religion."

"I never said I harbor malice toward religion."

"It's noticeable in your attitude. As I've mentioned previously, a person can learn much by listening to both what a person says and what he doesn't say." When I don't answer, she continues. "You do believe in God, don't you?"

"Perhaps."

"Perhaps?"

"Probably not."

"But you must believe in God and the saints."

"Why must I?"

"You believed in God as a child, did you not?"

I nod.

"When did you stop?"

"Oh, I probably lost track of Him a decade or so ago."

"You're saying you're an atheist? A nonbeliever?"

A *nonbeliever*. Yes, that's appropriate. Also appropriate is *cynic. Skeptic. Doubter. Rationalist.* I have a snobbish preference for *possessing a finely honed agnostic belief.*

Maria typically feels at liberty to speak openly about matters close to her heart. I sense this will be one of those chats.

"I guess if I had to describe my leanings, I'd use the term *spiritual numbness.*"

"If you don't believe in God, how will your soul receive its heavenly reward?"

"I don't notice *you* attending morning services," I chide her. "Or Sunday service, for that matter."

"I feel I can do more good for my fellow man by tending to his needs than by standing through a lengthy Divine Liturgy."

"At least we agree on something."

"What's that?"

"That the Orthodox liturgy is interminably long. And its old Slavic language is incomprehensible to most of the people it purportedly serves."

"I suppose the congregation does have a rather passive role in the service."

"Passive?" I explode. "Their contribution is to murmur 'amen,' cross themselves a few times, and beat their foreheads on the floor."

Andrey, you idiot! You allowed her to do it again. She goaded you into talking, even when you wanted to keep your thoughts to yourself.

"But the Church teaches us the principles and morals required to lead a devout life."

"Is it your conjecture that I'm dishonorable and evil?"

"Obviously not. But if you lack faith in God, I'm not at all sure where your soul will end up after you die."

"If a soul exists," I counter.

"What do you mean, *if* a soul exists?"

"It doesn't seem like a complicated statement."

"Of course souls exist. I have one. You have one."

"That's odd. Never in any of the cadavers I dissected in school did I stumble upon such a spiritual organ."

Exasperated white breath streams from her nostrils as she shifts the weight of her haversack. "All I can say is that I'll miss seeing you in Heaven."

We walk without talking as spits of cold rain fall on the dirt road. The smugness I feel for successfully provoking the chatterbox into silence is short-lived, dislodged by nagging remembrances of the Church.

The melodic but sterile chants.

The acrid fragrance of incense.

The reek of alcohol on my dear father's breath as he recited the Psalter.

I become aware that Maria has said something. "What?"

"I asked, weren't you raised in the Church?"

"Intimately."

"Pardon?"

"Intimately."

"What does 'intimately' mean?"

"It means 'in close association or familiarity.'"

"That answer isn't responsive to my question." When I don't elaborate, she asks, "Did you practice Orthodoxy as a child?"

"Intimately." *God, why won't she quit pressing me about this?*

"Stop being so ornery! I'm trying to show an interest in my traveling companion." If she weren't walking, I know she'd stomp her foot at this moment.

I parrot her. "'Traveling companion' implies a trip, usually for pleasure, with a specific destination in mind. A more apt label for this odyssey would be 'ludicrous misadventure.'"

"'Traveling companion' is as appropriate an application of a word as your use of the word 'intimately.'" She relishes going tit for tat.

"In point of fact, 'traveling companion' is not a word. It's a term."

She somehow manages to stomp her foot without missing a beat in her stride, and I fight the grin that clamors to surface. In some ways, she's so predictable. But I had forgotten her unparalleled skill at dramatic about-faces. When next she speaks, her voice is the gentle, maternal voice she uses with patients. "Why do you dislike the Church so much that you won't even talk about it?"

Why do you mind revealing your childhood, Andrey? She shared hers with you. Your childish secret serves no purpose.

"Because if I had been either of my two older brothers, I'd be a priest right now rather than a surgeon."

"I see." Pause. "I guess you were exposed to some things that we ordinary Christians aren't privy to. Things you found troublesome."

"I want no memories of the Church."

"Your shoulders always seem to carry a heavy weight."

"It's merely a lazy slouch."

"Maybe talking about it would lighten the load."

The peculiar thing is, I suddenly do want to tell her. She'll offer empathy, something I've had damn little of in my life.

I speak slowly, my voice staid. "Priests are inbred. And they're impoverished. They have no choice but to use every conceivable ruse to acquire the necessities of life, kopek by kopek."

"But priests are paid a salary."

I snort. "A priest can't begin to make ends meet on his salary. He's trapped in an archaic profession that can't support a family without milking parishioners who are as poor as himself. It destroys his sense of self-worth, so he drinks himself to an early grave."

Maria bides her time before edging the conversation forward. "At least the Church gives its sons an education."

"Let's trace that education, shall we? First, the boys are sent to the Church district school for six years, then on to the seminary. Both of which are appallingly expensive by the time you add clothing, room, board, bribes, and travel to and from the school."

"Bribes? How do bribes fit into all of this?"

"For the teachers. The superintendent. The inspector."

"Students have to bribe their way through school?"

I wonder if she's truly as interested as she portrays. Not that it really matters, because my memories are now boiling over. "A month or so before final examinations in the Church district schools, the teachers send their students home for a week with strict orders to return with a certain number of rubles. Anyone who brings back less than the designated amount remains in the same class. Anyone who brings nothing risks being expelled."

"So the fathers have no choice but to pay."

"If the boy doesn't show up with rubles, he's flogged. Then, as the boy rises from the floor, the teacher slaps his face or tears out whole tufts of hair."

"Those poor boys!"

"It's not just *those* boys. Be assured, I have *intimate* knowledge of this." I give her a long, sideways look.

"Oh. I can see why you'd be cynical." Her kind voice suddenly strikes me as irritating.

"I'm far more than *cynical* about classrooms filled with coughing, sneezing, wheezing boys. Classrooms so cold, snow is piled in heaps in the corners." I breathe deeply to calm myself. "The child pays a price that haunts him the rest of his life. And for what? They just breed more of themselves. There's such a surplus of clergy that seminary graduates have to settle for being sacristans or menial clerks."

"I didn't realize how complicated the structure is."

I give a caustic smile. "Most things are, once you're *intimately* familiar with them."

I need to stop talking before I tell her that the school day was only the beginning of a boy's nightmare. Before I tell her exactly what it was like to be a nine-year-old living in a filthy boardinghouse. The fear at school. The fear at home. The continuous fear.

Blood pulses through my temples, and my stomach pitches with razor-sharp memories.

WHAT'S WRONG? MY mother asks me. *Why are you crying?*

I'm afraid to go back to my boardinghouse on Monday.

Why?

The landlady sent me to buy some vodka, but it was time for class to begin, so I went to school instead. When I returned to the house for lunch, she beat me and said it will be even worse for me next week.

Your brothers managed, my mother says as she turns away. *They didn't whimper like you.*

My landlady is a young widow, a "special friend" of the school inspector. One evening, the inspector stops by while the widow is on an errand. He lowers himself into his favorite chair.

She beat you again? the inspector asks. *Would you like me to see to it that she never beats you again? Come here.* The inspector's open hand lies in his lap, his palm up. His fingers open and close in beckoning. Open and close. *Come closer. A favor for a favor.* His words are slow, his voice a subdued panting. Saliva glistens on his lips. *I'll show you what you can do . . .*

SLEET BEGINS TO pelt us. I was so self-absorbed in my tale of woe, I managed to miss the turnoff the driver described.

Where the fuck are we?

Maria, her windblown scarf slapping her face, shouts, "I think I saw a barn a short way back."

We retrace our steps, our long greatcoats doubling their weight with half-frozen rain. I tug my hat lower. Never have I seen such a disagreeable climate. The Crimea is worse than anyplace on earth. Except the boardinghouse.

AT LAST A desolate farmstead comes into view, and we let loose long, white sighs of relief. We dash through the cottage's doorway; the door itself is missing. The only living creature to be found is a lonely peahen in the front room, cawing out her warning to a vacant house that strangers are afoot.

Two rooms of the gutted cottage are reasonably intact. Shells and vandalism have demolished the other half. What walls remain are smoke-blackened. Any loose lumber has been pilfered.

We instinctively move to the back room, away from the gaping doorway and icy wind. Feeble light filters into the room from a small, high, glassless window. Ice pellets pound the tin roof. We gaze about the room. A soot-encased fireplace. A dusty icon. A few household utensils. A broken wine cask. Shattered crockery. Small piles of rags in the corners. All the remains of a family's life gone sadly awry.

My frigid toes feel in danger of breaking off. I blow on my shriveled fingers, but even my breath doesn't feel warm. I hear Maria's teeth chattering, and I look over at her. Ice crystals cling to her eyelashes and obscure the front of her coat.

If only we hadn't missed that turn, we'd be at the first aid station by now. If only. If only.

The one time in your life that you're loquacious, Andrey, and here's the price to pay.

We pool the contents of our haversacks—two blankets, two candles, matches, some sardines, a couple of biscuits. Maria suggests, "Maybe there's something worth burning where the barn used to be," and I nod. The peahen, crouched in the corner of the front room, gives a solitary screech as I walk past.

Ice and wind sting my face, and my boots crunch on frozen pellets as I poke about the rubble of rocks that was once the walls of the barn. All that remains standing is a portion of one wall. Foraging armies have looted the larger pieces of wood and all the buckets, tools, and tack. I find some wet, splintered remnants of wooden pens and fence posts, and I stuff a few handfuls of damp straw inside my great coat. The boards are neither long nor heavy, but the wind does its best to whip them out of my arms. I'll have to make numerous trips across the frozen yard.

The peahen cries her obligatory warning as I enter the front room.

"Shut up!"

The bird pays no heed to my words.

Maria has managed to start a sputtering fire using old rags and the wooden handles of some abandoned cooking utensils. She also pulled a tattered curtain across the open doorway between the front room and the main room, to keep in what little heat the fireplace generates. Plus, she wedged the broken wine cask and some rags into the little glassless window. I should acknowledge her ingenuity. Instead, I merely drop the wood and straw beside the fireplace.

I'm making my fourth and final trip back from the former barn when I hear a strange sound amid the howling of the wind.

Calm down, Andrey. Surely it's just hail beating against the stone house?

No, not hail.

Horse hooves.

I crouch behind the pile of stones. A solitary man dismounts in front of the cottage and removes a pistol from his holster. Sleet clouds my view, but I can see he's bundled in Western garments. My heart convulses; my testicles shrivel.

The man places a cautious foot across the doorless entry. The peahen screeches out her warning.

CHAPTER 14

February

1855

COLD SWEAT TRICKLES down the back of my neck as the man disappears into the hovel. The peahen repeats her alarm. I wait for a gunshot as the man dispatches the irksome bird, but the blast never comes. I breathe deep, trying to push down the panic. Without stopping to think, I grab a broken piece of wet board half the length of my arm.

My quaking legs sprint across the yard and past the man's horse, which flings its head and stomps its feet in cold misery. I flatten myself against the wall at one side of the entry, my heart hammering in my throat and throbbing in my ears as I raise the board like a club.

The front room is empty except for the peahen, which, extraordinarily, remains silent. Instead, I hear low voices.

I lick my lips as I creep across the earthen floor. Stomach hollow with terror, I take the final step into the entryway to the second room, fully in the line of sight.

The stranger is facing the doorway, his stalwart legs braced.

He instantly swings the pistol into perfect alignment with my chest.

I stop breathing.

Maria whirls about to face me, her purple lips in full smile.

"Be at ease," she tells me. "This man means us no harm. Come join us."

I keep the board poised in readiness, my muscles bound in petrified knots. There's no making sense of the scene before me.

She taps her foot impatiently. "I said for you to join us so we can finish introductions and I can tend to this fire." Then she says something that sounds like English.

The man, as immobile as a block of granite, continues to inspect me with trigger-happy eyes. Maria repeats her foreign words. With the reluctance of a dog abandoning a bone, the bulky man holsters the pistol. His steely gaze gores my eyeballs.

"Add the board to the fire," Maria tells me, "so this gentleman knows you mean him no harm."

My chest sinks, my shoulders slump, and my arm unceremoniously lowers the board to my side. In the space of four minutes, Maria has befriended the enemy. I entered the house ready for hand-to-hand combat with a formidable adversary, only to find her chatting with him in his native tongue.

Feeling as fragile as a spiderweb, I eye the foreigner, a bull of a man. Even the hair poking from beneath his cap is thick—brown and wavy, like his full beard. He appears to be in his thirties and eager to dispose of anyone who stands in his way. I glance at Maria in bewilderment. How could she be so naïve? She doesn't possess the survival skills of a three-day-old kid goat.

My attention reverts to the man, who studies me in return. His clothes are an odd assortment. An officer's cap with a broad gold band. A heavy military jacket. Cord breeches. Jack boots. Large spurs.

The man says something terse in English.

Maria wrinkles her brow, shakes her head, and replies with one word that has the intonation of a question.

The man drags his wary gaze away from me and directs it toward her. He neighs like a horse and, with his hands, creates a roof over his head.

Maria nods vigorously.

The man strides toward the doorway and brusquely motions me aside.

"Where's he going?" I ask Maria.

"To get his horse."

"What do you mean 'get his horse'? It's right outside."

"He's bringing it inside."

"He's bringing the horse into the house?"

Maria drops her chin and rolls her eyes at me. Her sigh makes it unequivocally clear that I have used up all her patience. "This can hardly be called a 'house.' The horse will stay in the other room with the peahen. Do you have another suggestion as to where to shelter the animal for the night?"

"For the night? That guy is staying with us for the entire night?"

Maria brings her chin upward so she can squint at the incredibly stupid man in front of her. In the dim light, I can see her eyes are green, which means she isn't truly as annoyed as she's letting on.

"It's very benevolent of you to make friendly with an Englishman. I just hope to hell we don't wake up tomorrow with a bullet through our heads."

"I can't think of a more illogical statement."

Hooves clomp across the stone entryway, followed by a whinny, then plodding across the dirt floor. The peahen goes berserk with her wailing. I drop onto my blanket, pull off my boots, and stretch my legs toward Maria's small but steady flames. As my toes thaw, I reach for the biscuits and sardines.

Maria lowers herself beside me. "We should wait until our visitor joins us."

My hands fall to my lap. "Visitor? The correct word is 'intruder.' I'm hungry, and I intend to eat."

"Stop acting like a cranky child."

I jerk an extended thumb over my shoulder toward the other room. "We are at war with that man. He's not an overnight guest or some long-lost relative."

Low, muffled words come from the front room.

"What's he doing?" I ask.

"Probably feeding the horse."

"The English hold dinner discussions with their equines?"

She glowers at me. "Why are you being so antagonistic?"

"Because we're spending a freezing night with an armed madman who talks to animals. Because his kind have done their best to blow apart our countrymen, and I've spent the past three months trying to put them back together."

Before Maria can respond to this, the Englishman enters the room and tosses his saddle bags and spurs in a corner. He nods at Maria, whose smile is wider than Sevastopol Bay, and he bestows a glare on me that's as sharp as a shard of ice.

I scowl back in equal measure.

He unrolls his blanket and sits cross-legged on the dirt near the fire. Waves of steam rise from his clothes, and the icicles on his beard turn into droplets. He points to himself. "William Howard Russell."

She points to herself. "Maria Ivanovna Kurbatova."

"Maria Ivanovna." He renders a gentlemanly nod of his head.

She points to me. "Andrey Yevgrafovich Rozhdestvensky."

He says something that resembles *Rusty-fencey* and gives a nod that's nothing more than an abrupt twitch.

The two of them begin talking in fits and starts, primarily in English. Maria does most of the talking, occasionally indicating me and seeming to mimic the work of medicine. Russell's speech grows animated, and Maria's jaw drops.

She turns to me, her green eyes radiant. "He said the English have women similar to the Sisters of Mercy."

They continue, Russell spouting a bunch of gobbledygook and Maria answering haltingly. After some time, he flaps his arms up and down at his sides. Maria throws her head back and belly laughs.

She turns to me. "It seems their officers can't resist the ducks on the Chernaia

River, despite the threat of the occasional Russian shot. Monsieur Russell joined today's outing. As they were returning to camp, he became separated from the rest of the party and lost his way in the terrible weather."

Russell opens his coat to allow the paltry warmth to penetrate his inner clothing, and I take note of the holster secured about his hips. Is that what he used to shoot ducks? A pistol?

Their conversation is resplendent with pantomimes. The motions of the barrel-chested Englishman, his thick arms and hands waving about, are laughable (if I were in a laughing mood). When comprehension in English and playacting is beyond reach, Maria tries French, which the visitor understands somewhat. Every so often, the two of them find their clumsy attempts at conversation so entertaining, they laugh at themselves with abandon. At such moments, the man's cheeks turn ruddy, transforming him into a jolly fellow. As soon as the uncontrolled chortling ends, however, he looks circumspectly at me.

Meanwhile, I sit in aloof silence. Their giddiness is rubbing my frayed nerves raw.

Maria relays the conversation to me in bits and pieces. Russell claims to not be in the military and has no official position or involvement in the war. He's merely a writer for *The Times* in London. The army offers him no protection, and he often finds himself in extreme danger. Maria is particularly intrigued that Russell writes about not only the great moments of battle but also the everyday lives of the men. Most of all, he says, he wants his readers to understand the heartbreaking tragedy of war.

I snort belligerently. Maria will believe anything.

"His story is impossible," I assert. "First, newspaper reporters don't cover wars in person. They rely on accounts from officers. Second, the government certainly wouldn't allow the newspaper to print all the details he provides."

"I questioned him about that, and he said it's true. The newspaper publishes every word he sends them. Even when he writes things that aren't nice about the army officers and the government or about how their troops suffer."

"Yes, tell him we've heard stories about that. We've heard how poorly they treat their men. And that they treat the Turks worse than dogs. Tell him we've heard all about it from their deserters."

"You're being intolerable. We have deserters too."

Perhaps I am unfairly critical of the Englishman who, thus far, has done nothing more damaging than glower. "By the way, an English gentleman isn't referred to as 'Monsieur.' The proper term is 'Mister.'"

"How do you know that? Are you sure?"

I shrug. "Ask him."

Maria's ensuing question involves pointing at me and the words *Monsieur* and *Mister*. When I hear Russell answer "Mister," I smirk and fold my arms across my chest in a juvenile display of triumph.

The supposed newspaperman and Maria decide it's time to eat. Russell pulls delicacies from his saddlebags: plum pudding, cigars, potted meat, cheese, and butter. ("His readers send them," Maria explains.) The items Maria and I brought from Sevastopol are added to Russell's spread.

Hope sprouts in me when Russell places a flask beside the food. Next to the flask, he sets a large mug. Into it he pours a splash of rum, which he proceeds to swallow in one gulp. He pours more rum into the mug and offers it to Maria. Her hand waves back and forth in front of her wrinkled nose, indicating she's not fond of hard liquor. However, she admires the engravings on the pewter mug.

"Tankard," Russell says.

She repeats the word several times, and Russell offers me the flask. I take as large a gulp as is polite and replace the flask on the blanket within easy reach of Russell and myself.

As we eat, Russell relays to Maria a lengthy narrative about the British. Their camp, she tells me, has turned the pleasant fishing village of Balaklava into a cess-pool, its streets full of fevers and dead Turks. Between ships in the harbor float the bloated carcasses of horses and camels and the feces of thousands of soldiers and sailors.

Meanwhile, on the plains, twenty-seven thousand soldiers are living, freez-ing, and dying in misery. The soldiers' coats are nothing more than rags tacked together. Every tree and bush was chopped down months ago for firewood, and two-thirds of the troops are sick with dysentery, typhus, pneumonia, or malnour-ishment. The horses that starve to death have their hides stripped off to be used for leggings, and those that are still alive are so desperate that they eat wooden wheel spokes and each other's manes and tails.

As Russell tells his story, his voice grows intense. Maria's translations become fewer and fewer, leaving me with little to do except sit and watch.

While her attention is monopolized by the Englishman, I spot a small pile of shattered china in the far corner of the room, within some hoops from a wine cask. In the jumble, I can see what appears to be a few scraps of wood. I rise and cross the room to the pile.

As I withdraw one of the wood fragments, a small creature darts out. The three of us jump like skittish colts. The creature leaps across the air and disappears behind Maria's tiny mound of firewood.

"Just a rat," I say, wishing my voice was more composed.

"It's not a rat. It's a cat." Maria turns and meows at Russell. She turns back to me. "You scared it."

"It scared me!"

She leans over, stretches the full length of her body, and places part of a sardine next to the firewood. After a few minutes, the cat builds up the courage to poke out its head and nab the fish before retreating behind the woodpile.

Without asking Russell's permission, Maria confiscates a tiny bit of his cheese and potted meat. On her rump, she slides across the dirt floor until she's beside the wood. She places a dollop of meat on the ground in front of her and patiently waits. Eventually hunger triumphs over fear, and the cat grabs the morsel and skedaddles back to safety.

Maria continues to play this game while she scoots, little by little, away from the woodpile. Russell and I sit in silence in the darkened room, lit only by the flicker of the weak fire, and watch the young woman coax the cat to her. Finally, with great persistence, she cajoles the scrawny tabby to climb onto her lap. He curls up in the dark, safe heat inside Maria's coat. The cat is a lanky adolescent, its matted, gray fur stretched over knobby bones.

Speaking softly, she announces, "I'll take him back to Sevastopol."

"We're not going to Sevastopol," I state flatly. "We're going, supposedly, to treat wounded soldiers—if any are still alive by the time we get there."

The conversation between Maria and Russell resumes, but Maria, out of courtesy to the teenage kitten on her lap, limits her pantomime. Russell likewise subdues his gestures and lowers his voice. I take a final swig of rum, place the nearly empty flask beside Russell for him to finish, and go outside to relieve myself in a snowdrift. The peahen treats me to a lusty wail both coming and going.

On my return, I notice that Russell has removed his holster and placed it on the floor within close reach.

I barge into their parley. "Ask him what kind of pistol that is."

Russell explains the mechanism to Maria, their heads bent together over the weapon. In due time, Maria informs me that this pistol is known as a Colt revolver. She explains in halting terms that the revolving cylinder has several ammunition chambers so it can be fired at a rate incredibly faster than a single-shot pistol.

I lose interest as the burly man and the large woman toil to understand one another. What requires fifteen minutes to laboriously communicate to each other takes Maria two minutes to convey to me. The lump under Maria's coat resettles itself into a more comfortable position. I decide to do likewise.

I stretch out on the blanket, half of it under me, half over me. My last thought before falling asleep is that Maria is divulging military secrets that cigars are impossible to come by in Sevastopol and that brooms are considered a luxury.

CHAPTER 15

February
1855

THE NEXT MORNING, I wake to two pairs of green eyes staring at me. One pair belongs to the woman stretched out on a blanket three feet away, parallel to me. The other set of eyes belongs to the cat, which sits with its back against Maria's neck, its tail wrapped securely around its paws as if holding down its feet.

I prop up on one elbow and locate Russell, still asleep, on the other side of Maria, perpendicular to us with his feet almost touching Maria's. All of us, except the cat, have slept in our coats, gloves, hats, and boots.

Faint sunlight seeps through the doorless front room. The fireplace is cold.

"You certainly slept a long time," Maria whispers. "Do you always require that much sleep?"

I lie back down and rest my head on the curve of my elbow. Why does she continuously bait me?

I close my eyes, but she doesn't intend for me to rest peacefully. "I can't wait to tell you all his stories. He's an amazing man!"

I open one eye. "So I noticed that you noticed."

Russell stirs and bids us good morning with a butchered, "*Dobroye utro.*" I have yet to hear a foreigner who can master the Slavic vowel.

I head outside to relieve myself, inciting the peahen to send up an early morning distress call. The snow is ankle deep, and the air is bitterly cold, but the precipitation and the wind have ceased. When I return to the cottage, Russell has his hat in hand and is running his fingers through his hair. He and Maria are laughing. The newspaperman's hair! It's shorter.

No, Andrey, not even Maria would do that. Would she?

But yes, she has indeed cut his hair. The woman possesses neither common sense nor a spit's worth of national dignity.

The three of us gather our few possessions. Maria lays out the sole remaining sardine for the cat. Russell tromps to the front room to saddle his horse.

After the peahen finishes her tirade, Maria tenderly promises the cat that she'll return for him in a couple of days on her way back to Sevastopol. She strokes the length of his body, and he lifts his nose to give her easy access under his chin.

While Maria exchanges some throaty feline mumbles with the cat, I walk into the front room where Russell is cinching his saddle. I awkwardly shift my weight from foot to foot as the man secures his bags. I should say something to him after spending the night with him in the midst of a war. But even if I could come up with something worth saying, I'd be just as well off to speak Russian to the horse as to the Englishman.

I'm unburdened of the task when Maria enters the room. She chatters in a mutated version of English merged with French. Russell responds in kind.

He turns to me and extends his hand to shake Western-style. I reciprocate. He does the same with Maria, who ignores the proffered hand and bestows three Russian kisses on alternating cheeks.

Maria and I hoist our haversacks. Just prior to stepping into the glistening daylight, she turns and waves an airy farewell to the kitten. Then to the peahen. The horse. The Englishman.

We're barely on the so-called road when I burst forth with, "You cut his hair!"

Maria looks over at me and nods.

"I'm astonished you did that!"

"It wasn't easy. The light was so poor, and I didn't have any scissors, so I had to use—"

"That's not what I mean. We are at war with those people, and you're giving them haircuts. For free, no less!"

Her eyes roll impatiently about their sockets. "It wasn't entirely free. He shared his meal with us. That plum pudding was good, wasn't it?"

How does a person respond to such absurdities?

Maria elaborates, "Besides, I'm not giving *them* haircuts. Only Monsieur Russell. He's a very nice man, Andrey, which you would have found out, had you made the effort to get to know him."

"And just how was I supposed to do that? I don't speak his language."

"Well, *I* managed."

Maria is in one of her feisty moods, and I have serious doubts that I possess the energy to tolerate it. "You have an aptitude for that sort of thing."

"What sort of thing?"

"Foreign languages. And . . . and chatting with people," I add.

"I found him to have a great deal of charm and good humor. And considerable courage."

"Courage?"

"Definitely. He's completely without protection here. The generals and such would be happy to see him killed so he'd stop reporting how badly England has bungled its war efforts."

"At least he has a gun. That's more than we have."

Maria exhales a long, white stream. "His courage goes deeper than mere physical bravery. He's not afraid to print the truth, even if it makes the generals hate him."

Her ceaseless accolades serve to escalate my ill-defined irritation toward Russell.

"His newspaper is the largest in the world, did you realize? And do you know what has happened as a result of his articles? His newspaper set up a fund for soldiers so that people can send money. Plus, depots were established all over England to collect linen to be made into bandages and dressings."

"You needn't say 'all over England' as if it's a gigantic place. The whole country is no bigger than one of our provinces." My comment is indeed extraneous to the conversation, but it seems important to put things in perspective.

Maria ignores me, pursuing her subject like a dog with a bone. "England may be smaller than Russia, but it has many of the same problems. He said there's a certain radical politician, high up in their government, who's quoted a lot in the newspaper. And he's as critical as *Monsieur* Russell about the handling of the war."

"Do you believe everything *Mister* Russell told you?"

"Printed copies of the newspaper are sent to *Monsieur* Russell, and the latest edition contains a quote from the politician about the war. *Monsieur* Russell was so impressed by the passage that he memorized it. I had him say it to me several times so I'd remember it. Do you want to hear?"

I don't answer. There's no need to.

"The politician said"—Maria inhales with theatrical drama—"'The angel of death has been abroad throughout the land; you may almost hear the beating of his wings.'"

My skepticism knows no bounds. "That was in the newspaper? Are you sure you translated it correctly?"

She nods. "The angel of death has been abroad throughout the land; you may almost hear the beating of his wings."

I must admit that my own sentiments often pursue a similar, though less poetic, vein. Touch the wounds. Smell the gangrene. Listen to the lungs rattle. *The angel of death . . . the beating of his wings.*

"Doesn't *Mister* Russell ever say anything favorable about his homeland?"

"He said Balaklava is on the mend. Huts are being built. Streets are becoming macadamized. Dead animals are collected and buried beneath lime and earth— oh, but I almost forgot the most exciting part! The British are building a railway! They're laying track even as we speak. It will run almost three miles and haul supplies and ammunition from the Balaklava harbor to their siege works. Horses will pull the cars up to the plain, then gravity will pull the cars back down."

I look over at her and stare, my eyes squinting and my mouth ajar. Has her captivation caused her to forget whose side of the war she's on?

"Oh," her eyebrows drop, "that isn't good for us, is it?"

"Not good at all."

"Do you think General Menshikov knows about this? Should we tell him?"

"I'm sure Menshikov already knows and has informed the Tsar, who will undoubtedly send Queen Victoria a note after the war, thanking her for building a railway on Russian soil."

She gives me a wry smile. We walk in silence, although not for long.

"Andrey." Her voice is solemn as her gloved hand touches my sleeve. "I want to thank you for trying to protect me last evening. It was very brave of you. For all we knew, he might have been a vindictive English lunatic."

Her earnestness, like all sentimentality, puts me ill at ease. I seek diversion. "He *is* a lunatic. He talks to animals."

"I talk to animals too. Do you think I'm a lunatic?" Her hand waves away the question. "It doesn't matter what you think. I'm sincere when I say how grateful I am that you would have saved me from harm. Had there indeed been any harm to save me from. It makes me think that perhaps you do care at least a tiny bit for me." With nervous little actions, she adjusts her scarf. "You truly were dashing, poised for combat with that old, termite-eaten board."

When she laughs that happy laugh, I can't resist joining her. "I'm just thankful I didn't have to go to fisticuffs with him. He's a big man."

"He is a very big man and as strong as a tree stump. And sometimes, while he was telling his stories, he had a fiery look about him, like he has quite a temper."

She clings to the topic of William Howard Russell like a terrier to a pant leg. My resentment resurfaces. "Speaking of temper, I wish you'd *temper* your enthusiasm."

"What do you mean?"

"Just listen to yourself. He's fiery. He's strong. He's compassionate. He's brave. He's fair. He's a magnificent writer at the world's largest newspaper. Are there any other accolades you'd like to bestow on him, or can we progress to another subject?"

She shoots me a smug smile. "I hope you're not tired of hearing his name, because you'll be hearing it quite frequently."

She's leading up to something, and I'm not going for the bait. "I simply don't think you should romanticize the man."

"I named the kitten Russell."

I stop dead in my tracks. She likewise halts and turns toward me. I blink at her several times before asking, "You named the goddamned cat *Russell*?"

"If you're reduced to cursing, there's little reason to continue this conversation." Her footsteps resume crunching on the ice-lacquered snow.

I stand motionless, staring at her back for moment before stretching out my legs to catch up with her. I inform her that she'll never find her way back to that place. "And if by some slim chance you do, the cat won't be there."

"Yes, I will, and yes, he will."

I don't really give a spit what she names the cat, so I have no cause to argue. Nonetheless, I'm compelled to present my case. "Cats aren't named Russell. They're called Vaska or Kira or maybe Martishka. But not Russell."

"A cat can have any name."

"You don't know if the cat is a male or a female."

"Russell is a fine name for either."

"May I remind you that your splendid *Mister* Russell is an enemy of Russia? He may not be in uniform, but he wants to see us beaten into the ground and then crushed like a worm. He desires to see all of Russia whimpering and groveling before his queen. And that includes you and me. And probably even that cat. For God's sake, get the fairy dust out of your eyes!"

Daggers shoot from those eyes, which have now faded to wintry gray. "He may be on the allies' side, but I made a friend last night. A friend I may never see again, but a friend nonetheless. And I will remember him and honor him by naming my other new friend after him!"

CHAPTER 16

February
1855

BY THE TIME Maria and I reach the site of the skirmish, triage and first aid are well under way. After spending only an additional two nights in the field, we're safely back on Sevastopol's north shore. Or so I thought. When Daniil seeks me out and pats his mustache twice, my head rears back with suspicion.

"You've been assigned to the first aid station at the Malakov Bastion."

My mouth falls open in disbelief and protest.

Daniil holds up a cautionary hand. "Pirogov wants all the medical students to have full exposure to military medicine—field conditions, main hospital, convalescent hospitals."

"I just returned from the goddamn field!"

My rejoinder is ignored. "You'll perform triage and administer first aid before the wounded are transported to the hospitals," Daniil continues. "Right now there's no action to speak of, other than some potshots. You'll only be there a week. Two at the most."

FUCK!

THE FERRY CASTS off as morning light appears in the east, and I snug up my collar and fold my arms against the damp cold. Over the sounds of the lapping waves, the breeze carries a defiant crackle from the rifle pits on the south side. The gray horizon beyond the city suddenly flashes with a violet light that pales to pink before fading away.

Maybe, Andrey, there really is a God, and this is His idea of atonement for having spat in His face.

Quivers shoot simultaneously down my spine and up my neck. Damn Pirogov! And damn the crowned heads and diplomats who should have settled this dispute sans gunpowder and blood!

When I and my nauseous fear reach the far shore, I square my shoulders and stride through the streets of a town I no longer recognize. Mutilation has blasted through Sevastopol like a typhoon.

The formidable Malakov Bastion is situated two and a half miles southeast of town, atop the most prominent hill on the southern horizon. The high ground itself is daunting; plus, our engineers and their sappers have recently bolstered it with walls, ditches, and dugouts. Gun placements had been dug into the hill's ground, then covered with thick timbers and earthworks to withstand the heaviest bombardment. Deep inside the hill, there's a first aid station that's supposedly the caliber of a hospital, amid a maze of bunkers, some apartments, and even a chapel. The Malakov is the preeminent fortification on Sevastopol's southern perimeter, and we Russians have no intention of losing it. The French bastards, meanwhile, have every intention of acquiring it.

Upon climbing to the top of the bastion, I find its elevated vantage point affords me a 360-degree view, even as far as the north shore. It also offers a bird's-eye view of the French guns to the south, which are pointed directly at me.

Encircling the top of the bastion is a head-high protective barrier constructed of fascines of sticks and branches, as well as gabions and bags stuffed with rocks and dirt. Poking through the parapet's embrasures are cannons, some of them massive, waiting to make themselves useful.

Within the fortification, disarray gives the impression that it's already been blown apart. Warfare's tools of the trade—rocks, sticks, rope, fist-size cannon-balls, broken boards, half-demolished wickerworks—blanket the hard-packed, stony earth like an obstacle course. Soldiers scurry in all directions, doing I don't know what.

I request directions to the first aid station and am pointed toward a passageway that leads down into the actual hill. There I find a subterranean room crammed with treatment tables, stools, crates, and chests of supplies.

A seasoned physician named Panfilov lays down the ground rules.

"Don't try any heroics. Ascertain if they're dead or alive. Stop the bleeding. Stabilize the fractures. Wrap any major wounds to keep out contamination. Give them a little morphine if they're in terrible agony. Send them to the main hospital. Don't even consider amputation. And don't go digging around for bullets. Let those fussy-britches at the hospitals do that." Realizing he's probably insulted me, he issues an apology of sorts. "Oh. Guess that's you, huh? Well, everyone has their job to do."

A crack splits the air above the earthworks. I flinch, but Panfilov assures me, "You'll get used to it."

It's pointless to pretend I'm not unnerved. "I've never been this close to the front lines."

Panfilov nods. "I was scared too, at first. But at some point during the nineteen years I've been patching men back together, I decided to let fate take its course. Besides, not all the racket you'll hear is necessarily bad. Some of it is our fire—that is to say, *your* protection. That explosion sounded like one of our thirteen-inch shells. It's a monstrous thing, as much as two men can lift into the mortar. Quite a spectacular sight when flung into the air. You can watch it rise until it gets out of sight. Then you see it off in the distance, when it explodes on the ground." Panfilov's hand follows the imaginary trajectory, his arm arching over his head like a ballerina's.

"I hope never to be any closer to the action than I am right now," I respond.

"I hope you aren't either. There's nothing so disagreeable as the singing of a Minié bullet as it zips past your ears." He swats at his ear as if shooing away a mosquito. "Quite different from a round ball, which whistles softly as it passes by." He places his finger vertically across his lips.

Panfilov's gesticulations dredge up recollections of crazy old Doctor Zaitsev. Do all military physicians end up so peculiar?

The first aid station remains tranquil for the rest of the day. I tend to a couple of frostbite cases and some minor injuries induced by clumsiness. But that night, my fitful sleep ends abruptly just after midnight when a volcanic *bang!* rocks the ground.

I bolt upright.

The orderlies, sleeping in their clothes for warmth, leap from their cots and careen toward the first aid center. I sit immobile on the cot, blanket pulled up to my neck, stomach constricted in fear. The cannonade is furious.

Please get me out of here, I plead to no one in particular.

I compel myself to rise and follow the moans and sobs toward the first aid station. On my heels is a hefty, gray-haired officer clutching a white kerchief.

"Can I tend to your hand, sir?" I ask the major general.

"Damn the French. Caught us with our pants down again." He holds forth a scorched, red palm. "In my haste to take leave of my quarters, I managed to knock over the lamp. Like a dimwit, I grabbed its hot chimney."

As the man lowers himself onto a three-legged stool, one of his beefy legs remains straight forward, its knee reluctant to bend.

"Make it double-snappy." The gritty voice is brusque but not harsh. "My own clumsiness has already cost me too much time."

I apply morphine to deaden the pain, then daub on burn ointment. My fingers, rigid with cold, wrap bandaging around his hand. Suddenly there's an ear-piercing explosion, and the earth shimmies beneath us.

"A gentle reminder of the French lads' dislike for us," the old warrior growls.

When my task is completed, the major general stands and tries to flex his hand, which, courtesy of the stiff linen, is now as unyielding as his knee.

"Don't expect much from that hand for the next week," I advise.

"My own dastardly, lamebrain fault." He salutes me, and I him. "Well done."

The flickering light reflects off faces contorted with pain as I move to my next patient.

THE POUNDING OF the guns is unrelenting through the dark hours. Shivering from the cold sweat on my skin, I progress from patient to patient. They lie on litters, on tables, on the ground. Disemboweled men. Weeping men. Cursing men. Oblivious men.

Before dawn, the roar of the French heavy artillery abates, only to be replaced by sorties of shot and shell from both sides. The medical personnel labor continuously, collecting the wounded, delivering them to the ambulance station, ministering to their wounds, and finally carting them to the main hospital on the south side of the bay.

A second day.

A third day.

Why, Andrey, are you patching up men so they can go out and kill other men? It's madness. Sheer madness!

By the fourth morning, a deficit of food and sleep has turned me into a walking corpse. Worse than my blurry vision and quivering muscles are my foggy thoughts as one soldier after another places his life in my exhausted care. The continuous blast of bullets and screaming of shells has untethered my mind.

Around midday, an eerie silence descends. We've run a white flag up the flagstaff, declaring an armistice so that the wounded can be collected.

I'm bandaging a man's head that was sliced open by a shell-splinter when Doctor Panfilov informs me that too many of the casualties are arriving at the dressing station beyond hope due to heavy blood loss. "The blockhead orderlies can't get the purpose of tourniquets through their thick skulls. Use this lull to go up top, and see if you can get a few of the wounded back here before they bleed to death. And try to teach those jughead orderlies why and how to apply a tourniquet."

The words shake me to the bone. "Me?" Certainly I, Andrey Yevgrafovich Rozhdestvensky, am not expected to go into the area where men's single, unified goal is to kill each other.

"I'll assign an orderly to go with you. Take plenty of compresses and tourniquets. Don't worry about morphine. Just stop the hemorrhaging." Panfilov hurries away, and an orderly hands me two haversacks filled with supplies.

On the verge of vomiting, I follow the young private to the top of the bastion. The pounding and screeching of artillery has been silenced. Below me, our soldiers are scouring the rocky terrain around Malakov Hill for dead and wounded. The French, less than a hundred yards away, are fanned out on the identical errand. Wind whips the white flags, and the crows and vultures enjoy a leisurely feast.

I narrow my viewpoint to the carnage that surrounds me atop the bastion. Faces jammed into the dirt. Men, scorched by explosions, draped over heavy ordnance. Bodies so smashed, it's difficult to credit they were ever human forms. Acid rises and burns my throat.

The angel of death . . . the beating of his wings. The words come unbidden. And I would have preferred they hadn't come at all.

For an hour I toil, stepping over the dead to get to the living. *Stop the hemorrhage, Andrey. Stop the hemorrhage.*

My God, the lust men have for other men's blood! So much for the rose-colored images of war that lured me to Sevastopol.

A shout—"The flags are coming down!"—is followed by a bright flash and the roar of a gun.

The enemy replies with murderous fire. I throw myself down, landing atop a dead soldier. As I roll off the body, the deafening thunder of a nearby Russian cannon rattles my whole being. The shot shrieks overhead, tearing toward the enemy.

I'm paralyzed with both terror and rage. All I want is to survive! Is that asking too fucking much!

I have no idea how long I lie here, eyes closed, limbs atremble. The splinter of a shell whirls past on its course of destruction. Whizzing bullets bury themselves in sandbags. Men scream. Fountains of dirt are thrown up all around the earthworks.

The wail of a nearby soldier stabs my ears. Fresh blood conceals his face like a shroud. I will myself to rise and tend to the man. My orderly has disappeared.

I'm surrounded by pandemonium. Piles of corpses. Men thrashing around in one another's blood. I reach inside myself and search for a hidden cache of courage, but all I find is the burning desire to survive.

I crouch low and hasten from this soldier to the next, blood and flesh flying into my face. A heavy pounder bounces along the ground and halts next to a mangled corpse that's missing its right temple, its brains spilling onto the ground. A ball whistles past me. Stones and deadly splinters fly through the air. I step over a body, its head whopped off at the neck as if with an axe. Twenty paces away, a soldier is hit by an exploding shell.

My ears ring. My head throbs. My jaw aches from clenching my teeth. A thick yellow pall blots out the sky. Acrid smoke and dust sear my nostrils and eyes until I can barely see through my tears.

I work on soldier after soldier until my supply of bandaging is exhausted. Then I toss aside the haversack, remove the shirts and trousers from dead soldiers, and shred them into strips. I move in a daze, rolling dead bodies off live ones. A canister explodes directly over my head. One of its fragments tears past me with an angry *whirr*.

I kneel beside a downed gunner whose hand holds back the intestines trying to spill from the gash in his belly. I begin wrapping the man's middle with the trouser leg from his dead comrade.

Above me, there's a whistle.

I look up. Sparks from a shell's fuse arc through the air. Closer . . . closer . . .

I want to scream, but my tongue adheres to my palate.

With a thud, the shell lands the mere length of a body away. Its fuse glows and hisses at me. Nearby soldiers dive for cover.

I stare at the shell.

My death. Very near.

Get rid of it.

Run, fool.

Get rid of it. Get rid of it. Get rid of it.

Unsure of what I'm doing or why, I hoist the shell, rest it against my chest, and carry it to the parapet. Time stands violently still as I shove it through an embrasure. As it falls, it explodes. Its splinters whistle and whine.

A roar encircles me.

I stare at the men, stupefied. Why are they shouting, "Hurrah"?

I glance down at my hands. They're covered with dirt and blood. Then I peer through the opening and down to where the demon shell has disintegrated. What just happened? What have I done? I can't figure out any of this.

I kneel and finish wrapping the herniated abdomen. When I stand up and step to one side, my foot lands on the upturned blade of a shovel. As its handle arcs upward toward me, I reflexively jump back in the direction I just came from, tripping over the newly bandaged man. I tumble sideways. A sharp pain stabs my temple as it strikes a stone abutment, and the sky crashes in on me.

CHAPTER 17

February
1855

A MAN'S FACE sways above mine. Why is someone holding open my eyelid?

"Where am I?" The croak of my own words pummels my head.

"You're in the hospital. You took a nasty blow."

I work in a hospital. But this isn't it. I slur, "Need drink."

"I'll find your girlfriend. That woman is kindness itself." The man gives an abbreviated smile and scurries off.

Girlfriend?

Sleep swallows me.

"ANDREY? ANDREY? CAN you hear me?"

With considerable effort, I drag open my eyelids. A round-faced woman with kind eyes is sitting on my bed.

"Maria?"

"Drink this." She cradles my head and lifts the cup to my lips. The liquid against my parched throat is almost as soothing as Maria's cool palm against my scalp. She gently lowers my head onto the hard mattress. My skull feels like a poker has been rammed clear through it.

I swivel my eyes toward her. "Pillow?"

"Pillow? There are no pillows left in the hospitals."

The tips of my fingers brush the bandage wrapped about the top of my head. "Hurts."

"Do you remember being at the Malakov?" she asks.

Malakov? I'm stationed at the hospital on the north shore. Malakov? I start to rotate my face toward hers, but nausea roils in me. "Sick."

Her fingers softly clasp my shoulder. "We'll talk later."

I waste no time lapsing into oblivion.

DURING BRIEF WAVES of muddleheaded consciousness, I assemble some murky fragments. Explosions. Armistice. More explosions. Dead soldiers. A headfirst tumble into a stone wall.

I want to rest in peace and quiet. Instead, all around me, day and night, are the sounds of other men. Hacking. Cursing. Sobbing. Praying. Shouting. Vomiting.

If I had a pillow, I'd put it over my head rather than under it.

I'M NOT SURE how much time has passed when Maria approaches my bed again. I find myself reaching for her hand. It's an alien gesture for me, but I'm so happy to see a familiar, caring face that my natural reserve deserts me. Her firm grip offers assurance that someone will help me get through this mess.

She sits beside me on the wafer-thin mattress. "How do you feel?"

"Rusty nail in my head. Ringing in my ears."

"Do you remember what happened at the Malakov?"

"Parts."

"Do you remember being a hero?"

"Hero?"

"Don't you remember that shell? The shell you picked up and tossed over the parapet?"

I stare at the rafters, trying to make sense of her blathering. Wait. Yes. I remember something. But I hadn't been a hero. I'd merely been scared, so scared my actions were impulsive. I hadn't tossed the shell, just rolled the heavy son-of-a-bitch. Hero? No, I'm a coward.

I study Maria's round, caring face. The woman can honey-coat even the ghastliest of life's calamities.

"It was ready to explode at any moment and, cool as a cucumber, you pitched it over the wall."

"Not exactly . . ."

"If it had burst where it fell, scores of men would have been killed."

I lack the stamina to refute her version of reality. "How do you know this?"

"Everyone knows. The men who witnessed it credit you with saving their lives."

"I was trying to save myself from—"

True to habit, she interrupts me. "Shush. It was a singular example of valor, and the men's commander plans to visit you to acknowledge your courage in person."

"Why do you always argue with me? I'm too tired."

"I'm not arguing with you. But that's the thanks I get for getting you off the floor and onto a bed."

"I rolled off the bed?"

"Don't be daft. When they brought you and hundreds of others to the main hospital, there weren't enough beds. Everyone was laid out on the floor. When I found you, I told them you were a physician and they secured a bed for you."

Somewhere in my foggy brain, it occurs to me that Maria doesn't belong at the main hospital on the south side. "Why aren't you at our hospital?"

Maria's eyes, normally steady and placid, suddenly flit about the ward. "When we heard about the horrific fighting, Sister Stakhovich temporarily assigned me here." Her hands flutter about, as if my question is challenging in its complexity. "Tomorrow I return to our hospital."

"How long have I been here?"

"Three days. Once you're able to eat on your own, they'll let you recuperate in your cottage. They don't let just anyone do that, but they think because you're a doctor, you can take care of yourself." She giggles as she rises from the bed. "I didn't have the heart to dispel their silly notion."

I hate that she's leaving. "Thank you for taking care of me."

She rests her hand on mine where it lies on the tattered blanket. Thick and red-knuckled, it's the most comforting hand in the world.

She's two beds away when she turns and wags a plump finger at me. "You need a haircut."

Nearby heads turn to scrutinize me.

THE FOLLOWING DAY, I awake from a nap to see Colya. His smile is so broad, his freckles seem to explode.

"Good day, Doctor Rozhdestvensky! My sergeant gave me permission to come in person to congratulate such an admired hero."

It's as if history has been rewritten. "Don't believe everything you hear. The tale has become a mix of fact and fantasy."

"Nevertheless, I'm proud to say I know you personally."

The preposterous story is sticking to me like a burr.

My eyes wander the length of the boy. In the few weeks since last I saw him, Colya has thinned out and stretched out. His ankles and wrists hang from faded garments that were probably passed down to him from a soldier who no longer had a need for clothing. "Where are you assigned?"

"I'm doing trench work."

That explains the dark circles beneath his eyes, as well as his cracked lips. As the engineers frantically struggle to bring the city's long-neglected perimeter fortifications up to the level of their exalted reputation, pitifully fed young men are worked almost to death, digging trenches in the frozen ground with pickaxes and cheap shovels. The fittest soldiers are used in place of pack animals to haul dirt and rocks, until they're admitted to the hospital, hollow-bellied and hollow-eyed.

"How are you holding up?" I ask, despite the observable answer.

The boy shrugs his far-too-thin shoulders. "Don't much care for it, but I do my part. Makes my muscles stronger, so I'll be ready to give the French a good licking when I get the chance."

"Aren't you afraid of grapeshot or bullets while you're working in the trenches?"

"Not really. I think more about the pouring rain and standing in slushy water." There's an adult's perception behind his haggard eyes. Colya is becoming a young man—a very fatigued, extremely underweight young man.

"Take care of yourself, Colya. I've seen too many frostbitten toes fall off."

With a heavy heart, I watch the weedy youth walk away in his faded uniform. He's too young to be facing the horrors of war. Hell, every soldier is too young to face such horrors.

LATER THAT AFTERNOON, I'm visited by the commander of the men I supposedly saved. But it isn't just their commander; it's their commander's commander's commander. A major general. And not just any major general. It's the major general with the burned hand, which now salutes me from my bedside.

In a huge bass voice, the officer identifies himself as Major General Tropinin and inquires about my recovery. I tell him that my head still hurts, I'm weak, and my ears ring as if there are harness bells in them but that I expect to be shipped back across the bay soon.

"Speaking of injuries," I ask, "how is your hand?"

"It's healing fine." He glances at the bandages. "I burned it on a lamp."

"Yes, I know. I'm the one who bandaged it."

He studies me, then breaks into a smile of wrinkles. "I didn't recognize you in that turban of bandages."

The major general explains that he came to the hospital to personally recognize my heroism. "As you surely knew, several cases of powder were only a few steps away. The devastation had that shell blown!" He continues to trumpet clichés: an *act of uncommon courage* and *nerves of oak* and the highly eloquent *triumph and disaster are but a moment apart.* His thunderous voice continues to capture the attention of other patients while my mind ponders the peculiarities of fate. Here I am, in the hospital because I'm an oaf, being honored for acting intuitively out of primal fear. There's no explaining the utter unpredictability of life.

"Thank you for your words, sir," I say, then sputter something about service to the Tsar.

Tropinin's thickset hand squeezes my shoulder. "I'm indebted to you, son, for what you did for my men."

He departs, and I watch him stride down the aisle of beds, his bum knee marring his gait. Halfway, he halts and pulls a blanket over a lifeless face.

I close my eyes.

The angel of death . . . the beating of his wings.

A lit shell. Cases of powder. That angel had breathed down my neck.

Then I think of Maria and grin. *A miss is as good as a mile.*

TROPININ IS BARELY out the door when I'm ousted from the hospital, transported across the bay to the north shore, and deposited in my cottage to recuperate. Several more days of bed rest are required before I can stand upright without feeling as if I'm in a rowboat in the midst of a cyclone. The perpetual hangover in my skull slowly clears, and the ringing in my ears—which has the aura of a mulish policeman who refuses to stop blowing his whistle—ultimately subsides.

By the time I finally return to work, winter has lost its bite. However, neither the balmy weather nor my return elicits much attention. Everyone is too busy dissecting the news that hit with the suddenness of a bombshell: Tsar Nicholas is dead. Tales buzz about the cause. Suicide, either gunshot or poison. Complications of the flu. Broken health due to his anguish over the war.

And how will thirty-six-year-old Alexander II handle the war? During the fifteen years prior to his ascent to the throne, he participated in both civil and military affairs without deviating from the reactionary political course set by his father. No one at the hospital expects any decisive initiatives from the new Tsar.

However, the reams of discussions about Nicholas and Alexander fall short when compared with Maria's kitten. The Sisters are enamored beyond reason with it.

ON MY FIRST day back at work, my stamina is depleted by noon. Hoping food will boost my vigor, I head toward the mess hall. My hands encircle the warm bowl—a thin, broth-based potato soup with a few forlorn sprigs of turnip greens floating about. Fresh vegetables are unavailable, and meat and dairy products are a twice-a-week luxury. As I bring the bowl to my lips, my thoughts hark back to my first meal in Sevastopol. Noodles covered with a cream sauce. Crayfish soup. Hot rolls with butter.

Using my palms as leverage, I push myself up from the bench and catch sight of the map of sinews, veins, and bones on the backs of my hands. Colya isn't the only one who has lost weight.

As I exit the mess hall, I see Maria for the first time since I've returned to the north side.

She asks, "Did you notice the flowers came out specifically to welcome you home?"

"Flowers?"

"Andrey Yevgrafovich, look around! They're all over the hillsides."

Sure enough, the earliest crocuses, veronicas, and hyacinths splash like tiny jewels across the hills. Something only a woman would notice.

A woman. A woman's gentle touch. Suddenly I want nothing so much as the feel of Maria's comb massaging my scalp.

"You sorely need a haircut!" She says at the precise moment I ask, "Would you cut my hair?"

CHAPTER 18

June
1855

OUR SPIES INFORM their commanders, and from there the rumors trickle down to the rank and file. Our enemies are suitably housed, adequately fed, and well supplied. By early May, the British boast a secure base, steamers, sturdy carts, horses, mules, ponies, buffaloes, camels, and oxen, as well as a railway. The upshot is a furious cannonade south of the city and a deluge of casualties into Sevastopol's hospitals.

A thick, caustic pall hangs over the plateau south of Sevastopol as the allies' guns creep ever closer. According to hearsay, fifty thousand Russians have been lost in battle, with an equal number of deaths due to illness. Another rumor comes directly from an artillery soldier under my care. He claims Russia is so low on ammunition and small mortar shells that his battery commander was ordered to limit fire to one shot for every four received from the allies.

Are these tales true? I don't know. But I can't ignore the naked truth that gnaws at my insides: the tide of war has turned against my homeland.

More Sisters of Mercy and medical students arrive. Mother Russia recruits German and American physicians and pays them better than she does her own sons. The insult!

Agitation churns within all of us. Some seek relief in alcohol. Others nurture pets, everything from dogs to caged garden snakes, a counterbalance to their feigned indifference to fear and death. The Sisters attach themselves to Maria's cat like ticks to a dog's underbelly. Russell is granted full run of the hospital, except for the operating theater. I admit that I'm surprised by the peacefulness that descends on the patients while they stroke the gray tabby. The cat has also gained my respect for keeping the mouse population under control.

A gaudy display of wild mint, parsley, and sage covers the valley floor, and delicate violets and snowdrops line the hard-packed soil of the north shore's few roads. Graceful bouquets of aromatic lavender appear in the hospital wards, courtesy of the Sisters.

While the rest of us bask in the delicious sunshine, Pirogov laments it. "The torrid heat will spawn fever and pestilence from the layers of human and animal matter that fester below the surface of the soil. With so much putrid flesh about, a poisonous effluvium is unavoidable."

True to Pirogov's prediction, fevers begin to ransack the troops. Although relief is available through quinine, hundreds of men die for lack of the drug. Such military incompetence is reprehensible!

The warm weather finds other ways to thwart our medical corps. Wounds crawl with maggots. Flies, fleas, and mosquitoes replace lice as the primary nuisance. Worse of all, dreaded cholera wields its deadly scythe, slaying half its victims.

Pirogov's praise of the Sisters of Mercy knows no bounds, and most of the physicians have sluggishly come to concur with his sentiments. One of the Sisters' unofficial tasks is to write to the families of dying or dead men, notifying them of their loved ones' fates. The letters provide great emotional benefit to the enlisted men, as the government takes no action to notify their families. And when wives and mothers invariably meet with defeat in their attempts to uncover the fate of their loved ones, the letters at least quell the anguish of uncertainty.

The Sisters also curtail thievery. Previously, each hospital division oversaw its own dispensary. But Pirogov turned the whole system upside down by placing the entire oversight in the hands of the Sisters. Lint, bandaging, laudanum, and quinine no longer vanish into thin air (or rather, into the black market).

Pirogov and the Sisters also join forces to ensure that all the victuals allotted to the soldiers—be it meat, eggs, cheese, or bread—actually reach the men before the rations mysteriously shrink in size or disappear altogether. Each piece of meat is weighed upon delivery to the kitchen, and the kettles are sealed so the contents can't be removed.

Meanwhile, the allies have upped the ante. Whenever our orderlies remove a corpse from one side of a hospital bed, they slide a living body onto it from the other side. Amputated fingers, hands, feet, and entire limbs are piled waist high in the corners of the operating room.

ONE EVENING, MARIA is scooping up Russell at the end of his daily hospital duties when she spots me. I've just finished a twelve-hour surgery shift. Everything aches, from my toes up to my forehead.

"Guess what arrived across enemy lines for me!" Her full-force squeal flattens the cat's ears. "A tankard."

"A what?"

"A tankard."

"What is a 'tankard'?" My brain hasn't the fortitude to tackle obscure words.

"Certainly you remember Monsieur Russell's big, heavy cup. Actually, it was more of a glass than a cup. But it wasn't really a glass either. Remember?"

So much has transpired since February that I have only the dimmest memory of the entire episode, let alone the specifics of a drinking vessel. "Why and where did you purchase a tankard?"

"I didn't purchase it. Russell's namesake sent it to me along with two bottles of beer. As a gift." She taps her foot robustly. "As I said, across enemy lines."

I squint at her, as though by seeing better, I would likewise hear better. "A gift?"

"He sent it with a carrier during the ceasefire, while the litter-bearers gathered up our wounded."

"Why would he send you a gift?"

"Because he's my friend. I told you he's my friend, but you didn't listen."

"So he sent you beer? And a glass?" I shift from one foot to the other, trying to ease the burden on my swollen feet.

"Not a glass. A tankard. I have his letter in my pocket. He had someone write it in Russian." She transfers the cat from the crook of one elbow to the other and rummages through pockets so cavernous, they could conceal a watermelon. "Here, hold Russell while I find the letter."

I look at the furball she extends in front of my chin. "Can't you just put it down?"

A little line descends the center of her brow. Lips pursed, she sets the cat on the floor. She finds the letter and paraphrases William Howard Russell's note.

"He's temporarily leaving the Crimea to meet his wife at Therapia. He would consider it a kindness if I'd keep the tankard as a remembrance of the extraordinary night we shared. The beer is called Oxford Audit, a good stout beer. In the years to come, when he looks back at his time spent in the Crimea, he will hold his evening with me as one of his fondest memories."

Maria sighs as if emitting stardust. She refolds the paper and buries it in her pocket. "Such an exceptionally nice man."

"Nice to you! He wanted to scatter my brains with his Colt revolver." I'm dead tired, and I simply cannot summon the patience to listen to Maria rhapsodize about the newspaperman.

Bashfulness floods her face. "That night, while you were asleep, he told me that he assumed you and I were lovers."

I emit a snicker, which grows into a chuckle. Then into an open laugh. I'm slap-happy from nonstop surgery. My nerves are stretched to the breaking point. After the horrors I face day and night, anxiety is a pressure cooker requiring an outlet. It finds that outlet in Maria's comment.

How absurdly hilarious that anyone, even an enemy of the Sovereign of Russia, would think the two of us are romantically involved. "I didn't realize your newspaperman had such a sense of humor!"

With blinding speed, Maria's eyes turn steely and slash through me like sabers. Her cheeks ripen to the color of plums. She scoops the cat into her arms and storms away.

I stand shell-shocked as she strides down the center aisle of beds, a tail flicking at the side of her waist. What the devil made her so mad?

CHAPTER 19

June
1855

FROM THAT DAY forth, silence sits like a block of ice between Maria and me. I try to remember at what point the exasperating conversation turned sour, but I quickly grow weary of second-guessing her motives. Maria is a bundle of moody, complex, and contradictory behaviors. Like all women, she blows hot, then cold.

A week into her silent treatment, I walk past her sitting beside a bed, writing a letter for a soldier. I purposefully and childishly bore an evil eye through the white scarf that shrouds her back. Engulfed by that juvenile task, I almost slam into litter-bearers carrying a soldier's body without a head.

I keep my hiss low so as not to upset the nearby patients. "Why did you bring him here?" I grimace as my hand pantomimes a slice across my neck.

"The fellow behind us is bringing his head," explains one of the bearers. "This soldier fought with great courage. Our Little Father will see that he survives to fight more battles!"

I'm speechless at the blockheads' blind faith in the Tsar's ability to resurrect life. Russian peasants are the most ignorant, backward souls in all of mankind.

"Take him directly to surgery," I say, knowing that my colleagues could use a hearty dose of comic relief. Their last good snort of merriment was during my bout of hiccups, which everyone agrees is a hard act to follow.

I assume Maria overheard the ludicrous conversation. Sharing a kindred sense of humor, she and I would typically exchange surreptitious looks of amusement. I glance toward her, thinking to catch her wide-mouthed, full-lipped smile. Instead, I see cool, pewter eyes devoid of mirth. She instantly resumes her letter writing.

Devil take her, I mouth. If Maria wants to stoke her animosities, by God, let her.

MORALE AMONG THE bone-weary troops drops lower every day. The summer sun bakes the earth, sending up shimmering heat waves from the white rocks in the distant hills. The nights are steam baths, making sleep elusive. Food is rationed. Basic supplies, including ammunition, are scarce and in some cases nonexistent. Men fight with empty bellies and empty guns.

Despite the ardent trench digging and artillery blasting, neither side gains ground. The siege seems interminable.

In the hospitals, stocks of morphine and chloroform are so low, they're reserved solely for officers. Without anesthesia, surgeries that involve the abdomen are banned, and limbs are amputated with the patient under the influence of vodka and the restraint of two or three strong orderlies. With each gruesome grind of my saw through muscle and bone, I yearn for the hapless victim to faint and end his gut-wrenching screams.

Even with our grueling work schedules, Daniil, Ignaty, and I manage an occasional game of skat. My companions have crevices around their mouths and exhaustion in their eyes. We try to fuel ourselves with alcohol, but it seems to have lost its magical power.

ONE OF THE physicians declares that we need a break from disease and death. He suggests a picnic. The idea catches fire and spreads throughout the north shore. Daniil and some of the seasoned veterans offer to staff the hospital on the day of the picnic, allowing the younger personnel to enjoy a brief furlough.

Scores of medical staff gather to revel away the June afternoon while columns of smoke rise south of the city. The chosen spot is the far eastern end of the bay, where a dry creek bed widens before ending in a cove that is sheltered from heavy swells.

The fierce afternoon sun is blocked by an overhang of trees that stood in creek water last winter, inaccessible to the axes of parties foraging for wood. A luxuriant growth of yellow and white jasmine fringes the area.

Despite food shortages, the staff has somehow scrounged up a mouthwatering banquet for this special occasion. Dark bread, cottage cheese, hard cheese, smoked fish, cucumbers, and three varieties of honey are laid out between basketfuls of apricots, melons, and cherries. Beverages are available from several large samovars, a cask of wine, a tub of peach brandy, and dozens of bottles of vodka.

Once stomachs are full and minds are abuzz with alcohol, some of the men bring out cards and dice. Others roll up their trousers and wade into the sparkling water. Like little boys, they skim stones across the surface of the waves and splash each other with water.

The Sisters eventually wander to the water's edge, remove their shoes, and allow the waves to lap at their stockinged feet. In the presence of a female audience, the men progress to footraces along the shoreline, using an old stone wall as part of an obstacle course. Ignaty wipes melon juice from his chin and joins the thick of the competition.

Soon the boozy men begin to slosh bare-chested in the cool water. I pour myself another glass of vodka, feeling sympathy for the Sisters as they sit with the heat trapped inside their brown habits. Little Soldier, meanwhile, is curious as to what lies beneath their somber garb.

Sluggish from an overextended stomach, I let out a satisfied grunt and stretch my back across the ground. A long line of storks flies overhead. Goldfinches, buntings, titlarks, and sparrows twill in the bushes. The day's sleepy warmth drags at my eyelids. By God, it's almost as if I'm partaking of a normal day in a normal life.

As the shadows thicken, everyone abandons the water. Some sing while others converse in low tones. When I rise to retrieve another glass of vodka, I catch sight of Maria and Ignaty seated on the ground, segregated from the others. Legs tucked under her, Maria twirls the stem of a wildflower. Ignaty, legs crossed, listens intently to her chatter. He lifts his hand and gently waves it beside her head, chasing away an insect.

Bands of gold and purple stretch across the sky, and crickets tune up their crooning instruments. It's a perfect evening for lovers. Except the lovers are Maria and Ignaty.

I divert my eyes and continue in my pursuit of vodka, and of an answer to what troubles me about the pair. I have nothing against Ignaty. Oh, sure, he's a little peculiar with his penchant for preciseness and his persistent head bobbing, but every person has quirks. And Ignaty is unquestionably an honest fellow. But . . .

But what, Andrey? But what?

I recall his question last winter about whether my relationship with Maria went further than friendship, and my answer in the clear negative—which still holds, of course. But as far as I know, the Tatar hadn't pursued his interest, probably because after all, Maria is . . . well . . . Maria is Maria. She's a large, amazingly plain woman. Even she admits she's homely. So what is that burly Tatar up to?

Despite Ignaty's unassuming personality, I've always intuited the purveyor possesses a certain baseness. Perhaps it's his coal black eyes that provoke my consternation. Or maybe his dusky complexion and blue-black beard lend him a bit of a fiendish appearance.

So, Andrey, what do you really know about your friend? Is Maria safe with him?

It's common knowledge that Tatars, like all Eastern people, are warm-blooded and licentious. And I know from our idle gab at the skat table that Ignaty is no exception. His quick smile, half concealed beneath his heavy moustache, gives the impression of something panting for release.

Andrey, maybe you should warn Maria to beware of . . .

Beware of what? What exactly are the Tatar's intentions? Not that it matters anyway, since I can't talk to her, because she's not talking to me.

I help load the empty baskets and samovars onto carts. As the light drains into the sea, the first of hundreds of summer stars make their appearance. In less than an hour, I'll be on my cot. Alone. Where will Ignaty and Maria be?

CHAPTER 20

June

1855

THE THIN GRUEL has become so grossly inadequate and the rotten salted meat so odious that I no longer take a midday meal at the mess hall. Instead, I head to my cottage, which is now overpowered with cigarette smoke and cramped with a fetid assortment of cots, trundle beds, and bunkbeds. I find a nap to be particularly useful when, as happened last night, my sleep is abruptly shattered by one of my cottage-mates leaping up in a hysterical dream frenzy and shoving his feet into his boots, shouting, "The British! They're invading!"

Following my noontime rest, I enter the hospital, trailed by a boy passing into his teen years.

"Excuse me, sir. Where can I find Maria Ivanovna Kurbatova?"

My eyes drop to the bouquet of wild lilies and orchids clutched in the boy's hand. Flowers? Who hired a messenger to deliver flowers to Maria? Ignaty? What's going on here? That's not how licentious Tatars behave.

"Sister Kurbatova is in the next ward. Just go through that door. She's the large woman." I make a hefty circle with my arms.

I peer through the doorway as the boy presents the bouquet to Maria. She squeals that the flowers are the most beautiful she has ever seen. The boy retraces his steps and is about to leave the building when he suddenly stops and curses like a sailor.

"Forgot the note." He withdraws a small, folded piece of paper from his shirt pocket.

I block his return to Maria. "I'm happy to hand deliver that note to Sister Kurbatova. You go on your way."

The boy offers no resistance, and as soon as he is gone, I unfold the scrap of paper. On one side are some calculations for a five percent dilution of something. I recognize Ignaty's precise handwriting from the skat tally sheets. The other side contains the words, *For your tankard*.

For your tankard, I mouth. The inference is that Ignaty has seen that ridiculous gift from the blasted Englishman. How much time does Maria spend with Ignaty?

A picture flashes through my thoughts of the two of them sipping wine from that damn tankard.

I hastily refold the note and tromp to the next ward. Maria is sitting beside a bed. Her head nods as she listens to a patient, her one hand holding the flowers while the other holds the patient's hand.

"May I speak with you, Sister Kurbatova?" I ask, my first words to her in weeks.

A flicker of surprise crosses her face. "Certainly."

"Perhaps in the supply room?"

She nods, her mouth set in a firm line.

Much to my relief, the supply room is vacant. I hand her the folded paper. "The boy forgot to give this to you. He asked me to deliver it."

Little frown lines appear on Maria's forehead. As she reads the note, however, the lines smooth away and a smile plays at her lips. Her eyes roll up to look at me. "Did you read this?"

"Of course not!" After a pause, I add, "But I assume it and the flowers are from Ignaty?"

"Yes, they are. Extremely thoughtful of him, don't you think, to have picked them himself?"

I'm tempted to ask, *How do you know he didn't pay that foul-mouthed kid to pick them?* But I exercise self-control.

She refolds the note and tucks it in her pocket. "Was there something else you wanted to speak with me about?" She lifts her chin. "I have work waiting for me. Plus, I should place these flowers in some water."

Probably in that goddamned tankard, I speculate.

Andrey, why are you so angry? You have no reason to feel cross with her, with Ignaty, or with William Howard Russell's tankard.

"Yes, I'd like to discuss something with you."

She shifts her weight, waiting for me to continue. The summer sun has added a golden hue to her pale skin, like a lightly toasted biscuit. It's rather becoming on her. But never mind that.

"It has been noticed that you and Ignaty have become quite friendly."

"Noticed? Noticed by whom? By you?"

"Yes . . . and others. I simply want to advise you to be careful. Ignaty is . . . Ignaty . . ." *Andrey, you idiot, why didn't you plan your words ahead of time?*

"Ignaty is what?" Her toe taps three times.

"I don't want to see you get in over your head."

"With Ignaty?"

"Yes, with Ignaty."

"Why does it bother you that Ignaty and I are friends?"

Why am I bothered that she and Ignaty are friends? I'm not sure why. "You are a fine woman and have much to offer a man. Ignaty is, well—"

"Is what?"

"Ignaty is good-natured enough, but a little lacking . . ." My voice drifts off as I picture my friend's head bobbing up and down like a cork in a brook. "He's a person of a different ilk."

"Ignaty isn't good enough for me? Is that what you're saying?"

"I think you deserve better."

"Better? By better, do you mean someone who is better looking?" Her sarcasm is biting. "Someone who has an inheritance? Someone who isn't a Tatar?"

"It has nothing to do with any of those things."

"What is it then?"

As I grapple for words, that quirky fair-play trait of mine tells me that to denigrate a good man like Ignaty would be morally wrong. Not to mention childish.

Hot color stains Maria's cheeks. "Are you telling me you care about who I see and don't see?"

"No, not exactly." I lick my lips.

"I'm sorry, Andrey, I'm confused. I thought who I keep company with is my concern. Not yours."

"Your well-being is my concern. I feel like a brother to you."

Her eyebrows leap skyward. "A brother?"

"Yes. A brother, looking after your well-being."

A deep freeze enters her voice. "And what do you know about my *well-being*? How do you know what I want or need? Have you ever asked? Have you ever acted as though you care? Did you ever think that I might want someone to occasionally treat me as if I'm special to him?" Her voice cracks. "Did you ever think that perhaps I occasionally need someone to comfort me? To put his arms around me?"

She swirls abruptly and stalks from the room. In her wake, several white petals glide to the floor. In the silence of the small room, I stoop and pick one up. As the tip of my finger strokes the delicate texture, I reflect on our discussion. It hadn't gone well. Not well at all.

CHAPTER 21

June
1855

I'M NOT ALLOWED time to fret about Maria, as the allies continue their full-scale bombardment of the noble city of Sevastopol. Pandemonium reigns in the hospital, and my sense of personal failure escalates as wounded soldiers enter our facility only to be butchered by their own countrymen. I have to concede that we doctors have a better kill rate with our knives and saws than the English and French have with their cannons and rifles.

Today's first patient screams as the shattered bones of his legs strike the operating table. With no chloroform available, his shrieking resumes when I begin the amputation. Needless to say, I'm relieved when the fellow passes out and his agony abates for the moment. My tension subsides, and I quickly amputate one leg and apply plaster of Paris to the other.

"Next."

Assistants lift the patient off the table, and I rinse my surgical knife in a bucket of red water, then hold it between my teeth while the next wounded soldier is positioned.

"Next."

"Next."

Bodies torn apart by lead and iron descend on the hospital faster than we physicians can funnel them through surgery. My heart grieves for the soldiers lying on the floor, listening to the death struggle as their comrades' chests fill with blood from a hemorrhaging vessel.

Well into the night, my knife cuts and my fingers probe. When the knife dulls, I hand it to an orderly to sharpen. Then I lean against the wall, dog tired, with my eyes closed, listening to blood dripping off a nearby surgical table into a pail below. How peculiar that over the frantic screaming, moaning, crying, and cursing, I'm able to hear the relentless, metallic *ping, ping, ping* of blood.

"Next."

"Next."

We physicians work eighteen-hour shifts. Eighteen hours on throbbing, swollen feet. Eighteen hours skidding on floorboards slippery with gore. Eighteen hours laboring in liquid heat without chloroform or morphine and with only short supplies of bandaging materials.

On the fourth day of the bombardment, I nod off to sleep while standing at the table awaiting the next patient. At this point, I'm incapable of giving my utmost. I fear (no, actually, I'm certain) that I'm making mistakes, taking short-cuts, being sloppy with the lives that have been entrusted into my hands.

Shortly after midnight, a handsome young man is placed on my surgical table. I lift one of the boy's eyelids and shrug. "Dead. He'll wait." My voice is hollow.

One of the older surgeons tosses a sharp look in my direction. "Take a rest, Rozhdestvensky. Be back here in four hours."

Outside the building, I continue to smell the necrotic flesh. The stink is entrenched in my sinuses. Never am I free from it.

The still air is sappy with moisture, and I wipe the perspiration from my forehead onto my bloody forearm. Knowing it's a waste of time and breath but unwilling to allow my discomfort to go unacknowledged, I damn the entire Crimean Peninsula aloud. I damn its biting winter, its scorching summer, its swarms of flies, its canopy of buzzers. I damn this god-awful place where the death of a man holds no more significance than the death of a beetle.

After a too-brief nap, I haul my aching body back to the operating theater. A chin-high pile of arms and legs is stacked in each corner, the butcher-surgeons having chalked up a productive night. I glance at the collection of knives and saws placed beside each table. Most of them are bloody. Some of them are rusty. All of them are dull.

By midmorning, I feel like lard about to melt. How the hell am I supposed to see the patient with sweat trailing into my eyes? As I drape a wet handkerchief around the back of my neck, a middle-aged private limps into the surgery room and hoists himself onto the table. I'd wager this brawny guy could win a tug of war with a draft horse.

While I rinse my hands and arms in the bucket of bloody water, the private points to a strip of tendon at the end of which dangles his foot. I shoo off the flies to get a better look at the floppy, lifeless appendage.

"You realize that this foot needs to be removed, don't you?" I ask.

"Figured as much. For the love of God, be quick!"

"It won't be a long operation. That, I can guarantee." I figure thirty seconds to slice through the strand of tissue and another two minutes to apply a dressing.

"That's good news, Officer Doctor. I don't want it said that I'm a slacker."

While I work on the subsequent patient, the litter-bearers tell of burial parties under so much pressure that they're burying presumed-dead soldiers before they actually die. My heat-baked mind begins to wander, imagining my body being thrown into a hole and landing with a thud on top of corpses. Dirt is shoveled in. Blackness engulfs me. I gasp, but there's no air.

I'm yanked back to reality by a sting on the back of my neck. *Fucking flies.* I swat away the offender.

A young soldier is placed on my table. A jagged bone sticks through the skin just above his elbow. Maggots wiggle in and out of the wound.

The private's words are barely audible. "It's not coming off."

"I'm sorry. Your arm has to be removed."

His lip curls. "You're not slicing it off like a chicken neck."

"It's badly tainted. You'll die if we don't take it off."

"I'll die if you *do* take it off."

"I understand your desire to keep your arm, but—"

"If you dare touch my arm, there'll be a hot place in Hell waiting for you!" The private's yell fills the room, which falls into a hush.

I instill an extra dose of sternness in my voice. "I'm trying to save your life."

"There's only one Savior, and you're not Him!"

With the quickness of a striking snake, the youth grabs a knife off the instrument table and raises it alongside his head, its tip directed at my neck. Two orderlies lunge for the boy and pin him flat against the table. The kid howls in agony at the torture to his broken bone. I throw my body crossways on the shins of his flailing legs while a third orderly wrenches the knife from his hand. The orderly secures the boy's legs to the table with a leather strap. The whole time, the boy hurls filthy oaths at us.

Heart still hammering, I swallow hard as I poise a knife above the boy's upper arm. I make the asinine mistake of looking at his horrified, heaving chest. My eyes dart to his face, which is contorted with fear and hatred. Rivulets of perspiration slide down my forehead and burn my eyes. Why isn't there any fucking chloroform?

My knife quivers. The room is airless.

You've amputated uncountable limbs without anesthesia. Do your job, Andrey. A clean, quick swipe.

"Get on with it," an orderly snarls.

I touch the blade to the skin and swiftly draw it across the flesh.

The private's scream is that of a rabbit in the talons of a bird of prey. Blood oozes from the sliced skin. I try to make a clean, quick slice, deep into the muscle, but the knife is too dull. The boy shrieks with pure anguish. Then, thankfully, he faints.

The orderlies release their grip, and two of them leave to assist other surgeons. The third ties a rope around the uppermost part of the arm and tightens it to serve as a tourniquet. I cast aside the knife in favor of the saw, a dull blade that carves its way through the young muscle. Stroke. Stroke. Once the saw scrapes against bone, I use my fingers to strip back the muscle from the humerus. When the area is free of tissue and in full view, I retrieve the saw, place its edge against the glistening bone, and drive the blade forward. Back and forth it grates, the fiendish grinding traveling up my own arm and reverberating round and round in my head.

At last, the orderly gives a final twist and tosses the appendage onto the heap with the others.

I gulp heavy, dead air as I stare at the bone and blood that cling to the saw's blade. My stomach churns. I toss the saw on the instrument table.

I pick up some silk and methodically ligate the bleeding vessels. Then I suture the skin closed. All the while, I'm surrounded by screams, sobs, and the infernal buzzing of flies. I swallow back the sour taste in my mouth.

"Find a dresser to bandage this boy," I bark to the orderly. Without a word to anyone, I bolt from the operating room and into the main ward, where the stench of dysentery rises from bedpans and feces-smeared men.

My stomach pushes burning liquid into my throat. I squat, seize a bedpan, and spew bile. Through a watery haze, I see yellow foam atop the bedpan's contents. My eyelids slam shut.

Behind me, a priest reassures a bedridden patient. "Begin each day on your knees in prayer. Do not fail to fulfill your duties to God and your country, and you will be granted eternal salvation."

I retch.

And retch again.

MY BREAKDOWN IN surgery slashed to shreds the meager self-respect I had acquired as a competent surgeon. I'm immediately reassigned to the postoperative and medical wards. Patients are packed together pell-mell—on beds, cots, mats on the floor—barely allowing passageway for their caregivers.

During my second morning, I tend to an undernourished private so desperate for a discharge, he deliberately shot himself in the foot. The angry red streaks of blood poisoning run up his leg. I estimate that his cot will be empty in three days at most.

As I turn from the patient, I catch sight of Daniil squatting on his haunches beside a boy sitting cross-legged on a floor mat. Daniil's blood-stained physician's coat has a cluster of silk ligatures threaded through one of the buttonholes. His hair is cloudy with dust, and a wet handkerchief drapes across the back of his neck.

Then I recognize Daniil's young patient, which is no small accomplishment given that half the boy's face is the color of claret wine, while the other half is wrapped diagonally in ribbons of bandaging.

"Colya! How badly are you hurt?"

"I'm a little banged up, that's all."

Daniil expands the summary. "His left eardrum is ruptured, and most of his ear is missing. You can see that his face was burned in an explosion, but there are no internal injuries."

"Doctor Berestnev says I might be deaf in that ear for the rest of my life." The boy doesn't sound overly concerned about the possibility.

"That may be a piece of good luck for you, Colya," chortles Daniil. "After you're married, be sure to keep your left side to your wife at all times!"

Colya grins, then informs me, "I was just telling Doctor Berestnev about the other hospital. I was originally taken there, and Maria happened to be there too, getting bandaged up herself. The moment she saw me, she insisted they transfer me here so I could be with my friends."

"Maria's in the hospital?" I ask, crimping my long legs to crouch beside Daniil and Colya.

"She was helping transport patients across the bay. The boat had just left the south shore when a bomb fragment grazed her. A cut right here." His finger tapped above his eyebrow. "She has a bandage like mine."

Maria, hit by a bomb fragment? Will we all be dead by the time this massacre is over? I struggle to find a bit of levity. "I can't wait to tease Maria about you two having matching bandages."

"Oh, you won't be seeing her," Colya says. "She won't be at this hospital anymore. She's been transferred."

"Transferred where?" I ask sharply.

"The death house."

Death house is the nickname of the facility on the north shore that houses those with cholera, gangrene, and other ailments that will soon take their lives.

Its purpose is to segregate hopeless cases from the other patients so their terminal agonies won't distress those who have at least a chance of living. Pirogov often expresses deep admiration for the Sisters on duty there. Tending to those who have been given up for lost is the most difficult and thankless task in the Crimea.

Daniil pats his moustache. "Who transferred her there? I'll see that she's reassigned to our hospital immediately."

"No, sir, you can't."

Daniil and I raise our eyebrows at the youngster.

"She volunteered to go there." We both stare at Colya, who is only too pleased to share his insider's knowledge with his elders. "She wants to work at the death house. To help those men face their final hours."

I remained crouched, in stunned silence, ignoring the pangs in my folded legs. When did Maria decide to undertake this most loathsome of tasks? And why? But then again, why should I know anything about her decisions? The two of us haven't engaged in a civil conversation since before the picnic.

I change the subject. "Tell us, Colya, how bad is the situation on the south side?"

"Real bad, sir, real bad. The streets are so full of round shot that wagons can't pass down them. Every building is damaged or blown up. And the streets are empty. All the women and children have left. And most of the prostitutes, too."

My eyes pop wide, as do Daniil's. Prostitutes? Little Colya is indeed growing up.

TWO DAYS LATER, I stop by the supply room for a couple of biscuits. I find only one remaining. As I crunch through its staleness, my gaze falls upon the samovar that has supplied me with hundreds of glasses of tea. Its brass is turning green, lending it a trounced, fatigued look. My finger taps the metal. Cold and empty. The war has defeated even the samovar.

I head to the mess hall, but its gluey porridge sticks to the roof of my mouth. I choke down half the swill before pushing it aside.

Back outside, I consider heading to my cottage to snatch a nap, but I lack the ambition to possibly run across—and have to chat with—whoever has taken over the cot next to mine. Its previous occupant committed suicide last evening.

Summer's sogginess and the thick smell of decaying life bear down on me, as though trapping me beneath swamp water. A squall of dark clouds builds to the west, and distant drums of thunder roll out their baritone notes. The breeze carries the clean scent of rain.

Perhaps I'll visit Maria.

Where did that harebrained notion come from? But once the idea is planted, it takes root.

Will she speak to me?

Give it a try, Andrey. After all, time heals most wounds.

CHAPTER 22

June
1855

A COUPLE DOZEN patients are taking in fresh air in the yard of the death house. Most lie on cots; only a couple sit in chairs. With the thunderclouds approaching, a handful of Sisters and orderlies are transferring the men onto litters and carrying them to shelter.

I assist with ferrying man after man into the building. In short order, my chest heaves in the oppressive sultry air, and my shoulders and arms are fatigued. How do the Sisters do it?

Once inside, I'm loath to inhale, so saturated is the room with the fetor of monstrous wounds. Most of the men are breathing cadavers, and the air is thick with their delirious moans.

Back outside, while toting my fifth patient, I cross paths with Maria, who is frantically gathering sheets and blankets from the clothesline. Her eyes go wide.

"Hello, Maria."

"Why are you here?" Her voice is neither friendly nor unfriendly.

"I'm helping," I say, and I move beyond earshot.

A cool gale charges through the midday heat. Stinging dust blasts my face, and the Sisters wrestle with their enormous scarves. The tethered horses whinny and stomp their feet. Lightning forks the sky, and the thunderclouds' black underbellies break open. I curse as the chilled rain streams down the back of my neck. No other place on earth can possibly have such savage weather.

Once the last patient is inside, I towel the men dry, wringing out the water from the same towel over and over into a bedpan. A raspy gurgle sputters behind me. I turn and am confronted with a man sealed beneath a mass of mustard-colored pus, some of it oozing, some crusted. Corruption seeps from his eyes and nostrils. The side of his nose is eroded away. His gaping mouth smells of rot. Noxious suppuration clings to his snaggletooth.

I gasp in recognition. This ulcerated, weeping heap of flesh is Puzanov, the veterinary surgeon.

My mind flashes to a page in my pathology textbook. Of course, it all makes sense. I'm looking at an advanced case of glanders, a disease acquired from horses and mules.

A bullet is the only kindness to a wounded horse. Would that we could offer Puzanov the same kindness.

I search for Maria and find her seated beside a bed, listening to a patient. I quietly approach her from the side. The air reeks of cholera feces. The patient's limbs are blue, and the muscles of his feet are curled in tight balls. His bones seem ready to bust through his skin. He begs Maria to find him a rabbi before the disease takes him.

In a flash, my sentiments switch from compassion to icy bitterness. The Russian Army has not a single rabbi. The monarchy exacts its soldiers' staunch loyalty but lacks the decency to allow them to die in the comfort of their own faith. There's only one true Church, and the rest be damned.

The man's body arches in convulsion. Foam oozes from the corners of his mouth as he heaves a terminal gasp. Maria rises and looks about for a litter-bearer.

I step up to the bed. "I'll help."

She turns and her left eyebrow rises quizzically. Above it is a partially healed cut, half the length of my little finger. I suspect it will leave a scar.

We move the dead Jew onto a stretcher and carry him to the back entrance. With my every step, death stares at me from all sides. The body needs to go promptly to the dead wagon, but demonic clouds are hurling down sheets of wind-driven rain. So we place the stretcher on the floor, where it takes up almost the entirety of the entryway's small vestibule. Standing side by side, we peer out the door's six-pane half window. Silence stretches taut between us.

You, Andrey, are a grown man. Act like one. Talk to her.

"Colya told me that you volunteered to work here."

Thunder clashes louder than the firing of a sixty-eight-pounder, but Maria remains as rigid as a statue, gazing at the curtain of rain. "He's recovering well?"

"Yes. Except he might be deaf in one ear."

"A shame." Her voice is devoid of emotion.

Does she plan to converse with me or just lob out detached expressions? I try again. "Are you happy working here?" As soon as the words pass through my lips, I realize their lunacy.

"Is anyone in Sevastopol happy?" Her inflection contains an unaccustomed acrimony.

"I admire your work." I hope my tone bears witness to the truth in my statement.

Her response is as empty as a dry husk. "Yes, many people have told me that."

The storm throws a ball of lightning to the ground. Instantaneous thunder rocks the building. For the most fleeting of moments, I have the urge to throw protective arms around her. Instead, I continue to stare at the deluge. "I think I owe you an apology."

She, likewise, persists in speaking to the window. "You *think* you owe me an apology? What do you *think* you owe me an apology for?"

You're being ridiculous, Andrey. If you're going to talk to the woman, at least look at her.

I turn toward Maria. The opaque light from the window pitches shadows across her face. "I had no right to interfere with your life. I was wrong, and I extend my apologies. Whom you see socially is your business, not mine."

Her voice sags as though timeworn. "And I gather you have no intention of making it your business."

What the hell does that mean?

At long last her face turns toward me. Weariness hangs in her eyes. "Never mind. Apology accepted. Let's drop the subject." Her voice is flat, flatter than neutral.

She resumes staring past the fogged window as acorn-size hail accumulates on the ground. "It won't be long before the days grow shorter." She turns fully toward me. "Do you think we'll still be here this winter?" Finally her voice emotes some nuance, even if it's worry and despair. But such an oddball question to put forth during the melting heat of summer! The answer, however, requires no thought.

I shake my head. "We can't survive another winter."

"What do you make of the activity along the south shore?"

Long lines of ox-drawn wagons on the south shore are depositing massive quantities of timber hauled from southern Russia. Reputedly, General Gorchakov ordered the construction of a gigantic pontoon bridge to span the entire distance, north to south, across the harbor. The tone of Maria's question entreats me to tell her that the hearsay is wrong, that Gorchakov isn't preparing for an evacuation. But although I desperately want to give her that assurance, I cannot.

I'd give anything to relieve her drained, fatigued appearance, the same appearance that all the medical staff share. I consider putting my arm around her shoulders and drawing her to me.

"Ruff. RUFF." The bark comes from the next room.

"Meow," comes a reply.

I wrinkle my forehead at Maria, and her mouth curves into a shallow smile. "It's the Cossacks."

I fold my arms across my chest. "Care to explain?"

"They're quite skilled at animal noises. They can sound like any animal that lives in the Caucasus. Wolves, jackals, dogs, cats, horses. Anything."

As if on cue, a long, high howl radiates.

"What's incredible is that the noises are signals. The Cossacks understand their meaning. Here in the hospital, they don't make the noises often, only when several of them feel well enough to neigh and purr and growl and bark. You should have seen Russell's expression the first time he heard them."

I laugh, a good old-fashioned, from-the-gut guffaw. And it feels good.

Maria breaks into a full-lipped grin, her telltale eyes a mossy hue. Everything will be fine between us.

CHAPTER 23

July
1855

THE WAR PLODS along aimlessly through the hot and foggy summer. Every medical man knows that fog portends cholera, so the hospital braces for an onslaught. I'm content to remain in the wards, away from surgery.

One morning before sunup, amid the quivering shadows of the oil lamps, I watch Father Arkhangelsky's flowing black robes move from one vile mattress to the next. Religion and war go hand-in-hand. Sprinkles of holy water encourage a recruit to be valiant in combat, and then the soldier is sprinkled again when he returns from battle with a bullet hole in his gut.

"All He asks is that you repent for your sins," intones Arkhangelsky. "And He will save you from the eternal damnations of a Hell worse than any you've seen on the battlefield."

I mutter under my breath, "If Hell is worse than this, then God must be an unimaginably vengeful bastard."

"What did you say?"

I whirl about to discover the question came from Daniil. "Just thinking out loud."

"I have a proposition for you." Daniil motions me to the supply room, where the samovar still sits cold and lonely. "Any desire to do a little surgery?"

"I'd prefer not to. But of course, I'll do whatever is required."

"This isn't ripped-flesh-and-shattered-bone surgery. This is the kind of stuff you'll be expected to do in civilian practice. A hernia repair."

"We're fixing hernias in the middle of a war?" I swat away a fly.

"A lieutenant general's son."

"Ah, I see. I assume there's chloroform available for a lieutenant general's son?"

"But of course." Suddenly the corners of Daniil's mouth droop. "By the way, Colya's going back to his division."

"But he's deaf. Can't he get discharged?"

"He's only deaf in one ear. That used to be enough, but no longer. The new Tsar is less fussy about who fights his battles."

THE DAY FOLLOWING the hernia repair, a robust hand clamps down on my shoulder. "Our paths cross again."

I instantly recognize the gravelly voice of Tropinin, the indomitable major general from the Malakov. I snap out a salute.

"And once again, I find myself indebted to you."

"I beg your pardon, sir?"

"That's my son you operated on yesterday. And you did a fine job. The color is already back in his cheeks."

"I'm pleased to hear that you are pleased, sir." *Pleased that you are pleased? Oh, Andrey, such inane blathering.*

The officer hacks a cough. "My only son. The joy and hope of my life."

"I trust you'll visit him during his stay. Good company always quickens the recovery."

"I certainly will. And if ever I can help you in any way, just let me know." He turns aside for another cough. "You made my son whole again, and I won't forget that. Nor will I forget the way you so coolly dropped that shell over the parapet." His hand goes to his throat.

"Is your throat bothering you, sir?"

"It's been on fire for a couple of days. It's nothing, I'm sure."

"Let's go to the light of the window, and I'll have a look."

Huge, cherry-red nodules flank both sides of his pharynx. My fingers inspect the underside of his jaw. His lymph nodes are enlarged.

"Sir, your tonsils need to be removed."

"I have no intention of undergoing an unnecessary operation in the middle of a war," he insists.

"If you don't care for this immediately, you'll be back in the hospital sooner than you think."

The old warrior refuses to budge until I bring forth the idea that he can recuperate in the officers' quarters with his son in the next bed. We make arrangements for surgery the following morning.

"Tropinin?" Daniil questions when I tell him about the impending tonsillectomy. "Tropinin's the lieutenant general who credits you with saving those men at the Malakov?"

"Quite a coincidence, eh? And by the way, he's only a major general."

Daniil shakes his head. "Just promoted to lieutenant general."

My eyebrows lift. "So I guess we can find a day or two's worth of morphine for a lieutenant general?"

"Oh, indubitably."

The surgery goes without a hitch. Just as during the hernia repair, Daniil stands beside me through the entire procedure, after which he praises me for its execution.

On the second day following the tonsillectomy, I approach the patient's bed to bid him good morning.

"Good morning to you, young Doctor Rozhdestvensky." The lieutenant general's thunderous voice has shriveled to weak and raspy.

"How are both Tropinins this morning?"

"The youngster is still asleep, but his father is fit as a fiddle."

I lower myself onto the bed and examine his throat. "You'll no longer need to have poultices applied to your neck. But you should continue to gargle with a solution of chlorate of potassium in water. Is your throat still painful?"

"It certainly is."

"I'll secure more morphine." I stand.

The general latches onto my arm. His large, grave face turns toward the sleeping boy in the next bed, then back at me. "A hernia can wrap around a man's balls and make him sterile, can't it?" He doesn't wait for an answer. "I'm beholden to you for saving my son's manhood. I swear, Rozhdestvensky, on the sacred name of Holy Friday, that I will light a candle for you every Sunday for what you did for my son—as well as for my men. You have my word on that, so help me God."

I look over at the younger Tropinin. He already has the bulky frame of his father. "I can tell you love your son very much."

"I get down on my knees and pray for his safety every day of my life. I could have had him assigned to an office position in St. Petersburg, but he wouldn't hear of it. Insisted on coming here. War holds such fascination for boys who haven't seen it up close." He snorts. "Yet in truth, it is one of the most hideous events to befall mankind."

"Then why do we keep having them?"

"Wars? Because those who don't learn from history are doomed to relive it. Only a soldier can know the true misery of war. I've spent six and twenty years of my life burying my comrades."

"What do you think our chances are, sir?"

"Our chances of winning this war? None."

"None?"

"None whatsoever. Sevastopol will fall like an apple plucked by birds."

My mouth goes dry, leaving my words sticky. "You sound certain of that."

"Leadership is nonexistent. When the posts aren't sound, the entire fence fails."

And it's not at all clear we're going to win.

Cold fear grips me with Tropinin's next words. "What we're witnessing now is only the lightning. The thunder is yet to come."

CHAPTER 24

August
1855

BY AUGUST, VIRTUALLY the whole of the Tsar's massive army is stationed on the Crimean Peninsula. On a typical day, 250 of those men are killed. After months of watching the allies creep closer to the city, General Gorchakov takes the offensive on the third Thursday of August. During the morning shift, the hospital is abuzz. Gorchakov, lacking both a plan and adequate artillery support, initiated a suicidal battle against the French under cover of the dawn fog.

I'm ordered to report immediately to the battle site to perform triage. Along with the order comes the warning, "Keep your ears forward."

Damn it to hell! Why was I picked for this misadventure?

I climb onto the seat of a two-wheeled cart that's part of a medical supply convoy headed southeast toward the Chernaia River. During the summer, the Chernaia is a shallow stream that flows between a succession of hillocks. The battle took place alongside it, in a flat valley less than a thousand yards wide. For the entire six-mile ride, my mind keeps repeating the same words, all of them foul.

Rumors sweep through our convoy of a total rout, with as many as eight thousand or even ten thousand Russians killed, wounded, or missing. My eyes scan the horizon, those hills that had been a delight of spring colors only a couple of months before. Now brown and bare, they radiate seething waves of heat on which glide telltale birds of prey.

By late morning, hundreds of retreating men are kicking up thick, hot road dust as they shuffle past the medical convoy on their return to Sevastopol. Their muskets are slung over drooping shoulders. Some clasp their hands over belly wounds, while others drag mutilated limbs. A few drop from sheer exhaustion. All beg for water.

I'm among the first medical personnel to arrive at the bivouac. The air is already foul with rot. Again we're assailed by the single word: "Water?" The allies have control of the Chernaia River.

If the battle of the Alma last September had given off the first whiff of defeat, the stench has now reached suffocating proportions alongside the Chernaia. I peer across the scorched, treeless landscape, carnage stretching all around me. If Hell exists, it must look like this. Helmets. Peakless forage caps. Knapsacks. Bayonets. Swords. Round shot. Men mangled beyond description. Corpses choking the slender river. Flailing horses that the vultures are already sampling. Human buzzards scavenging for a pair of boots or a trinket to hustle on the black market. Acres upon acres of suffering.

The angel of death . . . the beating of his wings.

I lift my haversack and head into the pockmarked valley. Before I've gone a dozen steps, I'm wiping the sweat from my forehead, cursing that a land so parched can have such soupy air. Only the crunch of my boots on the stony soil rises above the eerie silence. Sevastopol's clatter of shell and sputtering of musketry has become such a natural part of life, it's almost a comforting necessity.

I pick my way around corpses and horse carcasses and craters of congealed blood, all the while waving gnats away from my ears. It's easy to see where shot and shell ploughed through columns of men, mowing down whole sections. Interspersed among the Russian dead are the bodies of the red-trousered French. Friends and foes lie in tangled heaps like carcasses in the butcher's cart, flies swarming in and out of their open mouths.

I catch sight of movement under a jumble of dead bodies, and I work to free the man only to have his eyes roll back in death.

Through the gritty dust, I move from soldier to soldier, sorting those who have a chance of surviving from those who don't. I stem bleeding with compression bandages. I splint limbs. I wrap linen around abdomens threatening to herniate. In most cases, the best I can do is place a hand on the man's shoulder and say that I will send a litter. I merely shake my head at the pitiful cries: "For the love of God, a drop of water." I give wide berth to those who moan, "Shoot me."

I arch my back to relieve its spasms after the constant bending and stooping. Sweat streams like rainwater down my spine.

A single shot sounds in the hills, echoing from one side of the river to the other. I scan the area. Perhaps someone shooting a wounded horse? Or a renegade Russian fighting for access to river water?

Keep your ears forward.

Scores of riderless horses gallop about, many of them wounded and wild with fright. Hundreds more lie dying, each guarded by an army of flies. I close my ears to their gnashing teeth and high snickers of distress. I avert my eyes from their glaring eyeballs and the ants that crawl in and out of their distended nostrils. I'm here to doctor men, not horses.

As morning turns into afternoon, exhaustion scrambles my thoughts. My parched throat demands water. When I turn back toward the bivouac, I spot a man crawling on all fours. At the crunch of my boots on the hard soil, the man suddenly drops motionless to the ground.

"I'm Doctor Rozhdestvensky. Can I help you?"

The man reaches a beseeching hand in my direction. His head is a blackened, bloody mass of flesh: no eyes, no face. He's been dragging himself around the river valley completely blind. I help the man rise and slip an arm under his armpit and around his back. Together we walk back to the bivouac.

We're greeted by the smell of roasted meat. Someone has found a side of wild boar on one of the abandoned Russian wagons. By the time it's shared by all who are capable of eating, each person receives but a few bites.

Only a couple of dozen medical personnel have arrived. I swish my mouth with the allotted two swallows of rationed water, restock my haversack, and head back out.

Faces battered into jelly by rifle butts.

Skulls smashed like eggshells.

Soldiers who tore up clods of dirt with their hands during their final agonies.

A human limb blown off at the elbow, its fingers clutching an amulet, the remainder of the body nowhere to be seen.

A bayonet through a young soldier's stomach, skewering him to the bone-dry ground, a buzzard resting on its handle.

A shot rings out, and my eyes dart about the savage landscape.

Keep your ears forward.

I come upon a chestnut charger with white fetlocks. Its nose and mouth have been shot away. Yet the poor beast is still alive and standing, seemingly conscious of all that surrounds him.

I look into the clear eyes. *A bullet is the only kindness to a wounded horse in the field.*

"I'm sorry, fella. I don't have a bullet."

I find a bayonet beneath a dead soldier and return to the horse, which seems to be waiting for me. I glance at its patient, enduring eyes but have to quickly look away. I straighten my shoulders and tighten my grip on the bayonet. The still air is disturbed only by the vultures' flapping wings.

I thrust the three-edged bayonet into the horse's jugular vein. The animal screams and throws back its head, its once-calm eyes now rimmed with white fear. Blood streams down its neck as it falls to the ground. The desiccated soil turns maroon.

A *clang* resonates when I drop the bayonet on the stones. My vision clouds with a teary film.

I turn and begin walking, my boots grinding the gravel, pulses of nausea assailing my stomach. I stumble over a body that has not a shred of clothes left on it. All the man's hair and features are burnt away. His chest is torn open and covered with black flies.

In the blistering, ghostly quiet, I work my way toward the Traktir Bridge, where the largest number of casualties lie. On the other side of the river, the enemy performs the same chore. My every pace is marked by a corpse.

How much longer can the war carry on? Even the deepest well eventually runs dry.

I need water. I scrutinize the river—the allies' river—which is only a couple hundred feet away. No, too risky. I'd be a sitting duck for snipers.

A short distance to my left are two litter-bearers collecting the wounded. As I approach them to ask whether water has arrived at the bivouac, the defiant crackle of rifle fire splinters the air. The litter-bearers and I drop to the ground like stones. A shell explodes on the bank of the river, sending gravel flying. A few yards to my right, a hail of bullets tosses up puffs of dirt.

Blood roars in my ears. I swipe the grit from my eyes and spot the bridge. Sanctuary lies beneath its stone arches.

I race for the bridge. Behind me *pings* a volley of bullets. I push my legs harder. My heart ricochets against my ribs. When I reach the steep embankment, my chest is about to explode. I drop onto my buttocks and slide down the slope. Gasping for air, I stagger to my feet and sprint the remaining dozen paces around the corner of the arch and to the shaded underside of the bridge.

There, eyeing me at point-blank range, is the barrel of a pistol.

CHAPTER 25

August
1855

MY THROAT SUCKS a dry gasp. With excruciating slowness, I raise my open hands to shoulder level. The gun, held by a straight and steady arm, is pointed directly at my chest. A thick finger threatens to pull the trigger.

All of eternity holds its breath.

But the gun doesn't send a bullet blasting through my heart. My gaze creeps away from the cold steel and up the bulky arm. A sweat-soaked shirt clings to a barrel chest. Above that, in the foreboding shadows, is a man's dust-caked face, stamped with the ferocity of a wild beast.

Mother of God!

William Howard Russell.

Two frightened, angry men stand a half dozen paces apart, frozen in time, eyes bulging with stunned recognition.

The Englishman's free hand eventually signals for me to sit against the arch. My stare remains fixed on him as I slowly—very slowly—step backward, deeper into the shade.

I stumble over a body that gazes upward with sightless eyeballs.

Russell goes rigid. The revolver clicks. I thrust my hands higher beside my head. When the panic subsides, I take two more halting steps, reach behind me for the wall, and lower myself to the ground, muscles weak and trembling.

We endure this arrangement for what seems to be the remainder of the war. Although Russell occasionally glances at the area around the bridge, his pistol never wavers from me. All is quiet outside the bulwark of the bridge.

An idea surfaces. The tension in my abdomen relaxes ever so slightly. Do I dare?

"Russell," I breathe.

The reporter's eyebrows plummet into a scowl.

"Meow."

The frown lines between Russell's eyes deepen into crevices.

Slower than honey on a winter day, I bring my hands together an arm's length in front of my chest. I cup them as if holding something out to Russell.

His keen eyes oscillate between my face and hands.

With infinite slowness, I place one hand over the other and stroke the invisible object in the cupped hand. "Maria."

The newspaperman holds his revolver steady.

I raise my voice an octave. "Russell. Meow. Russell."

No response from the burly man.

"Maria," I repeat, then resume cooing to my hands. "Russell. Monsieur Russell. Meow."

A light appears in William Howard Russell's eyes. "Russell?"

I give a single, abbreviated nod. "Russell."

One side of Russell's mouth curves upward despite his obvious effort to stop it.

I nod again, my face solemn. "Russell. Meow." I tentatively lower my arms to my sides.

Despite this display of camaraderie, the bulky finger remains affixed to the pistol's trigger. The Englishman edges toward the outer corner of the arch and glances about. His eyes dart back to me. "Maria. *Privet.*"

I nod that yes, I'll convey the newspaperman's greeting. With breath-holding slowness, I bring my right hand toward my mouth, as if clutching the handle of a cup. "Tankard."

Russell's smile goes full blast, even showing his teeth. But it's short lived. His eyes flash about the riverbed. Apparently satisfied that all is clear, he gives me a curt tip of his head and bolts from the safety of the arches. The stocky Englishman sprints up the steep embankment, zigzagging between the dead French bodies that cover the rocky soil like wallpaper.

I collapse against the wall, but my eyes remain open, watchful. When all I hear is silence, I creep to the river and indulge in mouthfuls of water.

I can't wait to tell Maria.

CHAPTER 26

August
1855

FOLLOWING A NEAR-SLEEPLESS night spent prone on the ground, I raise my stiff, achy body, drink my allotted two swallows of water, and tie a damp rag over my mouth and nose to block the stench of hundreds of swollen, putrefying corpses. Eyes protrude from sockets. Blackened tongues loll out of mouths. But there are still no efforts to remove the dead.

Heat waves rise from the sweltering hills as I scour the valley for breathing bodies. As the hours creep beneath a pitiless blue sky, my thoughts grow sluggish. My brain feels like it's been boiled into a mush. I fantasize that yesterday's blind, faceless man is today crawling on hands and knees away from the bivouac. I imagine the mournful screams of wounded animals. I see belly wounds spilling out not intestines, but slithering snakes.

I drop to my knees and cradle my head in my hands. The world around me is gauzy and ill-focused. *Andrey, back to the bivouac! Now! Before your mind completely snaps!*

I wrest myself upright. Frantic, I stumble over man and beast, dead and alive. Staggering into camp, I swallow two mouthfuls of foul water and throw myself into the shade beneath a wagon.

LATE THAT MORNING, additional water reaches the bivouac, as do the burial parties and replacement medical personnel. I'm sent back to Sevastopol, where I drop onto my cot, grateful to be alive. To whom or what I'm grateful, I don't know.

I've been anchored in a leaden sleep for five dreamless hours when a hefty hand jiggles my shoulder. I lift impossibly heavy eyelids. The hand is Ignaty's. His other hand holds a jar with—could it be true?—two inches of vodka in the bottom of it.

"It's not much, but it's all yours." Ignaty grins, swirling the liquid in the surrogate bottle.

"Wherever did you get it?"

"Maria gave it to me."

"Maria?" I pull to a sitting position.

"But I had to swear by all that's holy that I would tell her immediately when you returned from the Chernaia."

I pour half of the burning liquid down my throat, then hold the remainder out to Ignaty. He shakes his head. "It's yours. Enjoy."

"Ignaty, you are a true friend. Nothing ever tasted sweeter."

"I wish I could claim the credit, but Maria's the one who sent it to you."

I lift the jar in a toast. "To Maria, the best Sister of Mercy ever to grace the Crimea." In her honor, I finish off the vodka.

"May I be blunt?" asks Ignaty, his tone somber.

"Of course."

"You stink like a camel trader."

I chortle. "Guess I'd better head to the bay. Care to come with me?"

"Sure. You might consider bringing a razor."

I put forth a pithy look at the bristly stubble coloring Ignaty's cheeks and chin midnight black. "Look who's talking."

During a long, indulgent soak in the sea, Ignaty updates me on what has transpired the past few days. First, the allies' artillery bombardment of Sevastopol intensified in a rage of fury. Russian losses from death and injury total nearly sixteen thousand from the bombardment alone, not counting the losses at the Chernaia River. An estimated four hundred guns are focused on Sevastopol at this very moment.

Second, the pontoon bridge across the harbor is nearly complete. It's over a thousand yards long and constructed of eighty-six linked pontoons, each secured to the sea by a pair of anchors. Although no official word has been given as to its purpose, the bridge is wide enough to allow for the passage of troops, carts, and all the items that would be moved during an evacuation.

"Andrey! Andrey!" A squeal comes from the cliff. "You're back! I'm coming down!"

"I'm buck naked, Maria. So is Ignaty." Even as I say the words, I wonder if she's already familiar with Ignaty's naked body.

"I've seen thousands of naked men. Do you look different?" She's in one of her feisty moods.

"Stay there. I'll be up directly."

After she retreats from the edge, Ignaty chuckles. "She's always a hundred laughs."

I let out a deep, haggard sigh as I stare at the now vacant cliff. "Yes, she's a merry sort, all right." I turn toward Ignaty. "You'll join us, won't you? Maybe she's found more vodka."

Ignaty declines the offer. "I have to get back to work. Besides, it's not me she wants to talk to."

"What do you mean? I thought you and she had become . . . romantic."

The tips of Ignaty's thick fingers massage his burly chest. "I wish that were true. She's a grand girl, the grandest I've ever known. God knows, I tried to sweep her off her feet. But she won't have me."

CHAPTER 27

August
1855

ON THE CLIFF overlooking the bay, Maria and I sit on the ground next to each other, our backs against a boulder as we watch puffs of smoke rise from distant artillery.

"Aren't you supposed to be at the death house?" I ask.

"No one keeps regular hours anymore. We work until we drop, snatch a few hours of sleep, then start all over again."

I can't help but notice the dark circles encasing her eyes, her sagging cheeks, and the drooping corners of her mouth. "Are you taking care of yourself?"

"Better than you're taking care of yourself. You're as skinny as a rail, and the sun has turned you as brown as an African."

I'm certain she meant the comment to be light-hearted, but I've always been sensitive about my lanky physique. Plus, I'm feeling tetchy as the effects of the vodka reverse themselves. A fierce craving urges me to return to my cot.

"Tell me everything that happened to you," she insists.

Unexpectedly, I find I lack the energy to relive the events. The last two days have depleted me beyond empty. Besides, how could anyone adequately describe the bloated bodies, the agonized horses, the gagging stench, man's unimaginable cruelty?

Nevertheless, I inhale and begin a leaden narrative. I have the impression she's listening with only half an ear, which aggravates me since I'm making a Herculean effort to accommodate her request. When her hands aren't fidgeting with the cross hanging from her neck, they're smoothing the front of her apron. Every time a shell arcs over the bay, she stops listening altogether, so I have to repeat myself. Only when I get to the part about William Howard Russell do I garner her full attention.

"I encountered a most unexpected person."

"Who?"

"Your chum, the newspaperman."

"Oh, you did not."

"Yes, I did. Spent what seemed like quite a long time with him."

"Stop teasing and tell me the truth."

"Believe what you want, but I'm telling you the truth. And I'm also telling you that I'm damn tired of looking down the barrel of that man's Colt revolver every time our paths cross."

I had assumed she wouldn't immediately credit my story. But now that I'm actually telling her, her disbelief is overtaxing my fatigued nerves. I run my hand through my hair, wishing that vodka jar had been full. "He was as close to me as you are right now."

She turns and squints full face at me. "Are you being truthful?"

"No, I'm a consummate liar."

Her full lips draw together like a purse string. "Why don't you just tell me what happened instead of beating around the bush and cracking dismal jokes."

"I am telling you what happened, but you refuse to believe me."

Not a trace of joviality can be found in either of our voices. I sigh and describe how Russell and I sought safety under the arches of the bridge.

Her eyes retrieve their life. "How incredible! Absolutely incredible!" Her hands fly to her cheeks. "What did he look like? Did he look the same? Did he need a haircut?"

Did he need a haircut? Did he need a fucking *haircut*? My frustration is so supreme, I'm about to burst like a corpse in the Chernaia Valley. Exhaustion pours through me. Every part of my body hurts, from the blisters on my feet to my sour stomach to my throbbing head. I have done everything possible and impossible in the name of my profession and my country. I'm sapped beyond anything recognizable as fatigue. Yet despite of all this, *despite all of this*, I'm forcing myself to listen to her drivel. By God, I deserve the Cross of Saint George for the valiant effort I'm putting forth this afternoon!

Maria jabbers some more. "Did he recognize you right away? Did you tell him we named the cat after him?"

I've been through Hell and back, and all this empty-headed woman can talk about is haircuts and cats. I've reached the limits of my endurance. Even my blood is angry as it pulses through my temples.

"First of all, *we* didn't name the cat. *You* did. And second, no one gives a fuck what the goddamned cat's name is!"

Thunderclouds gather across her face, and her eyes go as cold as slate. The flat of her hand smacks my cheek.

I stare at her and she at me.

Her lower lip quivers. "Oh, Andrey, I'm so sorry. Please forgive me. I'm so sorry."

She reaches her hand toward the hot spot on my cheek, and I flinch reflexively. My recoil upsets her further. "I'm so sorry. I'm so sorry." The three words keep tumbling out relentlessly, despairingly.

There's more going on here than I first recognized. Something is very amiss. "Maria, what's wrong?"

Her head drops into her hands, and I try to sift sense from the jagged words wedged between her convulsive throbs. "While you were gone . . . terrible. The town almost burned down. The ship blew up. The hospitals are a shambles. They say we're out of ammunition. And the bridge . . . the bridge spanning the bay . . . it can only mean one thing. We're going to lose. And they just keep pounding us, and pounding us . . ." She lifts her head and backhands the tears from her wet cheeks. "Do you have a handkerchief?"

I'm relieved to hear a rational question from her. "No, I don't."

As she gives one last sniffle, my anger abates. Maria is my friend, and she has a right to be overwrought. Hell, all of us have a right to be overwrought.

"I'm sorry too," I tell her. "I was so tied up with my own anguish that I completely overlooked yours."

She drops her head back against the boulder and shifts her bloodshot eyes skyward. "It's this ghastly war. Why are we involved in such a vile, bloody, pointless quarrel? Why does it matter who wields the firmest fist? What's the purpose of it all?"

"I don't know. I really don't know why men continue to search for glory in war. All they ever find is brutality."

She bends her knees and brings them as close as her large chest will allow. Her brown habit fans like a blanket around her. "Such senseless disregard for human life!" Her voice is small and distant. "Did you ever think you'd see such horrors?" She places her crossed arms on her knees and drops her forehead onto them.

I look at the white scarf across her slumped back. I had always thought of her as a strapping, rock-steady woman. Yet in the pale light of the dwindling Crimean sun, she appears very fragile. "I never dreamt there could be so much misery."

She lifts her head and turns her tear-stained face toward me. "Our existence doesn't even resemble life. It's complete lunacy. And the nightmare won't end. It. Just. Won't. End."

Maria's emotional collapse tears me asunder. Her strength and singularity of character have always seemed indomitable. But it turns out she's as vulnerable as anyone else.

Her words come back to me. *Did you ever think that perhaps I occasionally need someone to comfort me, to put his arms around me?*

It takes me a long time. I've never done this before, with anyone. With enormous hesitancy, I place my arm across her shoulders.

I keep my voice low. "I've learned that a person must blunt his emotions or risk becoming a madman."

"I've tried so hard. I've tried to toughen my heart, but I just can't." Her gasps send shudders through her. "My mind is spinning out of control."

She leans into me, and I sense some of her anguish and terror coming to rest on me. My other arm goes around her, and she curls into my embrace. Her face burrows against my chest, and her tears soak through my shirt. Her breath warms my skin.

"I want to be brave, but I'm scared. No one believes we can win. What will the end be like?"

In the eerie silence of the Chernaia Valley, I, too, heard the death knell of Sevastopol.

"Bombs pound every day." Her voice quivers with anguish. "Even when everything is quiet, there's pounding, pounding, pounding in my head. Merciful God, make it stop!"

I understand, all too clearly, what she's saying. For months, I've felt trapped in a labyrinth of unspeakable suffering, hurt, anger, agony. "Maria, you're one of the bravest people I know. More times than you'll ever realize, I've turned to you for strength."

"My strength is gone." She inhales a sob.

I grasp her shoulders and hold her at arm's length from me. My eyes lock on hers. "This war can't last much longer. But for as long as it does, we can turn to each other for strength. You might be getting a poor bargain in me. I'm certainly not known for my courage. But I'll do whatever I can for you."

I rise to my feet and offer my hand to help her up. Once standing, she releases my hand and wipes her cheek on her sleeve. "This isn't at all how I wanted to welcome you back." The corners of her mouth twitch like she's trying to smile, but the muscles of her face don't have the fortitude to lift them.

I shift my gaze toward the devastation on the south side of the bay. "All of us are strained far beyond a human being's limits."

CHAPTER 28

August–September

1855

MERCILESS, THE ALLIES make another lunge at the city. Sevastopol shudders as it confronts the rolling of musketry, the crash of steel, and the pounding of ordnance. Some days, more than two thousand of the city's defenders are killed.

Pure bedlam reigns in the hospitals. The wounded are deposited wherever space can be found. Two to a bed. On bloody cots. On pallets of straw. On tarpaulins on the ground. Some sufferers curl up as if in their mother's womb. Some lie on their backs, ramrod straight, already positioned for the coffin. Hospital personnel are like the walking dead. Despite our stalwart efforts, only a fraction of the patients receive any treatment whatsoever. For three weeks, I'm like a horse wearing blinders, focused only on what lies in front of me.

Midafternoon on the final Saturday in August, two rumors reach the north shore. First, the French flag is flying atop the Malakov. Second, General Gorchakov has ordered the evacuation of the entire south side of the city. What this means for our army, no one knows.

That evening, a senior physician informs me that I'll be leaving. As many of the wounded as possible are to be relocated to Simferopol, Belbek, and Bakhchisarai. I'll be stationed in Simferopol.

As the physician scurries away, I lean against a wall and close my eyes. My heart thumps inside a chest that seems incapable of taking in air. Inside me swirls a nightmarish cyclone of grief, foreboding, remorse, anger, despair, panic, and nausea.

When I inform Maria, her face goes pale and flaccid. She pleads for me to be careful, as if I'm a reckless gadabout. "And promise me that I'll see you again. Promise me."

"I promise you. After all, I can't go the rest of my life without locking horns in another querulous tête-à-tête with you."

I smile and reach out to pat her upper arm as I would do with Daniil or Colya. But she intercepts my hand and draws the back of my fingers across her cheek. "Of all the ties that must be broken," she gasps, "this is the one . . ." Her face crumples.

I'm relieved to hear a physician call for her assistance. I plant a light kiss on her cheek. "We'll see each other again."

As she disappears into the crush of wounded and medical staff, I cast a final glance about the converted biscuit factory that served for nearly a year as my workplace, my school, my home, and my prison. In this stone building, my youthful, ennobled romanticism about war gave way to wretched realism.

I walk out the main entrance and across the dirt road to a bluff that overlooks the churning waters of Sevastopol Bay. At dusk, humans, animals, conveyances, and artillery had commenced their exodus from the south shore across the newly completed pontoon bridge. Despite the massive weight atop the floating timbers, the structure holds firm.

White manes of allied bombs arc across the sky. Fountains of water shoot skyward. Waves heave the pontoon bridge. But the stoic retreat of tens of thousands of military personnel and civilians proceeds unabated. Russian discipline prevails.

The massive evacuation is anticipated to continue into the morning hours. As much as it sickens me to admit it, the undertaking is masterful in both its planning and its implementation.

An explosion rattles the ground beneath my feet. Then another. Our troops are blowing up their own batteries and powder magazines. The entire south side of the City of Imperial Power is becoming a sheet of flames, its crimson color reflecting off the seething water. The army is turning Sevastopol into 1812 Moscow all over again, burning the city to the ground rather than allowing it to fall into foreign hands.

The proud, beautiful port of Sevastopol will be nothing more than a decrepit scar. After three-quarters of a century of splendor and 349 days of siege, Catherine's ambitious stronghold in the Black Sea is being relinquished. The invincible Russian spirit has admitted defeat.

Emotional rawness catches in my throat. Damn it! Damn it all! How could the hasty, high-handed decisions of a few men have led to such limitless misery? My entire being screams for relief. I look about for something to punch my frustration into, but there's nothing to pummel. My hands grip the hair on both sides of my head. I pull and pull while my scalp screams in pain.

CHAPTER 29

September–November
1855

IT'S BEYOND BELIEF. Despite the evacuation and unmitigated destruction of Sevastopol, the war still doesn't end. The allies' and the Russian armies continue to duke it out at a weary pace.

To my dismay, but hardly to my surprise, conditions in Simferopol's hospitals are even ghastlier than they had been during my visit with Pirogov last winter. The hearsay is that thirteen thousand patients fill the hospitals, all the public buildings, and many private homes. Patients' clothes are half-rotted rags crawling with vermin. The air is saturated with putrefaction: putrid wounds, putrid breath, putrid bowels. On the floors, cockroaches and rats fastidiously maneuver around pools of blood. Those men fortunate to have a bed or cot share it with several others, lying on their sides or atop one another. Benches serve double duty, with patients both under and atop them. Most patients lie in a jumble on the floor, smeared with one another's blood and diarrhea.

My estimate is that only one out of every four men is in the hospital because of his wounds; the remaining three-quarters are sick. The real war isn't against military strategy and cannons. Disease is doing an outstanding job of decimating the army.

The impossible task of providing medical care during one of Russia's bloodiest and most underprovisioned campaigns has turned Doctor Orshansky, my rum-and-arrowroot mentor, into a casualty of the war. The chief medical officer committed suicide last spring.

I slog through my work duties demoralized, downhearted, and devoid of hope. I try to emotionally dissociate myself from the vast, hopeless suffering that surrounds me—an act of self-preservation. And I'm not alone. Behind closed doors, the medical personnel disguise their gloom with gruesome jokes, such as renaming Simferopol's medical facilities as the Gateway to the Grave. Or the catchy Odds-Are-Against-You Infirmary. The overall favorite is the Tsar's Morgue.

I identify two sources of solace in this hellhole. One is the city's black market trade in a wide variety of assorted foods, plus nonessentials such as tobacco, liquor, and shaving soap. The second is a clean, almost attractive Greek girl in the

Vladimirskaya district who offers her services cheaply. Little Soldier urges me to visit her often, and I comply whenever the occasional spare ruble presents itself.

FOLLOWING SEVASTOPOL'S EVACUATION, Daniil, Ignaty, and Maria were assigned to the tent city pitched two miles inland from the north shore. In September, Ignaty is transferred to a hospital pharmacy in Simferopol. Soon after, Maria also arrives in the city (along with her cat) and at the same hospital where I'm assigned.

What? How could happenstance once again place her and me side by side?

She wastes no time inviting Ignaty and me to an evening of "appreciation for the comfortable amiability of our friendship" that includes wine, cheese, pickled cucumbers, and preserved pears. After the meal, Ignaty produces his knife and whittles. Colya's name is brought up, but none of us know the boy's whereabouts. Or if he's even alive.

Maria's haircuts are soon in high demand, resulting in an income that exceeds that of the physicians.

One morning, Maria is lying in wait for me in the hospital supply room. "Where were you last evening? Ignaty and I looked all over for you. When I tell you who was visiting Simferopol, you will be very sorry you missed us. Very extremely sorry."

My hangover has no patience for Maria's hyperbole.

"You were awfully late getting home."

"And I'm paying penance for it this morning." I pick up a pair of scissors. Its blades are as dull as my mood.

"Think of someone you'd really like to see."

"Enough preamble. Just come out with it." I begin cutting segments of silk thread for later use.

She smirks at me with a half smile and a raised eyebrow. "Someone you haven't seen in two months."

"Daniil? Daniil's here?"

"*Was* here. He left at dawn."

Crap! "Where's he stationed? What did he say? Is he healthy?" I assail her with questions the same way she often bombards me.

"He's in charge of medical care in Bakhchisarai."

I internally kick myself. I had frittered away the hours with a bottle of vodka and the Greek girl when I could have spent time with Daniil and Ignaty. And, of course, Maria.

A medical student by the name of Nikitenko is also gathering supplies. Although I don't know Nikitenko well, I've bumped into him a time or two during my evening excursions about town.

"Sampling the wares at Vladimirskaya again, Rozhdestvensky?" Nikitenko winks at me before sauntering from the room.

Maria chills me with her wintry gray eyes. "Vladimirskaya?"

I refocus my attention on cutting strands of silk.

"A prostitute!" She breathes, more than says, the word.

This is ludicrous. Yes, I'm angry with myself for missing Daniil. However, I am accountable only to Andrey Yevgrafovich Rozhdestvensky, not to Maria Kurbatova.

"That's correct. Had I known Daniil was in town—"

"Why would you waste your rubles on a prostitute!" Her eyes are as menacing as an enemy's saber.

"Most of the men you work with have visited Vladimirskaya at one time or another." My throat is tight with anger. "There's nothing illegal about it. I don't have to justify to you how I spend my time or my rubles."

An ominous quiet surrounds us while her broad chest heaves. "Andrey Yevgrafovich, you're a fool." She twirls and storms from the room.

CHAPTER 30

November–January
1855-1856

THE WINTER OF 1855–56 requires so much stamina just to survive, Maria doesn't waste precious energy on anger directed at me. Fog, rain, and snow relentlessly pummel Simferopol. The Tsar's army dwindles daily by hundreds of men, primarily due to cold-weather maladies such as typhus and pneumonia. Meanwhile, the Russians and the allies persist in taking potshots at each other.

I greet each morning with apathy. Today, however, I awake with achy muscles and eyes that look like piss holes in the snow. During the afternoon, when I use the latrine, my breath catches at the sight of my abdomen.

Red spots.

The rash hasn't reached my arms or legs yet, but it will. It always does with typhus.

I'M ASSIGNED A cot in a school that has been appropriated as a hospital for officers. The improvised facility is crowded, clamorous, and corrupt smelling, but it's not as ghastly as the other options. At least everyone has a bed or cot to himself.

My fever and delirium bring forth the dead. Puzanov, the veterinarian. Orshansky, the medical director. A parade of former patients. The horse whose jugular I sliced.

I am dying, intones each ghoulish visitor, including the horse. *I cannot bear the thought of descending to my grave with my sins unforgiven.* Standing over all of us is my father, presiding like the Angel Gabriel himself, flapping his incense canister back and forth, and intoning, *Only through the agonized body of Christ will you find eternal salvation.*

In this nightmare I, too, am dead, but my father rebuffs me by withholding both blessing and incense.

The curses I hurl at this soulless man of God jolt me awake, my skin cold with sweat.

EVENTUALLY MY FEVER eases. When I regain my point of reference, I've been hospitalized for two weeks, and I'm as weak as a newborn.

One evening, after darkness settles on the wretched parody of human beings that we bedridden have become, someone steps through the doorway at the far end of the room. A flickering light slowly makes its way down the corridor of cots, its attendant inspecting each face.

As the lamp approaches, I see its bearer is Maria. What is she doing? She's not assigned here. My eyes follow her as she makes her solitary rounds, her beefy hand clutching her little lamp, her other hand tucking blankets around the men.

When she draws near, I feign sleep. She stands over me for what feels like an eternity. Finally, the light filtering through my eyelids falls away, and her footsteps recede. Such a tender-hearted woman! Why do I take her for granted?

Andrey, you're such a louse.

ALTHOUGH I'M A tad stronger each day, my complexion remains morbidly pale, my appetite is nonexistent, and my body is cadaverous. Some cases of typhus are slow to fully recover, and I'm not the least bit surprised that I'm one of them.

As I enter my third week in the hospital, Maria and her cat visit me. "It's well-nigh time you got well. Other people need this cot." Despite her sprightly tone, folds of tired skin tug at her eyes.

She dumps Russell beside me. The gray tabby settles alongside my leg, and his green eyes stare into mine while the tip of his tail weaves from side to side. I stroke him for Maria's sake.

I clear my throat in preparation for my much-practiced words. "Maria, I've been told that you visited me several times while I was insensible. Please realize that I speak not only for myself but for all your patients, both in Sevastopol and here. We are deeply grateful for your overflowing mercy and generosity. And I am personally grateful for your friendship. Many of us would not be alive today had you not bestowed us with your tender care."

Her eyebrows rise in surprise, the resulting wrinkles burying the little scar on her forehead. "Well, thank you. I must say, there were several times you seemed at the verge of death. But you never quite made it." She gives her happy laugh.

"I apologize for anything offensive I might have said. I'm told my curse words would make the devil himself blush."

"True enough, you did carry on like a lunatic. It concerned the others, but I saw it as not a bit out of the ordinary for you."

Her laugh sounds nothing short of marvelous, and without forethought, I reach up and grasp her big, work-roughened hand. Her broad grin slowly wanes bittersweet. "You look a little worse for wear. How about if I give you a shave?"

The next day, I'm discharged from the hospital. Bouts of chills linger, however, periodically racking my body. I sleep ten or eleven hours a day and do little in the remainder of my time except listen to the monotonous drum of sleet on the roof. My mind lacks focus. My appetite is nil. My shirt hangs from the knobs of my shoulders. I fear I have the glassy-eyed, faraway gaze of men who never completely return to their senses.

I'm physically and mentally off-kilter. It occurs to me that although a soldier's physical wounds are bandaged, no one tends to his deeper, intangible wounds.

How long will it take me to heal?

BY THE SECOND week of January, the army decides I'm more trouble than I'm worth. They're sending me home.

Home? Where is that? I know of no place to go other than Moscow. Will the university fulfill its promise and grant me a diploma? If so, what employer will hire me? My skills are limited to military medicine. I can't even deliver a baby.

I am a trained surgeon, however, even capable of performing tonsillectomies and hernia repairs, thanks to Daniil. I feel a profound need to thank him for being both mentor and friend. After scrounging up a relatively clean scrap of paper, I poise a pen above it and mull over various ways of expressing my appreciation. But I can't bring forth the right words. Later. I'll write the note later.

I summon all my energy and shamble to the hospital to share the news with Maria. Standing before me, her arms full of soiled hospital linen, she is uncharacteristically speechless. Her green eyes grow as big and round as lily pads. I expect them to start leaking.

But when at long last she speaks, her voice is monotone. "Such wonderful news. When will you leave?"

"In a couple of days. I need to obtain a letter stating I faithfully executed my duties here. I can't chance the university denying my diploma."

"A good idea. A very good idea." Her eyes dart erratically about the room, like a moth seeking light. "I'd better get this load to the laundry."

I watch her trudge away. It seems she could have been happier for me.

BY THE FOLLOWING day, Maria has done one of her famous changeabouts. "Where will you stay when you reach Moscow?" When I acknowledge I don't know, she asks bluntly, "Have you any rubles?"

I nod.

"Precious few, I assume." Her air of confidence implies she knows me at least as well as I know myself. "When you get to Moscow, you must go straightaway to my sister's apartment." She hands me a scrap of paper with an address on it. "You must go there. I'll post a letter to Vasilisa so she'll be expecting you. Will you do this for me? And for yourself?"

"It's a kind offer," I say. "I'll certainly give it some thought."

Her vexation is audible in the tap of her foot against the floorboards. "For once, please heed what I say. You have no money, no job, no family, no place to go. You're welcome at our apartment until you get on your feet. Russell and I will come directly there as soon as the war is over."

Not receiving an answer, she installs a decidedly obdurate look on her face, snatches the paper from me, and holds it a hand's length from my eyes. "The address is easy to find. Just a short distance west of the university."

I gently take the paper from her and put it in my pocket. "I promise you by all that's holy, I will give your suggestion sincere consideration."

"By all that's holy." She snorts her sarcasm. "Hearing those words from you certainly puts my mind at ease." She reaches into her cavernous pocket, pulls out two ten-ruble notes, and thrusts them into my hand.

I stare at the dog-eared notes before lifting my eyes to meet hers. "I can't take these."

"You must." Her words, rather than bubbling forth in their usual disjointed fashion, are slow and deliberate. "The convoy will take you only as far as the isthmus to the mainland. You're still weak. You'll need to hire transportation."

I hold forth the rubles to her. "When I volunteered to come to the Crimea, the government promised me transportation back to Moscow."

She plants her hands on her hips, conjuring the look of an unyielding oak. "The government? You're confusing words with reality."

I drop my hand back to my side. "Thank you. You are generous to a fault."

Big, silent tears slide down the round face that has made me laugh time and time again.

PART

Two

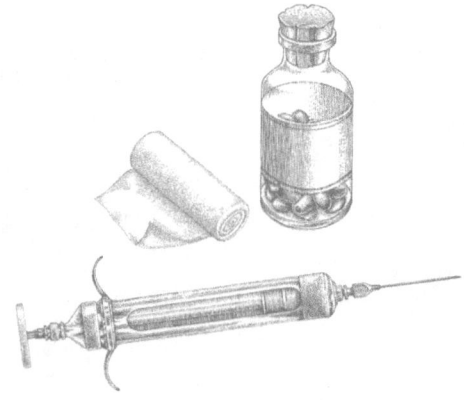

CHAPTER 31

October
1864

I FOLD BACK the verminous blanket and tap across the cadaverous chest with the tips of two fingers. The gray-faced man, who's probably a decade younger than his shriveled features suggest, drools spittle over his blood-caked lips and down his chin.

Which will kill him first, consumption or vodka? I muse over the answer with as much interest as I have in which cockroach will win the race across the grime-slick table.

During lapses in the consumptive's deep, juicy coughs, I explain the inevitable outcome to his haggard, very pregnant wife. Her onion-peel skin is so taut across her pallid, pockmarked face, she gives the impression of waiting in line to be the next corpse.

At her request, I examine one of the wheezing urchins who mill about. From my medical bag, I retrieve a bottle of camphor oil.

"I need to mix a few drops of this into some lard. Have you any?"

The mother's expression tells me that had any lard found its way into the two-room apartment, it would have been consumed posthaste. Instead, I add a trace of camphor to a tin of liniment. "Rub this onto their chests two times every day. It will help them breathe."

As the mother's chapped fingers reach for the canister, her life-weary eyes acknowledge that a single tin won't last long with her brood.

I chuck my instruments into my medical bag and glance at the grandmother slouched on a wooden stool beside the soot-caked window. Following the sale of her few remaining teeth to the local dentist for use as implants in a wealthy mouth, the desiccated old woman sank into a malnourished stupefaction. Death is tapping her shoulder too.

During moments of lucidity, she mumbles appeals to the dusty, sad-eyed icon angled next to her. The toddler on her lap, recognizing an opportunity when one presents itself, pushes his tiny fist past Grandma's pus-lacquered gums and explores the gaping black hole behind them.

I bid my farewell and curl my tall frame under the web of clotheslines, side-stepping two pale, snarl-haired girls wearing only their torn chemises as they play among unwashed dishes on the uneven floorboards. The heel of my boot slips on a greasy patch. When I grab the table to steady myself, my hand lands squarely on something gelatinous and unidentifiable.

I wipe my palm on the doorjamb as I enter the hall, a scowling passageway heavy with the mingled odor of fried onions and urine. I hurry past doorways shuttered only by dirty hanging sacks. On the other side of the first self-styled door is the laughing cackle of a card game. Behind the second, angry words. On the other side of the third, the moans of sex.

My eyes watering from the stink, I hasten my long legs down the narrow steps two at a time. A few steps ahead, a rat races me to the bottom of the staircase. I bolt from the building and sidestep an emaciated cur dog, oblivious to its surroundings. Its tail is curled between its rear legs, and it lacks the strength to hold up its head. The stringy mucus of distemper streams from its nostrils.

I question yet again why the devil I returned to Moscow. Where a couple hundred thousand people live stacked atop one another. Where autumn's long-awaited crispness is heavy with the stench of open sewers and kitchen slop on sidewalks. Where the water running down the narrow streets looks exactly like dysentery. Where the sky is overcast with gloomy factory coal-smoke.

But the question, Andrey, isn't merely why you returned to Moscow, but also what possessed you to agree to work for Doctor Seriyev?

Into my head pops another person's words. *Only a person who holds the welfare of suffering people above all other considerations has the right to call himself a true physician.*

Well, if Pirogov is correct that care of the patient requires caring for the patient, then I'm certain beyond any doubt that I'm not a true physician. I can't empathize with the ignorant and impoverished any more than I can dredge up compassion for the highbrows and social climbers whom I doctor in the grand residences along the Boulevard and the Garden Rings.

Of course, my questions are rhetorical, and I've asked them at least twice a day for eight years. When the army bid me adieu, my vision extended no further than leaving the Crimean Peninsula. My image of the future didn't include a destination. At a loss for where else to go, I landed back in Moscow. I found shelter at the fleabag Indigent Hostel, where I received room and board in exchange for providing minor medical services to my fellow residents, as well as the poor souls at the neighboring workhouse, where boys were taught cobbling and carpentry while girls learned sewing and housework.

Realizing I'd need a diploma in order to secure respectable employment, I promptly went to the university to start the bureaucratic wheels in motion.

Two months later, medical degree in hand, I scoured the city for work. My quest began at the Sheremetev Hospital, where I completely lost my bearings in its huge semicircle. Then I knocked on the doors of the Pavlov and the Golitsyn and eventually worked my way down to the Preobrazhenskaia Hospital for the Insane and the Mariinsky Hospital for the Indigent. No luck.

I was on the verge of taking a position as a hospital orderly when Doctor Seriyev offered employment. Seriyev has an aptitude for amassing rubles in a lucrative practice on the north side of the city. That deftness is accompanied by strong altruistic sentiment. He believes those who have been granted much in life are under obligation to give to those less fortunate. So two days a week, he offers free medical care to Moscow's poor.

Flush with rubles in my pocket, my first priority was to rent a room in a boardinghouse.

My second order of business was to purchase a thick pillow stuffed with cotton wadding.

My third action was to regret my choice of employer. Benevolent Doctor Seriyev is a noble-hearted person in his own mind. But as it turns out, rarely does he wade into the unwashed riffraff of Moscow's dark tenements. Instead he allows his young protégés to experience the mosaic of pain, hunger, disease, and early death that is passed from one destitute generation to the next.

And regarding my four-days-a-week house calls to Moscow's affluent, they're as repetitive as the drip of a melting icicle. Yesterday, for instance, I dressed the burnt finger of a girl in a brown boarding school frock who had snuck a cigarette. Next, I quietly referred a young debutante to a fellow colleague for termination of a pregnancy. Then I treated a countess for dropsy while she complained nonstop about her good-for-naught husband, her overpowering rosewater spurring on my headache all the while.

I remind myself that fair play is one of my few strong suits. Although I was bamboozled by Doctor Seriyev, I harbor no ill will toward him. He took me under his wing and patiently taught me the trade in civilian terms, which is a far cry from military medicine.

Every so often I accompany Doctor Seriyev to a professional meeting of local physicians, but I find the discussions supercilious and wearisome. I yawned through the dissertation on the latest treatment for gout. And as for the lecture on the current theory of how syphilis is spread . . . well, surely it will be as short lived as the previous theory. And the theory before that.

I feel worlds apart from my supposed colleagues. One young fellow had the audacity to recount that he had two patients who were both war veterans with leg amputations at the knee. He suggested the veterans save money by sharing a pair of boots. Although he received a hearty chuckle from his colleagues, nothing would have given me more pleasure than ripping out the schmuck's balls.

Ha, ha, ha, I wanted to shout, *you overprivileged, wet-behind-the-ears coxcomb! You didn't see the horrors I saw! A soldier cradling his intestines in his arms. Glistening gray matter oozing from a fissured skull. Breathing men buried beneath corpses.*

By the time the war ended in the spring of 1856, Russia had suffered incalculable losses and accrued no gains. For all the Empire benefitted from the heroics of its soldiers, the hundreds of thousands of gallant men and boys who sacrificed their lives might just as well have stayed home and blown out their own brains.

Today, as I walk past a drove of rats sending cooing pigeons to the windowsills, I mull over the question of why I keep bumping into the hardness of life. Why is my road always pitted with potholes?

I acknowledge it probably has more to do with my own internal perspective rather than with life's heavy-handedness. Perhaps I need to relax and enjoy the sweet pleasures that life offers.

And just what are those pleasures, Andrey?

Well, one partial pleasure is winter, and it's only a few short steps away. Winter's snow softens the hard world and hides the ugliness of poverty.

If only winter weren't so brutal on the homeless, poorly clad street urchins.

I don't particularly like the ruffian children who scratch and claw an alley-cat existence, but I understand their belligerence and deviousness. I recognize how, in Moscow's brain-numbing slums, children fall victim to plagues of mind and body that lead to crime, drunkenness, brutality, and debilitating illness. Children do what they must in order to survive. How well I know.

As I leave the filthy tenements behind me for the day, food regains its appeal. I approach a cheesemonger for a bit of brie. I wait to one side while a square-shouldered young man completes his purchase and drops some kopeks into the vendor's outstretched hand. The customer's index finger is missing.

My eyes dart to the fellow's profile. In lieu of an earlobe is an empty space.

"Col . . . Colya?"

CHAPTER 32

October

1864

THE YOUNG MAN turns toward me. "Doctor Rozhdestvensky?" True-hearted joy spreads across a face that bears only the palest remnants of its previous epidemic of freckles. We grab each other's shoulders and plant three alternating kisses. What's scratching across my cheeks? The stubble of a beard?

Colya takes a step back, his hands still grasping my shoulders. "I'm in a state of shock!" He pulls me to him, and we embrace in earnest and follow up with three more kisses. "Clearly this is a divine blessing!"

I have an almost irresistible urge to stick my pinky finger in my ear and clean out the debris. Yes, it is Colya, but he's stolen another person's voice, a bass voice that resonates with a deep knowledge of life.

Unable to countenance further displays of affection, I put some distance between us. "Oh, my. Look what a man you've become!"

His round cheeks have drawn in, his jaw has broadened, and his lips have lost their childish heart shape. The weedy youth has been replaced by a strapping young man of, what, twenty-four, twenty-five? He carries himself well despite his ill-fitting clothes and down-in-the-heels boots.

We move away from the cheesemonger, Colya with his purchase and I having forgotten completely about my brie. Colya shifts to my left side. "Can't hear much on this side." He playfully tugs at the remnant of his ear.

"Whatever are you doing in Moscow?"

"Getting an education." His eyes are still bright with the buoyancy of youth. "In fact, I'm in my final year of medical studies."

After several attempts, my breath grabs hold of my larynx. "Medicine?"

"Yes, sir. You and Doctor Berestnev inspired me. I want to help others, like you did."

I cock my head. *Inspired?* Colya is being chivalrous with his words. *Help others? Butcher others* would be more accurate. "The truth is, I sopped up no more than a mere drop in an ocean of blood."

"But you imbued me with a sense of purpose. More than you'll ever realize."

Well, fancy that! Colya, a physician.

The young man's eyes drop to his shoes. "I was never the same after that hor-rendous, bloody year. I learned there's nothing noble about war." He slowly raises his gaze, but his eyes remain hooded. "There's no glory in butchery. I want to make right all the harm I did to others."

The Crimea had laid waste to Colya's youth. That realization makes me feel far older than my own thirty-two years.

"Trust me, Colya, my perceptions about war were every bit as flawed as yours were."

"But despite the horrific conditions and the insurmountable obstacles, you and Doctor Berestnev accomplished wonders."

"Speaking of Doctor Berestnev, do you know what's become of him?"

The brightness drains from Colya's face, and his teeth pull on his lower lip. "I'm sorry to have to tell you this."

I know, even before the next words are spoken. An empty tingling starts in my scalp and works its way down to my gut. There it surges into heaving, ripping waves, as thick as the ones in Sevastopol Bay. I watch Colya's lips move, but I can't hear past the roaring in my ears. It doesn't matter. I know what the message is.

"How?" I choke out.

"Not long after you left, he was reassigned to Simferopol. An amputee went berserk and leapt from his bed with a knife. He slashed at the medical personnel. Doctor Berestnev's wounds weren't bad, but he got blood poisoning."

The angel of death . . . the beating of his wings.

My teeth are clenched so tight, they hurt. Oh, Daniil. Daniil. How much I owed you! And how little I gave you. I never told you what you meant to me. Never told you.

Colya's voice filters through my anguish. "Ignaty was with him when he died. He and I wanted to let you know, but we didn't know where you were."

"That damn war," I growl. "Those who started it should burn in Hell for eternity."

"But there's good news, too." Colya's resilient optimism comes shining through. "Guess who lives in Moscow? And not all that far from where we are right now." His cheeks would have puffed in a smile, had they any baby fat left in them.

"Ignaty?"

"Maria!"

My shoulders fall. "Maria?" Of course, I suspected she lived in Moscow, but I'd never tried to find her. Although I did think about it a couple of times.

"My path crossed hers, just like ours did today. She's the same old Maria."

"When did you see her?"

"About a year ago. She invited me for supper at her apartment. We had a swell evening talking about old times."

"She gave me her address before I left Simferopol. I guess I should pay her a visit." I do a quick mental search. Do I still have that slip of paper? Surely I do.

"Oh, she'd like that a lot. She's mentioned you several times. Wouldn't it be such fun for the three of us to get together?" His face turns sad. "Right now, however, I regret that I must go. I have obligations I must tend to directly."

"You've given me a lot to think about this evening, Colya. A lot indeed."

We exchange addresses and, promising to keep in touch, shake hands Western-style. In an unprecedented bout of sentimentality, I clasp my other hand over his.

"God take care of you until we meet again." With those words, the young man with nine fingers, one-and-a-half ears, and an endlessly sunny disposition disappears into Moscow's dreary masses.

MY FINGERS RAKE through my hair. Tonight will be worse than usual. Daniil. Dead.

I fling open the sole window of my cramped, third-floor boarding room, hoping to snare a stray breeze. Instead, all I get is an intimate view of the brick on the neighboring building.

I throw my first slug of vodka to the back of my throat. My fingers tighten around the empty glass as recollections assail me. Countless games of skat. Tea and conversation in the supply room. The sandy-haired man patting his mustache.

Daniil was the mentor I had hoped for. But the physician was more than a teacher. He bolstered my confidence. He gave his pupil the recognition when the credit belonged to the instructor. But beyond all that, Daniil gave me friendship, a rare commodity in my life.

A deep wave of regret shrouds me as I picture an unblemished scrap of paper lying on a table in Simferopol. Despite my good intentions, my words of gratitude will forever be left unsaid.

I lash out at myself with fury and pour another glass. I hoist the second drink to eye level and stare at the liquid I despise. Then I gulp it down greedily.

I pour a third glass but let it sit on my table.

Call my derangement whatever you please.

Psychic disorder.

Morose melancholia.

Mania.

Mental excitement.

Soft in the head.

Or my personal favorite, *a cracked bell in the tower.*

And what cracked it? The lunacy of the war. Which means I'm inherently a weakling. I've not heard of a single other veteran who brought his goblins and demons home with him.

I went to the Crimea to become tough. I wanted to be tested and hardened into a man. Instead, I left the peninsula as a cowering featherweight.

Why did Colya come out of the war not only unscathed but more insightful because of it, whereas I came out a nutcase? Possibly because I was a nutcase when I went in.

I glare at my bed, knowing what awaits me once I close my eyes. Hideous nightmares of bodies blown to pieces. The whites of horses' eyes. The yellow fog of battle. The uninterrupted *plop* of blood dripping from the surgery table into a bucket. All that I saw and heard and experienced—I tried my best to put the anguish behind me, but it won't release me.

Why can't the past stay in the past!

It's a rare night when I'm allowed five hours of sleep. I usually awake to a racing heart and clammy skin. Some mornings, the smell of charred flesh won't leave my nostrils—or the stench of gangrene. Shouldn't willpower quell the nighttime suffering? Mine certainly does not.

The word *suffering* connotes discomfort of the body. But what about suffering of the mind? Why can't doctors patch that up?

Here I am in overstuffed Moscow, as utterly alone as if stranded on a raft in the middle of the Black Sea. Daniil, Ignaty, Colya, Maria—they were the best comrades a man could have. But the war is over, and such friendships, even those that can be resurrected, won't have, can't have, the same intimacy.

A gray chill comes over me. Is it loneliness? I'm used to being alone. But not to being lonely.

I down the third drink and gird myself to resist a fourth. With a leaden ache in my stomach, I collapse on the mattress. Fully clothed except for my boots, I pull the sour blanket to my chin, put my hands behind my head, and yet again examine my life.

My unexcelled mediocrity has gotten me nowhere. Not only do I live in reclusive desolation, but I also sleepwalk through a career that benefits neither myself nor mankind. Why do I drift, day after day, without plan, purpose, or conviction? Part of the reason is my abhorrence of change.

I trace this loathing to a month I spent as a child at my uncle's parish in the country. The boy in me loved the outdoors, and my gaze followed the village peasant boys as they drove the cows into the pasture every morning and home again in the evening. A portion of me wanted to accompany the boys. The larger portion craved the safe familiarity of my uncle's home.

My uncle, under the mistaken assumption that my eyes were on the cattle, explained that cows live for tomorrow only to do the same things they did today. Back and forth. Pen to pasture. Pasture to pen. My uncle used the cows' unvarying routine as metaphoric guidance. "Humans are different from cattle. People enjoy trying new things."

The allegory convinced me that I should have been born a plodding bovine.

I finally yield to sleep. My vodka-laden brain takes its nightly voyage to the Crimea.

Blood squirts from a man's leg. Despite my valiant efforts, the blood keeps spraying the walls and ceiling. Colya and Daniil, their index fingers pointed at me, howl with ruthless laughter. A lone cow breaks out of Sevastopol's slaughter pens and runs through the gory surgery theater on its way back to its pasture.

The visions recede when I awake to the sound of the bells in Moscow's churches ringing out the midnight hour. In an effort to clear my mind of disheartening thoughts and gruesome dreams, I think about tomorrow, my day off work. I always feel uplifted when I fill my days constructively.

Let's see . . . something constructive.

Andrey, why don't you visit Maria?

Yes, indeed, that's constructive! The two of us will have a nice chat, and her intoxicating laughter will make me feel better.

Besides, I still owe her twenty rubles. It's a debt long past due.

CHAPTER 33

October
1864

LIGHT IS WIDENING the sky as I rummage through the contents of the top drawer of my dresser. True, it's been eight, almost nine years, but I can't imagine that I would have thrown it out. The slip of paper with Maria's address. It must be here.

Handkerchiefs. Epsom salts. Writing tablet. Penknife. Socks. Socks that need mending. I move to the second drawer. And the third. Did it somehow flutter under the dresser? No. Under the bed? No. Did I stick it in one of my books? I fan each book on my shelf.

When the dust settles and I finish sneezing, I look about the room. There's nowhere else it could be.

Damnation! On the back of my closed eyelids, I try to picture Maria's writing and the street name. All I can remember is that it's west of the university. But that leaves blocks and blocks of possibilities.

Somehow I'll find her. I'm amazed she hasn't already popped into my Moscow life. In the Crimea, regardless of where I was, she never failed to turn up. The memory buoys my spirits.

And anyway, how many women barbers can there be?

I ASK A milkman. "Tell me, please, do you know a woman named Maria Ivanovna Kurbatova? She lives in this neighborhood and barbers for a living. In her late twenties. About this tall." I gesture with my hands. "And this wide."

I receive a shake of the head.

I ask the same question of a vendor with a portable grinder in his pushcart. "Scissors to sharpen! Razors to sharpen!"

I ask the hawker bellowing, "Charcoal by the bushel! Charcoal by the frying pan!"

I ask the hotel concierge.

I ask a boy pushing a wheelbarrow of apples.

I query cabbies waiting for customers.

I rouse napping doormen.

I question men in business suits, the types who would seek out her barber services.

After three hours of searching, I succumb to a vendor calling, "Hot flaky *pirozhki*! Baked marvelously!" While handing over my coins, I pose my question.

Seated on a bench, devouring my beef-and-onion-stuffed bun, I shake my head in bewilderment. Maria makes friends so easily with anyone and everyone, she could befriend a corpse! How could an entire neighborhood not know such a gregarious person?

I scrutinize the beehive of people around me. I know her face too well. It isn't possible for our paths to cross and me not recognize her, even after eight years. I suppose she could have moved elsewhere in the city. Or gotten married.

I resume walking through the ragged smoke of street fires and past toddlers playing in gutters that overflow with kitchen slop. I ask children, shopkeepers, the corner constable. As the sun begins to settle behind the tallest buildings, I turn toward home.

Ahead of me, a couple dozen people are gathered along the train tracks.

"Doctor! We need a doctor!"

I elbow my way through the frantic throng. At the center are two teenage boys who have been hit by a train. One is somehow alive but newly missing a foot. Amazingly, he repeatedly asks for it, desperate for the ten rubles hidden in his boot.

"Give me your scarf," I demand of an onlooker. Crouching, I encircle the knitted muffler around the leg just below the fellow's calf. The tourniquet stanches the bleeding. I tear a single thread of yarn from the scarf with my teeth and place it around a pumping artery just above where the ankle was lopped off. Quicker than the eye can follow my fingers, I knot and tighten it like a ligature. I repeat the procedure with two more vessels. The action feels natural to my hands. I did it a thousand times in a converted biscuit factory.

"Get him directly to a doctor," I shout to no one in particular.

I swivel toward the other teenager. His chest is crushed and his face is unrecognizable. A priest kneels beside him. "Give Him your sins, and He'll give you His righteousness."

My teeth clamp together to trap my scream. *The boy is dead, you pompous ass! Dead!*

A woman grabs my elbow. "You're a kind man. They were just whippersnappers, calling each other's bluff."

I don't pause. I don't want gratitude or an explanation. I just want to be free of the entrenched memories.

Sweat streams from my pores as I weave my way out of the bystanders. My hand tunnels through my hair. I need a drink.

There she is.

Crossing the street, less than a store's width away. Her lumbering hips. Her thick, sloping shoulders. Wisps of chestnut hair poking from beneath her bonnet.

Maria!

CHAPTER 34

October

1864

I SPRINT TOWARD her, hands cupped around my mouth. "Maria!"

She continues to cross the street, seemingly oblivious to my shouts. Reaching the far side of the street, I'm only a step behind her.

"Maria!" I shout, practically in her ear. Still she doesn't glance my way.

I catch a glimpse of her profile before it's obscured by her bonnet as she turns onto the sidewalk. It's absolutely Maria. I stretch out my stride and step in front of her.

She abruptly halts.

I scour her face. It's her! But her face registers fear.

Incredulous, I stand with my neck drooped forward as she steps around me and hustles down the sidewalk.

I sprint to her side once more and gasp, "It's me, Andrey! Don't you recognize me?"

"Away with you," she snarls. Her eyes are round with fright. Patches of red color her cheeks.

I curve in front of her and grab each of her shoulders, forcing her to stop. "Why are you angry? Don't you want to see me?"

She twists to free herself. "Let go, or I'll scream!"

My forehead creases with befuddlement. It is Maria, isn't it? But no, she's missing something. The little scar above her left eyebrow.

"You're Maria's sister," I realize aloud.

The woman stops struggling and takes cautious measure of me.

"I'm Andrey. I knew Maria in the Crimea."

"Andriusha!" The woman's hands fly to her suddenly gleeful cheeks. "Maria will be beside herself!"

Andriusha? Maria never referred to me by my diminutive name. "I'm sorry," I say. "I must admit I've forgotten your name."

"Vasilisa. Come with me. Our apartment isn't far."

VASILISA AND I hatch a plan.

I wait outside the door.

"Mashenka," Vasilisa calls as she steps into the second-floor apartment. "Go to the hallway and see what the cat dragged in."

Maria appears from behind a screen partition, wiping her hands on her apron. I'm hit with a bit of a jolt, not having considered she'd be without the omnipresent white scarf. She's kept her hair short, an increasingly popular style among self-professed free-thinking women. Overall, the years have barely touched her appearance.

Halfway across the room, she catches sight of me. She turns as white and still as a marble statue. Then her great bosom heaves, and not with her voice but with her breath she utters, "Andrey," and her magnificent smile unfurls.

Her arms reach out as she dashes toward me. Reluctant to be swallowed in a fleshy embrace, I take hold of her hands and kiss her cheeks. She takes a half step back, and I look into her green eyes. I had forgotten that uncanny trait of her irises mirroring her mood.

"How? When?" Her chest continues to billow and collapse, as if it can't gather enough air to form words. "Where did Vasiusha find you?"

I cinch my chin to my collarbone and raise my arms out from my sides in the role of a bumbling blockhead. "Just wandering the streets and alleys of Moscow."

"He thought I was you," Vasilisa calls from across the room.

Maria's smile droops a wee bit. "You mistook her for me?"

Ever true to my character, I can't decipher the cause of her disappointment—if that's even what I'm witnessing. After all, hadn't Maria herself told me that the two sisters were practically identical?

"From behind! I saw her from behind." Once again, the blockhead raises his hopeless, helpless arms.

She dabs her moist eyes with her apron. "Come in!" She grasps my arm and leads me toward the only cushioned armchair, her gaze never leaving my face.

I glance about the room. Two unadorned rocking chairs. An equally modest mahogany wardrobe. A whitewashed corner cupboard. A couple of cheap wall prints. A small wooden table with four ladder-back chairs. The sole spot of color snares my eye: a bouquet of canary yellow tulips in the center of the table. Odd. It's the wrong time of year for tulips.

The room contains two interior doorways. One is a large archway, partially concealed by a folding partition and presumably leading to the kitchen. Through the other doorway, I glimpse the foot of a bed.

As we near the armchair, my mood dips. The cushioned seat is already occupied. "Look who's here!" Maria trills.

The gray tabby, curled full circle with its chin on its tail, opens one annoyed eye, then closes it.

"How magnificent!" Maria squeals. "You two fellows get to see each other again!"

She frees my arm and stands in front of the chair. A moment passes, and it occurs to me that she expects something. I bend and apply two strokes to the top of the cat's head, which is the size of a cabbage.

"Goodness, he's grown huge."

"Yes, my darling Russell is a big boy." She scoops the behemoth into her arms and deposits him on the rug.

Russell. I'd forgotten the cat had been bestowed with that preposterous name. Actually, I'd forgotten about the cat altogether. Apparently, I've forgotten a lot of things.

"Let's allow Uncle Andriusha to sit here, shall we?"

Uncle Andriusha? Suppressing a grimace, I settle into the chair. Maria places a small footstool at the tip of my tired feet.

"I'll finish cooking supper," Vasilisa says. "I hope you like potato soup, Andriusha." A replica of her sister, she doesn't bother to wait for an answer. She disappears behind the screen and calls, "Come here, Russellushka. I'll give you some cream."

Russellushka? I'm plagued with second thoughts about resurrecting this friendship.

Maria pulls one of the rocking chairs closer to me. "Oh, my." Her voice is resonant with disbelief as she sits down. "I'd given up hope."

"About what?"

"That we'd ever see you again."

"We?"

"Russell and I."

Russell and I? A shiver of annoyance bristles across both shoulder blades. I never cared for the cat. Its name chills me to the bone. And I resent the animal being treated as though it were a human. But annoyance is promptly replaced by a wrench of compunction in my gut. I had indeed taken an unforgivably long time getting in touch with her.

I segue with a dose of humor. "How could you have any doubt that I'd come looking for you, the person to whom I owe my life?"

"Owe your life?"

"Why, yes. If it weren't for you, that fiery-eyed Englishman would have made certain I left my brains under the Chernaia Bridge."

Her belly laugh erupts, and it makes me feel good. She leaps from the rocker. "I know you just sat down, but I must show you something. Two things, actually."

I wrest my long frame from the comfort of the armchair and follow her to the corner cupboard. She retrieves a small wooden figurine from one of the shelves. "It's Saint Nicholas."

I reach for the whittled Benefactor of Travelers and Soldiers and cradle him in my hand. "Ignaty?" The name is strangled by a tightness in my throat.

She nods. "He made it for me before we left Simferopol."

I'm assaulted by scattered images of that fine friendship. The walrus moustache over the flashing white teeth. Sinews of the thick neck. Perpetual head bobbing. Thick fingers clutching the playing cards. The banter between my two friends.

You be sure, when you leave here tonight, you're not too drunk to take your droppings with you.

I'll leave this place cleaner than I found it. You can bet your liver on that.

I look up from Saint Nicholas. "Do you hear from him?"

"We exchange letters. He's in Kazan."

"I chanced to stumble upon Colya recently. He told me about Ignaty. And also about Daniil."

Maria lowers her lids, and I stare down at Ignaty's handiwork.

Master your feelings, Andrey. If you don't, that tickle inside your nose is sure to spill from your eye.

As I replace the figurine on the shelf, I take note of the item next to it. That damned tankard from that damned Englishman. I assume that's the second thing she wants to show me. But I'm wrong.

From one of the drawers in the lower half of the cupboard, she removes a velvet box the size of her hand. She opens its hinged top as if it were a necklace case, then hands it to me. Lying atop the satin lining is a bronze metal attached to a gold ribbon.

"It's from Tsar Alexander," she says by way of explanation.

I look up quizzically.

"All the Sisters received one. Although some received it posthumously."

"A fitting tribute to your unparalleled efforts." Sincerity rings true in my voice. I hand it back to her. "The much-maligned Sisters deserve recognition for their selfless and unsurpassed contribution."

"They certainly do," calls Vasilisa as she places a soup kettle in the center of the table. "My sister was valiant in her efforts."

"Andrey's the one who was valiant," Maria says, tucking the velvet box into the drawer. With a twist of her eyebrows, she motions me toward the table. "Remember, Vasiusha, I told you how he dropped that horrible bomb over the parapet?"

I pull out the chair for Vasilisa as I explain, "That story is a half-truth that, thanks to the embellishment of *certain* romanticists, now has a narrative all its own."

Maria takes her own seat. "I'm afraid it's a permanent narrative. Everyone believes it."

"No one even remembers it, except you."

As Vasilisa ladles soup into my bowl, I realize this is the first time since I've been in Moscow that my fictionalized heroics have entered my mind. The event occurred in a moment of time no larger than a flyspeck, which is exactly how much import I attribute to it.

Over the meal, I tell them about my career in Moscow. Maria says she's still a traveling barber.

"Except now I'm a 'certified hair stylist.'" She points to the floor beside the main door. There lies the bedraggled haversack I saw over her shoulder countless times. "In addition to my barber supplies, I also carry *eau de cologne* and hair cream. I still cater to businessmen who haven't the time or inclination to leave their offices. I earn more trimming a moustache than trimming an entire head of hair." She gives her spectacular full-bodied laugh. "Thank goodness I specialize in men's hair. Nowadays, women want their own hair augmented with real hair from dead bodies. And the snobs will accept only a French hairdresser."

Vasilisa explains that she gave up the trade when she procured employment with steady weekly pay. She's a sales clerk at a posh flower shop specializing in hothouse plants.

"That explains the tulips," I say.

Maria nods. "We almost always have flowers. Free ones."

"Although they're usually past their last hurrah by the time my employer is willing to give them to me." Vasilisa's throaty laugh is identical to Maria's. I wonder if her green eyes turn gray, like her sister's.

After supper, I return to the relaxed comfort of the armchair. Immediately the cat appears and sits erect at the toe of my boot. Its unblinking eyes shoot daggers at me while its tail jerks back and forth along the floor boards like a horizontal pendulum.

"That cat's not going to jump on my lap, is it?"

"That cat has a name," Maria retorts, her foot peevishly tapping. "And so what if he jumps in your lap?"

My shoulders settle into the cushioned chair. Everything feels so familiar. So normal.

CHAPTER 35

October–March
1864-1865

WE SETTLE INTO a routine. The two sisters fuss over me like hens over their chicks. And I let them. I share their evening meal once a week. Flowers always grace the table, and a wholesome meal is followed by a board game. Sometimes I bring dry sausage, or fresh fruit when I can find it. And lemon drops—Vasilisa's favorite. Neither sister touches the vodka I keep in their corner cupboard, but Colya joins us every so often, and he tips the bottle freely.

Despite Maria's resolve to foster a friendship between me and the cat, no fondness develops. However, on blustery winter days when the wind strong-arms its way past the window sash, the behemoth will leap onto my warm lap, knead my crotch a few times, flop down, and curl nose-to-tail. In a half hour or so, after my legs have gone fully asleep, the cat gives a cavernous yawn, stretches, and glowers at me. Then it digs its claws into my thighs and bolts in disgust, graciously leaving behind a blanket of gray fur on my trousers.

Colya's favorite topic is politics, and his discourse usually starts at the local level. One evening he shares the timeworn rumor about Moscow's Mayor Korolev and his cronies settling in for a night of drinking. Korolev would set his silk top hat brim upward on the table, and their thirst wouldn't be quelled until the hat was full of champagne corks.

After giving the local scuttlebutt a thorough hashing, Colya ascends the political hierarchy and sings the praises of Alexander II. The young man is wedded to the belief that the Tsar's Great Reforms will right all of Russia's wrongs.

"I'd have had no hope of attending medical school if it weren't for his fee reduction at the universities. And his plans include admitting women to the universities."

"And you believe he'll take his overhaul of the judicial system to even further lengths?" I ask across Vasilisa's centerpiece of chrysanthemums and daisies.

"Definitely. Trial by jury, the right to legal counsel, equality of everyone before the court—and this is just the beginning of his vision."

I counter with, "From what I read, his new court system is corrupt and inefficient."

"Thank you for substantiating my point." He jabs a forefinger across the table toward me. "It's only because of Alexander's freedom of the press that you're presented with both sides of the story." His grin is wide. "Give him time. He'll remedy the problems."

I leave Colya to his illusions. My faith in Tsar Alexander left me somewhere in the Crimea.

At Christmastime, I give the sisters a subscription to the *Moscow Sheet*, a scandal-mongering local newspaper. Maria and Vasilisa lap up the tittle-tattle about prominent merchants, and they spend many an evening reading aloud its potboiler serial novels. In return, the two women surprise me with the very best of their barber skills. As hot towels steam my face and my legs stretch out on the footstool in a room of complete silence, my mind and my spirit are in complete repose, a novel and priceless experience for me.

The sisters and I often spend Sunday afternoons watching troika races or chortling at the antics of youngsters on the skating ponds. Then we head to their apartment for a lusty stew. Thanks to the two women, I explore more of Moscow than I have since my return from the Crimea. On some Sunday outings, I have a sister on each arm. Other Sundays, my only companion is Maria. On those occasions, I have the impression Vasilisa purposefully occupies her time with other activities. Perhaps she grows weary of seeing so much of me. Who can blame her?

THE SUNDAY PRIOR to Easter, Maria and I stroll arm in arm through the Pussy Willow Bazaar on the square near Saint Basil's Cathedral. On this day, peddlers specialize in toys and small animals, such as goldfish and tortoises, and the children turn out in droves.

In a temporary stall, the baker D. I. Filippov sells samples of his renowned Easter cakes. I buy a Warsaw baba and a Konigsberg marzipan, which Maria and I share as we lean our backs against a building, soaking up the luscious warmth of the sun-drenched bricks.

After two nights in a row of blissful sleep uninterrupted by jaunts to the Crimea, I feel unusually chipper. I offer a supportive smile to a toddler who is puffing her cheeks with all her might to spin her new pinwheel a feeble quarter-turn. Someone nearby throws a handful of grain into the air, and instantly a cloud of pigeons swoops down from the neighboring eaves. The swarm of birds startles another small child, and the breeze snatches his fluttering butterfly toy. The butterfly hopscotches through the stalls, and I give chase, my boots crunching on discarded sunflower hulls.

After I return the toy to the child, Maria observes, "I do believe you enjoy children more than you do adults."

"I'm not sure about that. Maybe I'm just more tolerant of children because they have fewer self-induced ailments. I know you get tired of hearing me gripe about my work, but—"

"I've told you before, I never tire of hearing about you or your work."

A fleeting pucker visits my forehead. At times, I know I provoke Maria to distraction, and vice versa. But there are moments when she seems to like me better than I like myself.

"This week, I treated a pillar of Moscow society who has sniffed so much tobacco dust, she now has a tumor in her nostril that completely obstructs her breathing. Not to mention a nauseatingly foul green discharge, not unlike the gangrene we saw in the Crimea. The very next day, I was in the lowest depths of the city when I encountered another damaged nose. But by the time I was summoned to treat this woman, she had been dead so long, her nose had been nibbled away by rats."

Maria scrunches her own nose in repulsion.

"What I'm saying, in a roundabout way, is that you're probably correct. I am more patient with children. Their misery isn't of their own making. It's brought upon them by the ignorance of their parents and the slow torture of poverty."

She nods. "Ignorance and poverty create vicious, ceaseless circles."

"Well put! The riffraff I tend to, and the riffraff they'll someday create in their hovels of wretchedness, have no prospect of education, no shelter from brutality, no opportunity for as much as a breath of fresh air." I run my tongue over my teeth to make certain I get every tasty morsel of the shamefully expensive Konigsberg marzipan. "Listen to what happened yesterday. One of my elite patients caught her massive skirt on fire at the hearth during an examination. I had to roll her up in a rug to save her life. There were several other ladies present. Of course, not one of them moved to help her."

"Because they were scared out of their wits, surely?"

"No. Because they couldn't bend over due to their enormous crinolines."

Ah, that unfettered laugh of Maria's, every bit as full and immense as the women's skirts!

The mirth leaves her voice sooner than I would have liked. "May I ask you this?" she begins. "Would you be happier working with children? Perhaps at the Foundling Home?"

"Foundling Home?"

The huge, cold, government-managed (or -mismanaged) orphanage that's known to be rampant with dysentery, congenital syphilis, and neglect? The place that serves as a depository for unwanted infants racing to see who can die first?

How did her brain concoct this ludicrous notion?

I strive for a smile that is two parts tolerance and one part annoyance. "I really don't consider that an option."

"What options *have* you considered? What do you picture yourself doing?"

I contemplate the question. "Nothing," I finally reply.

"How can you picture yourself doing nothing? Wouldn't it be easier to picture yourself doing something?"

Honest to God, she'd put a saint out of patience. "Rather than listening to you tell *me* what *I* should do, I'm telling *you* what *you* should do. You should invite Colya and me over for Easter dinner."

Her foot taps the cobblestones. "And *you* should buy Warsaw babas from Filippov's bakery to bring with you on Easter!" Her eyes glow emerald green.

CHAPTER 36

April
1865

"YOU FIND MY work acceptable?" The budding young woman stands an arm's distance from me as I sit on the edge of my bed, pulling on my boots.

I glance at the pile of clean laundry Klara has just placed beside me. "Why, yes, completely."

"Papa and I are struggling, you know." In the pockets of her apron, her hands move forward and back, billowing out the apron as well as the skirt under it. "The landlord threatens to put us out if we don't catch up on the rent." Her tongue slowly moistens her upper lip, then her lower one.

She fails miserably at portraying the coquette. Her intent, nevertheless, is unmistakable, and my heart bleeds that she's forced into such an egregious situation.

Klara's papa is one of the exceedingly few of my charitable patients whom I actually enjoy. The squatty little man is a chimneysweep and always endearingly cheerful. When I first met him, he was perpetually smudged with silt, and unfortunately, his terrible cough told me that his lungs were equally smutty. Over the past year, the sweep's hack has grown into a cavernous rumble. When blood began to rise with every cough, he could no longer work.

Whenever I visited him, Klara was by her father's bedside, and I learned that she takes in laundry. The father and daughter are the sum total of their family, and both worked hard to make ends barely meet. As a favor to the likable fellow and his devoted daughter, I hired Klara to pick up my laundry once a week. She's a wisp of a thing, polite and earnest in her work.

Today the lithe adolescent stands before me, skirt swaying, with her unexpected proposition.

"Klara, I'm very, very sorry about your situation."

"Some days, Papa can't even sit up in bed."

"Tell him I'll visit him soon. But all three of us know there's nothing I can do that will make him well."

She stares at the toes of her scuffed shoes poking from beneath her apron.

"I understand your offer, and I regret you're forced to make it. Paying you for laundry is a luxury for me. I haven't the rubles for . . . for anything else."

Her gaze rises. Her desperate eyes cling to mine while her teeth rake across her lower lip. "But we can still . . ." Again the skirt billows forward and back. "We can make a business arrangement."

"What are you suggesting?"

"Don't you work for a rich doctor? Maybe he knows of a hospital that would hire me. Maybe he has a friend who owns a fancy hotel. Hotels must have a lot of laundry. I could continue to take in laundry on the side. And I could repay your kindness in . . ." She again lowers her eyes. "In services." She lifts one foot and, beneath her skirt, rubs the back of her other calf.

I scratch my cheek and wait for my sense of fair play to forbid me from taking advantage of the girl's pitiable offer. But Little Soldier has eavesdropped on her suggestion and is staunchly voicing his opinion. My honorable words get wedged inside of me.

"I'll see what I can do, but I can't make any promises."

The skirt billows frenetically. "Oh, thank you, Doctor Rozhdestvensky! I'll make you happy. Just like I do with your laundry."

As I watch her leave, I think about how very young she is. Has she reached sixteen? Yet I'd bet a week's pay she isn't lacking experience.

CHAPTER 37

May

1865

WHEN THE SPRING bulbs flaunt their showy heads, Trubnaya Square fills on Sundays with the noises of a pet market. A popular custom is to purchase caged birds in order to set them free. During our visit to the Square, Maria hands over her kopeks, and I don't have the heart to tell her she's been duped. The birds, tamed by their owner, simply fly back to their cages, where they remain until the next unsuspecting animal lover appears.

As we continue our stroll through the square, we encounter a crowd gathered around a Bulgarian and his chained monkey.

"Show these nice folks how a peasant comes home drunk," the man tells the monkey.

As the little fellow dutifully does its tricks and turns its somersaults, it trembles from cold and fear. I'm moved to pity. The creature, so human in its appearance, was snatched away from its family of monkeys in the hot sun of Africa and hauled, alone and scared, to the cold of Russia.

Following its antics, the monkey leaps to its master's shoulder and holds out a wrinkled, supplicating palm to the crowd.

It's a hand I know intimately. It's my own as a child. My father, unable to make ends meet on his church salary, used every conceivable ruse to extract a few kopeks from parishioners who were as needy as he. Those ruses included having at least one of his children at his side.

A dry summer? my father wheedled. *Prayers for rain cost two rubles.* My young, upturned palm waits.

You can't find three rubles so your son can be christened? My hand extended still farther.

Later that afternoon at Maria's apartment, I drop into what I now deem *my* armchair while Maria describes to Vasilisa, complete with exuberant flapping of her hands, the monkey's antics.

Suddenly she stops smiling and turns to me. "Why are you scowling?" Her eyes have flecks of pale jade and streaks of slate gray. Her mood is shifting. Does anyone else in the entire world have eyes so talented?

"I didn't intend to scowl," I reply.

"You did scowl, intended or not. What did I say this time that you find so inappropriate?"

"You know the old saying. What you see depends on what you look for."

Apparently my attempt at levity has failed, because her hand goes to her hip. "You were definitely scowling."

I explain, "I'm confused as to why you'd pay to have captive birds released, and yet you think a monkey is adorable when it's every bit as captive."

"You're referring to its little chain?"

"The poor animal is miserable, trapped in an alien environment. Not so very different from all of us, captive in Sevastopol."

"Oh, how I wish you'd stop seeing demons in the dark." Sitting in her rocker, she throws one leg over the other and sets her foot to jouncing. "Why do you turn living into such a challenge?"

I think about last night's dream. In every direction around me, men lay gutted like sheep, a half million of them—the government's final war tally. *The angel of death . . . the beating of his wings.*

"We all have ghosts," I tell her. "What I wouldn't give to shake loose of the past!"

Apparently my words give her pause, because she falls silent. When she eventually speaks, her demeanor has reversed itself, swinging into an attitude of tender caring.

"What I'm saying is this. The war is over." Her eyes are soft as moss and her voice as warm as a caress. "If you can't stop living in its horrors, you'll never accept the fullness that life offers."

CHAPTER 38

May
1865

EVERY FEW MONTHS, Lenora Pavlovna, the gray-haired wife of a government administrator, summons me to drain out the fluid that her failing heart allows to accumulate in her abdomen. During the hour I'm in her bedroom, the girth around her middle shrinks from the size of a seven-month pregnancy to a normal, if flabby, belly. It's a rewarding task, and Lenora Pavlovna is so accustomed to the procedure and so complacent in her countenance that she spends the hour nestled among her pillows, quietly reading or sometimes dozing. She never exhausts my patience with idle chitchat.

While I swab iodine over her mountainous midriff, my mind travels down the list of this morning's scheduled appointments. My second patient will be a widow with painful varicose veins, a querulous old crone who complains about everything from the ridiculousness of Tsar Alexander's reforms to the abysmal way her daughter-in-law is raising her grandchildren. After that battle-axe, I'll visit a banker too busy to leave his office, who constantly seeks treatment for his dyspepsia, then fails to follow my advice.

Tomorrow I'll visit the homes of the less fortunate. Those who drew the short straw in life. Those without the means or wherewithal or desire to pull themselves up from the dregs of humanity.

So what's your point, Andrey?

My point is, I'm tired of walking past tenements, their open doors belching the stench of spoiled meat, stale piss, and vomit.

I'm tired of encountering teenage girls, desperate to escape hunger and beatings, their carnivorous eyes imploring me to avail myself of their offerings.

I'm tired of tired women who seem to never *not* be pregnant.

And here's what else. I'm tired of risking my safety on streets seething with vagrants, thieves, pickpockets, drunks, and gangs, all of them fueled by slum living.

I pick up a silver cannula and a fine-pointed steel trocar. My experienced patient turns her head to one side—the only discomfort she displays during the entire procedure.

"Just a prick," I tell her out of habit rather than as a point of information.

With the speed brought on by experience, I plunge in the silver cylinder. With efficiency of motion, I pull the trocar from the center of the cylinder and cap the cannula with a rubber tube to channel the stream of fluid into a bucket on the floor. While her stomach shrinks at an unhurried pace, the imperturbable lady settles in with Turgenev's *A Nest of the Gentry*. I'm left with little to do except listen to the throaty murmurings of pigeons outside the window and submerse myself in my own musings.

Lately, my thoughts have been barraged by the comments Maria made earlier this spring about the Imperial Foundling Home. *Would you be happier working with children? Perhaps at the Foundling Home?* I keep picturing the monstrous stone edifice on the bank of the Moskva River. I've even gone out of my way a couple of times to walk past it. Amazingly, I've never seen a child playing within the confines of its high wrought-iron fence. The rumor around the medical community is that it's a dungeon of disease and death.

How many babies and children live there? Supposedly thousands. The figure is plausible, considering the five-story structure covers an entire city block. People living cramped together, not unlike Sevastopol. Which means the emphasis should be on Pirogov's preventive medicine—hygiene, nutrition, smallpox inoculations, and so forth.

Lenora Pavlovna's bucket is full. I transfer the rubber hose to an empty one, without a pause in my thoughts.

Maria told me to picture myself doing *something*, not *nothing*. So I picture myself working in the Foundling Home and what that would entail.

Regular hours, which I lack as a general practitioner.

An easy walk from my apartment to work.

A government pension, some far-off day.

Perhaps even a positive influence on some child's life—a goal that, with my current clientele, I can never accomplish.

I clear my throat to interrupt my patient's reading. "Madame Pavlovna, am I correct that your husband holds a high position at the Foundling Home?"

She nods.

"I wonder if he'd consent to talk with me about possible employment."

"I'm absolutely certain he would. But whence comes this idea? Why are you seeking new employment?"

"As you know, Doctor Seriyev is getting older. It's only a matter of time before he shuts down his practice." The statement is somewhere within the bounds of reality. "I need to consider my options."

"Certainly you should speak to my husband." Lenora Pavlovna wags a playful forefinger at me. "But regardless of your employment, you must never abandon me. No one has as soft a touch as you, Doctor Rozhdestvensky."

"That's most kind of you to say," I reply, certain that her gratitude is reflected in Doctor Seriyev's bill.

"Give me your word that you'll continue my treatments."

"But of course!" I smile and nod. "Might I bend your ear a moment longer? My friend, a young woman, has suddenly lost her entire family and finds herself completely alone. She takes in laundry and is a hard, hard worker. And extremely honest and conscientious. She does a stellar job with my laundry. But as you and I realize, she can't support herself doing laundry, and she is about to be evicted from her single-room apartment. It would be invaluable for her to obtain steady wages as a laundress in a respected institution such as the Foundling Home. Might you also mention her plight to your husband? I'd regard it as a tremendous favor."

"And you can vouch for her good character?"

"Definitely. She's a topnotch young lady."

"Then I shall most assuredly mention it."

The flow of fluid ceases, and I withdraw the cannula. I say my customary, "There. All done. Feeling better?"

The woman fills her lungs with the first deep breath she's had in weeks. "Ah, much better. By the way, I do hate to trouble you, but while you are here, my constipation would benefit from your infusion of chamomile."

I reach into my leather bag and bring forth my enema equipment.

CHAPTER 39

June
1865

"WELL DONE, GREAT fellow!" I congratulate Colya.

"My little freckle-faced Colya. A physician!" Maria effuses.

Tonight's celebration at a restaurant is in honor of a life-altering event—Colya's graduation from medical school and his acceptance into advanced public health studies.

The three of us are jubilant, and our evening bursts with optimism. Maria's eyes beam greener, and her smile is wider than I've ever seen. This is thanks in part to Colya's accomplishment and in part to her mug of English ale, for which I paid a ridiculous amount, not to mention it's reminiscent of that puffed-up newspaperman.

The meal is enjoyable and long, and by the time we're ready to say our good-byes, darkness has fallen over the city. I offer to escort Maria to her apartment. A cool, light mist settles on our faces and coats as we walk.

Without prelude, I say, "I should have kept a journal in the Crimea. It would be good to have a written chronicle rather than scattered memories shuffling themselves around over time."

"Whatever provoked you to say such a thing at this particular moment?"

"The mist. It feels like the spray from the Black Sea, doesn't it?"

"You know what it feels like to me? It feels like you should have brought an umbrella."

"I didn't think of it. Why didn't you think of it?"

She ignores my playful tit for tat. "Do you know why you didn't think of it? You don't have time to plan for the future because you're too busy brooding about the past."

It's one of those moments when I want to put a clamp on her mouth. And tighten it. Instead, I say, "Our little sojourn at Sevastopol was a sobering experience. Wouldn't you agree?"

Again, my question is brushed aside. "I think you think too much. Sometimes I think you're still at war, this time with yourself."

In some regards, she's correct. A few days ago, a policeman chanced to blow his whistle close to my ear. I instantly flattened myself against a building, my heart frantic, my eyes searching the sky for falling shells. Quite embarrassing, to say the least.

"I had a pleasant day at work and a pleasant dinner," I reply. "Until this conversation."

"Then let's leave journals and the Black Sea and sobering experiences out of the conversation."

I yank my gloves tighter. Everyone likes Maria. Happy-go-lucky Maria. Maria of the charitable heart. So why does she go out of her way to provoke me and me alone?

My new job at the Foundling Home is providing me a gateway to both professional development and expanded sociability with my coworkers. And I'm actually having fun with the youngsters. Thank goodness for Lenora Pavlovna and her husband! I owe them a debt of gratitude. Since I gained employment at the orphanage, my optimism has blossomed. Or at least sprouted buds.

But Maria continues to harp on my failings. I'm making slow but substantial progress at tamping down my morose reactions to the war. Can't she see that I'm trying?

"Perhaps the fathomless, inconceivable suffering we saw didn't affect you the way it affected me," I retort. "But then again, you weren't at the Chernaia."

Her head spins toward me, her eyes smoldering in the light of the street lamp, her lips a rigid line. "And you didn't work in the death house." She might as well have added, *Checkmate.*

"I admit, my spirit is haunted by memories," I say, careful to keep my tone level. "And I fully realize a person can't live in the past and the present at the same time. I'm doing my damnedest to change my thinking. Would you please give me credit for that?"

She's silent a moment, then links her arm with mine. I'm sure the action is symbolic of her desire to put the argument behind us. Or maybe she's simply cold. Or possibly it's because we've just turned onto a deserted street that would be better termed an *alley*, its length lit with a single lamp and lined with decaying wooden warehouses.

Then I spot the real reason for her silence: on the opposite side of the street, a short distance ahead, three men have a woman cornered against the sideboards of a wagon.

Maria and I halt.

"You drank forty kopeks' worth," growls one of the men. "You only gave me twenty."

The girl's voice is young and tipsy. "The rest from my next pay."

"You pay up now," a second man demands with a German accent.

The young woman retorts, "This doesn't concern you."

"It concerns all of us," the German snarls. "You said you could afford the tavern."

I pull Maria backward around the corner of the building so that we're out of sight.

"You have my word," the girl wails. "My word is my bond."

The first man says, "You lying little whore, you pay up! Either that, or all three of us will have you until you're raw."

I poke my head around the corner just as a fist smashes into her stomach. Her body slams against the wagon and crumples forward.

A third voice asks, "Who's first?"

Maria's eyes are wide as she breathes, "Oh, my word!"

A speedy review of my life reveals not a single episode of valor, including the reputed one at the Malakov Bastion. And I see no reason to change course now.

Maria whispers, "What do we do?"

I glance at the street behind us, where we had walked under the safety of streetlights. And to where we could easily return.

From around the corner comes the clang of a metal chain against wood. I peek around the edge of the building. They've lowered the rear panel of the wagon and are pushing the girl toward it, a hand over her mouth.

I'm awash with the same nauseating, chilling panic I experienced at the Malakov. Fear shudders through me, constricting my stomach and strangling my throat. I know the terror that girl feels. And I can't walk away from her.

I lean close to Maria. "Run to the police station, the one near the restaurant. You know which one I mean?"

She gives a single nod.

"Send them here. Then go straight home. Stay on the main streets."

"What about you?"

"Run!" I thrust her in the direction from which we just came.

I take another glimpse around the corner. The thugs are probably armed to the teeth with knives, a gun, who knows what else. With my every nerve on fire, one numb foot somehow manages to advance in front of the other. Then again. And again.

One of the drunken scalawags is in the bed of the wagon, pulling the girl toward him, while the other two hoist her kicking legs over the dropped rear panel. She makes guttural noises, as if they've crammed something in her mouth.

I stop walking a good fifteen paces from the rear of the wagon and force sound through my tight throat. "What are you fellows up to?"

They pause and look across the street toward me. Close up, I can see they're young, just twenty or so.

"Get lost," shoots back the German, one of the two men standing on the street.

"I'm happy to oblige your wishes. If I can take her with me."

"'Happy to oblige our wishes,'" mocks the one in the wagon's bed. "Be gone, you skinny bastard. Or I'll beat your dogface to a jelly." He stands up, a hulking brute of a guy.

My voice strives to sound deep and authoritative. "Come on, fellows, everybody go home and sleep it off." I take a step forward. Followed by a second step. Then I stop.

"Maybe he wants a piece too," the third guy says.

The other two whoop at his witty postulation.

"Is that what you're after, string bean?" continues the comedian. "Climb up there and show us how to do it."

The two on the ground join Brute in the bed, and they drag the girl toward the front.

My entire body is cold with sweat. I need to buy time. God knows when the police will get here, if ever.

"Do you know her?" I ask.

"Shut the fuck up," the German directs.

Comic Guy is more informative. "Every man at the factory knows her."

Andrey, why are you defending a whore? Walk away now!

But I can't.

The girl struggles as they pin her flat on her back.

"So you've been with her before?" I try to sound curious.

"Like I said," slurs Comic Guy, "everybody's had her."

"Shut up." Brute cuffs the back of Comic Guy's head.

I oh-so-slowly move closer, stopping ten or so paces from the dropped rear panel. "Doesn't sound like she wants to get to know you three any better."

Brute rises into a tough-guy stance, legs wide, arms crossed, and looks down at me.

Shit. He looks massive.

"Get lost before I whip your ass!"

"I'm first," says the German over the sound of ripping material.

"The hell you are." Brute turns away from me and steps toward the girl. "They're my rubles she drank."

"While you guys are playing eeny meeny miny moe, I'll take the first stab at her." This comes from Comic Guy.

Brute pushes aside his buddies. "Get outta my way."

"Hold on!" I command with all the force I can muster. "I've got something to show you."

All three stop pawing the girl and look in my direction.

"You fellows have two choices." I quiver from my scalp to my toes. Can they hear it in my voice?

"Fuck off," the German says.

"If you come down from that wagon and go home, no one will be the wiser."

"Shut up, beanpole," Comic Guy says.

"Going home is the first option." How long can I draw this out? "The second option is to continue your shenanigans and spend the night in jail."

"Up your ass," sneers Brute. "I think your teeth oughta come out the back of your head."

The German follows up with, "One more word from you and—"

"The person who was walking with me is already at the police station," I continue. "Where his father is a captain."

The three hooligans, still crouched at the front of the wagon bed, look at me, then at each other.

"He's lying. He's alone."

"We don't know that."

"Don't be a gullible jackass. He's by himself."

"It's my twenty kopeks. I'll have her while you two stand guard."

"That's rape." My mouth is so dry, my tongue sticks to the roof of my mouth. "And it won't be just her word against yours. I'm a witness."

"Not for long, you scrawny jackass." Brute rises and walks to the rear of the wagon bed, his boots scraping the wagon's floorboards.

My every muscle goes rigid.

"Ignore the runt. He'll go away," suggests the German.

"Yeah, let's get on with it," urges Comic Guy.

Brute lurches back to the other two drunken rogues, then squats down.

Last chance, Andrey. "Take a look at this." When I've gotten the attention of Comic Guy and the German, I whip a slender object from my vest pocket. Its metal reflects the dim light from the sole streetlamp at the corner. I wave it quickly, not letting them get a good look.

The two men holding the girl stop short. "What's he got?" asks the German.

"It's a scalpel." I draw out my words, trying to buy time. "A very sharp surgical instrument. You see, I'm a physician, and I used it just minutes ago to lance a boil on a child's asshole. My assistant is fetching the police."

The German says, "He's lying. He ain't got nothing."

"He ain't lying. I saw it," insists Comic Guy.

Brute again stands up and comes toward me, a little less swagger in his step.

"You take one step closer and I'll lance your face, starting with your eyeballs," I inform Brute as I slice the air in front of me. Miraculously, the metal throws off a sinister glint in the lamplight. "This little beauty is sharper than any knife." Somehow I manage to take a step closer. "Anybody touches that girl, I'll whack off both your balls with a single slice."

"Go ahead and try, asshole." Hands on his hips, Brute billows out his chest.

Coming from the cross street is the sound of horse hooves and metal wheels on cobblestones. The punks hear it too and utter all manner of sacrilegious words.

Brute vaults off the back of the wagon and bolts into the darkness. The German tries to vault over the sideboards, but the girl, much to her credit, grabs his leg, and he tumbles face-first to the ground. A young policeman leaps from his wagon, stomps his boot in the middle of the German's back, and slaps on handcuffs.

Comic Guy races to the back end of the wagon. As he leaps off, a second policeman, one with bushy side whiskers, lands a good whack on the goon's head with a baton. He falls face-first to the street. Side Whiskers kneels atop him and whips out his handcuffs.

My chest deflates as I let loose the air I've been storing, and I drop my apartment's skeleton key back into my vest pocket. I put a boot across Comic Guy's face, pinning his cheek to the cobblestones. Why I did that, I'm not certain, other than to feel as if I've contributed something.

Once Comic Guy is handcuffed, I back away, my chest heaving as if I've just gone fisticuffs with all three goons.

"It's . . . it's the girl's fault," the German stammers as the young policeman drags him to his feet. "She promised us . . . certain things. We just wanted to collect."

"You're the fellow who was with the woman who reported this?" asks Side Whiskers.

I nod as I climb into the wagon's bed. "There's a third who ran off." I move toward the girl, who has lost all her bravado and is huddling in a front corner. I squat beside her. "Are you hurt?"

She shakes her head.

The young policeman asks the girl, "You know these fellows?"

She mewls, "I work with them at the glass factory."

"Ha!" cries Comic Guy. "She does more than work with us!"

"That true?" the two policemen ask her simultaneously.

"Of course not!" Her voice trembles.

"Oh, it's true, all right," insists the German, blood streaming from his nose. "I swear on the name of sweet Mary, Mother of God."

"For money? Or pleasure?" the young policeman asks.

"Money," the German confirms. "Sometimes for fancy clothes or baubles."

"I ain't never!" the girl screams.

"You a prostitute?" Side Whiskers asks.

"I ain't never laid with a man. Never!"

Side Whiskers continues as if the girl hadn't spoken. "If you take money, then you'd better have a yellow ticket."

Her head pulls back. "A what?"

"A yellow ticket. A prostitute's license."

The girl swings her head from side to side, her eyes wide with either disbelief or fright.

I interrupt with, "Here's the story I overheard." I sit atop the sideboard and tell them about the twenty kopeks.

"Only one way to know who's telling the truth," Side Whiskers announces. "Lock them all up for the night. The Women's Clinic physician can examine her in the morning."

I'm familiar enough with the term *Women's Clinic physician* to know his job is to check prostitutes for disease and to examine for virginity. I lay odds he won't find the latter.

All right, Andrey. You've come this far. Finish the job.

Another part of me rebels. *Why should I? How she lives her life is her business.*

Because she had the daylights scared out of her tonight. Give her a chance to redeem herself.

"No need to wait until morning," I announce. "I'm a physician. I can verify her virginity or lack thereof."

The policeman eyes me from under the brim of his cap. "Do you know this girl?"

"Never laid eyes on her until a few moments ago."

FOLLOWING THE EXAMINATION, the girl's face is filled with the sincerest gratitude and the early tint of bruises. I estimate her to be in her late teens. "I live with my uncle. He'll be eternally grateful. He'll reimburse you for the cab, plus lots more."

The church bells have already tolled two in the morning by the time the cabby pulls up to a refined, one-story house built of blocks of cut stone. Light flickers through the front windows. The girl leaps from the cab at the same instant the front door flings open. "My darling Daria! Come into my arms!"

I tell the driver to wait, and then I follow Daria into the antechamber, hoping she's correct about the cab fare.

"Uncle Tima! It was horrid!" Daria wails to a bald man in a housecoat and slippers, whose hangdog jowls suggest he was once thick of neck and heavy of barrel.

I stand quietly to one side, hands clasped in front of me, while Daria describes the unprovoked attack by the three thugs from the factory, including how I single-handedly fought them off until the police arrived. Tears flow down her cheeks. "The most awful! But this man—the bravest man ever—saved me."

While she details the ghastly conditions at the police station, I look closer at Uncle Tima. In the sallow lamplight, wrinkles cross-hatch his leathery cheeks. Deep in my mind's recesses, a familiar chord is struck, but my brain is too exhausted to place him.

I return my attention to Daria, flinching with guilt as she describes how "this most marvelous physician declared beyond any doubt that I'm a virgin, which immediately ended the whole problem. But now I'll have to find work somewhere else. Those hoodlums will have it in for me."

"Under no circumstances will you go back to that horrid factory." Uncle Tima turns to me, grabs my hand, and pumps it like a well handle. "My soul, we can't thank you enough." He takes an ungainly step back, as if one of his knees won't bend.

My breath catches noisily halfway between my front teeth and the back of my throat. "General . . ." What was the fellow's name? "Lieutenant General Tropinin?"

Uncle Tima looks at me from under dropped brows. "Where do I know you from?"

"I removed your tonsils, sir."

"Well! Saints in Heaven!" His hand again pumps mine as his fossilized face creases into a wide smile. And now it's the general's turn to sing my praises to Daria, describing how I risked life and limb to save his men from a shell ready to explode at any moment. "Not to mention, removed my dastardly tonsils. And brilliantly performed a tricky surgery on your Cousin Fedya."

Tropinin extends an arm toward the divan. "Come sit with us while Daria's nerves settle."

"As much as I would like to, sir, I'm afraid my cab is waiting. I have to report to work first thing in the morning."

"Are you still with the army?"

"No, sir. I'm at the Imperial Foundling Home."

"Well, Doctor, if you ever grow weary of all those children and want a career change, come see me. Though I'm retired, I still have friends in high places at the Ministry of Internal Affairs."

"Thank you, sir. I'll keep that kind offer in mind. And if I may say so, retirement appears to suit you quite well."

"Appearances are deceiving." He launches into a loquacious inventory of his ailments. His sciatica burns so bad he sometimes can't stand, and his recurring Crimean fever leaves him weak with aches, shaking chills, and insomnia. "They dose me with various nostrums, but nothing helps."

When he begins detailing the paroxysms of his ague, I plead that, as much as I hate to, I'd best be off before my cabbie's bill rises any higher. True to Daria's promise, Uncle Tima presses some crumpled rubles into my hand, then instructs me to come back for a good, long visit.

"Tropinin. Of all people," I mutter as I climb into the carriage. The utter unpredictability of life.

CHAPTER 40

May
1866

SHORT OF STUFFING a sock in his mouth, I can't get Colya to stop talking about Alexander's latest debacle—the zemstvo.

Created by statute in 1864, zemstvos are institutions of local government at the provincial and district levels. They hire staff and carry out the responsibilities that previously fell to the nobility prior to the 1861 emancipation of the serfs. The all-encompassing duties include the establishment, provision, and maintenance of schools, libraries, roads, agricultural assistance, famine relief, fire protection, veterinary services, and—of prime interest to Colya—medical care. With a medical degree in his hand, plus the first of three years of advanced public health studies under his belt, he has his sights set on eventually securing a position as a zemstvo physician.

Colya trumpets the regime's spiel while he, Maria, and I enjoy a noonday meal at a café. "Zemstvos will place self-government into the hands of the people they serve. It's a turning point in our country's history!"

I'm convinced that his youthful enthusiasm overlooks two insurmountable obstacles. First, the statute requires the nobility and the peasants—two social ranks with deep, long-standing hostilities toward one another—to jointly organize and administer the myriad programs involved. Second, although St. Petersburg will provide a trifling subsidy, each zemstvo must raise the bulk of its funding through taxation of its populace. My head wags as I recall the insubstantial district towns and squalid villages I passed through while on my way to and from the Crimea.

Last summer, as a greenhorn physician, Colya worked as an apprentice to a trailblazing zemstvo physician in what Colya lauded as "the pastoral countryside of Tambov province." He had intended to resume his training there this summer, but the zemstvo physician was transferred to Penza, and Colya will be joining him there.

"But that's fine! I'll gain new perspectives!" the giddy young man tells Maria and me. "The location isn't important, as long as I'm part of pioneering free rural health care! Do you realize the peasants have never had *any* medical care whatsoever? Zemstvo medicine is like nothing Russia's far-flung villages have ever seen!"

"That's certainly true," I agree, biting my tongue to keep from adding: *Russia has never seen anything like it, because the peasants, uneducated and indigent, are incapable of an undertaking of that magnitude.*

"Consider how the honorable work of a community physician can contribute to a village's health. Decrease infant mortality. Boost nutrition. Improve basic sanitation." Colya's eyes are afire with the combination of youth and ambition. "The peasantry will have all their medical and public health needs met. And without paying a single fee!"

And what do you think taxation is, if not a fee? But I keep my thoughts to myself as I study the moonstruck young man across the table. Colya's utopian belief in zemstvo medicine is every bit as unrealistic as his starry-eyed view of war was. *But then again, Andrey, which is worse—your self-defeating realism or Colya's optimistic pipe dreams?*

Maria's foot taps my ankle, hinting that it's time to give Colya his gift. I reach under the table and retrieve a present wrapped in wallpaper that Maria has cajoled from one of her clients. "A little present from Maria and me, to take with you this summer." I hand it across the table.

Colya gasps as he unwraps the heavy book and fans the pages. "Oh, my!" He faces the book toward Maria as if she hadn't seen its cover: *Principles of War Surgery* by N. I. Pirogov. I'm delighted with Colya's response to the gift. The book is newly published, and it was no small task to secure a copy.

Maria quips, "Hopefully you won't find much need for war surgery in Penza."

I add, "But Pirogov includes a great amount on preventive medicine that will definitely be of use to you."

"I heard an interesting bit of news about another one of our friends from the war." Maria pops a bite of asparagus into her mouth and lets the suspense build while she chews. "Guess where William Howard Russell is."

Suddenly my food looks far less appetizing and the wine far more appealing. "Oh, do tell."

She ignores my unmistakable sarcasm. "The United States of America."

Colya's head jolts back. "The United States of America?"

"Well, actually, he's back in England now. He was thrown out of the United States of America."

I give a mighty *harrumph* and order another bottle of wine.

"He reported on their civil war from the front lines, just as he did in our war.

After one of the battles, he wrote that the Northern soldiers lacked discipline and courage. The Union leaders got very angry."

"How did you hear of this?" Colya asks.

"One of my good customers has connections in England. He knows that I know Monsieur Russell, so he relayed the story to me. Life is so full of coincidences!"

I refuse to comment on Mister Russell. Instead, I wonder if any of the American physicians who were in the Crimea also served in the war across the ocean.

Good God Almighty, Andrey. Maria is right about one thing: I spend far too much time inside my head, brooding about the past.

OF THE TWO bottles of wine, Maria drinks a single glass. The remainder is split between Colya and me. Small wonder that as I saunter from the restaurant, the afternoon takes on rosy tones. Springtime has burnished the rough edges of the city. Life rejuvenates itself as the earliest buds appear. And a country halfway around the world has banned the egoist Russell from its shores.

I stop by the Foundling Home to pick up my pay.

After I pocket the rubles, I check on two of my favorite patients, a set of twins with whooping cough. I also chat with a couple of nursemaids who are wheeling their infants about, then scan the physicians' bulletin board for upcoming seminars. Little Soldier is feeling feisty, so I keep my eyes open for Klara.

Immediately upon gaining employment as a laundress at the Foundling Home, Klara willingly lifted her skirt for me. The little pixie is most accommodating of my needs, either when she picks up my laundry or drops it off, and occasionally in a walk-in linen closet at the far end of one of the orphanage's interminably long wings. By the time her father died, a peculiar friendship had developed between her and me, and together we mourned his death.

As it turns out, this afternoon Klara is receptive to a break from her laundry duties. Her young body is limber enough to flex into any position required by shelving, brooms, and stacks of blankets in the linen closet. And her young mind is pliant enough to not distress itself over our eccentric, acrobatic gyrations. Both of these are, in my view, gratifying attributes.

Klara is as obliging as usual. Until the chief housekeeper opens the closet door.

CHAPTER 41

May
1866

WE'RE BOTH FIRED. My self-contempt for involving Klara in this incident is deep, and I want to make amends. After her father's death, however, she moved from their old apartment, and I don't know how to locate her. She no longer appears at my apartment to collect my laundry.

I'm gutted. For the first week, I anchor myself in my darkened room, curled up like a fetus under my blanket. Most of my so-called nutrition comes from a bottle. Demons of the darkest night are regular visitors in my nightmares.

A meat butcher is dressed in only a surgeon's bloodied oil-cloth apron.

I'm covered in flies, fleas, maggots, lice.

Rats nibble off all my toes.

Cholera diarrhea drips from my hair.

The incense scar on my hand turns blue. Then the entire hand goes blue and falls off.

I'm wearing a shirt and no trousers, and the Sisters of Mercy pull their voluminous white scarfs over their faces to conceal their laughter.

During the second week, I curse hotly all day, every day—long-winded strings of foul curses aimed at my own stupidity. The guy in the next apartment bangs on the wall for me to shut up.

By the end of the second week, I'm sober enough to calculate that, if I scrimp, I can live off my savings without employment for about a year. But to plunder my nest egg would be idiotic. I need to pound the streets to find a job. Immersing myself in self-pity, however, occupies all my time.

Are there any friends who could help me find employment?

Who can I count as friends anyway? There are only three. One is a young man who is at his summer internship in Penza. It would probably be best to confess the truth to Colya. Word of the bizarre incident might filter through Moscow's medical community. Colya is a male and old enough to understand.

My other friends are two sisters, one of whom aggravates me to no end and would string me up by my toenails if she were to find out about Klara. Probably an out-and-out lie would be the best strategy.

I concoct a story about how I met with bad luck when the Foundling Home, which forbids its physicians to engage in the private practice of medicine, got wind that I'm still earning income from the regular tapping of Lenora Pavlovna's abdomen. Wanting to make a point to its other physicians, the Foundling Home laid my head on the chopping block.

Yes, a very good piece of fiction.

In my small shaving mirror, I see black-encircled eyes, cheeks so gaunt they belong on a cadaver, and the pinched lips of a pissed-off fish.

I eventually wash my rancid body, shave two weeks' stubble from my face, and slump from the boardinghouse. Over the next five days, I visit every hospital in the city and every factory that has a physician on its payroll. The responses are all variations of the same theme: *We'll add you to our list of applicants.*

The government continually recruits physicians to Siberia. But besides being a homebound bovine that shuns new pastures, I know I don't have the mettle for that frozen no-man's-land.

I make a rare appearance at a meeting of the Moscow Medical Society. My colleagues give half-hearted promises that they'll pass my name along if they hear of any available positions. More than a few of them slap me on the back, expressing their high regard for my resourcefulness with women. Despite all the glad-handing, I'm a laughingstock.

When I return to my boardinghouse, I stand outside staring at the brick building. I've lived here longer than any of the other tenants. The weeks spiraled into ten years, and I've yet to make a proper home for myself. How has so much time trickled unnoticed through the hourglass? My gaze slowly lifts to the third-story windows. I'm reluctant to climb the dark, sagging stairs to my soulless cell, where I know I'll toss back a slug of vodka, then another and another, until oblivion sets in.

Not only am I drinking too much, but I've been drinking too much for quite a long time. And I'm well aware of the health consequences. But vodka is my hermitage.

Loath to yield to the call of the bottle, I sit down on the front steps of my building and drag my fingers through my hair, hoping the cool night air will congeal my muddled thoughts.

The disheartening truth of the matter is, Maria is correct. I've plodded through three and a half decades, master neither of myself nor of events.

Yet is she truly correct?

Or are you, Andrey, selling yourself short?

As a youngster trapped in the Church like a butterfly in a jar, hadn't I sorted through my limited options and found an escape route through medicine? And hadn't I, of my own volition, chosen to go to the Crimea? And hadn't I determined the fate of my career when I sought employment at the Foundling Home? And hadn't things been getting better there?

Then why do I feel I've roamed through life without becoming part of it?

Because you've contributed nothing of value to mankind, Andrey. And at this rate, you never will.

Assuming a typical life expectancy, I'm past life's midpoint. What do I want from my remaining years? And how do I go about obtaining it?

The answer to the first question isn't difficult. An honest, productive career. Contentment and rational stability. A quiet life and a quiet death. To make a positive difference, however small.

As for the second question, I feel the truth beating inside me. I need to make a clean break from both Moscow and alcohol.

My head bows until my chin rests on my chest. I press my thumb and forefinger against the bridge of my nose, as if the action might stimulate some logical thought. Apparently, it works. Across my memory march the words of a young medical student.

Honorable work.

Pastoral countryside.

What other quixotic expressions had Colya used regarding the zemstvos?

Pioneering free rural health.

Community physician.

Community physician, I repeat, liking its sound.

All at once, I see a slit of hope in the darkness. I'd receive a dependable paycheck from the government. And life in a small provincial town would be productive, peaceful, and predictable.

Can this bovine brain break free of its pen and graze new pastures?

CHAPTER 42

June–December
1866

I WRITE TO Colya to ask whether there's a zemstvo position vacant in Tambov now that his mentor has transferred to Penza. Colya is a treasure trove of information. Currently, about fifty physicians practice zemstvo medicine in eighteen provinces. This coming year, that should increase to three hundred physicians in thirty provinces. And the number will continue to climb thereafter.

"But," Colya warns, "numerous applicants vie for each position."

And yes, his mentor's previous position is vacant. The district town of Petrovka in Tambov province.

IT'S ONLY BEEN a year, but Lieutenant General Tropinin's descent has been steep. His flesh has melted away like wax from a candle, rendering his face a mask of heavy, grayish wrinkles. His eyes appear sunken halfway to the back of his skull.

"Tell me again where you want to go." His voice is raspy, and his head quivers with the tremors of old age.

"Here, I'll write it down for you."

> Andrey Yevgrafovich Rozhdestvensky wants position as zemstvo physician
>> Petrovka, in Tambov province
>> Served in Crimean War
>> 10 years in Moscow working with indigents and specializing
> in diseases of children

I add my name and address and place the paper in Tropinin's tremulous hand. The general reads the words aloud, getting most of them correct. I'm filled with melancholy at the thought that this shriveled man, in days gone by, had such a towering command of his soldiers.

To my enormous relief, Daria arrives for a visit. She's frenzied with excitement to once again see her benefactor, bestowing me with more kisses and hugs than my mother did during the entirety of my childhood. While she sits on the arm of her uncle's chair, I weave my story about my altruistic desire to enter zemstvo service.

"Of course Uncle Tima and I will see to it! You needn't worry about a thing. Isn't that correct, Uncle Tima?" She hugs a withered back that is bent like top-heavy bluebells.

Tropinin's hand cups around his tuft of ear hairs. "What did you say?"

"We'll contact the necessary people to get Doctor Rozhdestvensky assigned where he wants to be."

"Indubitably!" His jowls flap. "It's the least I can do for the man who saved my men from that shell at the Malakov! And saved my little niece from those scalawags! And saved my son from having strangulated balls!"

THE GENERAL HAS a willing heart, but his memory is another matter. However, subsequent to some dogged prodding from Daria and me, he finally pulls some dusty strings and secures for me the position of Petrovka's zemstvo physician. This incredible, eleven-year chain of events is pure, dumb luck on my part, although some would hold God to be the responsible party.

My departure for the three-hundred-mile trip happens to fall on the worst day of the worst head cold I've ever had. My throat screams, and my cranium feels as though it's crammed with cotton wadding. I'm laid low by sweats and chills, and when I try to blow my nose, my ears pop like muskets.

The coachman is tinkering with the brake lever. The horses have yet to be hitched. I drop onto a bench inside the stable, let my head fall back against the wall, and close my eyes. At least it's December. The roads are frozen hard, not like the slurries of Crimean mud that snared wheels and hooves during my last quest for a fresh start.

Just listen to yourself, Andrey! Musket-popping ears! Crimean mud slurries! Enough is enough. As of today, in taking this very first step toward your new life, you will no longer be ensnared by the past.

"You're flushed."

My eyes pop open to discover Maria is standing in front of me. She pulls off her glove and places the back of her hand against my forehead. "Do you ache all over?"

"Even my teeth hurt. But I'm glad you came to see me off."

"Such a miserable way for you to start a long, cold journey."

"And you know how my head colds turn into the croup." My words remind me that Maria knows more about me than anyone else in the world. I'll miss that companionship.

"You'll be comforted to know that you'll be traveling with a friend. Someone who will keep your lap warm."

She bends sideways and slides her hand through the handle of a box beside her. She hoists the wood-and-metal carton in front of my face. From between vertical bars, blazing disdain shoots from the slits of two green eyes.

"What is this?" I demand.

"Russell is going with you."

Andrey, stay calm. It's merely a fever-induced hallucination.

She gingerly places the box on the pavers and herself on the bench beside me. "He hasn't been happy since the fire."

Last month, Maria's landlady hired workmen to paint the woebegone hallways. Unfortunately, spilt turpentine met up with a lit match near the sisters' apartment, and the damage required Maria and Vasilisa to temporarily lodge with a cousin and her family. The cat provokes sneezing fits and throbbing headaches in the cousin. And her children (whom Maria labels as "black-hearted hooligans") torment the beast to no end.

"The workmen keep extending the finish date on our apartment," she explains. "Now it won't be ready for another two months."

"Surely you can find someone local to take him temporarily."

She begins to detail, one by one, the excuses of the other people she's asked. She's well aware that her prattle will wear me down.

I hold up my palm to curtail her saga. "I understand, but—"

"Russellushka will adore the open spaces of provincial life." Her boot lightly taps the metal bars. "I had this custom-made. I painted the inscription myself, in case he gets separated from you."

I bend down to examine the miniature version of a circus lion's cage.

RUSSELL

TRAVELING COMPANION OF

ANDREY YEVGRAFOVICH ROZHDESTVENSKY

WHILE LEANING FORWARD, I feel the crash of thunderous waves of mucus against my forehead. When I straighten back up, a horrific mudslide careens down the inside of my skull.

"Maria." I close my eyes while I put my thoughts into polite words. "Maria, I know saying goodbye . . . I mean, to Russell, to the cat . . . must cut you to the quick. You shouldn't part with him."

She gives a slurpy sniffle. "You've been his friend since he was a kitten. He adores you. Besides, surely you'll return to Moscow for a visit. You can bring him back to me. Or who knows, maybe someday I'll go on a little holiday to the countryside and retrieve him."

"Let's think about this logically. First of all, my trip to Petrovka will take at least a week, assuming nothing on the carriage breaks and there are no winter storms. He can't stay inside the coach the whole time." I wave a hand in front of my crinkled nose. "The other passengers won't appreciate when he—"

"That's why I'm giving you this." From her reticule, she brings forth a thin rope contorted into several loops. "Vasilisa designed it. This smaller loop goes over his head and around his neck. And the larger one goes around his chest, like a horse harness. When the coach stops for any reason, you can take him outside so he can . . ." Her voice drops to a whisper. "You know."

I blink at her. Here is a woman who worked in the Crimean War death house, but who can't bring herself to say the word *poo*.

I move along to my second line of defense. "I know nothing about caring for a cat."

Her eyes take on the perturbed hue of cool mercury. "What's there to know? He needs food and water and love." Now that she has the bit in her mouth, she isn't about to be waylaid. "It will all work out." She hands me several cans of sardines. "For Russell. Not for you."

"Boarding!" the coachman calls.

Maria's aplomb disintegrates. Her voice cracks. Her eyelids flutter. "I'll miss you both unspeakably." She puts a hand on my shoulder. "May Christ guard you."

"Yes. Wouldn't it be just lovely if he'd do that?"

Behind the tears, her eyes darken, and I regret my sarcasm. "I'm sorry. I know I'm difficult to get along with. You and Vasilisa have been saints to put up with me."

"Love doesn't demand perfection." Her breath catches in her throat in miniature hiccups.

I pick up my suitcase and medical bag and shuffle along with the other five passengers to the carriage. Maria and the cat are at my side as we wait for the other travelers to hand over their baggage.

"Oh! What an incredibly handsome cat!"

Maria and I look down to see a woman, bent in half, cooing into the crate. "Russell, is it? And you're the traveling companion?" She points at me with a long, gloved forefinger. "You will let me hold him, won't you? Does he purr? What fun!"

I fully expect the woman to clap her hands together like an excited three-year-old. Maria pitches me a self-satisfied smirk. *I told you everything would be all right.*

I hand my suitcase and medical bag to the coachman, and Maria and I step to one side and face one another. She sets the miniature lion cage beside my foot.

"As soon as you arrive in Petrovka, you must write me straightaway. I must know that you're both safe."

I kiss her cheeks three times. "Farewell, Maria."

Standing on her toes, she hugs my neck, and her lips graze my ear. "May your hopes and dreams be fulfilled."

When she pulls back, I respond with all sincerity. "I'm not certain I've ever had any."

"It's just as well," she replies. "They end up crumbling into dust."

PART

Three

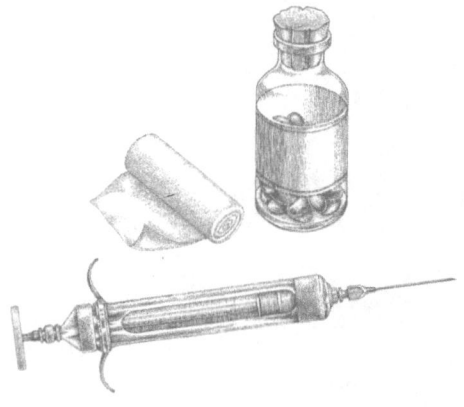

CHAPTER 43

December
1866

THE COACH PASSES through a single-bell-tower village. Then another. Another. The endless procession reinforces my long-held belief that the glorious expanse of Russia is nothing more than an interminable string of miserably poor villages set against a backdrop of bleak, frozen fields.

I'm sick as a dog. I sleep the days away under a lap blanket, my hat pulled low over my ears to block the ceaseless jangle of harness bells. Meanwhile, the cat makes his rounds from lap to lap. He avoids his new roommate like the plague.

On the fourth day, I catch a pungent whiff of someone feeding the cat sardines. Ah ha! The contagion is vacating my head in favor of my chest. I'm on the mend.

"Look!" one of the passengers exclaims. "We're in Tambov!"

I squint through the web of frost on the window. The wooden direction post, having lost its battle against the wind, tilts away from the road, the provincial name half buried in a snowdrift. Good! Petrovka should be just two more days of travel.

But the following afternoon, the driver pulls the horses to a halt. "Andrey Yevgrafovich Rozhdestvensky," he hollers. "Your stop."

My coat sleeve wipes the fog from the window. All I see is a shivering jumble of huts and barns in a frigid world of blowing snow. This is a district capital? Impossible!

I push open the door and lean into the howling north wind. "This isn't my destination," I call to the driver, who is atop the coach retrieving my baggage.

"This is where you get off."

"But . . . but no! This isn't it."

The driver descends the back ladder and sets my suitcase and medical bag behind the coach. I put on my muffler and gloves and step out of the coach into a cold that boggles the imagination. I clamp my arms across my chest, braced against both air made of ice and the notion that I might take my luggage and join this abysmal world.

"Where are we?" I inquire.

"Exactly where we're supposed to be. Petrovo, in Tambov province."

"Petrovo? No, I'm headed for Petrovka."

The driver lowers his scarf to allow a long, exasperated white sigh to pass beneath his icy moustache. "I don't know where you're headed, but this route doesn't go to Petrovka. My bill of lading says to drop you off in Petrovo." He looks about, seemingly a little disoriented himself. "Guess this spot is as good a place as any to let you off." His thick glove gestures at a weather-beaten hut with the word MERCANTILE slopped in white on the planks above the door. "Unless you want me to take you to the orphanage the nuns run." He motions vaguely farther down the narrow road before stepping up into the coach to retrieve the cat in its cage.

"N-no." Desperation grips my voice at the possibility of being stranded in this sinkhole. "This isn't where I belong. Look, perhaps I'm supposed to meet another coach headed to Petrovka?" It's an entreaty more than a question.

"Maybe." The driver sets down the cat, spits tobacco-stained saliva in the snow, and brusquely taps the toe of his boot against my suitcase. "But this is the end of the route for you, as far as I'm concerned." He repositions his muffler over the lower half of his face and climbs into his open-air seat. He pulls the sheepskin over his legs and sets the horses in motion.

As the coach departs, the blood drains from my face and limbs and pools God-knows-where. The air is so cold, it hurts to breathe. The wind is even more biting than it was in Sevast—

No! I forbid my diseased memories to get the better of me!

My eyes water, and my ears are mutating into icicles. I turn up my coat's fur collar, pull my fur hat down to eyebrow level, and raise my scarf over my nose and mouth. I pivot in a dejected circle, taking in the forlorn village huddled against the growling winds.

Lining what appears to be the sole road are bedraggled wooden fences, each meeting end-to-end with the next. Behind the fences are the hand-hewn planks and low-slung roofs of the huts and barns. A covered well sits at the road's wide spot in the center of the town. Farther down the road is a squatty little church in no better condition than the huts, which themselves look like listing woodpiles. The tiny thread of a road stretches out until it disappears into the great Russian vastness. There's no evidence of the orphanage the coach driver mentioned. The sole hint that the village is inhabited is the sooty gray smoke that belches from the chimneys and rises to meet heavy clouds of the same color. The only sound is the wind whistling between the boards of fences and gusting through the bare limbs of the disappoint-ingly few trees. It catches hold of my hacking cough and carries it down the road.

My guts twist with equal measures of panic and self-loathing. If ever a grown man wanted to cry . . .

Rather than stand here and freeze, I examine my only two options. I can inquire at the Mercantile. Or I can seek assistance at the church.

There's really only one choice, isn't there, Andrey?

The creak of wooden hinges announces my arrival at the Mercantile, but the woman seated behind the counter on the far side of the room pays me no notice. Perhaps she didn't hear me over the wind's howl, which the rough-hewn log walls do little to stifle. I set the suitcase, medical bag, and cage to one side, free my mouth from the muffler, and approach the counter, which is a high, wooden trestle table.

"Hello?" I hail the woman, who wears a calico blouse and skirt, a knitted shawl pulled tight across her shoulders, and a babushka tied under her chin.

"Hold on," the woman mutters as she flicks the beads of her abacus. She enters the sum in a notebook, then she flicks some more. Her hands, red and creased, are staunch with sinews.

I glance about the store. It's poorly stocked, but the wall shelves are orderly. Clothing: fur hats, bulky leather gloves, two pairs of leather boots. Fabric: mainly cheap chintz and calico, along with a few spools of decorative braid and ribbons. Staples: matches, salt, kerosene. Colorful pottery: mugs, bowls, and a few platters, their quality craftsmanship incongruent with the other merchandise.

On the floor in a corner is a horse harness plus a few iron implements: shovels, axes, scythes.

Safely stashed on shelves behind the woman are small items that could be easily snitched: sewing and knitting needles, thimbles, thread, knives, scissors. Hanging on the wall are three small mirrors interspersed among an equal number of icons, cheap prints with garish frames.

In a front corner is the sole window, its glass murky with layers of grime. Near it are three square tables, each surrounded by rustic benches, the seats darkened from use. Next to the wall, a samovar sits on a cheap set of unpainted drawers.

And hurrah for the huge whitewashed clay stove! It consumes a quarter of the floor space and radiates the most luscious heat I've felt in days.

I might have been ignored for the rest of the afternoon had the cat not meowed. The woman looks up from her figures, her eyebrows sternly knitted above discerning eyes.

"Yes?"

I approach the counter, side-stepping a pile of tanned hides. No sooner does my mouth open than a spasm grabs hold of my chest. The dour woman strums her chapped fingers on the tabletop, impatient for my hacking to subside.

"Excuse me," I wheeze. "I'm a physician who is supposed to be stationed at the zemstvo in Petrovka. Somehow my orders got all afoul, and I was delivered here. Can you tell me, is there a carriage that could take me to Petrovka?"

The woman shook her babushka'd head. "None to be had."

"But there must be."

"Naw. The only regular route through here is the one that dropped you off."

"I must get to Petrovka. Do you have any suggestions?"

She props her elbows on the table, her fists providing a resting place for the lines that radiate downward from her mouth. I guess her to be between forty and fifty, though her leathered skin undoubtedly adds years to her appearance. "I suppose you could hire someone with a sledge to take you. But we'd have to find out which direction Petrovka is."

"I've seen it on a map. It's in the northern part of Tambov province." I may as well be speaking Chinese, the woman's expression remains so blank. If only Maria were here. She'd have the woman chatting in no time.

Russell meows again. The woman frowns down at his cage. "It's not black, is it? Black cats are bad luck, you know."

"He's gray. I think he might have to relieve himself."

Her eyes display not the slightest comprehension.

"Pee," I clarify. "Excuse me for a moment." I slip the rope harness out of my pocket and drape it around the cat. As I depart, I glance over my shoulder to see her careworn face pucker in a suppressed laugh.

Outside, my cheeks feel like they're being lacerated by tiny icicles. After placing Russell on the packed snow of the road, I shove my gloved hands deep in my coat pockets and peer in both directions in whirling disbelief.

Andrey, how on earth did you wind up in the middle of nowhere, tethered to a cat? Life can play cruel tricks, but this is viciously sadistic.

While Russell gives thoughtful attention to the task at hand, I desperately try to gather my wits. The Mercantile woman is obviously incapable of helping, and asking at the church is at the bottom of my short list of options. And just how far down the windswept road is the supposed orphanage?

Jangling harness bells divert my attention to a wagon on wooden runners coming toward me. The driver's eyes are the sole part of him that isn't bundled, and their gaze never leaves me as he directs his horse to turn onto a wide path alongside the store. Russell is daintily gathering white snow over the patch of yellow, but I don't give him time to tidy up. I scoop him under my arm and hasten back into the warmth.

"Thank you for your time," I tell the woman, who hasn't moved from the stool behind the table. "I'll follow your suggestion and find someone to take me to Petrovka." I deposit the cat into his cage and retrieve my suitcase and medical bag.

"I wouldn't be so quick to leave if I were you."

"Pardon?"

"We've been expecting you. You're the doctor from Moscow."

I slowly replace my items on the floor. Why the hell didn't she say so before!

"The government told us about you. We thought you'd arrive a month ago, but . . ." Her shrug suggests, *What can you expect from the government?*

From a back room, boots clomp across a wood floor, and soon the man who had been driving the sledge passes through the curtained doorway directly behind the woman. He has removed his hat and untied his muffler, exposing a brown beard with silver threads that reaches halfway down his breast bone and is as thick as a wolf's winter coat.

"This is Feodor Nikiforovich Zhemchuzhnikov," the woman says. "And I'm Elizaveta Vorontsova." Her crusty demeanor softens as she looks up at the man standing directly beside her, only a sliver of light between them. "This is the doctor we've been hearing about. Finally got here."

The wolf's coat parts between the moustache and the beard, and I think I detect the glimmer of a smile. But probably not. "Welcome to our village." Zhemchuzhnikov removes his hand from the pocket of his sheepskin coat and extends it Western-style.

I set down my luggage and cross the rough plank floor to shake his hand. "Andrey Yevgrafovich Rozhdestvensky."

"Feodor and me run this store," Vorontsova says. Now that I'm closer, I notice that the sinewy woman has a sizable belly.

"Actually, Elizaveta runs it," Zhemchuzhnikov says. "I simply give her a hand when I have time."

I glance about the room appreciatively. "You must have an aptitude for business, Elizaveta Vorontsova."

"I have very little except common sense and motivation." In no mood for flattery, she again looks at Zhemchuzhnikov. "He brought his cat with him."

Zhemchuzhnikov, one eyebrow raised, peers at the baggage across the room.

"A gift from a dear friend." I'm grateful for the stirrings of a good, deep cough so I don't have to elaborate.

"They didn't tell us where your hospital would be," Zhemchuzhnikov says. "Or where you'd live."

I assume *they* is a general term for *the government.* "Actually, there's been a bit of a mix-up. I'm supposed to be stationed in Petrovka, not in—where am I?"

"Petrovo," she says.

"Petrovo, yes, thank you. But until we get this blunder set right, I'm in need of somewhere to stay. Is there a hotel, perhaps?" I ask without a trace of optimism.

Puzzled lines form between the man's eyebrows, while the woman bestows another vacuous stare on me. Eventually the two of them put their heads together, and at long last, Zhemchuzhnikov turns back toward me. "The owner of this estate, Maximov, can probably help you sort through this. He'll put you up for a night or two."

"Those are welcome words, Feodor Nikiforovich. Where do I find this Maximov?"

"I just returned from his place. If you'll help me unload the kegs in my wagon, I'll take you there."

"Kegs?"

"From Maximov's distillery. When his kegs wear out, he sells them to us. Then we patch the leaks with tar and sell them to the villagers."

As I and Zhemchuzhnikov haul a half dozen empty wooden kegs, Elizaveta Vorontsova clears space for them in the store. I wonder about the relationship between these two. *He sells them to us,* the man had said. *Then we sell them to the villagers.* Yet Zhemchuzhnikov had claimed, *I simply give her a hand when I have time.* Although they appear to be about the same age, they don't resemble brother and sister. And their lack of wedding rings implies they aren't married to each other or anyone else. And what's the significance of the woman's bloated abdomen?

Andrey, don't burden yourself with other people's situations. You've enough problems of your own.

The task finished, Zhemchuzhnikov and I climb onto the sledge. As we turn onto the road, he points at a ramshackle hut that makes all the others appear stalwart. It lacks a door or any glass in its single window, and holes gape in the thatch on its roof.

"That's the only vacant *izba* in town."

"Izba?"

"House."

My insides snicker. To call any of these structures a *house* is the grossest form of flattery.

Zhemchuzhnikov continues, "Don't think it would make a good hospital, though. Been empty since the Widow Shabanova died, years and years ago."

I'm tempted to reply that a hospital isn't a concern, because I'm headed for Petrovka. But instead I ask, "How many houses are in Petrovo?"

"Fifty-two, including the empty one."

"And how many people?"

"Between four and five hundred. Somebody's always dying or being born."

Ten people in each squatty little hovel? *Andrey, you've hit rock bottom.*

CHAPTER 44

December
1866

CROSSING A NARROW wooden bridge that spans a frozen, insignificant river, we leave behind the winter-ravaged village. The sledge climbs toward a stately, two-story red brick house atop a gently sloping hill that appears custom designed for winter toboggans.

Zhemchuzhnikov bypasses the white porte-cochere and follows the snow-packed lane around the house to a humble rear entrance. The sledge is slowing to a halt when a woman's head pokes out the door.

I step from the sledge, so preoccupied with peering at the woman that I fail to notice the shined-to-perfection patch of ice beneath my foot. My boots grapple for traction while my arms whirl around and around like pinwheels. A stinging blast of wind slams into me. Needless to say, I end up on the seat of my pants. The clownish mishap sets off a coughing spasm, adding insult to injury.

Magnificent first impression, Andrey! You look like a blundering oaf and sound like a consumptive.

While I gracelessly gather myself off the ground, a white goose appears from nowhere and circles about me, its neck stretched in a threat and its honk out-shouting the wind's shriek. I guardedly slide my feet along the ice-bound path to the door while Zhemchuzhnikov moves with the agility of a speed skater.

"Dasha, this is the zemstvo doctor we were promised," Zhemchuzhnikov explains.

"Andrey Yevgrafovich Rozhdestvensky." As my head bows, my eyes skim over the woman from top to bottom, then back up again. She bears the austere, wrung-out features of a servant, but she lacks the conventional little lace cap and white pinafore I'm accustomed to seeing in Moscow. The sleeves of her calico blouse are rolled up as if she's about to plunge her arms into a laundry tub. Her blouse is belted at the waist and falls over a broadcloth skirt without petticoats.

"I'm afraid there's been a bit of a mix-up," I sputter.

Zhemchuzhnikov adds, "We hope Monsieur Maximov can help sort things out."

"I'm sure he can." The woman takes measure of me, and I sense that she finds me wanting. She opens the door wide, keeping her blue eyes narrow. "Wait in the kitchen while I fetch him."

My gaze follows her as she moves deeper into the house. The thick waistline. The bountiful hips. The sway of her skirt. I feel a prick of nostalgia for the two sisters in Moscow.

I'm in the throes of a coughing conniption when Dasha returns, followed by a broad-shouldered, clean-shaven man near my age. Dark locks tumble rakishly over his forehead while thick curls cascade over the back of his collar.

"Back so soon, Feodor?" Maximov's strong chin widens into a generous smile of perfectly straight, white teeth.

"This fellow is in a bind," Zhemchuzhnikov explains. "Perhaps you have some advice?"

I give my full name and extend a hand.

"Anton Stepanovich Maximov" comes the reply.

During our handshake, I take note of Maximov's callused palm and dirty nails. His hand is no stranger to work. This rounds out the portrait of a laborer, formed by the curly fleece of his sheepskin vest placed over a thick red shirt, which is tucked in to nankeen trousers.

In concise terms, I explain my predicament, concluding with, "I'm hoping you can suggest a means to get to Petrovka."

"You could hire one of Feodor's nephews to take you. But are you sure you're supposed to be in Petrovka?" The back of his hand rubs his jawbone. "You see, we heard that a physician is coming here." He brings forth a contagious laugh. "An unlikely place to assign a physician, eh? I don't mean to alarm you, but I wonder if you haven't stumbled upon your new home."

Heated panic rips through my hair, my toenails, and everything in between. "I hardly think so. I was assigned to the district capital town of Petrovka."

He smiles. "I'm sure the ride from Moscow was wearisome, and your throat sounds a little worse for wear. Why not stay with us a few days while I contact someone who can get to the bottom of this?"

"I . . . I hate imposing," I stammer unconvincingly.

"Your other option is to curl up in a barn in the village." Maximov's grin is resplendent with charisma, and I find myself drawn to it. "Feodor, I'll write a note to Victor Vladimirovich Rusakov. Have one of your nephews take it to him tomorrow."

Dasha, whose eyes had been tracking the conversation, leaves the kitchen.

"Rusakov has spent the past half dozen years collecting political contacts. I'll ask him to come by here so you can explain your situation. He'll know how to handle it. Trouble is, his position requires substantial travel, so I can't say for certain when we'll see him."

Dasha returns, having retrieved a piece of paper, pen, and ink. While Maximov scribbles a message, I retrieve my baggage from the sledge. Zhemchuzhnikov is leaving with note in hand when I reenter the kitchen. Dasha's eyes instantly drop to the cage.

"Follow me," she orders.

As she leads me through the dining room, I note that the furniture, although of fine quality, has seen better days. Wallpaper peels above the arch of the doorway, and plaster does the same on the ceiling. Even prior to the serfs' emancipation, this must have been a modest but far from affluent estate.

When we reach the parlor, Maximov is already settled on the divan. I head for a high-backed, brass-studded leather chair, its cushion's generous divot suggestive of a comfort sorely lacking during my carriage journey. As I set my belongings on a worn patch of carpet at my feet, Dasha keeps a wary eye on the cage.

"I wager you'd like to clean the travel out of your clothes," Maximov says. "Dasha, get one of the village girls up here tomorrow to launder Doctor Rozhdestvensky's clothes."

"Please, call me Andrey."

"And likewise, I'm Anton."

"Is that a cat?" Dasha blurts, deep suspicion in her voice.

"Yes. It was given to me by a very dear friend who could no longer keep it."

"It's big. What's his name?"

I shift uncomfortably. "Russell. A British name."

Try as she might, Dasha can't twist her Slavic tongue around the foreign name. "Can I take him out of his box?"

Perplexed by the universal reaction of women to the cat, I reply, "If you wish."

Her lace-up boots fly across the room, and she drops onto all fours and coos, in a pose reminiscent of the cat's Moscow owner. The cat saunters out, peruses his surroundings, then stretches as if to imply, *I can be comfortable here.*

"What a fabulously handsome fellow!" Dasha's coarse features soften into a smile that puts sparkle in her eyes and color in her cheeks as she lavishes Russell with full body strokes. She's actually attractive, I realize, and I guess her to be slightly older than myself. "Would you like some milk? Come with me to the kitchen." She rises, and—my eyes must be deceiving me—the cat does as it's told.

I raise incredulous hands, palms facing Anton. "That devil of a cat never listens to a thing I say."

"Women have a way with animals, don't they?" Anton snickers. "I bet you're as thirsty as the cat. That cough will benefit from some nice, hot *sbiten*. I'll get us both some."

As Anton follows the trail of Dasha and Russell, my fingers rake through my hair, and my eyes flick about the room. Specifically, they're scouting for a liquor cabinet. Or a decanter. A breakfront containing wine glasses, snifters, cordial glasses. Some evidence of liquor in the house. But there's nothing. Damn!

I lean forward to peruse the bulging contents of two mahogany bookcases. Lermontov. Herzen. Turgenev. Goncharov. Someone—Anton, perhaps—appreciates good literature.

My thoughts wander to the relationship between Anton and Dasha. Wife? No. Servant? No. Mistress? Maybe. But she's woefully plain for someone of Anton's position in life and abundant good looks.

When Anton returns, he is without the enigmatic Dasha. He hands me a tall, glazed mug. I wrap my cold-stiff fingers around it, and its steaming heat pulls my grip in tighter. I settle against the soft comfort of the chair and take a sip. The warmth of the water, honey, and spices soothes my beleaguered throat. The house mutes the sound of wind, leaving only the ticking of twigs against a window. I could nestle here quite comfortably for the remainder of the week.

"So, is there a bottle shop in this village?" Even to my own ears, I sound like a panting dog waiting for a reassuring pat on the head from its owner.

Anton's left eye narrows a sliver while the same side of his mouth curls upward, as if he's just unearthed my secret. "Not anymore. When Elizaveta and Feodor bought the tavern, they stopped selling alcohol and expanded the rest of the inventory. By the way, don't buy their tea. Tastes like boiled cat piss."

I give a hearty laugh. "Elizaveta and Feodor. I'm not clear on their affiliation."

"Been lovers since they were teenagers." Anton's tone couldn't have been more casual. "But they couldn't marry because of the Church's ban on the children of godparents marrying each other. So when their respective spouses died, they teamed up financially. I loaned Elizaveta the rubles for the property and merchandise."

"You loaned the money to . . . Elizaveta?"

He nods. "Feodor has a sharp and analytical mind. But Elizaveta is the one with a knack for commerce. Plus an indomitable spirit. I was a just a kid when she was a teenager, but I remember her knocking on our door, doggedly peddling wild mushrooms, berries, meadow flowers, whatever. And believe me, the Mercantile is doing remarkably well. It's the only store within a half-day ride."

"Elizaveta, she's . . ." It's ill-mannered of me to say this, but I forge ahead. "She's a grouchy old thing. Or does she simply not like strangers?"

"She's grumpy, that's for sure. A hard life molded her into a hard woman."

"So Elizaveta and Feodor live at the Mercantile?"

"Elizaveta does, but Feodor lives in one of the old serf cottages out back." Anton vaguely gestures somewhere behind the estate house. "But he's rarely there." He winks and gives a devilish grin.

"It's none of my business, but Elizaveta looks as if she's with child."

Anton's face loses its animation. "I'm worried about her. Over the past year, she's become bloated, especially her belly. Feodor's worried too. Perhaps you'll take a look at her?"

"I will." I toast my host with my mug. "*If* I'm in Petrovo long enough."

"Oh, you will be. Resign yourself to that reality." After beaming another grin, Anton sips his sbiten. "My guess is, you're wondering about my relationship with Dasha."

My head jerks back. "You're quite unreserved, aren't you?"

"If you're curious, here's our story. She was a housegirl here. Known me since I was a little boy. And she still puts up with me." His expression turns melancholic. "She's one of the handful of house serfs who stayed on following emancipation. Most of them ran off to the cities, which was fine, since we couldn't afford to keep but a few of them. Dasha does the cooking and housework. And I oversee the distillery and the fields. Yes, it's a scandalous relationship, but we're happy with it, and we ignore the criticism." He exhales a slow, somber sigh. "I've known my share of women, but I had to become a trustworthy friend to myself before I could expect a good woman like her to do the same."

"So do I understand correctly that Feodor works for you? And at the Mercantile?"

"The Zhemchuzhnikov family has more brains and ambition than all the rest of the village families put together. My father recognized that, and he paid Feodor a few kopeks to lend a hand at the distillery when he was a teenager. The kid learned the entire business, everything from where to get the best prices on kegs to fabricating the sheet metal to selecting the best potatoes. I lavish false praise on myself when I say that I oversee the distillery. In truth, Zhemchuzhnikov runs it."

"I take it your father is deceased."

"A year ago, almost to the day. My brother and one of my sisters choose to live in the glitter of St. Petersburg. They share custody of my mother."

"You and Dasha live in this big house alone?"

"My daughter lives with us. But she's staying at the orphanage for a few days."

I cock my head in confusion. "The orphanage down the road from the village?"

"It's a long story. Suffice to say that she was raised there until I discovered I was the father of an eight-year-old. Although Anastasia sometimes stays here at the estate house, she misses her friends and regards the orphanage as her home. So she divides her time between us."

"I see," I reply, though actually I don't see at all.

"The orphanage is run by three dozen nuns, one of whom is my youngest sister. Except for a few donations, they're self-supporting. They raise their own food and fiber and sell the excess. And they sell pottery." He holds up his mug as an example of their work.

"I believe I saw some of their pottery at the Mercantile."

"That Elizaveta, she has a knack for marketing."

I view this as an opening to the subject that's gnawing my insides. "So if the building was a tavern, why did she stop selling liquor? Seems as if that would be her most lucrative commodity." I run my fingers through my hair. After a day like this, God Almighty, do I need a drink!

"Completely correct. The tavern did a roaring trade. If the peasants weren't in the fields, they were in the tavern. Laughter spilled nonstop from that building. But last winter, a peasant froze to death on the road one night after drinking at her tavern. Straight off, Elizaveta stopped serving liquor." Anton sips his sbiten, and his gaze wanders to the far side of parlor. "I don't know for certain, but I suspect her sentiments run deeper than that single incident. I think she realizes the ruin that vodka brings to the peasant families. There's no worse yoke that God could have placed around the peasants' necks." His eyes return to mine. "Nor around mine. That's why I had to quit."

"You no longer drink, then? But you used to?"

"Every waking hour." His dazzling smile widens. "Life seems so much easier when you drink."

"I know." Now it's my turn to let my gaze traipse across the room. But actually, I'm looking inside myself, at my own lack of self-discipline. I haven't even the will to try to stop drinking. Aware of Anton's silence, I wrench myself back to the tangible world. "Was it hard to quit?"

"Hard? Oh, perhaps a little painful. Somewhat akin to a medieval torture rack. Or being strung up by your thumbs."

My throat constricts, craving vodka's relaxing warmth.

"I was thirty-two when I came to my senses." Anton's chuckle is sardonic, his face mirthless. "A year ago, once again, almost to the day."

I cock my head in surprise. Anton appears to be at ease with his life and his position in the world, not a bit like a man who would require the fortitude of a bottle. "Do you mind if I ask how it came about?"

"My quitting? A trilogy of influences. First, I woke up one afternoon with the worst devil of a hangover. My sister, the nun, needed me, but I was too debilitated to be of any help. Second, that very same day, I discovered I had a daughter. Third, at about that time, the death of my father heightened my sensibilities. So my liquor-scrambled brain took an unsparing look at the wreck I had become, and I had to confront the demon inside."

"How long did the pain last?"

"For the first half of this year. I lived in a dark hell, feeling more like a tortured creature than a human being. There were days on end when I couldn't sleep, and other days when all I did was sleep. My thoughts verged on demented, scattering themselves everywhere like a blast from a shotgun." Anton half grins. "But things got better, although the cravings are still with me. And it helps to be surrounded by caring women. My sister Elena. My daughter. And that fine woman in the other room." He hoists his mug toward the kitchen.

"I see," I say again.

Anton looks at me, and his grin drops. "If you need anything, perhaps some words of encouragement or simply someone to rip the bottle away from your lips, I'm here to help. Anytime of the day or night."

My cheeks grow warm. Anton wasted no time in pegging me as an overimbiber. I stretch my lips into what I hope is a smile. "That's kind of you. But I won't be here. I'll be in Petrovka."

Anton throws his head back in a full laugh. "Oh, Andrey," he says, as if addressing a young boy. "Have you ever tried to untangle a bureaucratic snarl?"

CHAPTER 45

December
1866

SHROUDED IN A sleep-fog, I'm vaguely aware of the crocheted canopy above me, but I'm unable to rouse myself. Not that I'm really trying. The downy mattress is too inviting, the clean sheets too luscious, the snug coverlet too persuasive.

Then I awake to the chilling reality that I'm marooned in a miserable, woebegone village so frigid and remote, it might as well be in Siberia. And all because a senile general mixed up a couple of letters in a name. Ugh! The utter unpredictability of life.

A world of worries tries to smother me, but I refuse to succumb until I luxuriate in the delectable plumpness of my pillow and the indulgent tatting of the pillowcase. After a few moments of this refined pampering, a bout of homesickness carries me across the frozen miles. I fancy myself basking in a state of pure, gentle bliss while two Moscow sisters coddle me with steamy towels and kind words.

Something moves against my leg. What the devil? I lift the coverlet. Green eyes glower at me, rankled that their sleep was disturbed.

"How did you get under there?" I swear the cat was outside the room last night when I closed the bedroom door. Damned if I'll share a bed with a cat. Especially one with a galling British name.

I'm in a tiny windowless room directly off the kitchen that was formerly a servant's quarters and that now serves as Anton's daughter's bedroom when she stays at the estate house during the winter. As Anton explained last evening, the second floor is currently shut off at the top of the stairs to conserve wood during the winter. Anton and Dasha's bedroom furniture is temporarily downstairs in the study.

I sniffle and hack a few times as I get dressed, but a good night's sleep seems to have tempered my cold.

"Good morning, Doctor!" Anton waves me toward the third place setting on the kitchen table. Based on his hat-flattened hair and ruddy cheeks, I surmise he's already been outside this morning.

Dasha springs from her seat. Before I can settle onto the wooden ladder-back chair, she has scooped steamy porridge into a ceramic bowl. She points to each cut-glass saucer on the table, a habit presumably ingrained during her years as a servant. "Pickled plums. Honey. Gooseberry preserves."

The bowl, creamer, and biscuit platter look like the ceramic handiwork of the nuns. Their straight, unembellished lines are at variance with the ornate silverware, which is out of keeping with the square, bare-bones table and chairs. The lord of the estate definitely does not stand on ceremony.

Dasha calls a guttural word that resembles, "Russell!" She sets down a chipped saucer containing a splash of cream. "Does he like liver pâté?"

Devoid of any notion of what the cat likes except sardines, I reply, "Oh, yes. Very much."

Dasha places a dollop of pâté on a small square of butcher paper, and the cat scampers over and laps it up. She retakes her seat. "After you went to bed, Russell meowed at your door so pathetically that I let him into your room. I hope you don't mind. I assumed he's accustomed to sharing your bed."

I lack the impetus to explain that the only thing I and the cat share is a mutual antipathy.

Anton flips open his pocket watch. "I'm due to meet Zhemchuzhnikov in the distillery. We're experimenting with honey to make mead. What are your plans for the day?"

"I need to buy a few things at the Mercantile."

Anton wipes the corners of his mouth with his napkin. "While you're in the village, go out to the orphanage and meet my sister." He rises from the table. "Take your medical bag with you. The nuns will undoubtedly ask you to tend to a sick child or two."

I wipe my dripping nose and make no commitments.

I TRUDGE ACROSS the ice-bound bridge toward the village, my gloved hands deep in my coat pockets as the wind bites and the sun struggles to break through the heavy clouds.

> I'm cold.
> I'm sick.
> I'm broke.
> I'm lonely.
> I'm regretful.

I'm scared.

And I have no idea where I am.

The words have a dishearteningly familiar ring. *Golly gee, Andrey, you've made real progress during the past dozen years, haven't you?*

When I reach the warmth of the Mercantile, neither of the people behind the counter is Elizaveta. Instead, propped on stools are two boys who share the mischievous look of lifelong collaborators in tomfoolery. One of the boys swipes his forehead to push aside his hair, which is cut in the peasants' ubiquitous inverted-bowl style. "Good day to you, sir."

"Good day." I glance about the store. "I'd like to buy some items, but I don't see what I'm after."

"Auntie Elizaveta," the boy calls over his shoulder toward the curtained doorway. "A customer."

"Who is it?"

"The new doctor."

The new doctor? Tongues certainly cluck in this village.

"She'll be right here," the boy assures me. I can't help but notice his peculiar ears. Not only are they large, but they're pointed like a wolf's, and they lie flat as though buttoned to his head.

A draft of cold air assails the back of my neck as the door opens and promptly closes. A girl bounds around me. She's about the same age as the boys, whom I assume are on the brink of puberty. She flashes a wide, easy smile at everyone, me included, and pulls off her hat. Luxuriant dark curls flow down her back. A feminine version of Anton, no doubt about it.

As comfortable as if in her own—what was the word Feodor used? Ah, yes, izba—the girl goes behind the counter and removes her coat. Her left sleeve hangs limp. But it's not completely empty. Near her shoulder, her arm moves quite a bit. Her right arm gives the boy with the wolf ears a playful shove. "How many times have I told you? A gentleman gives up his chair to a lady."

"First of all," the boy retorts, "this is a stool, not a chair. Second of all . . ." His head pivots in both directions. "I don't see no lady." He returns her prankish nudge.

The girl's sigh is one of deep exasperation as her finger twirls a long lock of hair. Her foot begins to tap peevishly, and I feel a powerful pull of nostalgia for Maria and all that is familiar in Moscow.

"A gentleman would also introduce a lady to a visitor," she chides.

The boy with the run-of-the-mill ears takes over. "This is the new doctor." He extends an upward palm toward me, and then he gestures to the girl. "And this is Anastasia."

The girl gives a theatrical curtsy. "Anastasia Antonovna Maximova."

"Doctor Rozhdestvensky." I bestow a deep nod of my head.

Auntie Elizaveta emerges from the other side of the curtain, scowling as though she has a bug up her ass.

The three children scurry from behind the counter like spiders, all legs and arms and elbows and knees. They cluster together just behind me.

As Elizaveta steps up to the counter, I note the bobbing of her large abdomen and her ashen complexion. Her lips, which I had initially assumed were thin with displeasure, are in reality almost bloodless. I've tapped too many abdomens not to recognize heart failure. But Elizaveta Vorontsova's problems aren't my problems, I tell myself. And they never will be.

"I'd like to purchase a straight razor."

"A what?" she asks.

It dawns on me that Anton and I are probably the only men in the village lacking full beards. I mimic the use of a straight razor against my cheek.

"Don't have those. But Feodor will get you one on his next trip to Sukanovo."

I have no inkling what or where Sukanovo is. "Also, I need a cheap pair of leather gloves."

"Cheap?"

I refrain from slapping my forehead. Of course, to a peasant, nothing is cheap. "Not fancy. Plain leather gloves for work."

She retrieves a pair from the shelf behind her. "Seventy kopeks. Pay for the beard-knife when you pick it up." She holds out her palm. The tips of her fingers are an unhealthy blue. I speculate that Auntie Elizaveta will be dead long before her nephew reaches manhood.

As I turn from the counter, the pointy-eared boy says, "I'm Platon Vorontsov. This is Anastasia Antonovna Maximova."

The girl's fist punches his upper arm. "I already introduced myself."

"I'm acquainted with Mademoiselle Maximova's father." My use of the French term receives the expected giggles.

Platon indicates the other boy. "That's Filip Zhemchuzhnikov."

"You're related to Feodor Zhemchuzhnikov?"

"My uncle."

"Those three are stuck together tighter than bark to a tree. Just like me, my sister, and Feodor at their age." Elizaveta's brown eyes are softly muted for a speck of a moment before she retreats to the back room.

As I wrap my muffler about my neck, Platon says to the Zhemchuzhnikov boy, "Come on, let's figure out where to put those steps." One of his legs bounces feverishly.

Filip Zhemchuzhnikov groans. "You dream up more work to do than anybody."

"You're building steps?" I ask.

"This spring, we'll cut them into the hill," Platon explains, "so next winter when we sled, it's easier to climb back up."

"Don't forget you need to split wood today," his aunt's voice resonates from the back room.

"Doctor," Anastasia says, "could you come to the orphanage? The Sisters want to meet you."

The Sisters already know of my arrival? Gossip must be the lifeblood of this barren hellhole.

"I'll do my best to stop by." Again, no commitments. I nod my goodbye and return to the frozen outside.

As I recover from a coughing seizure, a woman steps up to me. She's bundled from head to toe except for her face, which is as wrinkled as a raisin.

"You the new doctor? Come with me." She gestures with her fingerless gloves. "My baby's dying."

CHAPTER 46

December
1866

I BEND LOW to follow the woman through the squatty door of her izba, where I'm greeted by the indignant cluck of a hen. We're in a windowless, dirt-floor vestibule that stretches the meager width of the hut. As my eyes adjust to what little light slithers between the ill-fitting logs of the walls, I realize the hen is just one of several, along with a couple of geese and a grunting sow with a passel of little ones. The smell of fresh manure is unmistakable, and unless my nose deceives me, human waste is also part of the aroma.

The woman clears a path through the menagerie of critters. Holding my breath, I trail her the few steps required to cross the unheated entryway. The woman swings open a second plank door hinged on a wooden peg. A dusty sheepskin lines the inside of the doorway in an attempt to block the cold. I hope it thwarts the stink as well.

But the miserable inner room has a composite smell of its own. Smoke. Rancid grease. Vinegar. Unwashed clothes. The stench of humanity.

I'd guess the hut to be about five times the size of my hole-in-the-wall Moscow room, and the massive clay stove takes up a good portion of that space. The single room serves as kitchen, bedroom, and work and living area. It's alive with the motion and voices of at least a dozen people, half of them small children.

So, Andrey, your talent for failure has led to this.

Without undue preliminaries such as introductions, the woman directs me, "Over here." As she tromps across the dirt floor, a toddler teeters up to her, its arms extended. "Get away with you," she mutters, bestowing the kid with a glancing blow of her foot.

She leads me to a creative contraption, a cradle lined with moldy straw and hanging from ropes looped over a rafter. Inside is a baby bound from head to toe in grimy linens, as rigid as one of Pirogov's plaster of Paris casts. Only the child's face—eyes closed, mouth slack—is visible.

"He just lies there doing nothing. Hardly even wants to eat." She jabs her hands onto her hips as if her sick child is nothing more than an intolerable nuisance.

"Please remove the"—wrappings? verminous rags?—"the swaddling, so I can examine the baby," I request.

The woman's jagged, filth-blackened fingernails begin the lengthy process of unfurling the layers of linen while I scan the gloom. The only source of light comes from a single ice-glazed window. "I need more light so I can examine the child."

"Pyotr, burn a splinter," she calls to a pale, sunken-chested boy around ten years of age, who's perched on the edge of the table.

Pyotr removes his finger from his nose, lowers his rag-encased feet to the dirt floor, and sets fire to a single splinter hanging from a rafter.

After the woman tosses the baby's grimy linen onto the dirt floor, she looks about and hollers, "Over here, Pyotr, where it can do some good!"

The half-wit plods over with the splinter. His hair is as greasy as tallow, and his face is smudged with the same soot that covers everything. "I'm Dmitry," he tells the woman, presumably his mother.

The woman grunts and casts an embarrassed glance my way. "I have so many, you understand," she explains through the dark nubs of her teeth.

No words can describe the desolation I feel at this moment.

Heat rolls from the huge clay stove, transforming my coat's ice pellets into steam. Sweat accumulates around my collar and trickles down my back. I unbutton my coat but leave it on; there isn't a soot-free surface on which to place it. I'm already picturing myself returning to the estate house, freezing naked outside the door after divesting myself of all my clothes, the bedbugs, and the lice.

"When was this baby born?" I don't bother to ask the tiny boy's name. If the mother is unconcerned about her children's names, why should I care?

"In the summer."

Pyotr/Dmitry's added light supplies as much illumination as a single match. I look at the baby's pus-rimmed eyes, the distended abdomen, the skeletal arms and legs, and the wispy hair on a head that's oversized for its body. "So he's about half a year old?"

She peers at me as if I'm as thick in the head as Pyotr/Dmitry. "Naw. One year and a half."

I swallow back my horrified response and ask instead, "Is the baby still receiving breast milk?"

"Naw. Dried up during the Time of Suffering."

I don't know when or what the Time of Suffering was, but I guess it to be quite awhile ago. "What are you feeding him?"

"Gruel with a nip of hemp oil, but he'll hardly eat any of it."

"He needs the nutrition of milk. Have you some milk?"

"Naw. Had to sell one cow to pay the taxes. The other cow is between calves. No milk for at least two months."

"So this baby won't have any milk until March?"

"Naw. Then Lent's upon us. No milk for any us."

Speechless, I look at the woman. At the baby. At Pyotr/Dmitry. At the rough-hewn man at the table who's pulling up his shirt to scratch his belly. At the six inquisitive young faces lined up just beyond the dull light of the burning splinter. None of these people will receive any dairy nutrition until after Easter.

"What about eggs? Have you some eggs?"

"Two or three a week." In response to my mute stare, she adds, "It's winter."

Ah, right. Winter. Hens prefer to drop their eggs on warm, sun-filled days. "Soft cook an egg every day and mix it with the baby's gruel."

The words wash over the family as if I'd never spoken.

I try again, this time letting my voice resonate: *Don't question my orders.* "An egg every day. Also, find some milk to give him."

The man with the itchy belly responds with icy belligerence. "Can't give him what we don't have."

"You must. Or he's certain to die."

"Jesus took a forty-day fast." The rough old cob raises a dirty wooden cup to his lips, drains it, and burps.

I stare at the guy's furrowed forehead and wonder if there's any brain matter behind it. Then my blood begins to simmer. The sanctimonious Church, demanding sacrificial obedience while killing its congregation. "I repeat, without the nutrition of milk and eggs, he is certain to die this winter."

"Can't you do something for him?" the woman pleads. "I'd hate to lose a boy."

So the implication is that to lose a girl is no great catastrophe? "I have nothing to offer that will save him, other than my advice." I can't resist adding, "Your other option is to summon the priest. I'm sure that for a few kopeks, he'll furnish a prayer or two."

The man at the table responds, "We'll just have to believe in God's mercy."

I must get out of this stuffy, filthy, rancid room. Now.

"I wish I could do more." My perspiration-drenched clothes cling to my skin as I back away from the cradle.

"There's no cure for bad luck." The woman's shawl-draped shoulders shrug with fatalism. "We have to lose some. Otherwise there's not enough room in the izba for them all." She calls to one of the urchins, "Lena, get the doctor an onion."

I must credit the family for their integrity. They compensate me for my time despite my inability to help the baby. To be honest, even the milk and eggs wouldn't have helped him. The rich food would have provoked diarrhea, which would have pushed his tiny body over the brink. The child is sure to die within the next couple of days.

AT THE DINNER table, Anton snaps out his snow-white napkin and tucks it into his collar. "Dasha told me you were treated to an intimate view of peasant life. Many thanks, by the way, for the onion." He winks.

"I don't believe I've ever seen a lower, more beastly set of people." My lip curls. "And I'm speaking of both genders."

"Don't be too hard on them. In point of fact, until five years ago, they were regarded as little more than beasts of burden. Their changeover will require decades. Perhaps generations."

Suddenly it dawns on me that until emancipation, Dasha had been a serf, one of those "beastly people." *Andrey, you're such a shithead!* I quickly change topics. "I encountered Anastasia at the Mercantile."

With a daffy grin pasted on his face, Anton bobs his head up and down as if he is expecting more from me. Eventually it strikes me that, yes, of course he is. He's a father.

"I must say, she is a lovely girl, both to look at and to talk with."

Anton continues his giddy head bouncing, nearly a vertical quiver now.

I add, "Very polite. And quite articulate."

Anton puffs like a tom turkey. "I tutored her and Dasha at the same time."

Following the meal, Dasha clears the table of plates and returns to the dining room carrying a silver pedestal candy dish, atop which are three dark mounds. As she leans over to place the dish in the center of the table, Anton gives her bottom a risqué pat.

I'm taken aback by the familiarity between the couple. Although they are obviously intimate with one another, such playfulness in the presence of other people transgresses the limits of propriety. But my gut instinct is that Anton Stepanovich Maximov, blessed with a ridiculous amount of charm, has spent much of his life beyond the rules of propriety.

Anton contemplatively scratches his chin and pursues the topic of his daughter.

"I'd really like to find an instructor for Anastasia's voice. She sings like an angel." He looks to Dasha for verification.

"Antoshka's not exaggerating. She sings sweeter than wine."

My ears hone in on the word *wine*.

Dasha gives the candy dish a small push in my direction, bidding me to take one of the brown globs.

"She belongs on the stage." The proud papa raises his hands helplessly, bewildered as to how any offspring from his loins could possess such a rare and extraordinary talent. "Trouble is, the nearest voice instructor is in Tambov, the provincial capital. Anastasia would have to attend boarding school there. Don't know that I can bear to part with her."

"Perhaps she can be persuaded to give us a concert sometime," I suggest.

Dasha quickly agrees. "That would be lovely." She scoots the candy dish closer to me, her eyebrows arching with encouragement. To end her torture, I select one of the lumps. In a flash, she puts one in front of Anton and snatches the remaining one for herself.

My thumb and forefinger lift the brown nugget to eye level. "I hate to show my ignorance, but what is this?"

"A bonbon," Dasha says.

"A what?"

Anton explains, "My sister, the nun, has a herd of Russian Swiss cattle, which produces more milk than even the orphanage can consume. Have you ever had chocolate, Andrey?"

"Once, in Moscow. I found it to be overrated."

"Precisely. My sister is experimenting with the addition of milk to reduce its bitterness."

"We agreed to be her tasters." Dasha runs her tongue around her lips.

I take a nibble from the bonbon. "Say! This is scrumptious!"

The three of us spend a delectable moment in silent chewing.

"At the risk of being too blunt, I couldn't help but notice your daughter's arm." I hoist the final morsel of bonbon into my mouth.

"Just born that way," Anton mumbles through chocolate and nuts. "Her arm is half the length and thickness of a normal limb. As useless as a broken wing."

"You know, I saw an arm like that once before, while employed at the Imperial Foundling Home."

"Oh? You worked at the Foundling Home? Then you know all about the diseases in an orphanage!" Anton's palm smacks the table, as though it went without saying that I'd be overjoyed to spend my future tending to the ailments at the orphanage.

I keep the topic where it belongs. "Speaking of Anastasia, I must give her bedroom back. She'll expect it when she visits here."

"Then where would you stay?" Anton thumps his fingertips against his forehead as though the answer is obvious. "But of course! You made arrangements today to board with that peasant family."

I give my host a very evil eye. "Actually, I was wondering about one of the cottages, your former serfs' quarters."

"I won't hear of it. You must stay here in the estate house."

"But the rooms downstairs are all taken, and it's pointless to heat the upstairs just for me. I can live quite contentedly in a single room. And I can chop my own firewood for exercise."

And if I chance upon some vodka, I can drink in private to my heart's content.

Eventually Anton agrees, on two conditions. First, I must share my meals with them. "Having you here is like a breath of fresh air."

"And the second condition?"

"Take the cat with you."

"Aw, Antoshka." Dasha droops like a butterfly whose wings have been pulled off. "It does no harm for Russell to stay here."

"I don't want the cat in bed with me. Or scratching at my bedroom door."

"But . . . ," Dasha bleats.

"I said *no*, Dasha. Andrey is welcome to bring the cat with him when he visits, but I won't have it living in this house."

I hold my hand up to stop the squabble. "I agree completely with you, Anton. He's my cat, and I take responsibility for him."

Dasha slouches against the lyre-back chair and stares at her lap.

I seek a new subject. "How do you two occupy yourselves in the evenings?"

Anton answers, "When Anastasia is here, we usually play board games."

"Do you ever play cards?" My gaze roves from Anton to Dasha, who doesn't look up from her pout, and back to Anton.

He replies, "I've been known to shuffle a few decks."

"Which game do you prefer?"

He lifts a casual hand off the tabletop. "No real preference."

"Have you played skat?"

"Sure. Dasha hasn't, but we can teach her. It will give her a chance to practice arithmetic. But no betting. Not allowed in this house."

I retrieve the dog-eared deck from my suitcase. With my first shuffle, a scrap of yellowed paper falls from between the cards. I pick it up from the table.

Maria's Moscow address. The one she scribbled for me when I left Simferopol, eleven years ago.

A whisper of melancholy quivers in my chest.

CHAPTER 47

January
1867

I GIVE ONE of the former serf cottages an exhaustive cleaning and borrow a few household items (including a pillow) from Dasha. Except for a bed and an outmoded wash basin hauled down from Anton's attic, the furniture is spartan, handhewn, and replete with splinters. A piddling amount of sunlight enters through the solitary window. All in all, though, the single-room cottage is reminiscent of my Moscow cubbyhole, so I'm content with my surroundings.

Dasha overfills my stomach three times a day. I awake each morning with a furball pressed against the small of my back, as well as a profound feeling of isolation. Where's my career? Where are my Moscow friends? Where's my comfortable chair at the sisters' apartment? Where are all the places Maria and I went, all the things we did?

Sometimes I roll over and philosophize with the cat. "I do everything in my power to avoid change. So why does my life slip and slide all over Russia?"

His comeback is a yawn that threatens to dislodge his jaw.

"And on a less philosophical level—why can't you sleep in the barn with the other cats?"

He curls into a self-assured circle.

"One of these mornings, I'm going to give you a boot out the door that will carry you all the way to Moscow."

This threat elicits no response. The cat merely follows me to the estate house for a breakfast of liver paté, after which he naps. Then he demands attention from Dasha. Then he sinks into another nap.

DURING THE THIRD week of the new year, Anton receives a response from Victor Vladimirovich Rusakov. In a brief note delivered via messenger, Rusakov says he'll visit Anton and me on Friday, weather permitting.

I ask Anton, "And how will he help me get to Petrovka?"

He explains that Victor grew up on a nearby estate and that the two families were close friends. "He and I were playmates, of a sort. As a young man, Victor developed a fanatical passion for the equality of human rights. When the serfs were emancipated six years ago, Victor obtained the newly created position of local peace mediator, which means he guides both the former serfs and their former owners through the post-emancipation negotiations. It's a tortuous, anger-charged process. Everyone, whether nobleman or peasant, is convinced he's being cheated out of what is rightfully his."

"Sounds like a miserable way to earn a living."

"In more ways than one. He still resides on his family's estate with his wife and son, but he's rarely home. Not only does he cover a large territory, but he's constantly at meetings in Tambov. Because of that, he has a very long reach. He's on a first-name basis with the highest of the high hats in the provincial government. If there's a way to maneuver through the bureaucratic behemoth, Victor will get it done."

If there's a way. A dissonant chord resonates deep in my marrow.

RUSAKOV TURNS OUT to be a good listener, a skill that I assume he honed as a mediator between the peasants and their previous masters. Rusakov, Anton, and I sit in the parlor while I recount the enfeebled Lieutenant General Tropinin's promise and the resulting mishap.

Rusakov sinks back in the wing chair and contemplatively strokes his well-kept beard. "Next week I'm attending a provincial assembly meeting in Tambov. I'll explain your predicament to the Zemstvo Executive Board. Several factors are in your favor. First, once the mistake is called to the attention of the Executive Board, they won't want to waste time and resources overseeing a physician in this tiny corner of the province. Second, our district seat, Sukhanovo, will surely balk at funding two physicians, one of which is located in the hinterland. Third, Petrovka is undoubtedly clamoring for its own zemstvo physician."

Rusakov holds up a cautionary index finger. "But here's what we're up against. The mills of Slav officialdom turn slowly at best. Often, they won't turn at all without greasing. Have you any rubles you can part with?"

I shake my head. "I've been without income for seven months."

Rusakov levels his eyes at me, a gesture that I suppose was also polished during his mediation work. "Are you absolutely certain you want to go to Petrovka? If you stay here, you're just a half day's jaunt from Sukhanovo, where you can partake of culture, make purchases, have intellectual discussions with your fellow physicians, and if you're so inclined, find a pleasant woman."

"I'm completely certain."

"Then look at it this way. A dozen little villages just like Petrovo are within a two-hour ride from here. The peasants pass from birth to sickness to death without any contact with a medical person. Tending to Petrovo and its neighboring villages on the outskirts of the district will be a low, or possibly nonexistent, priority for the zemstvo physician in Sukhanovo. You are our peasants' only prospect for hope. I know Petrovo looks like a sad little crossroads. But think of the impact you can have on the lives here. And subsequently, on the lives of future generations."

Rusakov is nowhere near finished, but my head is already shaking so hard, it rattles.

"Hear me out," he insists. "Your patient load here would be immeasurably lighter compared with Petrovka. And you'll spend less time on the road than you would if you were the sole medical benefactor for the entire district of Petrovka. That means less time fighting winter blizzards and summer dust."

"No. I can't. I'm not cut out for a life so completely . . ." *Think of a polite word, Andrey.* "So completely rural."

Rusakov sighs. "I'll talk to the necessary people. But if you change your mind, get word to me. It could very well be that God dropped you off in our little corner of the world as a gift both to us and to you."

I steady my eyes to keep them from rolling in derision. God will just have to find another gift for this dismal cranny. "I won't change my mind. The people here are . . . they're . . ." How to finish? I'm at a loss.

"I know. I agree," Victor says, as if I had made an outstandingly perceptive observation. "They're obtuse, superstitious, ill-mannered, and dirty. Their heads seem as empty as their pockets. And that's exactly why they need us."

Us? I snicker silently. Rusakov is a madman if he thinks I'll squander the rest of my life in this Hell on earth.

"Keep in mind, Andrey Yevgrafovich, that although you'll be headquartered in the district capital of Petrovka, the outlying villages you'll serve aren't a whit better than what you see here."

We're interrupted by the cat, who saunters into the parlor, settles himself into a sitting position, and stares up at me, ready to pounce. I call for Dasha. She scoops Russell into her arms and heads toward the kitchen, informing him in no uncertain terms that people's laps are a no-no when company is present.

I use the cat's interruption to shift topics. "Anton tells me your position requires quite a bit of travel."

"Indeed. It's no small task to keep almost six thousand residents at peace when all of them, the nobility and their former serfs alike, feel certain they've been swindled."

"Swindled in what way?"

Anton springs from his chair. "I think now would be a good time for some tea cakes."

"I'll keep it short," Rusakov promises me as Anton heads toward the kitchen. "Obviously, both the peasants and the landowners need land in order to survive. My job is to see to it that the land is divided fairly."

"That sounds like a heavy mantle to bear."

"The estate owners would rise in revolt if forced to give their land—the very land their noble forefathers acquired through their sweat, their rubles, and their loyalty to the Sovereign—scot-free to the emancipated peasantry. However, the State Treasury can't afford to indemnify the landowners, impoverished as it is by that misbegotten war in the Crimea."

I nod. How well I understand that.

"The peasants, meanwhile, have worked the land since time immemorial and consider themselves inseparable from it. And in truth, they are. Without land, they'd perish."

"Quite a quandary."

"Indeed. Once the landowner and the peasants strike a *fair* agreement, the government reimburses the former serf owner for his land by giving him government bonds. The peasants make payments to the government for the land that's now legally theirs. And from those rubles, the government makes good on the bonds it issued the original landowners."

When Dasha enters the room carrying a full serving tray, Anton is directly behind her. And trailing them is a gray cat, which, with feline obstinacy, makes a beeline for my lap.

After Anton presents Victor and me with tea, sugar cubes, and bite-size tea cakes, he says, "It's largely because of this gentleman's power of persuasion that our region didn't erupt in riots and insurrections during the transition. Plus, he doesn't burden the peasants with paperwork or formalities."

Victor's head rears back in surprise. "I appreciate hearing that, Anton."

Dasha sets her tray on the sideboard and marches toward me, her hands ready to nab Russell from my lap. But I wave her away. If locked in another room or thrown outside, the cat would just scratch and howl and make everyone miserable. Best to confine the torture to one person. I scoot to one side of the chair's cushion and place the cat lengthwise beside my thigh. Russell closes his eyes, content with his position in life.

"I'm still unclear about something," I confess. "What's your relationship, Anton, to the villagers?"

Anton settles back into his chair. "They were my father's serfs until they were emancipated. When he died, my siblings placed management of the estate in my hands, of all the unlikely places. I chose to treat the freed serfs like sharecroppers. Therefore, they work the land that has remained part of the Maximov estate following emancipation. My family gets a portion of that crop, and the peasants keep the remainder." He slips a sugar crystal between his teeth and sips his tea.

"And the peasants also till the land they were allotted as part of their emancipation, the land they're making payments on?"

"Correct. They keep the whole of their crop from those parcels of land."

"That's hardly true, Anton," interjects Victor. "They're neck-deep in debt to the government. Virtually their entire crop income goes toward making their land payment."

Anton's eyes narrow. "Victor, you know that's an exaggeration."

I feel heat gathering under both men's collars. "Excuse me if I'm butting my nose in where it doesn't belong, but Anton, between your government bonds and your sharecropped land, your estate is financially sound, correct?"

The angles of Anton's jaw tense. "My father, my father's father, his father, etcetera—all of them paid hard-earned rubles for Petrovo's serfs. When the Tsar waved his magic wand, *poof!* Those assets were wiped off our balance sheets. That's just one financial blow Petrovo took. Want to hear the others?"

Even I can hear the hesitation in my voice as I say, "Of course."

"On the land that remains in the estate, I now have to share my crop with the peasants who till my soil, whereas before emancipation, that labor was essentially free. Keep in mind that the estate lost a full third of its land to the freed serfs. And all I have to show for that land is a paper promise that the government will compensate me for the loss in some distant year." His thumb drums the arm of his chair. "Perhaps I shouldn't mention it in your presence as a zemstvo employee, but I now also have zemstvo taxes to pay."

Victor resumes his role as neutral peacemaker. "So you can see, Andrey, why many estate owners chose to sell all their remaining land and their promissory notes outright and move to the cities. By the way," Victor turns to Anton, "someone made an offer on our estate, and Father actually accepted it."

The conversation misses a beat before Anton asks, "So that's the end of it?" All acrimony seems to have been blown out of him.

"Actually, the pieces have fallen into place nicely. I had planned to move my family off the estate anyway. I simply can't make ends meet on the pittance paid to peace mediators. I've accepted a provincial position in Tambov, and we'll live there." Victor taps his forehead, as if wondering what had become of his brain. "I hope I'm up to the challenge of working with those knucklehead bureaucrats in Tambov. At least the peasants are accustomed to working together on public affairs in their villages. They understand give and take, compromise, and lines of authority."

Anton winks at me. "At heart, Victor's actually a peasant."

"Will your new job still involve emancipation issues?" I ask.

"Oh, yes. I can't bail out now. In Moscow, you didn't feel the effect of emancipation to the degree we did in the countryside. Our old world was turned upside down, and a new era has begun. I want to ensure that era is just and equitable."

CHAPTER 48

February
1867

I SUSPECT SEVERAL weeks will pass before I receive a response from Victor Rusakov. The same goes for a swallow of vodka. I receive a letter from Colya, however, and Maria sends weekly, voluminous letters, with a note from Vasilisa squeezed into the same envelope. The newsy dispatches are enjoyable, but they leave me with an ache to spend an evening together as a foursome in the sisters' apartment.

I set about the task of occupying my time. I read at least one of Anton's books every week and discover the activity brings me a great deal of solace. Anton teaches me the fundamentals of billiards, and I rather enjoy the genial man-to-man competition. Occasionally Anton's sister Elena visits from the orphanage. Not only is she a delight to be around, but her skill at billiards rivals Anton's.

I also spend considerable time plotting ways to avoid the priest, who never tires of stopping by the estate house in pursuit of meeting the new doctor. Exercise is plentiful thanks to chopping firewood, plus walks to the village and the orphanage.

My ice-bound evenings are filled with Anton, Dasha, or Anastasia. Russell keeps an eye on things from the rug in front of the fireplace, the tip of his tail flicking with approval. The evenings filled with cards and board games are almost as enjoyable as those with the two sisters in Moscow. Almost.

I spend many hours in the village, where some peasant is always in need of care. I leave the squatty huts with payment in kind: pickled cucumbers, loaves of rye bread, dried peas, garlic cloves, honey.

On occasion, Platon accompanies me. The boy stands quietly to one side, silent except for his perpetually bouncing leg, an outlet for his boundless energy. He hands me instruments when instructed, and he helps with bandaging. On our way back to the Mercantile, Platon quizzes me about the whys and wherefores of what we've just seen and done. The boy has an irrepressible curiosity. It leaves me chagrined: Platon is enthused about medicine in a way I never have been. But then again, Platon is enthused about life in a way I never have been.

The orphanage perches on a bluff overlooking the river, a half mile or so east of the village. During my trek, I'm engulfed in the deep silence of the snow-shrouded blackland prairie. Not a door slams. Not a peddler hawks. Not a train whistles.

At the orphanage, I treat the occasional sick or injured child. I also taste test the chocolate candies Anton's sister makes, try my hand at the pottery wheel, and describe to the children the purpose of each instrument in my black bag. Unlike the mangy village children, the orphans are clean and exposed to at least a rudimentary education.

There's one fly in the ointment regarding the orphanage. The nuns. Well, not the nuns per se, but their drab brown habits and the crosses hanging from their necks. They keep my memories of the war close at hand.

Nevertheless, my nightmares have dwindled to one every week or two. Maybe the fresh air acts as a tonic for soothing my anxieties. Or maybe the exertion of walking and splitting wood settles me in for a good night's sleep. Or, most likely, my relentless worries about getting to Petrovka leave me no time for dark ruminations about the past. Thus, at the top of my meager list of regular self-imposed duties, I stop by the Mercantile as often as possible, antsy for a letter from Rusakov.

AT BREAKFAST ONE Siberian-cold morning, Dasha announces that I am in horrific need of a haircut, and that this morning would be a dandy time to do it. She positions one of the old ladder-back chairs in the middle of the kitchen floor. The room is delectably warm, and as she slides the comb through my hair, I'm almost as cozy as when the sisters pampered me at Christmas. But not quite. Those steamy face towels were sublime.

Dasha shares several of Maria's traits. Besides her pear shape, she's also a chatterbox. "No news yet from Victor Vladimirovich Rusakov?"

"No. But I expect wading through the bureaucracy will take awhile."

"Then the best thing you can do is enjoy the spare time God has given you. Not a thing can be done to speed up the government. Soon enough your nose will be to the grindstone again."

"A valid point. But I do worry that I'm a burden. I wish I could compensate you and Anton in some way."

"Don't give it another thought. During the endless winter, it's nice to have another person in this big house. If it weren't for you, I wouldn't know how to play skat. I can tell Antoshka enjoys the challenge of it."

"Well, I'm glad I brought at least one thing of value into your household." I really wish she'd be quiet so I can relish the comb skimming across my scalp.

"You don't talk much about your life," she probes.

True enough. Only one person knows the story of my life, and even she knows only bits and pieces.

Dasha's scissors point toward my hand resting atop the cat. "That scar, did you get that during the war?"

"No. Merely a burn from a childhood mishap." I expertly shift the topic off myself. "Is there anyone in the village who served in the war?"

"Oh, no. Those who were conscripted never returned. For a peasant, military service is a life sentence."

Yeah, for me, too.

She announces that my hair again looks respectable, and I gather up my medical bag and head to the village.

DESPITE MY EARNEST attempt to follow Dasha's advice to "enjoy the spare time God has given," my nerves are frayed from fretting over my dwindling supply of rubles. Not to mention, I'm short on bismuth, liniment, and tincture of iodine and completely out of camphor and bandaging. And I'll be damned if I'll spend my few remaining rubles on medicine for the peasants.

In late February, I help the newest daughter-in-law of the Karpov family with the difficult delivery of her first baby. I'm a far more convenient choice than fetching the midwife, who not only lives an hour's ride away but also requires steep compensation. I'm not surprised to find myself in the bathhouse with four female members of the Karpov family. I've learned during my not-brief-enough stay in Petrovo that the bathhouse is the preferred location to give birth. The act of birthing and the newborn itself are both impure and, according to peasant folklore, would taint the izba.

When the young Karpova woman successfully brings forth a son, the four women cross and recross themselves, thanking God for His goodness. They assure me, "It's God's will that you came to our village." They swaddle the newborn, prop the exhausted new mother between them, and head for the izba so that the baby's father can inspect him. I trail after them, bending nearly in half to avoid the purple onions hanging from the izba's beam.

"A boy!" The baby's grandfather has a long, skinny face with an overbite that would rival a turtle's. "Good job, Slava!"

While the men in the household offer congratulatory slaps on the new father's shoulder, the women focus their attention on the elderly matriarch. She holds the infant near the mouth of the ponderous clay stove and sprinkles his bald head with ashes, beseeching the family's ancestors to grant him their protection.

With the newborn's future secure in his grandmother's hands, the father, grandfather, and two uncles (all of whom share the turtle overbite) pass the celebratory bottle around the rough-hewn table. The bottle slides across the boards to one of the uncles, who wipes a drip from his nose onto his shirtsleeve, its material faded from much sun and lye soap. He proceeds to take a drink, then wipes the mouth of the bottle with the same shirtsleeve. The uncle offers the bottle to me.

The entirety of my body throbs for the burning liquid. As always, the craving for vodka gnaws at me like the giant rats in Moscow's slums. Fortunately, the shirtsleeve-cleansing endows me with the willpower to resist.

It's been two months since I last tossed back any vodka. Anton assures me that in another month or two, the urge will lose its fierceness. I have my doubts, but at least I've successfully weathered today's opportunity.

The baby's grandmother compensates me with beet soup for my services. "Bring back the empty crock," she whistles through her remaining teeth.

I head to the Mercantile to check my mail yet again. The day is a breathtaking juxtaposition of a pristine blue sky above a horizon of purest white. How amazing that such lovely surroundings are home to such gray, dull, bowed people, which to my way of thinking includes everyone in Petrovo over the age of twenty. The women are bulky, dour creatures, and their husbands are built of burly beards and leathery sinews. Once or twice a year, when the occasional wanderlust infiltrates their leaden existence, they'll hitch the wagon for a half-day outing in the district capital of Sukhanovo. Neither the men nor the women exhibit much insight into their past or present, or much vision regarding their future. Petrovo is a village without hope.

Yet my gut feeling is that if Maria were in my shoes, she'd somehow intuit how to elevate the boorish lives of these pitiable clods. *Just be glad, Maria, that you're not in this inescapable pit of squalor. The wretchedness would tax even your good cheer.*

Inside the Mercantile, Filip Zhemchuzhnikov, Platon, and Anastasia are seated at one of the three tables. Elizaveta is on a stool behind the counter, knocking the abacus beads to and fro. Wordlessly, she hands me the estate's mail. I thumb through it: a copy of the *Moscow News*, a letter to Anton from his sister in St. Petersburg. And finally, a letter from Victor Rusakov!

CHAPTER 49

February

1867

MY LEGS STRETCH their length as I race to the shaft of light from the solitary window. Gripping the envelope like a drowning man clutches the riverbank, I rip open the seal.

> Greetings, Andrey Yevgrafovich.
>
> I fear I have little to report in the way of progress. Every authority I spoke with at both the district and the provincial levels said the predicament is beyond his jurisdiction. The next person with whom I must confer is currently away on official business in St. Petersburg and won't return for several weeks.

My arm drops limply to my side, and I stare out the window at the forlorn water well in the middle of the forlorn village.

God dropped you off in our little corner of the world as a gift to both us and you. Rusakov's words during our meeting planted seeds of doubt in me. Those seeds are now taking root, leaving me to wonder exactly how much effort Rusakov is putting into my relocation. Increasingly, I feel like a dog that won't stop gnawing on a bone with no meat on it.

Saints above, Andrey, how did your life's path take such a fork?

Because I bungled it. I had a purposeful job. Spare rubles. Friends.

Now I'm living in a nightmare.

So what are my options?

One. Continue down the impenetrable path of trying to get to Petrovka.

Two. Hightail it back to Moscow and dump the cat on Maria's lap.

Three. Weigh myself down with a sack of rocks and jump off the bridge. Except I'd have to wait until spring, when the river thaws.

Ass-deep in self-pity, I run my fingers through my hair, longing to get fully stewed tonight. Alcohol not being an option, however, I'll pour all my doubts and desperation into a letter to Maria.

In the meantime, I tug the corners of my lips into a smile. "Good afternoon, *les trois mousquetaires!*" Last week, I assigned the nickname to the inseparable threesome. Of course, the reference to the French novel had required a bit of explaining on my part, but the trio was delighted by the allusion.

The Moscow newspaper is spread out between them. Filip's and Anastasia's reading skills are on an equal footing, Filip being raised in the village's only literate household. Platon lags considerably behind, having only his two chums to teach him. The threesome commonly asks me to decipher words in the newspaper, which invariably unleashes a torrent of questions from Platon.

I lower myself onto a wobbly, three-legged stool. Platon studies my lips as I pronounce and explain each multisyllable word. Then the youngster positions his deep-set eyes close to the newsprint to silently assimilate the combination of letters and sounds and meanings.

After the burdensome words are unraveled, Platon says, "An article in last week's paper said that a sta . . . a sta . . . anyway, someone important guessed there's eighty million people in Russia. How do you write a number that big?"

I fish the pencil stub from my medical bag and write the figure in the margin of the newspaper. Platon is awestruck. "Seven zeros? Not possible!"

I assure him that it is indeed possible. "Eighty million. Which is also the number of questions you ask."

The boy takes the teasing in stride, and I write *statistician* in the newsprint's white space. "Is this the person who estimated the number?"

Platon's head bobs up and down, his pointed ears at full attention as usual.

"Stat-i-stish-uhn," I pronounce. "It's a person who analyzes numbers and information and makes predictions about the future."

"Like when we have a starry night at the New Year, and it means we'll have lots of lambs born in the spring?"

"Not exactly. A statistician learns his trade at a university."

"Oh. University." The boyishly expectant face plummets into solemn hopelessness. Platon's eyes dart toward his auntie Elizaveta, then back to the penciled *statistician*. The meaning of his unintentional pantomime is obvious. Platon has a better chance of sprouting wings and flying to the moon than attending a university. Such a shame. The boy has a sharp mind that's open, inquisitive, and direct. He's the complete antithesis of me.

Platon's disappointment over his nil prospects of receiving an education quickly dissipates. Or is purposefully pushed aside. "Hey, Doctor Rozhdestvensky, do you ever catch crayfish?"

"Crayfish? I did when I was your age."

"We're having a crayfish-catching contest this summer." His leg bounces with enthusiasm. "We have the location and the rules and everything figured out. We'll even have prizes."

"Prizes?"

"From the attic at the estate house," Anastasia explains as she twirls a dark curl around her index finger. "There are games and toys from when Father and Sister Elena were young. I'm sure he'll let us use them as prizes."

"We're going there now," Filip says to me. "Come with us."

"Confession first." The voice is female and stern and originates from behind the counter.

Platon's eyelids lower. "I'll meet you there when I'm finished with confession."

Filip hoots. "Ha! With your sins, you'll be there until tomorrow." Filip gives his friend a playful but manly fist jab to the shoulder. Platon shoves back as Anastasia rolls her eyes at the boyish behavior.

"How about this idea?" I suggest. "After confession, come to the estate house, and les trois mousquetaires can search the attic. I'll ask Dasha to make supper for all of us. Then Platon and Filip, you can spend the night in the cottage with me."

"Wow!"

"That will be so much fun!"

"Make sure you attend the Divine Liturgy tomorrow morning," tolls the familiar voice behind the abacus.

"I will," Platon promises.

"This evening, we'll play some games," I suggest. Something that will stimulate Platon's young mind.

Filip and Anastasia race from the Mercantile. Even as Platon trudges off to atone for his sins, he holds himself as straight as a fencepost. A real fencepost, not one of Petrovo's battered ones.

As I rub my thumb across the letter I hold in my lap, I glance at my other hand resting on the table, involuntarily encircling an imaginary glass of vodka. Panic swells inside me. It's the same morose fear that strangled me in the Crimea, the terror that I'm trapped here for the whole of eternity. I clench my fist, my teeth, my eyelids. My chest feels as though it's about to explode. I'm a prisoner in the wretched depths of Russia's backcountry.

I pry my eyes open. If I continue to wallow in a pit of gloom, I'll lose my mind.

Instead, I reflect on my evening and my houseguests. Three young, bright minds suffocating in the obscurity of Petrovo. But Anton will see to it that his beautiful daughter has the option of a life far more expansive than Petrovo. Zhemchuzhnikov is destined to work in the fields the rest of his life, but he seems utterly content with this prospect.

Yet what about Platon, with his wiry energy, watchful eyes, and eighty million questions? It's the middle of winter, and he's already planning a summer crayfish contest. Most boys his age slide through the day with nary a thought for tomorrow, let alone half a year from now. Given a chance, Platon would tower above the intellectual level of the gray peasant masses.

An idea has been festering for the past week, one that I need to broach with Elizaveta. Now is as good a time as any. If only she weren't so formidable! I'd sooner walk off a roof than confront that woman. I gather my medical bag, my crock of beet soup, and my courage and force my legs toward the counter.

"I hope you don't mind my inviting Platon to spend the night with me," I begin.

"Just make sure he gets to the church in the morning."

"I think he will enjoy this evening. Something new for him. He's a very inquisitive boy."

"He's a handful."

"Have you ever considered his attending school?"

The cold, hard look that settles on her face tells me that this subject has already been broached and that she's finished with it. "Did he talk to you about this? I told him, the answer will always be *no*."

"Don't blame Platon. He didn't speak with me about it. Not at all. It's just that he has such an active mind, he really needs schooling. Otherwise his mind will collapse from lack of use."

"Reading isn't worth an ox fart. Literate or illiterate, he'll remain behind the plough."

"That would be such a waste of his budding intellect. With an education, his horizons will extend as far as his ambition will take him."

"Can't afford to send him to school. He's just now at the age when he's finally some help to me."

"Certainly we can find a way to accomplish something this important."

To hoist herself off the stool, Elizaveta places a hand under her pendulous abdomen, much the way a very pregnant woman does. "Don't go raising his hopes." She turns away from me and begins flicking the back shelves with a homemade duster of rooster tail feathers. Her chest heaves for air from the simple exertion.

"Forgive me for being presumptive." I search for a smaller word. "I don't mean to pry where I shouldn't. But as a physician, I can't help but notice that a large amount of fluid, that is to say *water*, is in your abdomen. I mean, your belly. I'd be happy to examine you. Perhaps there's a treatment that can make you feel better."

"I feel well enough."

"Your belly has gradually gotten bigger over the past couple of years?"

"Yeah." She sidesteps to dust farther along the shelf.

"Did you have a bad accident at some point in your life?"

"Why do you ask that?"

"You have a limp. I wonder if it possibly has some bearing on the situation with your belly."

"A damaged knee. Never healed right. It's nothing." The set of her jaw seals the topic closed.

"What about a grave illness at some point?"

"I almost died once." Her tone is as bland as if she were announcing she's about to dig up some potatoes to toss in the soup pot.

"You almost died once?"

She hangs the feather duster on a nail in the wall and turns toward me. "I was fifteen. The village was starving that winter. All my family got the fever and flu. They got better. I didn't."

"How long were you sick?"

"Christmas until . . ." Elizaveta squints, looking into the past. "Until after Easter."

"So you had a snotty nose, coughing, chills. Anything else?"

"A rash."

"A rash. Where?"

"On my body."

"Where on your body?"

"First here." She points to her chest. "Then here." Her hand swivels around to her back. "And here." Her thighs.

Hundreds of orphans at the Foundling Home parade across my memory.

"You were very lucky you didn't die. Do you ever have pain in your chest?"

She shrugs. "Sometimes."

"As a youngster, you had a disease called scarlet fever. And believe it or not, the water in your belly is from the illness."

"What took so long?"

"The sickness damaged your heart. Now your heart has become so weak, it doesn't have the strength to push your blood through your body. And that's why you gasp for breath sometimes."

She shifts her weight. "You said maybe there's a cure."

"Not a cure. But, yes, there is a treatment that will make the swelling go away for a while, and you'll feel better."

"An herb of some sort?"

"It's a procedure, one that I've—"

"A procedure?"

"A treatment that I've done scores of times—"

"Scores?"

"Many, many, many times in Moscow. I push a needle through your skin and into your belly and take out the water."

Her eyelids pinch as she draws her head back in disbelief. "A sewing needle in my belly? That's crazy."

"It's like a large sewing needle, but its center is hollow. I poke it in your belly, and the water there flows out. I've done it so often that I can do it in my sleep. And you'll immediately feel good, like your old self."

She crosses her arms and flattens them tight against her chest. "I feel fine."

"Is that so? Then why did you dust only the two bottom shelves? Why not the top shelf? Is it because you haven't the strength to climb onto the stool? You're afraid you'll lose your balance?"

"Enough talk!" Her fist wallops the countertop. "No needles. And no school."

CHAPTER 50

March–April
1867

PLATON CAN'T SEE well. When deciphering words, the boy tilts forward until the tip of his nose almost scrapes the newsprint. His response is the same when I ask him to retrieve something from my medical bag.

During a breakfast in March, Anton inadvertently opens the door to this topic. "I need to make a few purchases in Tambov. I might take Anastasia with me to meet with a voice instructor, to get a professional opinion of her talent."

My ears perk up. Just the opening I've been waiting for.

"You do agree, don't you, that she has an exquisite voice? It's not merely my fatherly pride, is it?"

I've never heard Anton needy for reassurance. "Her voice is exceptional. With proper training, it's anyone's guess how far she can go with it."

Anton grins, showing the blackberry preserves smeared across his teeth.

"I wonder . . . When you go to Tambov, might you accept an extra passenger or two?" I ask. "Victor's letter arrived over a month ago, and I've heard nothing since. Perhaps I should personally cajole, bully, and bribe the zemstvo officials."

"Superb idea." Anton pushes the platter of eggs and kidney sauté toward me. "Finish that off. I'm quite full." He swipes a napkin across his lips. "Wait a minute. You said a passenger or *two*?"

"Well, yes." I scoop the eggs onto my plate. "Have you noticed that Platon's vision is abysmal? How he puts everything close to his eyes?"

Anton's eyebrows rise. "Go on."

"The boy needs spectacles. And Elizaveta would never consider purchasing them."

"Ahhh. You're fond of that boy, aren't you?"

Fond of the boy? No, that's not the case. Not really. I open my mouth to say so, until a bit of the past sidles up to me. I remember Daniil's soft spot for Colya. How bewildering it had seemed back then that Daniil, or anyone, could develop a deep attachment to someone merely passing through his life.

So Andrey, have you grown fond of Platon? Aware that my silence has stretched on too long, I sidestep the question. "His mind, even in its impoverished state, is sharp as a tack. He possesses untold potential, just as Anastasia does. But he'll never break loose of Petrovo's shackles if he can't see."

"Agreed. The lad is entombed in this village. But—"

I interrupt. "A village that is devoid of intellectual pursuits."

"That's true. But just for a moment, view it from Elizaveta's perspective."

"Which is?"

"Above all else, let me repeat, *above all else*, what matters is his duty to his family. And by extension, to the village. As a person, he matters little."

"Your point is valid," I reply. "However, a gifted mind cannot be allowed to stagnate in darkness. It would be criminal to allow Platon's view of the world to be confined to this small plot of earth."

Anton nods. "He's undeniably a good kid. Anastasia worships him. Yes, of course, bring him along."

I look down at my plate. I hate, absolutely despise, requesting favors. "I really wish I didn't have to ask you this, but would you loan me the money for his spectacles? Just until I start working. I swear, I'm good for the debt."

Anton leans back in his chair, taking so long to answer that embarrassment creeps up my neck.

"In my youthful days, my mind—like Platon's—was, as you say, 'sharp as a tack.' Alcohol dulled my intellect, but I can still finagle a way to remedy a problem."

None of this sounds optimistic, but I wait for him to continue.

"Let me make a deal with Elizaveta. I need some drainage ditches cleaned out. I'll tell her I'll pay Platon to clean out the ditches, but the only pay he'll receive is the spectacles. She'll have to either take it or leave it. But be warned: given her mulishness, she might just leave it."

SHE TAKES IT. Although not at first.

"Aw, come on, Elizaveta," Anton wheedled. "At least think about it. Don't you want Platon to learn arithmetic so he could help at the Mercantile? He can't do arithmetic if he can't see the numbers."

She answers Anton by leveling her eyes at me. "How stupid do you think I am? You don't care about numbers. You care about books." Her fists go to her hips. "He's. Not. Going. To. School."

I smile benevolently. "My entire intention for coming here today was in my capacity as a physician. I diagnosed that Platon can't see well."

"*Humph.*"

"But now that you've brought up the subject, I'll repeat what I told you last time. The boy should receive an education."

Elizaveta gives me a look that would freeze Hell.

"Now hear me out," I begin.

"No. You hear me." Her chin juts forward. "I need that boy helping me at the store. You yourself said my health ain't good. I can't tend this place by myself. And Feodor can't afford to stay here and help me. He needs to earn rubles at the distillery."

I take a big gulp of air. I rehearsed these words many times while lying in bed, absentmindedly petting Russell. "Platon is like a young sapling. Given a chance, he can stretch and grow and reach for the sky. But a great tree will not grow from barren soil. It must be nourished."

"He's nourished enough at the supper table." She pulls her shawl close. "Get it through your head. He'll spend his life in the fields and behind this counter."

I defer the conversation to Anton, who, drawing upon every morsel of his charm, persuades her at least to allow Platon to get the spectacles.

FACING A COLD April wind on the way home from the provincial capital, everyone in the wagon is silent except Anton. He hums a merry little tune while loosely holding the reins. The apple of his eye made a favorable impression on the voice instructor, and she and Anton hashed out the details of training, room, and board.

Platon doesn't have time to talk. Leaning against the sideboards of the wagon's bed, he surveys endless fields of young rye, as if he's been dropped into a new world. A world without fuzzy edges. A world of detail and clarity.

"How are things looking?" Anton asks him.

Platon glances about the wagon's bed at the various purchases Anton made while in Tambov. "I can see the letters on the boxes and crates!" He pulls off a glove and scans his hand. "Look! A hangnail!" He pushes the wire-rimmed spectacles farther up his nose, his smile exuberant.

Anastasia, seated cross-legged in the wagon's bed directly behind her father, has also been tight-lipped. She twirls a long lock around her forefinger while she stares at something only she can see: the perils and possibilities of leaving home.

I, too, am silent as I repeatedly relive my infuriating encounter with the zemstvo official. Only the presence of the children in the wagon keeps my firestorm of obscenities in check. Unable to hold back any longer, I blurt, "A complete nincompoop."

Anton gives me a fleeting look. "Pardon?"

I jerk the muffler down from my mouth. "That snot-nosed pup was a complete nincompoop. He said that yes, he had spoken with Victor, but the matter is out of his hands. The authority to make those changes is in St. Petersburg. The little bureaucratic pisspot talked in circles, insisting it isn't his responsibility."

Anton nods sympathetically.

"Confound it! The whole organization is a shambles!"

"Undoubtedly."

"How does Victor deal with those government loafers?"

"He's bitten his tongue so many times, he barely has one left."

"Does the government purposefully hire employees who are spineless, apathetic, and half-witted?"

Anton's rakish smile dimples his cheeks. "Correct me if I'm wrong, but aren't you seeking a government position?"

I mouth a silent *Fuck you* at him, then pull the muffler back up and mutter into it.

Anton dons one of his enchanting, lopsided grins. "Do you want to repeat that, or is it for your ears only?"

I swipe the scarf out of the way. "I said that if ever I wanted a drink, it's now." I don't admit to him that I was so angry when I left the little bureaucratic weasel, I went directly to a bottle shop. But I somehow scrounged up the wherewithal to leave empty-handed.

Anton nods. "I must say, you've done admirably well these past months. I'm surprised you haven't tapped one of the barrels in the distillery."

"Apparently you've been eavesdropping on my thoughts."

"I'm sure temptation abounds when you're doctoring the peasants. They swear by salted vodka for a stomachache. And nothing helps a cold like vodka with pepper."

"Oh, indeed. They're very creative in their reasons for tipping the bottle."

"You've heard the saying: The more brilliant a person, the more ingenious his rationale for drinking. That's why I excelled at imbibing." He winks. "Maintain eternal vigilance, Andrey."

I'm sick and tired of fighting the bottle. And I'm fed up with continuously running into brick walls. I've had enough of being trapped in limbo. I'm wiped out by living like an indigent. I want a peaceful, orderly existence. Is that asking too damn much?

Anton seems to sense my thoughts. "It appears one barricade after another thwarts your quest to reach Petrovka. Sometimes fate lets the blows fall little by little to allow a person to build the strength to face reality."

I narrow my eyes at my friend, striving for the cool disdain that Russell has perfected.

"The peasants are surprisingly accepting of you, and trust me, they're suspicious of anyone who steps into their world."

"You really understand the villagers."

"They're part and parcel of my existence. I palled around with them as a kid. I watched them beget their own families. I've seen more than a few of them die. They're ignorant of books, scornful of outside ideas, and indifferent to the ways of the modern world. They have little experience with anything except hardship and deprivation. That makes them suspicious but not stupid. You could open many eyes and minds, Andrey."

"You've gone completely thick in the head."

"Probably true." He bestows the road ahead of us with a wry *harrumph*. "Craziness definitely runs in my family."

A moment passes before he continues.

"If an altruistic rationale doesn't resonate with you, then look at it this way. Starting in May, Anastasia will spend five days a week in Tambov. If you leave Petrovo, I'll have no one to talk with except Dasha and occasionally my sister Elena. You do realize, don't you, that there'll be one very lonely estate owner in the middle of Russia's grain fields?"

An uninvited but vivid memory rises. A blank scrap of paper on a table in Simferopol. The words of gratitude for Daniil that I was unable to articulate. I never want to sidestep that opportunity again.

"Anton, I . . ." I swallow back the lump in my throat. "I want you to know how much I appreciate all you've done for me. You're a good man, and I . . . I place enormous value on our friendship. I'll treasure it all of my days."

There. I said it. For the first time in my life, I've shared my deepest sentiments. And I'm gratified to receive Anton's wide smile in return.

CHAPTER 51

May
1867

Petrovo
16 May 1867

Greetings My Dearest Maria & Vasilisa,

I beg that you forgive the tardiness of my response to your last letter. I delayed writing until I had something of substance to tell you. However, my future remains uncertain. The zemstvo is such a fledgling government institution, no one is clear about its functions, organization, funding, or staffing, let alone how to deal with a misplaced physician mired on a windswept dot in the middle of Russia's grain fields. Having met with defeat at the provincial capital, I sent my appeal to the bureaucrats in St. Petersburg. My letter of a month ago remains unanswered.

But enough about me. Let me promptly give you news about your favorite fellow. With the warm weather, Russell no longer feels compelled to share my blankets. He now prefers to sleep atop the bedsheets at the foot of the mattress. At cockcrow, he rises and gives a good, long stretch. He believes I should do the same. Several times a day, he finds rousing joy in chatting with the squirrels outside the window.

Your previous letter requested that I detail village life. Allow me to start with the bench I am sitting on outside the Mercantile. It is crude, flimsy, decaying, paintless, backless, and uncomfortable. However, from my vantage point on the bench, I have an unrestricted view of the village square (a term that is indeed grandiose for the muddy wallow that encircles the listing, thatched-roof lean-to that shelters the public well).

Leaving the well is a woman wearing the ever-present babushka wrapped about her head and carrying a yoke across her shoulders. At each end hangs a bucket. No wonder the work-weary backs of peasant women are bent like sickles. When the housewives aren't cooking, weaving, washing clothes, tending a garden, or hatching children, they're slaving away in the fields. Their faces are as creased as the bark of an oak.

On the far side of the village-square quagmire, a bull-shouldered peasant is trying unsuccessfully to pull a wagon with a broken wheel. He has no horse because last week he beat his old nag to death. This week, he's wailing about his loss.

I'm also privy to a view in both directions of Petrovo's sole road. (I assure you that "road" is an embellished term.) Not a single one of the teetering shanties that serve as houses has ever been graced with the slap of a paintbrush. The plank boards are as parched as the peasants' faces, which have been behind the same type of wooden plow, tilling the same fields for centuries.

As I look toward the peasant's hut next to the Mercantile, my eyes settle on a mud-caked pig that oinks with hungry vigor as it paces the road outside the gate. The peasants let the pigs roam loose at night so they'll eat the refuse and keep things tidy. A peasant boy emerges from the hut, kicking aside the hens. The boy opens the gate and lets the pig into the dirt yard. Based on the pig's grunts and complaints, it's deeply aggrieved as it pokes about the yard. When it bestows the rooster with an impertinent snort, the cock bristles his multicolored feathers and gives a lusty crow. Finally, the boy tosses some kitchen scraps into a hollowed-out split log. Head buried in the trough, the pig seems content.

About to enter the Mercantile is a peasant wearing the ubiquitous faded trousers and linen shirt, complete with patches on the elbows. But wait. First he stops outside the door, occludes one nostril with his finger, and empties the thick, yellow mucus of the other nostril onto the ground. Perhaps he is to be commended for completing the act *prior* to entering the Mercantile.

I hope that I've sketched a vivid picture of rural life for you and that this letter finds you both well.

Andriusha

Moscow
9 May 1867

My dear friend and mentor,

I hadn't heard from you in such a long time, I was worried about your safety. But after reading your recent letter, my main worry is your sanity!

Having been raised in a village very much like Petrovo as you describe it, I can understand the jolt you've experienced. But that's exactly why I chose to extend my medical studies to specialize in public health.

A simple glance at Russia's staggering rural problems should make even the most obtuse person aware of how much can be accomplished.

Epidemics of typhoid fever, cholera, diphtheria, smallpox.

Undernourishment.

Lack of hygiene.

A passive fatalism that illness is sent directly from God.

To my way of thinking, the real challenge of a zemstvo physician is to rid the countryside of its dangerous lifestyles without using confrontation and coercion. The physician must become part of the village and gain the peasantry's confidence, which is an agonizingly slow process.

Sometimes in bed at night, I stare at the ceiling, pondering the decade since the war. During those years, Alexander emancipated twenty-five million serfs, created a new judicial system, revamped the military and the universities, and founded institutions of self-government for city and countryside alike. Yet a quarter of all peasant infants die before they reach one year of age. Of the remaining, less than half will reach adulthood. How can this happen when the problems (as well as their solutions) are so basic?

Disease and health go hand in hand with society's customs, mores, habits, child rearing, education, housing, hygiene, nutrition, and so on. I often recall Doctor Pirogov's statement that disease won't be curtailed until physicians spend as much time on preventive medicine as they do on treatment of the sick.

Have you had enough of my rhetoric?

When I was debating whether to take my advanced studies, you advised me to keep an open mind and seriously consider my options and their consequences: income, professional fulfillment, personal happiness. Please forgive my presumptuousness, but I encourage you to do the same. I know you don't hold much credence in religion, but maybe Petrovo is where Divine Providence (or fate, if you prefer) wants you to be.

With the fondest of regards,
Colya

I REREAD THE letter I am about to post to Maria and Vasilisa, and I acknowledge that my depiction of the peasants is probably too derogatory. Ridicule solves nothing.

I also reread the letter I just received from Colya. His points are valid. The peasants' abominable health and abbreviated life span are attributable to two shortfalls. First, their lack of understanding of basic health principles. And second, the absence of an infrastructure to deliver even minimal health care. These are both staggering problems, but young men like Colya will chip away at them.

An unbidden sense of guilt befalls me. Why am I pushing these undertakings onto Colya's generation? I ponder my life experiences, both the ones I intended and the ones I never expected.

My education at the university.

My maturation during the war.

Pirogov's tutoring on preventive principles.

My experience with Moscow's impoverished.

The knowledge about childhood diseases (and childhood in general) that I gained at the Foundling Home.

Truth be told, the sum total of my background is quite rich.

A pervading impression keeps swirling through my mind, like an eddy in Petrovo's river. Has the time perhaps arrived to call upon my knowledge and skills to create a more noble life? Isn't every man obliged to give back to society? And not just according to what he received from it, but at a higher level?

How odd! Somehow, amid all the muck and poverty of Petrovo, might I have found not only the vitality I've always lacked but, paradoxically, the peace and rest I've been seeking?

CHAPTER 52

May
1867

"DO YOU WANT to hold or stab?" I ask Platon.

Platon's leg pulses up and down while he weighs the two undesirable options. We're sitting on the brick pavers of a small room in the estate's horse stable that houses a table and two chairs, plus assorted animal medicines. Russell is on my lap, his legs tucked under him, his eyes closed, oblivious to what's in store for him.

Even through my trousers and the cat's fur, I can feel the heat of Russell's feverish body. A bite wound on his neck has festered into an egg-sized pocket of pus. It's his third abscess since we arrived in Petrovo.

I ask the cheeky tom, "How do you manage to get in fights with the barn cats? You're either in the cottage or the estate house twenty-three hours a day."

"I'll hold," Platon announces with finality.

"Use every bit of strength you have."

As I thrust the cat into the grain sack, he becomes a lightning bolt of energy. Gathering all his legs—which now number at least eight—into the sack requires Herculean strength and dexterity. It results in several oozing claw marks that extend from my fingers up to my elbows.

Panting from the first phase of the medical procedure, I twist the sack closed and secure it with twine tied in a miller's knot. Russell lies still, apparently having worn himself out.

"The tighter you hold him, the quicker it will be over."

Platon swallows, pushes his spectacles up his nose, throws back his shoulders, and employs both hands and one leg to anchor the sacked cat against the floor.

My pocket knife cuts a small slit in the sack, exposing the swollen pocket of pus. I give one quick jab through the skin with the point of the lancet. The cat screams like a locomotive whistle. Legs fly every which way. Claws pierce the cloth sack.

While I squeeze the blood-tinged pus from the swelling, Russell threatens me with screeches, hisses, and growls. Working fast, I don't look at Platon, but I'm aware that the boy's knuckles are blanched as they hold the thrashing beast. Russell's theatrics rise to a crescendo as I splash on tincture of iodine.

"Hold tight while I undo the knot," I wheeze, winded more from tension than from exertion. Russell stops his caterwauling but continues to battle the sack. I pull the rope free. "Let him go."

The gray tabby shoots from the sack and ricochets about the room in search of an escape route. I fling open the door, and Russell is out in less than a blink. Platon and I watch as he runs flat-out through the wide stable entrance and past Dasha's scarecrow, disappearing among her vegetable plants.

I stand with my head high and my chest out. "That wasn't too bad, was it."

Platon agrees it hadn't gone badly, not badly at all. He asserts this while his lungs are still gulping for air.

I wonder how many more of Russell's fight wounds I'll have to contend with. Out of the blue, I recollect that the veterinary surgeon was recently at the estate house to castrate a colt. My thoughts churn. Castrated horses are calmer and less quarrelsome. If I could change Russell from a "stallion" into a "gelding," would that stop his sparring matches?

During the war, Daniil removed a gangrenous testicle from a wounded private. He said the procedure was easier than amputating a finger. But how would I physically hold the cat still?

Perhaps the physician from the neighboring estate would sell me a bottle of chloroform. Shouldn't the drug work the same in cats as in humans?

Platon and I lean against the stable wall, the sun-warmed red bricks melting the tension from our muscles. My gaze falls on Anton and Dasha seated at a little iron table on the terrace in the speckled shade of a black alder tree. On one side of the couple, crocuses, tulips, irises, and narcissus eke out an existence in a raggedy garden that at one time was probably manicured. Behind them is an arbor enlaced with vines. Beyond the arbor is an unending expanse of green rye, heads rippling in the gentlest of breezes. Aloft, swallows cut through the air. The goose, strolling with dignified grandeur an arm's length from the twosome, adds the final touch to the bucolic scene.

I contemplate the odd pairing. Anton is a remarkably handsome member of the nobility. Dasha is plain of face and built like a milkmaid. She will never be well received by society. Yet I sense a quiet comfort in their life together, as well as ardent devotion.

Unexpectedly, I perceive a deep hole in my chest, as if the surgery knife had been plunged into me rather than Russell. Would the warmth of family life always evade me? Am I even capable of partaking in such unequivocal devotion?

Platon interrupts my pensive thoughts. "You did real good doctoring the cat,

Doctor Rozhdestvensky. Too bad you didn't become a veterinary surgeon instead of a human surgeon."

The boy's comment deposits me face-to-face with Puzanov in Sevastopol's death house. I hear the moans. I smell the rot.

"Becoming a physician seemed like the best choice at the time," I reply.

"But . . . but you do *like* being a physician, don't you?" The boy's peculiar pointed ears seem as erect as a dog's as he waits for an answer.

I'm let off the hook when a well-appointed, enclosed carriage crossing the bridge snares our attention. The carriage ascends the road to the estate house, a trail of dust in its wake, and the two dappled grays come to a stop under the porte-cochere. With great trumpeting and flapping of wings, the goose announces the visitors, and Anton and Dasha rise to greet their company.

"Must be Anton Stepanovich's cousin and her son," I say. "They're staying here a few days on their way back to Moscow."

The coachman places a stool below the door. From the open doorway extends a long, slender arm, covered at the top with a short, puffed sleeve. Next comes a white-stockinged calf. Clutching a full skirt is a woman in her midtwenties. She stoops low to avoid hitting her feathered hat on the door frame, then offers Anton her cheek to kiss. Her bodice stretches across breasts that are abundantly ample for such a delicate waistline.

Need I say I pay scant attention to the schoolboy in knee pants who leaps from the carriage?

Platon breathes, "Look at those fancy clothes."

"I'm looking."

What I don't tell Platon is that, according to Anton, Cousin Nadya has a penchant not only for fancy clothes and carriages, but also for beds other than her husband's. Provoked to his limits, her husband sent her and her finery packing. In dire financial straits, she headed lickety-split for the Ural Mountains and the loving arms and purse of her widowed mother. Her mother, however, felt compelled to teach her a lesson and sent her back to Moscow empty-handed. Anton confided in me, "Hope she doesn't become a hanger-on, living off me for months."

My gaze dallies on the tantalizing sway of Cousin Nadya's skirt as the foursome move toward the estate house.

Platon isn't as absorbed as Little Soldier and I are in the skirt's subtle movement. "How long does it take to become a physician?" he asks.

"Huh? Lots of years of school. Including medical studies at the university."

"The university in Moscow?"

"That's one. But there are others also."

Platon is reverential as he repeats, "Moscow."

I look over to find that Platon's gaze has shifted toward the vast rye fields. This isn't the first time I've caught the boy peering through his spectacles at distant horizons, horizons much too far away for anyone else to see.

CHAPTER 53

June
1867

SUCH A GLORIOUS June! The grounds of the estate house are immersed in the ambrosial scents of peonies and roses, and the days are delectable shirtsleeve temperatures. And the night sky, unobscured by Moscow's lights, speaks of both infinity and our own impermanence.

But first and foremost among the glories of June is Nadya, one fine specimen of a woman.

When I was first introduced to her, she extended her hand to me and insisted that I, as a friend of Cousin Anton, call her by her diminutive, Nadya. As I graciously clasped the tips of her fingers, warmth spread to my thighs. Her sapphire eyes snared me like a fishhook.

Every evening, Anton and Dasha invite me to join them, Nadya, and her son, Vanya, for dinner. Prior to dinner, Nadya, Vanya, and I play croquet. Anastasia joins us on days she's home from her Tambov school. During our first game of croquet, the goose lowers its head and, neck extended, charges toward Nadya's skirt. Although I move to brush aside the little tyrant with my foot, I'm too slow. The sole of the delicate lady's shoe has already landed an effective, full-force slam against the feathered chest. From then on, the goose critiques our shots from a safe distance.

When the lemony sun turns honey-colored and the crickets urge the darkness to arrive, Anastasia goes to the kitchen to help Dasha, and Nadya tells Vanya to wash up for dinner. As far as I can tell, Nadya never helps Dasha with either the cooking or the cleanup. This bothers me somewhat. But not excessively.

Nadya and I retire to the little iron table on the terrace, where her easy conversation is a soft breeze that carries me away with her. On those occasions when I say something even remotely humorous, she titters as carefree as a little girl, leaning sideways toward me until her shoulder brushes mine. My cheeks burn like hot embers, and Little Soldier pants zealously.

At my prompting, she describes how, as a child, she and her family would visit Petrovo yearly. "Cousin Anton always made such a fuss over us. Even as a boy,

Antoshka would show us the distillery's valves and coils and explain how they worked. All of us thought there was nothing Cousin Anton couldn't accomplish. And he'd take me, the city girl, for canoe rides and long walks in the woods, frightening me to death with tales about goblins."

Nadya confirms my suspicions that Anton was indeed quite a gadabout in his younger years. "That rascal was so charming, he'd snap his fingers, and girls instantly fell under his spell." Her dimples deepen as she gives an impish shrug of her slender shoulders.

Jasmine covers the arbor, and all around us, poppies, marigolds, and delphiniums flaunt their vibrancy. In the fields behind us ripples a sea of ripening grain. But all that beauty pales in comparison to the loose auburn tendrils from Nadya's chignon that trail down her ivory neck and spill over the shawl broach securing the gauzy material taut across her comely breasts.

Too soon, the throaty frogs in the pond start their jabbering, and Dasha waves us to the dinner table.

Following a dessert of Elena's bonbons, Nadya tucks Vanya into bed. Then Anastasia sometimes leads us in a song, or we might play board games. But my favorite pastime is charades, its pantomimes provoking Nadya to crumple in rapturous, uncontrollable giggles.

I fully realize I'm wearing my heart on my sleeve. Nadya has taken my breath away, along with my common sense and my urgency to leave Petrovo. In fact, she's taken everything away except my ambitious Little Soldier.

PARTWAY INTO THE second week, Anton announces that the time has arrived for his daughter to learn how to dance. It's up to him and Nadya to teach Anastasia, Dasha, and me. My heart plummets, knowing I'll look every bit the fool. However, it turns out that all three of us novices are more comical than elegant. I find my laughter every bit as spontaneous and unconstrained as when I was with Daniil and Ignaty at the card table or with the sisters in their apartment.

Within a week, Dasha and I are able to lumber through the rudimentary steps. Anastasia, with her youthful, supple mind and body, is a quick learner. Nadya, of course, is poised and lissome. But Anton outdoes us all, skipping the mazurka as if he mastered it during his diaper days.

After Anastasia goes to bed, Anton brings forth the cards. We endeavor to teach skat to Nadya, but the complex rules won't take hold in her pretty head.

Instead, we opt for whist, which Anton plays with the same competence as he dances, putting the rest of us to shame.

NADYA HAS BEEN at the estate house for three weeks when Anastasia announces during dessert that *les trois mousquetaires* will be having a picnic in the woods later this week. "Or maybe at the hunting cabin."

Her father's response is succinct and uncontestable. "No, you're not."

All our heads swivel to stare at Anton.

Anastasia resorts to a woeful bleat that she's heard Dasha successfully employ many times over. "Aw, Papa, why not?"

"You can wheedle me with 'Aw, Papa,' but I'm telling you that you are not going without a chaperone."

Ahhh, a chaperone. This summer, I've noticed Anastasia is sprouting breasts, and apparently, her father has also noticed. Anastasia alone for hours in the woods, or possibly a hunting cabin, with two pubescent boys . . . Anton's decision is probably a wise one.

A verbal back-and-forth ensues between father and daughter, until Cousin Nadya gibes, "Oh, Anton, you're being a hypocritical, old fuddy-duddy." Her blue eyes are devilish, almost to the point of wrathful.

The calm in his voice is deadly. "You stay out of this."

Shocked by Anton's acerbic response, Dasha and I exchange bewildered glances. Anastasia throws her napkin on her plate, leaps from the table, and bolts toward her room.

Anton jabs the tines of his fork at her retreating back. "Mind your manners, young lady! Excuse yourself before leaving the table."

"I excuse myself!" she flings over her shoulder.

The table is swathed in silence as Anton, Dasha, Nadya, Vanya, and I push our ginger cake about our plates. Nadya eventually says to her son, "I think this would be a good evening for us to retire early."

When just three of us remain at the table, I solicitously ask, "What would you think, Anton, if all of us, including the two boys, go on a picnic together?"

Dasha supports me with, "It's the perfect time of year."

CHAPTER 54

June
1867

WHEN THE DAY of the picnic rolls around, Nadya's visit has entered its second month. She's officially a sponger, a hanger-on. During her stay, Little Soldier has partaken in a dizzying amount of stretching exercise. I constantly remind him that he and I have seen enough breasts to know that none are as full or as sprightly when devoid of a corset, but he insists that Nadya's would shatter that tenet. I decide it's time to pick up the pace and find out firsthand.

On the day of the picnic, the adults ride in the carriage while the youngsters jostle in the bed of a wagon among food, chairs, a table, a samovar, plates, cups, utensils, and two quilts that have seen far better days. Anton selects an enchanting glen downriver from Petrovo on the estate of Victor Rusakov's father, ownership of which will transfer to its new owner next month. Tall, leafy trees provide ideal shade for picnickers, while an open glade supplies space for the fledglings to play blind man's bluff or vulture-and-chickens. The location abuts a widened, meandering portion of the river that's only waist deep. Filip and Platon scramble to the edge of the slow-moving water to skip stones across its surface.

I slip back to Sevastopol. A June picnic. Skipping stones. Ignaty. Maria. I also recall drinking cup after cup of vodka. But today, astonishingly, I don't want a drink. I am bravely and objectively able to meet both the present and the future without the crutch of alcohol. Today, I have no desire for it.

Good for you, Andrey!

Twirling a strand of hair around her index finger, Anastasia scrutinizes the two boys, then the four adults, apparently trying to determine which is less boring: tossing rocks into a river or listening to prattle about the weather and politics. She offers to take Vanya with her to the riverbank. "If you agree, Cousin Nadya."

"Yes, but do promise to keep a close watch on him."

Nadya looks luscious in the dappled shade. She, Dasha, Anton, and I fritter away time with an assortment of topics, starting with a highbrow deliberation about the military action between Prussia and Austria, followed by a discussion of Nadya's impression of Moscow's new zoo. Finally, we sink into gossip about a young woman on a nearby estate who suddenly advanced her October wedding date to next month. Regardless of the topic, Nadya's participation seems dry and cheerless while she frenetically fans her neck as if she's about to melt.

She suggests it's time to eat, and as we seem to have run dry of scuttlebutt, we set out the food and supplies. The adults settle onto chairs at the table while the children sprawl about on a quilt. Dasha's picnic baskets include tongue with potatoes, herring and beet salad, stewed dried pears, and *krendels*. Everyone digs in except Nadya, who occupies herself with flicking ants off the table and backhanding bees away from the honey cakes. Her bracelets jangle and her rings flash. I'm not an expert on women's finery, but I did learn a thing or two while administering to Doctor Seriyev's affluent patients. Nadya's jewelry seems tawdry to me. I recall Anton's description of how her former husband had sent her packing, putting her in dire financial straits. Had she liquidated her valuables, leaving her with only baubles?

A cough comes from the quilt, and Nadya peers at her son. "You coughed several times down by the river. Do you feel all right?"

"Yes, Mama."

Nadya sighs as she swats a grasshopper from her skirt. "If it doesn't offend anyone, I think I'll take a brief nap in the carriage. I didn't sleep well last night, and the heat is draining me. Vanya, come with me and rest for a while. I don't want you succumbing to the croup again."

Despite being utterly bewitched by Nadya, I'm relieved when she disappears into the carriage. I've had enough of her slapping at bugs and fanning her neck.

Perhaps I'm a little intolerant today because I also didn't sleep well last night. I was visited by a Crimean dream, the first one in over a month. I stepped over an arm that was attached to nothing. Then another one. And another. On and on they stretched, the whole length of the Chernaia River. Each arm was one I had amputated.

I stretch out for a nap in the shade. The sky soon turns brooding, and I have no objection when Dasha suggests we return to the estate house early.

TALK ABOUT GOING to Hell in a handbasket. What have I done wrong?

The day after the picnic, my surgical knife dethroned Russell's testicles. The anesthesia and the castration both came off precisely as I had hoped. Four hours after I tied my final knot, Russell stood on all fours and lapped up the bits of salted cod I had saved for him from my noon meal.

However, the following day, he refused to eat, and today he's lying limp on his side, without even a flick of his tail. How have things gone so askew?

For the twentieth time today, I lift his tail. The surgical site is swollen and pink, but no worse than the stump of a soldier's arm.

I gently press his ear between my thumb and forefinger. "You're feverish."

Russell opens his eyes and gives a feeble, heartrending *meow*.

"Eat something. Please." I again go through my assortment of feline delicacies. "Look, cream from the orphanage's best cow." I put a couple of drops on Russell's tongue. He swallows it, so I add a few more drops. This time, however, he shakes his head and sends it flying.

"How about one of these sardines Dasha sent over especially for you. Yummm." I hold the pearly sliver against Russell's nose, but he turns his head away from the offending fish.

"Try some chicken. I shredded it just for you." I put a smidgen in Russell's mouth, but the pink tongue sends the piece sailing back at me.

What if he dies? How can I possibly tell Maria that I killed her Russell?

THE FOLLOWING MORNING, his eyes are dull, and his coat is matted. When I try to get him to swallow a little food, the inside of his mouth is as dry as the Crimean hills. I put some water on the little tongue. Most runs out the side, but perhaps a dribble or two goes down his gullet.

"I've finally come to like you, you little bastard, and you want to die on me," I whisper.

I'm startled by a knock on the door. It's Feodor Zhemchuzhnikov, cap in hand, head tucked.

"Excuse me for troubling you, Doctor Rozhdestvensky. Elizaveta didn't want me to come here, but I told her she needs you. She can't go on like this."

"Like what?"

"She can't even get off the mattress."

"Because she's so bloated?"

Zhemchuzhnikov nods. "And she's panting like a dog."

ELIZAVETA, AS PALE as milk, is lying on a bed in the backroom of the Mercantile. The room's tallow candles stink like slaughterhouse entrails.

I lean over the prostrate woman and softly ask, "Are you ready for my help? I can make you feel better in no time."

From behind me, Feodor asks, "What ails her?"

I turn toward him. "She didn't tell you?"

"She said the illness is left over from when she was a teenager."

"You knew her back then, correct? When she was sick with fever and rash?"

"Oh, yes. We all prayed for her day and night. We wanted to light candles in the church and keep the icon candle burning. But we'd had poor crops for two years and didn't have kopeks for food, let alone candles."

"The illness is known as scarlet fever. Most of her body got well, but her heart didn't. It's stiff and scarred."

"She'll never get better?"

"Her heart will never get better, so, yes, basically she'll never get well."

"She's going to die?"

"The truth, Feodor, is that her damaged heart will eventually steal her life. But in the meantime, I can make her feel better by taking away the swelling."

Feodor stands over her, and they search each other's eyes, engaged in a long, silent conversation. Feodor turns toward me. "Do whatever you can. I don't want to lose her sooner than I have to." He lowers himself onto a three-legged stool beside the bed and grasps her hand while I begin the process.

By the time I'm finished and am curling up my rubber tubing, Elizaveta feels well enough to sit up in bed with her back against the wall. Feodor's face is sheer joy as he asks what fair payment would be.

"Perhaps you can repay me with advice rather than rubles. Do you remember my cat, the big gray tom? I'm afraid he has blood poisoning. Any suggestions on what I can do?"

Elizaveta's answer is succinct. "Garlic tonic."

"What's that?"

Without doubt, she's feeling her old self because she squints at me as if to say *How in the world did you become a physician and not learn about garlic tonic?* She rattles off the instructions.

"Slice garlic into a mound this big." She gestures the size with her hands. "Pour one-fourth bucket of boiling water over it. Let it sit for twelve hours. Add honey so it's the consistency of syrup."

As she speaks, I try to keep my head from swaying back and forth in skepticism. Nothing but a witch's brew.

She concludes with, "Feodor, give him the garlic as payment."

I RETURN TO my cottage to find Russell's hold on life is tenuous. I never thought I'd live to see the day when I'd know this cat so well, I can tell how awful he feels. He can't moan like a human, and he doesn't have sad eyes like a dog. Yet it's easy to see Russell is badly ailing.

"I swear by my whole being, if you get better, I'll never say another mean thing to you or about you," I tell him as I scale back the tonic's ingredients to cat-sized portions.

I glance at my pocket watch. Twelve hours would put it in the middle of the night. Nine hours will be long enough.

I spend the rest of the day and into the evening with Russell. I periodically offer him cream, sardines, and chicken. But the cat scorns them all, flinging the distasteful items far and wide.

As I sweep up the rebuffed food, I tell Russell, "You *will* swallow the garlic tonic, by God."

For the second time today, someone knocks on my door. I open it to reveal Nadya, her arm around her son.

CHAPTER 55

June
1867

NADYA IS JAW-DROPPING in a scarlet silk dressing gown. My gaze skims down the filmy material as it cleaves to the curves of her breasts before cinching into folds under a braided sash at her waist. Her auburn hair cascades loosely about her shoulders.

Little Soldier takes notice.

"Nadya. And Vanya. Such a nice surprise!"

Her smile brings forth deep dimples, then her expression turns sheepish. "I so regret bothering you at this hour." She holds forth a tin lantern and peers about the single room. "Did I hear you talking to someone?"

"No, no. Merely humming a little tune to myself."

"Could I impose upon you to take a peek at Vanya?" Her lips pucker with worry as her lissome arm wraps about her son's shoulders. "He had a slight cough all day. As soon as he went to bed, he coughed and coughed and couldn't stop. Frightened me to death."

"Come in. Let's have a look," I tell the boy while coveting his mother.

Nadya draws up the skirt of her robe and steps across the threshold, trailed by her son and a flowery fragrance. Her eyes dart to the blanket on the floor.

"Please excuse my cat. He's been sick."

"Yes, Dasha mentioned something about that." Nadya isn't interested in pursuing the topic, a reaction I find perfectly understandable.

I instruct Nadya to direct her lantern's light to the back of her son's mouth while I look at his pharynx. "Does your throat hurt?"

He shakes his head.

My palm feels for fever on the youngster's forehead. I palpate the lymph nodes on each side of the boy's neck. A slight pressure from my thumb on Vanya's windpipe elicits a coughing fit.

At my direction, Nadya removes Vanya's nightshirt.

I place my hand flat upon Vanya's bare chest and tap the center of my middle finger with the tip of my other middle finger. I incrementally move my hand across the boy's chest, tapping as I go. "I'm listening for dullness or other unusual sounds in the front of your lungs," I explain to the boy. "Turn around, and I'll do the same on your back."

When I'm finished, I tell his mother to replace his shirt.

As Nadya bends over her son, the hem of her night-robe lifts to expose her calves, flaming my fantasies. Little Soldier grows restless, urging me to loosen the sash. Slip my hand inside. Cup her buttocks.

Instead, I explain that the boy's throat is slightly inflamed. "Nothing serious. And we want to ensure it stays that way."

Nadya's coquettish dimples reappear. "Your words are so reassuring." From beneath her thick lashes, her eyes snare mine for a long moment. "You have such a knack with children. How in the world did a man like you escape marriage?"

The warm swell rising within me is interrupted by Vanya wandering, hand extended, toward Russell.

"Don't touch that!" his mother lashes out. "It's sick." Her countenance flips back to one of a devoted parent. "Vanya, sweetheart, scurry back to the estate house and get into bed. You need all the rest you can get. I'll be right there to tuck you in, as soon as I ask the doctor a few questions."

From the doorway, she watches him make his way safely to the estate house, then closes the door. She turns, and her eyes beseech mine for reassurance. "But why did he have such a terrible coughing attack when we went to bed?"

"Possibly the change in posture, more blood in his head and neck area. Or perhaps he merely inhaled some dust."

"Dust. That wouldn't surprise me, considering Dasha's housekeeping." Her lips slide to one side in repugnance. Suddenly her eyes go wide, and the flat of her hand flies to the hollow at the base of her throat. Her spread fingers rise and fall with the billowing of her chest. She leans close to me and whispers, "You don't think it's whooping cough, do you?" Her distraught hand slides down to her waist, further tightening the material across her breasts.

"No, I don't. Vanya's system is merely run down from all the traveling, the new experiences, the changes in his diet. I recommend lots of rest, plus give him a smidgeon of hot wine twice a day. And I'm certain I saw some mint lozenges somewhere in the estate house. Probably in the larder. Ask Dasha. She'll know."

"Dasha." Nadya's eyes roll in derision. "To this day, I am in dismay that Cousin Anton is living openly with her. I remember coming here as a child. Dasha was a mere housegirl. A serf!" She swallows as if cleansing her mouth of its distaste. "But then again, nothing stays the same, does it? I mean, Petrovo isn't exactly prospering under Anton's care. Isn't it peculiar how things turn out?" Her delicate hand again rises to her creamy throat and toys with the trim on her dressing gown.

My insides bristle at the snooty comment about Dasha, who is shouldering the workload of at least four previous house serfs. And it's quite cheeky of Nadya to pass scornful judgment on Petrovo when the serfs' emancipation has pulled the rug out from under the Maximov family. Especially considering Nadya is currently without a roof over her own head.

I repeat my reply. "I'm certain Dasha can find the mint lozenges for you."

Little vertical lines erupt between her eyebrows, then disappear. "I can't possibly thank you enough for your time and advice." Her voice is the audible equivalent of a caress along the long, sleek back of a cat.

Her hand unexpectedly reaches out as though she were about to reinforce her words by placing her palm on my chest. Then she pulls back, blushing. "If something were to happen to Vanya . . ." The dark-lashed eyes squeeze closed. "I can't imagine anything worse."

Pinching the upper part of her nose, she glides toward a ladder-back chair. Beneath the flowing silk, her lithe body moves with the fluidity of a snake. She grips the wooden chair as if in need of support. "Sometimes I feel so very alone and vulnerable in the world." Her bosom rises and falls in a gasp.

Heat surges in my groin. I envision pressing her to me, sliding my hand into her low neckline, bringing my lips to her nipple . . .

Then I swim up to the surface of reality as Maria's voice in Simferopol resonates in my head. *Andrey Yevgrafovich, you're a fool.* Little Soldier shrivels protectively into himself.

My memory moves forward a few days, when Maria did an about-face and handed me rubles for my return trip to Moscow. Rubles I would have possessed had I not squandered them on the Greek girl.

I haul my attention to the present moment and the ochre lamplight flickering on Nadya's cheeks. She tucks in her chin, and her sapphire eyes roll upward, beckoning me.

Maria's words again tumble forth from another time and place. *She knows exactly what those dreamy blue eyes can do to a man.*

I'm as bewitched by Nadya as I was a dozen years ago by Sister Vasilisa. Evidently, I didn't learn my lesson very well.

Nadya murmurs, "Don't you feel alone in this desolate village?"

"Yes, on occasion."

"You said you don't hold much hope that you'll obtain the zemstvo position you want. I'll be leaving Petrovo in a couple of days. Why not return to Moscow with me?" She cocks her pretty head and lifts her eyebrows like question marks. "I have connections for your employment. Lucrative employment. We could enjoy the good life." Her voice is as smooth and slippery as river stones.

My world pivots. She and I are walking arm in arm toward our nicely appointed apartment for a rousing time between the sheets.

Hold on, Andrey, you nincompoop. Take a long look at yourself and your unexcelled mediocrity. Pale, undistinguished face. Hair becoming increasingly thin. Scrawny physique that's sprouting a paunch thanks to Dasha's good cooking.

A vibrant young woman would have no use for such a lackluster man, except for possibly two things. First, to regain her lost respectability by resuming her status as a married woman. Second, to enjoy the rubles I would earn hand over fist as a Moscow physician. Ha! A delusion if ever there was one! Besides, just where would Nadya get those career connections? Anton implied she'd done a top-notch job of befouling her reputation with Moscow's upper echelon.

I longed for this woman with a high passion. But at this moment, I find her conniving, pathetic, and desperate.

Nadya purrs, "Doesn't Moscow's good life sound appealing? Its comforts. Its culture. Its daily pleasures."

Ooooh! Daily pleasures!

Andrey, get back on track! She's trouble, pure and simple.

"Certainly it sounds appealing, but I'm not ready to abandon my goal of zemstvo medicine. The peasants are without health care of any kind, leaving them condemned to short, impoverished lives."

Nadya's expression is dull with apathy.

My thoughts shift to another woman's animated face as we strolled through Moscow's Pussy Willow Bazaar. *I've told you before, I never tire of hearing about your work.* I do believe Maria meant those words.

I take a physical and emotional step back to study the enticing woman before me. It occurs to me that Nadya is malnourished. Clearly not in her sensuous body, but somewhere deeper, in something Maria would call a soul. She possesses neither Elizaveta's steadfastness nor Dasha's devotion.

Meanwhile, Little Soldier once again feels randy. *Don't abandon me now, Andrey! Not now!*

But a voice inside me counters with, *This woman is so desperate for money, she'll stoop to playing fast and loose with a poor country doctor.*

Nadya runs the tip of her tongue across her upper lip, leaving behind a dewy moistness. I'm struck by the impression of a serpent's tongue seeking prey.

I need to slay this serpent. Once and for all.

But Little Soldier, his passion at a feverish pitch, is screaming, *She's ours for the taking! Come on, buddy, reach for her. Now, Andrey. Now!*

And I could. Yet that familiar sense of fair play is once again chiding me. It would be criminal of me to lead Nadya on for the sole purpose of getting her in bed. But this time my hesitation is more than just fair play. Nadya is dangerous. If I succumb to her charms this evening, then refuse to legitimize the relationship, she'll carve me into buzzard bait.

Having lost the thread of our conversation, I pursue a neutral topic. "Put your mind at ease regarding Vanya. With your tender care, your son is in no danger." My groin is throbbing as I gather my words. "I don't mean to be rude, and please forgive me if that's how I appear. However, I must excuse myself and tend to my cat."

Her eyes widen with surprise, then narrow to slits. "Good night, Andrey. I leave you to your cat."

She sails past me, leaving a trail rife with the aura of excess. Excess perfume. Excess theatrics. Excess self-absorption.

Little Soldier withers as he accepts defeat.

I, on the other hand, stand taller. *Hooray for you, Andrey! At least you've gained some wisdom and willpower over the years.*

Nearly nine hours have passed since I brewed up Russell's garlic potion, so I add the honey to the concoction. Realizing it's a last-ditch and probably futile effort, I sit on the floor, put a smudge of the sticky glop on the tip of my index finger, pry the cat's mouth open, and smear the syrup on the roof of his mouth. Russell gives a rapid-fire shake of his head. But at least some of the so-called medicine goes down his gullet.

I give him another dose, then a third.

Russell's patience wears thin, and he rises and staggers a few steps before collapsing back onto the blanket. Against my will, my vision grows filmy as I watch him lying limp and miserable. I'm overcome with the compassion that can be felt only by a soul, an organ I swore didn't exist.

I pick up the broom and resume the task that Nadya interrupted. The sound of the bristles grazing the floorboards stirs up images of a long-ago day. Maria and I in the mess hall, Maria beside herself for want of a broom. Maria. The quintessence of hard work, integrity, and honesty. The antithesis of Nadya.

What was it Ignaty had said about Maria? *She's a grand girl, the grandest I've ever known.*

"Indeed she is," I murmur.

But over the sound of my own mutter, I hear her words, and they rattle my brain like a clap of thunder: *Did you ever think that perhaps I occasionally need someone to comfort me, to put his arms around me?*

My arms?

A warm dizziness enfolds me, and I clutch the broom handle for support.

My arms belong around Maria?

All this time, have I been blind to what was right in front of me?

CHAPTER 56

June
1867

IN A PARALYSIS of shock, I lower myself onto a chair. Every hair on my body stands straight out. My fingers and toes tingle.

Maria? Little Soldier is baffled.

Yes, Maria.

The moment I met Maria, I squarely embedded her in a mold. For the next decade, I stubbornly refused to release her from it.

The thought of a sensual Maria rocks me back on my heels. Her soft, full lips burgeoning with greed. Her majestic breasts supplying countless hours of diversion. Her robust hips warm between the bedsheets.

I imagine those emerald eyes steamy with yearning. I feel the enticement of her thighs wrapped around me with unconstrained desire. My body grows warm and my skin becomes moist as Maria attracts me with an irresistible force.

My heart pounds. My cheeks flame. Blood throbs in my ears. I'm as giddy as deliriously bubbly champagne.

My recollections of the past take on an entirely different hue. They're like bolts of lightning across the night sky, illuminating the entire countryside. How Maria's happy laugh lifted me up. How agitated I felt at the thought of her with Ignaty or the newspaperman. How she has crept into my thoughts each and every day since my arrival in Petrovo.

As I remember every unheeded feeling, sorrow creeps in. I mourn the time I wasted, plodding along, taking her sustained, unbroken commitment for granted.

Andrey, no one walks this earth who is stupider than you.

A rustle on the blanket yanks me back to my current responsibilities. "Is this why she sent you? As a constant reminder of our time together, both during the war and in Moscow?" I look down at Russell and feel absolute tenderness for the helpless creature. I whisper to him, "I know someone who will make you feel better."

I am writing this, Maria, in the dead of night, unable to sleep due to the most peculiar sensation in my chest. I was quite slow to recognize that it is my heart throbbing with the purest longing for you.

How do I tell you that I'm a complete blockhead? But I don't need to tell you, do I? Because you've known for years that I was so caught up with my own woes, I couldn't see the most precious thing to have ever entered my life. You, my loving and lovable Maria.

The revelation hit me like a fist. I guess my true feelings had been unavailable to me for so long, I couldn't recognize them. It's a pathetic excuse, but it's all I have to offer, and I hope you'll accept it.

Without my being cognizant of it, you come to me every day on a tidal wave of thoughts. Something as simple as the fragrance of wildflowers along Petrovo's road reminds me of our spring in Sevastopol. Just the other day, ~~I was plucking maggots out of a wound and pictured you in the hospit~~

Hmm. I'll have to rewrite the letter, inserting a more aesthetically tasteful memory.

At this moment, the taste in my mouth is so bitter, I feel as though I've swallowed a cupful of gall. I've squandered so much time that we could have been together. And yet I don't believe we could have shared a life together before this moment. Only now am I capable of giving you the love you deserve, of honoring you the way you deserve, of taking care of you the way you deserve.

Before leaving Moscow, I reflected at length on what I desired for the remainder of my time on earth. I came up with the following:

An honest, productive career

Contentment and rational stability

A quiet life, a quiet death

But now I've added another desire—to love and be loved. Shall we make the journey together? What I'm saying, Maria, is that I hope you'll agree to marry me and—

I set down my pen. I need to talk to Anton before finishing the letter.

CHAPTER 57

June
1867

AT DAWN'S FIRST glimmer, I awake to an owl hooting the cessation of his nightly pursuits. A familiar warmth is curled against my back.

"How in the world did you find the strength to jump up here?"

Russell slits apart his eyelids, stretches one foreleg straight out in front of him, then reshutters his eyes.

I follow his lead and plunge my head back into the pillow.

Outside, the goose honks, *Breakfast!*

Not only am I guilty each morning of tossing stale bread to that self-pro-claimed autocrat, but somehow the pond's ducks caught wind of my generosity and have started demanding handouts. On the far side of the gurgling river, from one end of the village to the other, competition is intense for the title of Most Boisterous Rooster. Toss in the wake-up calls of the songbirds, and it's altogether quite a lovely opus.

I swing my legs out of bed and lower my bed partner to the floor. He pads a few steps then weakly flops down. But at least he's resting on his chest rather than prostrate on his side. I line up his buffet: cream, sardines, chicken. Russell sniffs each selection and takes a few laps of cream. I kneel beside him and make an offering of garlic tonic. Russell will have none of it. "Listen up, I won't have you suffer a relapse."

Russell turns his face away from his tormenter.

"Maria is anxious to see you."

The big head swirls back toward me. Is there a knowing look in the green stare?

Quick as a hornet's sting, I grab the scruff of his neck, paint the roof of his mouth with the goo, and clamp his mouth closed. He's beyond outraged. I fling a leg across his back, pinning him to floor.

"Swallow!" When he does, I perform a controlled release, and he sprints a safe distance from me and glares. "You rest and grow stronger, hear me?"

He's not the type to hold a grudge. Either that, or he has a short attention span. His head abruptly jerks toward the window where, outside, a couple of sparrows squabble halfheartedly.

I hoist myself from the floor and peer out the window. In the mild morning light, gauzy vapors swirl up from the river to halo each peasant hut. Men head to the fields to cut hay. Harshness and labor juxtaposed with pastoral beauty: a romantic fantasy favored by so many authors these days. Yet at moments like this, the illusion is very near to accurate.

"I have to go the village for a while," I inform Russell. "When I return"—I shake an admonishing finger—"garlic tonic."

MEDICAL BAG IN hand, I check on Elizaveta, who is up and about, her color and breathing restored. She thanks me for giving her life back, even if it is just temporarily.

"If you really want to thank me, consider Platon's situation—"

"The answer is still *no*," she interjects. "You can't eat books."

"But surely the boy is too precious a melon to lie wasting on the vine."

"I need him here, where he can be of use."

"He'll come home on the weekends and work in the store. And he'll be here all summer for fieldwork. Plus . . ." I pause for effect, knowing this could be the clincher. "He could write letters for the villagers and earn a few kopeks. And good Christians will always pay someone to read the Psalter at funerals."

Just as I suspected, the prospect of additional revenue snares the entrepreneur's attention.

"Talk it over with Feodor," I suggest. "There's still some time before Platon needs to register for autumn classes."

As I head toward the Mercantile's door, the priest enters, his dusty black robes swishing with each stride. He halts, blocking my exit and smiling gamely. "Doctor Rozhdestvensky, at last. I'm here to pray for Elizaveta. So fortunate that we finally have a chance to meet."

I extend my open hand, chest level, palm toward him. "Let's get right to it, shall we?"

His smile tightens.

"The Church has left me cynical and tattered, and I want nothing more to do with it. I do not intend to have this discussion a second time."

I push past him as his smile withers.

I'm dumbfounded that not only did my voice portray force, but my words were in logical order.

Well done, Andrey.

Even more amazing is that I've come to terms with my past—the Church, my family, the war. And it feels damn good.

I lower my lengthy body onto the backless bench outside the Mercantile, where Anton and I agreed to meet. As I look about, the day seems flooded with light. On a similar rickety bench beside the well, a grandmama naps, her chin sunk on her ample bosom as a gust of warm air billows her skirt. Kids gallop about, playing tag, their faces alive with joy. In a small cove where women are washing clothes, Filip Zhemchuzhnikov and Platon set about launching a canoe. Using a decayed board, Platon, in the rear, pushes from shore. Once settled into the dawdling current, they began a hearty rendition of "Down Mother Volga":

> Down the Volga River
> from the lower town,
> the boat is coming,
> like an arrow coming.

The words fade as they pass under the bridge. I can't help but chuckle. No doubt their trip "down Mother Volga" will last less than five minutes. Below the orphanage, they'll cast a rope to the waiting Anastasia, who will haul them to shore. Then they'll tow their vessel upstream and repeat the whole adventure.

I'm jabbed by a pang of jealousy. The boys lap up life's joy in a way I never did as a youngster.

But you know what, Andrey? You're no longer that youngster. You're no longer a victim of your youth.

"And it's about time," I say under my breath.

A shadow falls over me, cast by a stringy man whose face is a web of creases. He's the grandfather of a mischievous toddler who had wedged a pebble up his nose. My forceps easily extracted it. Now the peasant, hat in hand, thrusts an unadorned cake at me.

"My wife sent it. For your help with Misha."

"That's most kind of you, but it was a simple procedure. I really can't—"

"You know the saying: A house is beautiful not because of its walls, but because of its cakes."

I shake my head. "I can't accept this."

The peasant is a stubborn, old donkey. "My wife told me, 'Be sure the kind doctor gets this.'" He gives me a snide man-to-man smile that implies, *You know how women are.*

I rise and take the cake. The peasant grabs and presses my free hand in gratitude, then hurries on his way.

You know, Andrey, there are worse places to live. And you're needed here.

By Elizaveta, whose heart you'll treat with foxglove, once your supplies arrive.

By Platon, who will get an education, by God!

By the orphanage's myriad children.

By hapless peasants scattered throughout nearby nameless villages.

By Anton, so he can maintain a sane mind while isolated among the—what did Victor Rusakov call them?—obtuse, superstitious, ill-mannered, dirty peasants.

How would Pirogov tackle this bleak morass of ill health, with its confounding factors of poverty and ignorance? One of his first undertakings would be to administer smallpox inoculations to the whole of the village. And he'd finagle a way to secure some of the orphanage's excess milk for the malnourished children in the village.

The whole framework of this destitute village is dysfunctional. Remedying the problems will be a monumental challenge. But, unlike the deep abyss of urban poverty in Moscow, it's not an insurmountable one.

In this small population, records could be kept year after year on longevity of life, body weight, infant mortality rate. Then the information could be analyzed, and the improvement measured and used to—

"So what's up your sleeve that you wanted to meet on this side of the river?" Anton swings down from the saddle.

I wave away the stirred-up dust. "I'd like your opinion on something." I motion for my friend to follow me across the road to the long-abandoned izba Feodor had pointed out that frigid winter day I arrived in Petrovo. "Do you think there's any possible way this ramshackle hut could be turned into a medical clinic?"

Anton's smile bursts ear to ear as he slaps me on the back. Apparently on second thought, he deems a smack to be insufficient and tosses his arms around me in a bear hug. "I knew you'd eventually come to your senses."

"Or perhaps I've lost what little sense I once possessed." I shove my pursed lips to one side of my face.

Anton furrows his brow. "You're confident of your choice?"

"Overall, yes. Oh, I know there'll be days when I regret my decision. Days when I can't stand the smell of another unwashed body. Days when I don't want to enter another filthy izba. But yes, I actually do want to use my training to ease the plight of these people."

Anton gives me another jubilant wallop, nearly knocking the wind out of me. He squints at the disintegrating remains of the hut. "Tell me what you have in mind."

"A small waiting room. And a second room to examine patients. A supply closet. And two rooms for my personal needs."

Anton angles his head toward the hut's remnants. "Let's look inside."

The door is missing. As I duck my head to pass beneath the lintel, nesting swallows scatter through what was once a roof. My chest caves as I look about the tiny, soot-darkened izba. The caulk between the wall boards is missing. The dirt floor is gummy from a recent rain. A musty odor emanates from moldy hay and rodent droppings. The glass is gone from the sole window. The great stove, the centerpiece of every izba, is crumbling from neglect, its whitewash part of a far distant past.

"Phew!" Anton exhales. "Not much here to work with."

Back outside, we take inventory of the yard: weeds, a half-standing fence, a barn in the same condition as the izba. Grim and cross-armed, we return to the road and stare at the desolation.

"Here's what we'll do," Anton announces. "The izba is beyond repair. We'll tear it down. The peasants will help—they love community projects. Gives them an excuse to get drunk. Plus, the nuns will probably make the orphans pitch in, too."

"What about the stove? Should we salvage that?"

Anton shakes his head. "It was built without a chimney, which means the smoke stays in the hut. Unbearable." He folds his bottom lip between his thumb and forefinger, his thoughts hard at work. "Victor will convince the zemstvo to build new buildings for you."

"Buildings? Meaning more than one?"

"Exactly. A clinic near the road, with two rooms plus storage. Behind it, a breezeway to your three-room house." Ideas continue to gush forth. "Each building will have its own iron stove. And wood floors, of course. And we'll patch up the barn. You'll need it for your carriage, horse, chickens, those types of things."

Irina Osokina and her barefoot son amble up to me. The ten-year-old has a fountain of blood spewing from his mouth.

My head jerks back. "Oh, my goodness! What happened?"

Osokina replies, "A horse kicked out his two front teeth. But that's not why we're here."

"But those were his adult teeth!" I exclaim. "They won't grow back."

Osokina's concerns differ from mine. "The blockhead's own fault. Careless. Far better the hoof went to his teeth than to have his brains lying about the ground."

"I . . . I . . . suppose so."

The mother puts the episode behind her. "He's got a tick in his ear we can't reach. I heard from Magda Karpova that you pulled a rock out of Misha's nose. Can your gadget yank out the tick?"

I'll forever be at a loss to comprehend peasant reasoning.

While I pluck out the offending bug, Anton wanders about the yard, stepping off distances and tapping the barn's rotted boards.

After Osokina and her bloody-faced son go on their way, Anton returns to the front of the hovel. "There's a good spot between the house and the barn where you can put your garden. Soil looks fertile. Probably has years of manure in it." He folds his arms and gazes with enthusiasm at the possibilities that continue to elude me. "So. What do you think?"

"I think if you say it can be done, then it can be done."

Anton's face turns solemn. "But here's what you have to promise me in return." He jabs my chest with an extended forefinger. "When you move away from the estate house, Dasha will want you to leave the cat with her." He gives a single *don't-you-dare* shake of his head and lightly punches my shoulder. "With that, I'm off to the orphanage to help my sister clean out a cow's tainted hoof. Let's draft a letter to Victor this evening."

"I genuinely appreciate your help," I tell him. "Beyond words."

Anton reaches one hand around my arm clutching the medical bag and one hand around the arm cradling the cake, and gives three manly slaps to my shoulder blades. Who'd have thought Anton became so physical when in a gleeful mood?

He mounts his horse but pauses when he sees Platon and Filip in the canoe, pushing off from the shore. "Using splintered boards to steer a canoe." He shakes his head woefully. "Guess I need to show them how to make paddles."

I expect him to prod the horse, but he remains motionless as he watches the boys drift downstream. When at long last he speaks, his tone is rich with melancholy. "I made that canoe."

I cock my head. "You did?"

He looks down at me, the corners of his mouth in an uncustomary droop. "As a boy. With my father and Nadya's father and her brother. All three are dead now." His gaze floats back to the dancing, sunlit waves. "Back then, life bubbled just like that river."

At last, he kicks the horse.

As the cloud of dust disappears down the road, my spirits turn somber. I contemplate my friend's unusually pensive mood. I swear that behind me, the river gives a soulful sigh.

My attention is diverted when a nearby cock stretches in a lusty crow and flirtatiously sashays past three hens. *Well, Andrey, this isolated nook is where you and Maria will build a life together.* I take a deep, satisfying breath. Until Petrovo, I had drifted along like Platon's ineptly guided canoe. But now, everything is in its place. I can begin the business of living.

I SMEAR A huge glob of garlic tonic on the roof of Russell's mouth, then hold his mouth closed until he swallows the potion. When I let go, he turns his back to me and struts off. Now that we have the hang of this routine, he's probably healthy enough to discontinue it.

Let's see, Andrey, where did you leave off?

What I'm saying, Maria, is that I hope you'll agree to marry me and live in Petrovo. Yes, this is where I belong. In this small hamlet, I can't melt into the background as I did in the clamor of Moscow. I've come to realize it's not just a matter of finding the right path for myself. I also need to help others find their path, to be of service to those who are less fortunate.

I've hurt you many times and in many ways. It's presumptuous of me to swagger in at this late stage and expect you to say yes. I pray you can overlook all the years I kept my feelings hidden, even from myself.

My decision doesn't surprise you, does it? You know me better than anyone. I confess that I was an idiot and that I will probably always remain one. But I also confess that my heart has opened, and a new man has been forged.

The villagers will quickly befriend you. The world always seems to welcome you, benevolent Sister of Mercy, wherever you may be.

If you don't mind living where the wind whips ice pellets in your face in the winter and hot dust in the summer . . . where twin ruts through grain fields are aggrandized as "roads" and regress into muddy sinkholes every spring . . . where gossip is the lifeblood of the women . . . where goat droppings are ~~scattered like bullets on the streets of Sevastopol~~ always underfoot . . .

Yes, I definitely need to rewrite this letter.

If you don't mind being married to a man who wears the unpretentious clothes of a peasant, then a home awaits you here. I must warn you, your house will be "cozy," similar in size to the cottage where you, I, an Englishman, a gray kitten, a gelding, and a peahen shared a frigid winter night.

Say the word, Maria, and I'll come to Moscow to escort you to your new home, humble though it may be. Russell is waiting for you.

THE END

FROM THE

Author

Dear Valued Reader,

After thirty fulfilling years, I took down my veterinary shingle and began seriously pursuing what I had kept on the back burner—creative writing. Recalling how inspired I was as a fifth-grader watching *Fiddler on the Roof*, I researched rural 1800s Russia with the goal of writing *Who Is to Blame?*, my first novel. *How Did I Get Here?* is the second in the Petrovo series, with more in the works.

My mind weaves stories that have a common thread—time is inevitably accompanied by change. Change within us. Change in the world around us. My responsibility is to pen those stories in a way that you'll find compelling, that offers meaningful life lessons, and that you'll want to share with others.

I hope my tales convey the grayness and the grandeur of 19th-century Russia. Check my website for updates on forthcoming books in the Petrovo series.

Jane

JaneMarlowBooks.com

Reading Group
GUIDE

1. Identify each of the changes Andrey undergoes as he's held in the limbo of Petrovo. Are all the changes for the best?

2. Here's a line that was cut from the novel prior to publication: *Lives pivot on small moments. Which way they pivot is up to the person.* Can you give an example from the story? Can you give an example from your own life?

3. A person can overcome a miserable childhood, but it requires great strength and endurance. Have you ever identified an undesirable behavior in yourself that can be traced back to childhood? Were you able to remedy that behavior? How much effort and time was required?

4. The U.S. Department of Veterans Affairs estimates that post-traumatic stress disorder (PTSD) afflicts between 10 and 30 percent of the veterans of U.S. wars since Vietnam. Assuming PTSD affected soldiers of *all* wars, why did Andrey believe he was the only weakling affected by the painful experiences of the Crimea? In the mid-1800s, were any resources available to help Andrey?

5. Once the inducing event is over, PTSD symptoms sometimes decrease with time. Were Andrey's lessening symptoms due to the passage of time? Or to changes in the environment when he relocated from the hectic city to the countryside? Or to becoming sober (i.e., did alcohol fuel his anxiety?)

6. Since the mid-1800s, a mountainous body of knowledge has been amassed regarding disease transmission and treatment, as well as advancements in surgical techniques. Can you name a few obsolete medical beliefs that held sway in this story?

7. In the final chapter, Andrey decides to minister to Petrovo's peasants by focusing on nutrition, child-rearing, vaccinations, cleanliness, etc. Today, these measures are termed "population-based medicine," also known as "preventive medicine" and "public health." Do the following statements surprise you? *In the United States, 80–90 percent of the improvements in mortality and morbidity can be credited to the public health system. Medicine, with all its pharmaceutical and technological advances, is credited with the remaining 10–20 percent. Yet less than 1 percent of the dollars spent on health care in the United States go toward public health.*

Hello,

READERS!

JUST BECAUSE YOU finished reading the story doesn't mean we have to say goodbye.

Are you interested in the 19th-century Motherland's tsars, reforms, nobility, peasants, war, and culture? In other words, are you curious about what Russia was like before Putin? Before Stalin? Before the Revolution?

Let's keep in touch with my free, 100-percent no-obligation smiles-letter ("e-newsletters" are way too ho-hum!).

Petrovo Potpourri isn't about me. It isn't about things you can buy. It's about knowledge you can glean. It's about chuckling while you learn.

* Free book giveaways
* Behind-the-scenes stories about composing novels, including bloopers
* A foretaste of the next novel in the Petrovo Series
* Wisdom and wisecracks from renowned Russian writers
* Russian proverbs that run amok in translation
* Can that be true? Historical tidbits
* Featured fiction & nonfiction books that delve into Russia's bygone years
* Objets d'art
* In-box delivery four times a year
* No sales gimmicks. No spam. Not ever.

Petrovo Potpourri isn't information quicksand. It's a ten-minute breather during your day. Submit to some well-earned smiles.

View the newsletter's latest edition at
www.JaneMarlowBooks.com/contact

www.ingramcontent.com/pod-product-compliance
Lightning Source LLC
Chambersburg PA
CBHW030531120726
47904CB00005B/1724